"So that my soul chooses strangling, and death rather than my life."

Job 7:15

Kris Allis

A FALSE START

This book is a work of fiction. Names, characters, places, and incidents are the product of the author's imagination or are used fictitiously. Any resemblance to actual events, locales, or persons, living or dead, is coincidental.

T.S.W. Wordsmith LLC
Powder Springs, Ga. 30127

Printed in the United States of America

First Edition

Library of Congress Control Number: 2014942990

ISBN 978-0-692-23232-3

For Butch, Richard, Shanna, and Casi

I love you all!

ACKNOWLEDGEMENTS

I would not have been able to complete this novel without the support of my family. I want to thank Richard for all of his input, especially about the title; Cassandra and Tishanna for their giving spirits; and Gilbert Denton for allowing me to be me.

I would like to extend a special offering of gratitude to my three best friends known affectionately to each other as Dragon, Shakes and Bibbit for their never ending belief in me.

I want to thank my editor, Helga Schier, for her assistance.

A special thanks to Elayne Morton for always supporting me in whatever I do, and to the ladies of her book club "Sister to Sister"— Angela Allen, Celestia Brown, Valerie Browning, Linda Cain, Doris Carter, Gloria Farris, Norma McClendon, Lauraetta Starks, Regina Toliver and Karen Williams. They were an instant motivation for my next novel—they wanted a sequel.

I want to give a big thank you to my nephew, Bernard, for all of his help.

I am also grateful to Gail Stiles and Brenda Ceo for their assistance. Thank you so much, ladies!

Thanks to Darcy Evans Photography for the perfect photo!

A False Start

Chapter One

The woman driving the red sports car felt the bump and realized that she must have run over something. A quick glance in her rear view mirror confirmed her suspicions. What appeared to be a human body was lying in the street and traffic had stopped in the lane she had just traveled. *Oh no! Did I hit that person?* she asked herself. Terribly late for a doctor's appointment she'd already cancelled three times, she had tried to get through the intersection before the light turned red. She would have missed the appointment again if she had stopped. This couldn't be happening to her. If that person was dead and they caught her, she was in a world of trouble. She had to keep going.

She glanced at the clock on her dashboard. They would not start looking for her right away so she made a U-turn a few blocks down and headed back up to the East Side. Making the appointment was no longer an option. She had to get off this island as soon as possible. But where should she go? And then she knew. She kept hearing sirens, but decided that they couldn't be for her. It was too soon. If they were coming for her, they were going to have a chase on their hands; she was not going down easily. The traffic was worse than any day she'd been on the streets.

And why in the hell was the air so darn foggy? It was so heavy it almost looked like smoke. And papers flying in the air! She turned her music up louder—she'd just gotten a new CD by Mary J. Blige. As she sang along with it, she was sure that percolating was exactly what needed to be done—it was definitely slow going. There was no break in the traffic, but at least it was moving. She kept hearing sirens, imagining a police car pulling her over any minute.

Three hours later, she crossed into Connecticut. She stopped for gas and when she went in to pay, the cashier was glued to the television. He was watching a news report, but she didn't have time to figure out what it was about. If he was watching news about her accident she had better get out of there. She put the cash on the counter and left without as much as a glance at the television screen. Hopefully, he was too engrossed in whatever he was watching to pay any attention to her. She got back on the road and headed deep into the state.

She finally stopped at the house where she'd spent most of her life with her grandparents. Her grandmother had died first, leaving her grandfather alone for the last ten years of his life. The BMW had been a surprise birthday gift nine months earlier, but her grandfather died before he could transfer the title. She didn't feel rushed to do it because he'd left everything to her, including this fifteen acre semi-farm. So far, she had done nothing with the property. The barn was still in good shape; her grandfather had invested in a good sturdy barn door with an excellent locking apparatus just before he had the heart attack. She pulled her car inside, got out, took all of her belongings, and glanced at her beloved little auto one last time. She opened the storage cabinet, pulled out one of the automobile covers for her grandfather's old cars, covered the red BMW, and then locked away the only evidence of her crime.

The house still smelled like her grandmother. How was that possible? The woman had died over ten years ago. All of the furniture was covered, but the floors were clean and free of dust, thanks to Mabel, her grandparents' caretaker, who insisted on coming by once a week to make sure things were in order. A quick search of the cabinets in the kitchen was fruitless. The booze her grandfather had kept hidden behind the chafing dishes was gone. She sighed deeply and quietly slipped back outside, locking the door behind her. She'd been here long enough.

She had planned to buy a sports utility vehicle. Now was as good a time as any. She urgently needed another drink first. The accident and that long drive had been too much to bear without a good stiff drink or two. She truly hoped that the person was not dead. She shuddered at the thought of being on trial for vehicular homicide, leaving the scene of a crime, and drunk driving. She would have no defense and the judge would throw the book at her. No, she had done the best thing for everyone, herself included.

Returning to the city, she would report the BMW stolen. She also made a mental note to establish an alibi as well. Realizing that she'd done all that she could do, she pulled on her sweater and set out for the old McHenry farm to hitch a ride back to the city with Marvin. Marvin would be home. He probably wasn't drunk because it wasn't yet five o'clock. He had convinced himself that he wasn't a problem drinker because he didn't drink until after five, but he drank about as much as she did. If she rewarded him with a good bottle of scotch he'd forget all about wondering what she was doing out there without a car.

The leaves were beginning to fall and the pathway leading to the McHenry's property was covered with them. Hearing the crunch and feeling the crisp texture under her feet brought back many memories of a life long ago, when everything was still new and fresh and no one ever treated her differently because she was a female. When she was a little girl she had many friends, both boys and girls. No one warned her about it being a man's world.

Maybe she should give up her job, sell her condo, and move back here where life was simple. Just as quickly she decided that her grandparents' home was too big and vast and the liquor stores too far away. She'd probably get bored, and when she was bored she drank too much. In fact she drank too much when she felt any kind of emotion. Her chances of getting sober and staying sober were better in the city where her work distracted her. If God let her get away with this hit-and-run today, she would never put another drop of alcohol in her mouth. And that was a true story.

Chapter Two

Designed by Minuru Yamasaki, a Japanese-American, the twin towers of the World Trade Center were a symbol of world peace and a representation of man's belief in humanity. To Yamasaki the center had a more meaningful purpose than just providing space for tenants.

Opened in 1970, both towers were a breathtaking sight, standing 110 stories high. More than five hundred businesses with at least fifty thousand employees called the place home. There was a shopping mall in the lower level and an outdoor plaza. Windows on the World, a restaurant on the 106th floor of the North Tower, had an observation deck providing breathtaking vistas on a clear day.

The tour guides would recount that the buildings weighed more than 1.5 million tons, contained 194 passenger elevators, 43, 600 windows, 198 miles of heating ducts, 23,000 florescent light bulbs, and that the express elevator could reach the 110th floor in 4.8 minutes.

Felton Dade, a New York City police detective, had lived in New York for the past eleven years. He had come to the big city to live with his older sister when he was twenty-two and fresh out of the United States Air Force. He loved New York; the people, the food, the streets, the theater, and the skyline, dominated by the World Trade Center.

Dressed casually in a Brooks Brothers brown jacket, khaki pants, white shirt, and no tie, his six-foot frame fitting comfortably in his Ford Explorer, he waited for the traffic to move. He had just crossed the Brooklyn Bridge on his way to work. He glanced in the mirror to make sure that he'd washed all the sleep from his light brown eyes. He was clean-shaven, not even a trace of stubble on his dark brown skin. He knew he was handsome, but tried to keep it to himself. His eyes were drawn to the North Tower and the smoke coming from the top of the building. He quickly tuned into a news broadcast. That's when the nightmare began.

"An airplane has just crashed into the World Trade Center North Tower. We are getting reports of fire on the top floors and plenty of smoke."

Not again, he thought. Planes often flew low in the Manhattan skyline; it was probably an accident. He had continued slowly on his way to work, listening to the broadcast, and glancing up at the building from time to time. A few minutes later, his police radio squawked a report of a hit-and-run on Broadway. He wasn't too far away and traffic was turning into a parking lot to make way for emergency vehicles and fire engines headed for the Towers.

Ordinarily, he didn't show up for hit-and-run accidents; his duties no longer required wearing a uniform or quick response to traffic accidents, but what the heck? He was close and the traffic wasn't moving. He could walk to the scene faster than he could drive. He'd pulled over to the curb, turned on his flashing lights, got out, and started walking.

Papers were flying in the air, dust was everywhere, and the air was getting a little smoky. He'd looked back again at the fire and smoke coming from the tower, as did most pedestrians. Some of them had stopped to describe the scene to persons on their cell phones; others used their phones to take pictures.

Arriving at the scene, Felton forced his way through the crowd in time to see people crowded around a person lying on the sidewalk. From his vantage point, he saw another woman lying in the street, obviously dead—her body mangled, lying face down with her bloody blond head twisted at an awkward, angle. At that moment a cruiser and an ambulance arrived almost simultaneously.

"Get back! Everybody get back!" Felton yelled at the crowd, holding up his badge to identify himself. One of the guys in the cruiser joined him, moving people away from the scene.

Another cruiser arrived and soon Felton and the other officers were canvassing the witnesses. Most claimed that a red sports car had sped through the intersection, running a red light. Depending on who was asked, the driver had been male or female, African American or white, and age twenty to forty. All agreed that the operator of the vehicle had not so much as slowed down. The woman in the street never had a chance—the woman on the sidewalk had fainted in the process.

Minutes later, she was put into an ambulance. Her vital signs were good, so the attendants were directed to take her to New York Presbyterian Hospital.

"Has anyone got ID on the women? We need to notify next of kin!" Felton yelled out as the ambulance pulled away.

"It's on you, man," one of the officers replied, tossing a black leather purse to Felton—the contents scattering everywhere. He gathered everything he could see, went through it, and identified the woman as Jessica Woods. There was a paper with a name and phone number on it. Felton dialed, confirmed that the person answering was next of kin, and gave information about the incident.

Felton had been too busy with the crowd to go near either victim, but the other officers let him know that a thorough search near the dead woman had produced no signs of a purse or any other identification. None of them noticed the passport that was shuffled along by the crowd until it landed in the street and promptly disappeared into the gutter, as he headed back to his car.

He was worried. He had not been able to reach his sister or his niece. Both women worked in the South Tower. He'd been in contact with his fellow officers by radio and learned that both Towers had collapsed while he was wrapping up the scene of the hit-and-run. He knew that all emergency vehicles and rescue units had been dispatched to the site.

He also knew what he had to do. He had to get uptown and get the boys, Nathan and Justin. His niece, their mother, would go there first if she was alright. If she wasn't…he didn't want to finish the thought. Her boys would be scared. The faster he could get to them the better.

Chapter Three

Sometimes the simplest thing can change a life forever. For Kathy Stockton it was a phone call. She sat at a desk in the room that was once her father's office, writing the date, *September 11, 2001*, on a check, when the ringing of the phone startled her. Her family had never appreciated unexpected calls, hence the non-published phone number. Glancing impatiently at the caller ID display she saw NYPD. This was not to be ignored.

"Hello?" she answered.

"Mrs. Stockton? Kathy Woods Stockton?"

"Yes, this is Kathy," she responded hesitantly.

"This is Detective Felton Dade of the NYPD. A young woman identified as Jessica B. Woods was taken by ambulance to the New York Presbyterian Hospital a few minutes ago. She had a piece of paper with your name, address, and phone number in her purse. Do you know this young lady?"

"My God is she hurt? What happened?" Kathy asked.

"Do you know her?" Detective Dade demanded again.

"Yes, I mean I've never met her, but she's my brother's widow. Has she been in an accident? Has she been hurt?"

"Well, yes and no. Witnesses reported that she tried to save a woman from walking into the path of a car. Unfortunately, the woman died at the scene, and Mrs. Woods fainted and hit her head against the curb. Can you go to the hospital? You seem to be her only next-of-kin at the moment."

"Yes," Kathy replied. "I can be there in a few minutes."

"Thank you, Mrs. Stockton. Someone from the department will come round to talk to you later."

Kathy hung up and just stood there a moment, looking around the room. Everything was almost the same as when her father sat at the Louis XIV desk for the last time. The wood paneling, the wood floors, the books on the shelves and the wide doorway that led to the master bedroom remained unchanged, occupying the entire third floor of the family home.

Kathy had added rose-colored bedding, window treatments, and carpet to create a more modern look. The master bathroom had been beautifully redone with marble everywhere. Renovating the rest of the house had been a major undertaking, but it had been done. She now had a flawless kitchen of epic proportions with a full breakfast area. There were four floors in all, plus a finished cellar. It was easily one of the most prestigious brownstones on her Upper East Side block. What Kathy loved more than anything was the privacy the home afforded; in New York privacy was a privilege.

A natural redhead who'd opted for unique by wearing brown contacts to cover her obligatory green eyes, Kathy was very well preserved at age forty two. So much so that she could easily pass for thirty if one chose not to notice the crinkled wisdom around her eyes.

When she was worried or upset her brow wrinkled. It was wrinkled now. Jessica was in the hospital? She had just talked to her the day before. Jessica had told her that she would arrive in New York early this morning. Kathy knew that she had landed at LaGuardia on time, because the funeral director telephoned to inform her that he was at the airport and had met Jessica. Kathy had hoped to meet her sister-in-law at the airport, but Jessica had insisted on accompanying the mortician to the mortuary with her husband's ashes and then getting her own transportation to the family house. Had she gotten lost somewhere? Kathy shuddered. Troy Woods should have been there. It was just not a good time for him to be dead.

Troy Woods, Kathy's only brother, had been killed in a freak accident four days earlier while on the job. He was sixteen years her senior and they had not been close. Kathy had married and moved to Georgia while he called Texas home and they rarely saw each other, despite maintaining the family home in New York. He and Jessica married on impulse in Las Vegas on a Friday and two weeks later he was gone, just one day before he'd planned to bring his new bride to meet her.

Jessica had been due to arrive at Kathy's home any minute. A memorial service was to be held by the end of the week, and so far, no arrangements had been made. If only their mother were still alive; everything would have been taken care of by now in her usual quiet and efficient manner. Kathy sighed at the memory of her mother. She had been gone for fifteen years, but it still felt as if it had been yesterday that she'd filled the house with her presence.

Kathy grabbed her purse and a red jacket and took a quick glance in the mirror. The jacket clashed with the purple dress she was wearing, but she had no time to coordinate. Instead, she threw a black scarf over her shoulders and then headed down to the garage.

She sat in the car for minutes waiting to navigate into the traffic from her driveway. She couldn't help thinking that if Troy had brought his young wife home to New York to meet Kathy and the rest of the aunts, uncles, and cousins immediately, perhaps none of this would have happened. He might still be alive. Most people liked to think that when it was their time to go, it was their time to go, but Kathy felt that some people contributed to the timing of their departure.

She sighed, as she wished that she had gotten to know her brother better. By the time she was old enough to show any interest, he was out of the house. He and their father had argued a lot about Troy's lack of desire to follow his father's footsteps down Wall Street. Instead, he wanted to build things. Kathy vividly remembered the morning he left. Her mother cried all day and did not speak to their father for weeks. She blamed him at first, but, as time passed, everyone got over it.

Troy came home for Christmas occasionally, but spent most of his time partying, so Kathy never had a chance to even talk to him. Now he was dead. Kathy never knew his friends, not to mention the women he dated. Certainly there was no reason for her to be surprised that she had no clue about the woman he'd chosen to spend the rest of his life with.

Even their young lives had been different—Troy had attended private school while Kathy had begged her parents to go to public school. She remembered how upset her mother had been.

"Why do you want to go to public school?" her mother asked incredulously.

"Daddy went to public school. He said that he worked hard and made something of himself—that he learned to get along with all kinds of people! I want to be like daddy," Kathy replied.

After days of tears and tantrums, her parents relented and enrolled her in third grade at PS 3222. Her mother had shaken her head in disapproval, but her father understood. He said Kathy had the same do or die attitude that was so prevalent with his ancestors. He seemed proud of her and gave her his support and approval.

"I worked for every penny I've earned and I had to get out there among common people to do it," he'd said whenever Kathy's mom suggested putting Kathy back into private school.

And she'd blossomed. She'd made friends and she'd seen what it was like for a person not to have a silver spoon anywhere near the mouth, and still be happy—still succeed. She'd learned to be just plain old Kathy instead of a haughty little rich girl with a tiny circle of boring friends. She'd been a daddy's girl for sure, while Troy showed more affection for their mother.

All the time that she and Troy had lost—the times they could have gotten together were now gone forever. Kathy felt a deep sense of loss and sadness brewing on the inside. And now Jessica was hurt. When it rained, often it poured.

Chapter Four

Getting to the hospital proved to be extremely difficult. The traffic was heavier than usual and a never ending stream of police cars, fire trucks, and emergency vehicles clogged the streets. Something big must have happened. It took Kathy forever to find a place to park near the hospital.

Inside she was asked to wait for the doctor in a small alcove just outside the double doors leading into the bowels of the emergency room, marked *Authorized Personnel Only*. Hospital personnel were running to and fro as if a time bomb were ticking. People were everywhere. Most of them were crying. Many of them looked scared.

"Are you waiting to see me?" a voice behind her suddenly asked. She turned to see a rather squat, comfortable looking, older gentlemen without a strand of grey hair, wearing a white lab coat and holding a clipboard in his hands.

"I'm Dr. Jennings Ford." He extended a hand to her.

"Kathy Stockton. I'm pleased to meet you, Dr. Ford. I'm Jessica Woods' sister-in-law. How is she?"

He smiled and guided Kathy away from the door, out of the way of a stretcher transporting a female covered in blood and dirt. Kathy wondered what could have happened to generate so much dust that it had infused the woman's hair and clothing.

"Witnesses say your sister-in-law tried to save a woman who stepped right into the path of an oncoming car. The woman was killed instantly and your sister-in-law literally passed out at the sight of it. It was a terrifying thing to witness, I'm sure."

"I can imagine. May I see her?"

His expression subtly changed to serious.

"Well, she is heavily sedated and is unconscious at the moment. Your sister-in-law has some bruises and tenderness to palpitation in the left upper quadrant of her abdomen. That suggests that she may have an injury to her spleen. Her blood pressure is a little elevated which is a good sign. We'd rather see it a little high than low. However, her injuries are so severe that we are sure that they did not come from fainting on the sidewalk. Allow me to be blunt, Mrs. Stockton. She is bruised all over her body, and the nature of these bruises is consistent with injuries from repeated beatings."

Kathy couldn't help but gasp. Somehow, Jessica had taken a wrong turn and landed in the middle of trouble. What could have happened?

"I hate to be the bearer of bad news," the doctor continued. "It is a bit hectic here right now, given that we're beginning to see more and more victims from the World Trade Center, but I did want to take a look at her now to make sure she doesn't have more serious internal injuries."

"My goodness, by all means do whatever it takes to get her better and back on her feet. I will complete any paper work you need. I just want to help in any way that I can." Kathy could feel her level of emotional disturbance rising. And what did the World Trade Center have to do with anything?

"I'd also like to mention that it seems the blows were placed carefully, so that clothing would hide any injuries."

"How is that significant?" Kathy asked, her sense of dread added to the mix. None of this was making sense.

"Well, we see this type of abuse quite often, Mrs. Stockton. Is your brother with you?"

"No my brother is deceased. Jessica just flew in this morning from Texas for his memorial services. She and I have never met."

The doctor raised his eyebrows. At that moment a young woman ran toward the automatic doors that led to the outside, screaming hysterically. Kathy briefly wondered what was going on with everyone, but immediately snapped her focus back to the doctor. If she was hearing correctly, this doctor thought that Troy had been abusing Jessica.

"You see, they were just recently married," she explained, somehow wanting to make sure the doctor understood that there were no ill feelings between Jessica and her brother. "He was killed in an accident before we could all be formally introduced."

"I see. Then your brother is likely not responsible for these recent bruises."

"I beg your pardon? Dr. Ford, how dare you insinuate that my brother would do anything to hurt his wife!" Kathy was indignant now. She didn't know her brother that well, but she did know that he wouldn't beat a woman. Their parents had taught him better than that.

"Please accept my apologies. As I said, we see this type of abuse very often, and more often than not the husband or a boyfriend is responsible."

"Why don't you ask her who beat her?" Kathy snapped. She was completely dumbfounded. Had Jessica blamed Troy?

"We did, but she can't remember anything, not even her own name."

"What? You're telling me that she doesn't know who she is? What's wrong with her?"

"She has amnesia. I believe it's temporary, which is quite common after injuries to the head. But I won't know for sure until we do some further testing. You may come with me to see her briefly."

Kathy wasn't ready to see her. Not until she digested all of the information she had just received.

"It won't do any good. I don't know her, and she doesn't know me—or anything else, it seems. I won't disturb her until after you've done what you feel is necessary."

"Fine. I just need to know that you understand the gravity of the situation. Someone has violently abused this woman."

Kathy understood perfectly. She realized that the man was doing his job and from the looks and sounds of things around her, he was very busy. Everybody was busy. More and more people were coming into the emergency room. The waiting area was so crowded, only standing room remained. What in the world was going on? She'd find out soon enough. Right now, she needed to take responsibility for Jessica and clear up any misconceptions this doctor might have about her brother.

"I will cover all of her expenses. And let me assure you that my brother would never do anything like this. I don't know my sister-in-law and I don't know where she's been or who could have done this to her, but it wasn't my brother."

The doctor nodded, barely concealing his skepticism.

"Well, if you would just have a seat in the waiting area, I'll get started, and as soon as she is conscious again, we'll come for you."

He turned and walked through the double doors. Kathy walked toward the overflowing waiting area and noticed immediately that everyone's eyes were glued to the television screen mounted high on the wall. She looked up too and there, right before her eyes, an airplane flew directly into the North Tower of the World Trade Center; the impact caused the building to burst into flames.

The captions running across the bottom of the screen explained that an apparent terrorist attack had occurred. Kathy watched in horror as an almost identical scene played out with the South Tower. An airplane crashed into the steel structure and ignited an inferno. Smoke billowed from the windows of the floors that had been hit. Glass and steel tumbled to the ground. And to her dismay, Kathy realized that people were trying to escape the deadly fire by jumping to their deaths.

News reporters were running with their cameramen following them as they tried to tell the world what was happening. Firemen and policemen were running towards the scene, as civilians were desperately trying to get away. Then she watched the South Tower collapsing to the ground as well as the Marriot World Trade Center; the time caption read 9:59 a.m. The North Tower collapsed less than half an hour later, at 10:28 a.m. No one in the room spoke. The reporter's voice fell on every person, as they realized that terror had come to America.

The longer she watched the more anxious she became. Ironically, the South Tower collapsed first even though it was the second to be hit. Was this all? Was another attack planned? Here in New York, or elsewhere? Were they still in danger? She looked around the room: some people were crying, some remained solemn and dumbstruck. Tears quietly streamed down Kathy's face. All of this had happened while she had been sitting at her desk unaware, writing checks to charities.

She moved closer into the crowd, as people made room for her. Watching as the most prominent buildings of the city's skyline disintegrated, falling to the ground like a child's toy, she imagined a kindred spirit beginning to form amongst those waiting at this hospital and at others around the city.

Chapter Five

Dr. Jennings Ford rubbed his head—a habit when he was under extreme duress—while looking at the mess that had become his emergency room. Today he was the attending physician and it was his job to coordinate the nurses, doctors, and support staff. When the call came in that there had been an attack on the World Trade Center, he had called them all together and reminded them of the disaster preparedness drill.

"Remember your training. We've practiced this many times. This is the real thing. But you are ready. You are in control and you will function efficiently as long as you don't panic."

They were ready when the first ambulance arrived, and the next one, and the next one, and for the ones that had not arrived yet. For all of his advice and show of strength, he felt panic creeping in now. But not because of the extraordinary horror of the scene at the World Trade Center. No, it was ordinary horror of abuse. He wanted to call the police. It was his duty to report domestic abuse, but he had no one to lay the blame on. According to Kathy Stockton, Jessica Woods was a widow. Her husband was dead. But someone had beaten this girl in the last eight hours. He took a few deep breaths to calm himself. He had a job to do, and all of his life when confronted with work that needed doing he had sucked in his gut and got the job done.

It was his task to perform triage, a method of determining the urgency of patient care and how to prioritize it. Ordinarily he never would have put Jessica Woods in a room for immediate treatment when every other patient coming in was covered with dust or bleeding. Her top had come up when the attendants shifted her from the ambulance stretcher, revealing a myriad of angry bruises, causing him to suspect that she could be injured internally.

He signaled his nurse and gave her instructions for the tests he was going to run and then walked back into the small cubicle where Jessica lay. She was a lovely woman. He felt a stab of pity for her. He checked her vital signs again—pleased that nothing had changed.

Dr. Ford had been educated at Johns Hopkins and NYU. All of his studies and his practice had prepared him for a day like this. But nothing prepared him for man's inhumanity to man.

He had a friend on staff at NYU Downtown Hospital who'd taken a few minutes to call to warn him.

"Jennings, get ready for something you've never seen in your life. The World Trade Center has been hit. We have an onslaught of patients, and we'll never be able to handle them all."

Dr. Ford had heard the fear in his friend's voice and he knew that something big was coming. New York Presbyterian, a university hospital, was among the best hospitals in the world. With its more than 2,000 beds, it was the largest, non-profit, non-sectarian hospital in the country. Composed of two medical centers, it was connected with two Ivy League medical schools, Columbia University's College of Physicians and Surgeons and Weill Cornell Medical College.

For a few minutes he watched the broadcast on the small wall television in front of Jessica's bed. He watched the planes hit the Twin Towers. He refused to allow himself to fear. If the whole city was in trouble and they were all headed for death by terrorists, he would go down doing what he loved. He would let his anger compel him to action. The panic that had threatened to take over began to subside as he released the sides of the bed in preparation for the staff when they arrived to whisk her away to the CT scanner.

Chapter Six

Hours later—hours Kathy had spent staring at the TV screen like everyone else— Dr. Ford came back to tell her more about Jessica Woods' condition. Extensive testing that included a CT scan, a complete blood count, and back X-rays had determined that Jessica had a slight abdominal contusion and minor pelvic fractures as a result of blunt force trauma. There was no trauma to the brain, so the amnesia likely had nothing to do with falling on the sidewalk. Dr. Ford explained that amnesia could sometimes be psychological, and if so, was usually temporary. Should it prove to be psychological he would have to suggest special care.

"A recent death can cause this kind of trauma, as could a violent beating. When you combine these two incidents with seeing someone killed by a car, it's quite plausible that her mind has shut down," he said.

"What will happen next?"

"We want to keep her for twenty-four hours for observation. After that, she will be dismissed to go home. Her treatment will include bed rest and pain medication for the fractures and contusion. Her memory will have to take care of itself. The best thing to do is to talk about her former life in hopes that something will trigger a memory. It could happen quickly or it could take some time."

"I have no idea about her former life. I will be no help at all, except for talking about my brother. She'll be on her own trying to remember."

The doctor smiled. He seemed impatient as he pulled a pad from inside his coat and looked at it. Kathy could not blame him; he probably had other patients waiting.

"The hospital has therapeutic staff that can help. I'll give you some recommendations for psychologists and therapists before you leave. In the meantime, you may see her now."

"Thank you, Dr. Ford."

"I also need to inform you that it is my duty to report the abuse to the authorities."

Kathy paused momentarily, considering the doctor's comment.

"I understand. Like I told you, I am sure my brother had nothing to do with this. I'll tell the authorities that and whenever Jessica remembers what happened; she should be able to clear it all up."

Dr. Ford nodded, asked Kathy to follow him to Jessica's room, and stood aside to allow her to enter. The young woman lying in the bed was beautiful. Even though her body was covered, the outline clearly revealed a flawless figure. She was obviously taller than Kathy's five feet and she looked to be about a size ten. Her blond hair was thick, and long, and obviously from a bottle. Although she looked Caucasian, Kathy easily discerned that she was African American, with skin reminding one of café au lait. Her full lips were natural—not the result of a few injections.

Kathy chuckled as the thought occurred to her that Jessica's ethnicity had probably made them get married so quickly and without the family present. Having waited until after the wedding to meet her, the family would know that the case was closed and any advice or snide comment was moot. *Really Troy?* Kathy thought to herself. He was not the first Woods family member to fall in love or marry someone of a different race.

As Kathy approached, she could see the look of confusion on the young woman's face.

"Hello, Jessica! How are you feeling?" she asked.

Chapter Seven

The young woman watched as the strange woman with red hair approached her bed. "Who . . .?" was all that would come out. She closed her mouth and tried to swallow, but there was no moisture. She needed something to drink badly. In addition to overwhelming thirst, she felt a deep foreboding inside, all the way down to her belly, and she was absolutely certain that the feeling attached to this foreboding was fear. Strong, unadulterated fear.

"Just a minute, Jessica, I'll get you some water," said the stranger as she poured water into a cup from a plastic pitcher by the bed.

"Who are you and why am I here?" While waiting for the stranger to answer, the young woman quickly scanned the room and determined that she was in a hospital. When she lifted her head to see better, intense pain dictated that she make no more sudden movements.

"Hello, Miss Jessica. How are you doing?" This time the question came from a very stern looking nurse who'd just come into the room. *Jessica. Is that me?* The name felt peculiar and unnatural, but that thought was quickly replaced with a more pressing concern: her mouth was dry and her tongue felt stuck to the roof of her mouth. This must have been obvious because the nurse placed a straw in the cup and lifted it to allow Jessica to drink greedily.

"That medicine will do that to you. Makes you thirsty, I know. My name is Geraldine Wilson and I'll be your nurse today. Does your head still hurt?" Geraldine was an attractive, buxom, African American woman whose soothing voice belied the austere expression on her face.

"Why am I here?" Jessica asked again, this time looking at the nurse.

The strange redhead and the nurse exchanged looks.

"I'll take care of her, Nurse Wilson. If we need anything I'll come right out and get you." The stranger placed her hand firmly in the middle of the nurse's back, turned her toward the door and guided her out, closing the door behind her. She returned to Jessica's bedside.

"Sweetie, I'm Kathy Stockton, Troy's sister. You're in the hospital because you fainted as you witnessed a horrible accident. It was just more than you could bear. The doctor said you must have hit your head hard when you hit the ground, because you can't remember anything. The amnesia is temporary, so don't you worry. I'm so happy to finally meet you."

"Who is Troy?" Jessica asked, regarding Kathy suspiciously.

"Your husband."

Jessica slowly sat up in the bed. She suddenly had a strong urge to flee. Something was wrong and she didn't know what. She just had an eerie feeling that all was not well. She looked around for her clothes and decided that they must be in what appeared to be a little closet. She pulled the tubes from her arm, swung her legs to the side of her bed, and stood. Immediately a sharp pain buckled her knees. She fell back on the bed to get her bearings.

"What are you doing? The doctor said you need to rest," Kathy protested.

"You don't understand, I can't stay here, I have to go." Jessica felt tears welling up in her eyes. She did not want to lose control in front of this strange woman, but she felt the urge to get up and leave, but wasn't certain where she was supposed to go. She concentrated, but nothing came to mind. Apparently, her name was Jessica, but beyond that she knew nothing.

"I understand. You've just had a very traumatic experience. You saw a woman get crushed to death by an automobile right in front of your eyes. You have to lie down right now and rest." Kathy gently pushed Jessica back down on the bed. "I know you have a lot to say, but now is not the time." She pushed the button on the side of the bed to call the nurse.

"We need some help here?" Nurse Wilson asked just seconds later.

"Yes, she's trying to get out of bed," Kathy replied.

"Miss Jessica, you have to rest now. Why don't I get something to help you relax?" offered the nurse patiently.

"No, I don't need medication. I need to get out of here."

"You'll be able to leave soon. In the meantime you've got to get some rest and try to stay calm."

"I can't stay here, but I don't know where to go."

"I know, dear. The doctor left orders about that. If you become agitated, we are to keep you comfortable with a mild sedative. You've been in a lot of pain. We don't want you to hurt yourself. " The nurse gently pushed Jessica back onto the bed and then skillfully administered additional medication through the IV.

"I feel like I'm supposed to be somewhere," Jessica protested.

"Calm down, Miss Jessica. You're going to be just fine. This amnesia is temporary, but I know it's a little frightening. Just relax, this medicine will help you."

"Where is the doctor?" Jessica inquired, beginning to feel drowsy.

"He's making rounds. He'll be in to see you later," Nurse Wilson answered.

"When exactly will that be?" Kathy asked.

"He should be back later on this evening. Is there anything I can get for you, Mrs. Stockton?"

"No, I'm fine."

The nurse left the room, closing the door behind her as Jessica felt herself drifting away.

Chapter Eight

Kathy Stockton took a long look at Jessica, who, aided by the medication, had quickly settled down. She wished they could have met under different circumstances. It was very fortunate that Kathy's name, address, and phone number was found in her purse; without that the likelihood of her getting lost as just another Jane Doe was a definite probability. She moved closer to the bed.

"Jessica?" No response. She gently lifted the covers and the gown, gasping at the sight of the profusion of bruises on Jessica's abdomen and legs. She felt pity for the pain that she must have endured. It was a blessing that she couldn't remember the feeling of fists pounding into her flesh right now.

Kathy found Jessica's purse in the closet. She wasn't prying; she just wanted to see if she could find the name or number of a friend. Troy had mentioned that Jessica had no family; her parents had died when she was very young and she'd been raised in an orphan's home somewhere in New Mexico.

A wallet with five hundred dollars in twenties, an American Express Card, and a Visa; a slip of paper with Kathy's name and number on it; along with a compact, lipstick, and gum were the contents of the purse. *No driver's license*. Kathy smacked her own forehead. Of course! Troy had mentioned that his new wife didn't drive—he'd joked about New York City being the best place for her to learn.

Many thoughts swirled through Kathy's head as she tried to come to grips with the fact that she was on her own with the memorial arrangements and Troy's estate; not to mention trying to piece together what had happened to Jessica. Sighing deeply, she quietly left the room.

She waded back through a sea of people crowded into the lobby of the hospital. Once on the sidewalk, she realized driving her car was out of the question. Traffic was literally at a standstill. There were police officers in the street clearing lanes to allow emergency vehicles to enter and exit the emergency room. She was afraid. No one had said anything on the news about any attacks elsewhere in the city, but that did not mean that the danger was past.

The Pentagon had been attacked as well. Should she be out on the street? Was she safer on the inside? She glanced at her watch. It was 12:45 p.m. The first plane had hit at 8:46 a.m., the second one at 9:03 a.m. Surely the terrorists would not wait this long to attack again. A well-organized plan would need to be executed swiftly. Perhaps the danger was past. She started to walk down the sidewalk, away from the hospital.

As she passed the cars, she could hear snatches of news being reported. It seemed like everyone was listening to the radios, but not one beat of music thumped from any vehicle. New Yorkers were famous for honking horns when traffic backed up, yet there was not a single blast. Not a sound. She quickened her pace. Many other people walked along the street so she became a little less apprehensive. She had to get to the mortuary. According to the news, many casualties were expected, which meant that the undertakers were going to be busy. She walked straight ahead about three blocks, turned a corner and then walked four.

Arriving at the funeral home twenty-five minutes later, the funeral director, James Citoff, a solemn looking man with very cold hands, greeted her with a handshake. It is never a good time to visit a funeral home, but when it involves family, it is particularly depressing. Kathy felt a deep sadness as she remembered the last time she'd been in the presence of this man with the frigid hands.

"How are you, Mr. Citoff? It's been quite a day so far hasn't it?"

"Indeed," Mr. Citoff held his hand out to guide Kathy down a long hallway that led past viewing rooms and the chapels. As they walked, he spoke to her with professionalism, seemingly ignoring her reference to the attack on the World Trade Center.

"You have my condolences, Mrs. Stockton. It's nice to see you again, even though present circumstances are not more cheerful. I understand that Troy was the last of your immediate family?"

"Yes. As you know, my sister-in-law was to help with the arrangements, but she's in the hospital. Mrs. Woods witnessed a hit-and-run accident that killed a woman literally in front of her eyes. She fainted and injured herself in the fall, so much so that she's lost her memory."

"I'm sorry to hear that. For a moment I thought you were going to tell me that she'd been a victim of the attack on the Trade Center."

They'd reached the door to his office. He led the way inside and indicated a chair for Kathy to sit down. She looked around and noted that since the last time she'd been here he'd added a new desk. It was solid mahogany and very large. On the desk lay a folder. He sat down and opened it while he continued to speak.

"As long as I've lived in this country not once did I ever think that something like those planes crashing into the towers would happen, but I've decided to carry on with business as usual."

"I feel the same way. Did Mrs. Woods accompany you here with my brother's remains?" Kathy asked.

"Yes, she did. She left here walking, said she was going to take the subway. I assumed she was going to your house. That was around 8:00 a.m. this morning. "

"I don't understand why she'd try to get around a city that she knew nothing about. I'll just have to wait— right now she doesn't even know who she is."

"That's a shame. Perhaps she's lucky not to know what has happened—not experiencing the fear and the dread that we all are feeling right now. I wish there was something more I could do to help."

"Thank you, Mr. Citoff. In Jessica's absence, it's up to me to finalize my brother's memorial service. I believe I'll let her choose an urn for his remains later."

"I understand, Mrs. Stockton. Come with me please. Will you be holding the services here?"

"Yes. I think that's the best choice."

"Well, let's start by choosing one of our chapels."

Two hours later, Kathy left the funeral home with Troy's services planned for September 13th at 2:00 p.m. She was deeply disturbed and a little angry that she had not seen her brother's body. Jessica had him cremated immediately due to the condition of his corpse. Several of his employees were present when the accident occurred and they all verified his identity. Jessica likely had felt it was best that Kathy remember him the way he'd looked the last time she saw him.

Given some time to think, she had come to two conclusions, neither of which made much sense. Either Jessica had run into foul play and had been beaten by some unknown person or persons in the past and again yesterday for some reason yet to be discovered, or Troy was responsible. She hated to think that her brother was an abuser, but that was the thought that nagged on in the back of her mind. It was theoretically possible (though unlikely) that he had beaten her in the past. But the doctor said that some of the injuries had occurred within the last twenty-four hours. Obviously, Troy could not be responsible for those injuries because he had been dead by then.

Chapter Nine

At 8:49 a.m. Dr. Foley Brogdon left the meeting on the 61st floor of the South Tower bound for the room with refreshments and poured himself a cup of coffee. Tall, blond, and handsome, he looked as if he'd stepped out of a fashion ad for his navy blue Armani suit. The yellow shirt and golden tie drew attention to his perfect tan. He turned to take his first sip and saw fire coming from the North Tower. Papers were flying everywhere and he could have sworn that a person had just fallen out of a window. A minute later a guy stuck his head into the room and announced:

"A plane crashed into the North Tower. I don't know what the hell is going on, but some people are starting to get out of here. But finish your coffee; you know what I'm saying?"

Foley smiled. He knew exactly what he was saying. He gulped the liquid down and crossed the hall to his meeting. They had reached a critical point in the discussion about the implementation of a new cosmetic procedure for necks and, if there was no emergency, the right thing to do was finish. Every cosmetic surgeon knew how lucrative it was to transform a wrinkled and saggy neck into youthful smoothness without visible scars. And this new procedure could be done without surgery or Botox. No one had moved.

He sat down, turned his attention to the speaker and then it hit him. *Anissa!* He wanted to talk to her, let her know that something had happened. On his way out into the hall he glanced at his watch and noted the time; 9:03 a.m. Almost simultaneously he felt the building shudder. What in the world? He tried his cell phone but could get no reception.

At this point, an announcement came over the PA system, requesting that everyone begin evacuating the building. They were to use the stairs. He went back into the meeting room, grabbed his briefcase, and joined the crowd. It was a narrow stairwell and the people were moving in a slow and orderly fashion. They were down at about the fortieth floor when they all heard a muffled sound that sounded like distant thunder followed by a violent vibration.

The lights went out for a brief moment. A few people started to wonder aloud about what had happened, but everyone kept moving. Foley prided himself on remaining calm in the face of calamity; however, this time he felt his palms beginning to perspire and his heartbeat quicken. Something was terribly wrong. He moved a little faster, remembering to be as polite as possible as he managed to squeeze past people and attempt a faster descent. He wanted to get to Anissa; she would be in a quandary, worrying about him.

When he reached the thirtieth floor, someone yelled that they could return to their offices. He made his way out onto the floor, trying to find a phone, breathing a sigh of relief. Congestion was created from people trying to return to their offices while others were still trying to get to the exit. All this really slowed him down. He finally found an office and a phone, rang the Marriot, and got a recording telling him that all circuits were busy. He did not have the patience to wait, but stood there, tapping his feet when another announcement directed everyone to resume evacuation. *Could these people make up their minds?* He looked at his watch again and it was 9:40 a.m. He went back to the stairwell and pushed his way into the crowd—rejoining their slow descent.

On the fourth floor, all hell broke loose. This time the vibration seemed to shake the world but everyone kept moving. Panic spread like wildfire. They reached the bottom floor and exited into calf high water—electrical wires dangling everywhere, as they continued to move forward. Foley was beginning to doubt that he'd get out alive. He did not scare easily but he was frightened now. People were beginning to shove and push, but Foley planted his feet on the ground and held his place in the throng.

They finally emerged into an opaque and white dust cloud. It was daylight, but he could not see through the cloud. His eyes began to burn and breathing became difficult.

"Get away from the building! Get away from the building!" A male voice ordered loudly.

"We gotta take Vesey Street!" somebody in the crowd ahead yelled.

"Get across the Tolin Plaza!"

"We can't get across the Plaza!"

"Come on! Let's go by the Custom House!"

There were too many voices, too much distraction, and too many directions to follow. Foley had no idea where he was; he just kept his head down and followed the people in front of him.

He found himself walking underneath a protective eave as they continued their harrowing journey. Foley would think back later and remember this as the longest walk he had ever made. He covered his face with his jacket and used his briefcase to protect his head from falling debris. They kept going and he found himself descending stairs to what he assumed was Vesey Street. From there, the crowd just kept moving forward.

"Get as far away from the building as possible! Move toward the piers! They're loading up ferries. Keep moving!"

Foley was trying to stay calm. He knew that as soon as he could get to a safe place with a phone, he would find out what had happened and begin to right his world again.

They reached the pier and Foley was eventually shuffled onto a Coast Guard vessel that moved away from the island of Manhattan as a loud noise reverberated. He looked behind him, and what he saw filled him with terror. There were huge clouds of smoke and dust. The Towers were gone.

Foley was frantic with worry. *Where was Anissa?* He had heard enough from members of the Coast Guard and the conversations among the other passengers to know that airplanes had crashed into the World Trade Center. The last time he'd seen her was this morning in their hotel room at the Marriot as he was leaving to go to the medical conference in the South Tower.

When the ferry docked in New Jersey, there were crowds of people everywhere, staring across the river at the smoke where the twin towers had stood. A huge line for the phone formed in front of the ticket office at the Ferry station. Foley forced his way through and walked until he found a little diner, threw fifty dollars on the counter, and asked to use the phone. He dialed his parents' home. While waiting for someone to answer, he looked down at his two thousand dollar pants, now covered with ash and soot, and his shoes that were functional, comfortable, and pricey. He was filthy! Every eye in the place was focused on the television behind the bar.

"Hello!" It was his mother, Lacy Brogdon.

"Mom, have you heard the news?"

"Oh F J, you're alive! Thank God! Foley!" Lacy called to her husband. "Foley it's FJ! He's still breathing!!"

"FJ? Son we've been calling your cell phone for hours! " His dad was on the phone now.

"Hello, daddy. My phone is useless. I'm fine, but I don't know where Niss is. I left her at the Marriot. We all had to get out of the towers and I had no way to get to back over to the hotel."

"The Marriott is gone, son. Came down like building blocks. Do you think she got out? Surely she got out. I tell you what I'm going to do. I've got friends. I'll get in touch with someone with authority in that town and we'll find her. She's got to be alright son. Don't you worry. Where are you?"

"Jersey City. I came over with the Coast Guard. They're sending everybody out of there on the water. There're so many boats in that water. Man! What happened, daddy?"

As soon as the words were out of his mouth Foley looked at the television screen and saw the first airplane flying into the North Tower, as his father replied.

"Some planes flew into the buildings. That's all I know now. They're suggesting it was a terrorist attack, but I don't know. How are you, son? Did you get hurt at all?"

"Just wet and dirty. I was at the conference and Niss stayed at the hotel. I tried to call over to the Marriott, but couldn't connect."

"I'm glad you're okay and we're going to find Anissa, too. Listen, you remember Paul Laferty? Well his son and daughter-in-law are at Port Liberty near the water. They live in a big octagonal condo that you can't miss. Just sit tight. I'll get their number and you get on over there with them. You can't get home and we can't come to you, because all planes in the country have been grounded. You're not going to be able to go back over to Manhattan right now either. You hang tight where you are and I'll make some calls. Here's your mother."

Foley's mom came back on the line and explained that his dad was searching for the phone numbers of friends of his in the New York Mayor's office. The elder Mr. Brogdon felt sure that someone would help him find out where his daughter-in-law was or at least get him to someone who could.

"Son, your father wants me to get the phone number where we can reach you. We're going to contact a few people who can help find Anissa. We'll get back to you," his mother said.

After Foley hung up, a waitress poured more coffee and directed him to the restroom where he could wash up. Everyone in the small establishment tried to be as kind as possible as they all attempted to find out as much as they could. He had been there, but didn't know any more than they did; less probably, because the other customers at the diner had watched TV all morning. Foley was horrified at the scene of airplanes flying directly into the Twin Towers. His heart threatened to stop when he saw both buildings collapse to the ground and heard that the Marriott had come down, too.

Twenty minutes later, Foley had downed three cups of coffee and was feeling pretty wired, but he had convinced himself that Anissa couldn't be dead. They had evacuated both towers and the hotel, and he could visualize her being shuffled along in a crowd, maybe onto a ferry. There had been many survivors, people like him who'd been able to get out in time. Why hadn't they stayed at the Waldorf Hotel? Because he had wanted to be close to his conference since he was one of the keynote speakers.

He was trying to build a strong, professional network. He was doing this for her, so that she would have all the finer things in life. Why did he bring her with him? If she'd stayed at home he would know exactly where she was. She was upset about losing the baby and he had thought a trip to New York would cheer her up. One of his new-found friends, Clyde, the diner owner, handed him the phone.

"Hello, daddy. What did you find out?"

"Well it's pretty chaotic over there. Everybody I talked to suggested that you get somewhere safe and tune in to the news. In the meantime, I'm going to do everything I can from this end. I've got folks at work for me as we speak. They'll get out and scout around. We'll find Anissa. Don't you worry, son. Actually, Anissa will probably contact us as soon as she can. I know how much you two love each other. She's probably worried sick about you, too. I've got the address over there in Port Liberty. I've already talked to Paul Jr.'s wife. She's there with the children and she's expecting you. You got pen and paper? I've got the phone number, too."

Foley ended the call. He left a hundred dollar tip on the counter and walked out. He really hated leaving tips like that to people for only a few minutes of their time, but he'd learned from dining with Anissa that a big tip ensured gratitude and respect from the recipients. It had become a habit even in her absence.

He'd decided to pick up a few things so he could clean himself up. He pulled up the collar of his jacket and strode purposefully down the sidewalk. The only thoughts running through his mind were about Anissa. He considered going back to the docks to search for her, but decided against it. He'd need a bullhorn and a platform to stand on. Neither of which were available to him.

It seemed unfair to him that able-bodied people were not allowed to return to Manhattan. He looked back towards the pier and could still see the smoke across the river. He would wait until morning. After that, only God could stop him from searching for her. He checked his phone again. Still no service.

Chapter Ten

As soon as Kathy was home, she made a telephone call.

"Hello," the voice answered. Kathy felt pleasantness begin in her secret place, travel up to her belly, and languish at the sound of his voice. She loved his voice; to her it was extremely seductive.

"Hi," she said breathlessly.

"Hi, yourself," said Geoffrey Winston, Kathy's lover and friend. "I've been worried about you. I started calling the minute I heard. Are you alright?"

Kathy moved to a window and looked out over the horizon. Was it her imagination or could she see smoke? She walked over and flipped on the TV.

"Yes, thank you. You know I'm on the East Side. Far away from what must be complete chaos. And I didn't find out about it until I got to the hospital. Remember me telling you that my sister-in-law was coming today?"

"I do."

"Well, she fainted in the street and hit her head on a curb after seeing some woman get run down by a car. She's in the hospital with amnesia. And according to the doctor, someone has been beating the crap out of her." Kathy watched the scene at the Pentagon. It too had been attacked by an airplane and looked like a war zone. According to the report, hijackers had flown into the western side of the building, causing a partial collapse, with ensuing fires and casualties.

"Are you serious?" Geoffrey asked.

"Yes. Can you believe that?" Kathy answered, refocusing her attention to Geoffrey.

"So she doesn't know who you are? And you can't get any information from her because she doesn't remember anything?"

The image of the plane flying into Tower One flashed on the screen. Kathy turned away and kicked her shoes off. She'd seen enough.

"You got it, Mr. Quick Draw McGraw!" she said, trying to sound cheerful. "What a dilemma! The doctor says she needs to stay at the hospital overnight. I'll be bringing her home then and we'll just wait out her memory. The amnesia is temporary, so perhaps things will come back to her soon."

"So what about the arrangements for your brother's memorial service?"

Kathy began to climb the stairs toward her bedroom, removing her scarf and her jacket as she moved.

"I've arranged everything. The memorial is Thursday. Are you coming?" She asked.

"Of course. I'm not even going to try to fly. You know they've grounded every plane in the country. I've got a few more things to throw in the suitcase and then I'm out of here. I'm driving up. I'll stop over somewhere for the night and should arrive tomorrow night."

"Good! I can't wait to see you. In the meantime, how about a little phone sex? I'm so wound up I feel like I could snap!"

"We can't have that. Go to your bedroom."

Kathy reached the third floor and quickly went into her bedroom. She picked up the remote receiver and lay down on her back across the bed; the excitement of what was about to come was almost unbearable.

"I'm here," she whispered.

"Uncover your breasts," he breathed into the phone.

She pulled the dress over her head and hurriedly stripped down to her panties. They'd done this enough times for her to know that he wanted her private parts covered for now.

"I'm looking down at them." And indeed she was.

She was very proud of her bosom. It took twenty-four years and thirty pounds before she had cleavage. When she dropped the extra pounds, the boobs stayed big, just a little softer and not nearly as perky.

"Wet the palms of your hands and place them over your nipples."

She clicked the receiver to speaker phone and then licked her tongue in the palm of each hand until they were good and moist and lay back on the bed.

"Ready," she said.

"Move your hands in circular motions," he directed.

She began to move her hands and as she did, her breath caught in her throat. She loved doing this with him. It felt so deliciously wicked.

"Now imagine that your hands are my hands. Next, I want you to wet your fingertips and then I want you to gently tug at each nipple as you imagine my mouth on them. Do you feel me?"

"Yes," she sighed.

"Now take off your panties."

She did.

"Open your legs and spread yourself open just like when we're together."

She did.

"Now with your thumb go to the sacred spot and with light pressure begin a slow circular motion and move your hips slowly. Wait for it. Now go faster, matching the movement with your hips. Faster. Faster. Are you arriving?"

She was breathing loudly and the wonderful feelings enveloping her clitoris were sending her over the edge. She moaned. And then released. Wonderful, sweet, release.

"And so you've come. I love you, Kathy."

"I know. Finish packing and call me when you get on the road."

"Will do. I wish I could put that thumb in my mouth."

"You shall."

"Bye, my love."

"Bye." Kathy ended the call and settled back for round two on her own.

Later, she showered, made some coffee and sat down to watch the news. She drank the entire cup and then started making phone calls. She needed to know that her aunts, uncles, and cousins were safe and to let them know about Troy's memorial service and Jessica's amnesia.

Chapter Eleven

Felton Dade had dropped off his nephews at a friend's house and was almost to the site of the attack now known as Ground Zero. It was the exclusive domain of the New York Police Department and Fire Department.

United Airlines Flight 175 had crashed into the South Tower between the 77th and the 85th floors. His sister and his niece worked on the 96th floor. From the brief snatches of news reports that he'd seen on television and what he'd heard on the radio, unless they got out before impact, the chances for their survival were slim.

He had served in the Air Force for four years. He came away with the knowledge of how to thoroughly assess a situation, leaving no room for sugarcoating. Expecting the worst caused good news to become great. He'd been praying nonstop.

Thanks to his military training, he knew how to case a scene, weigh the resources available, ponder what was needed, and how to best resolve the issue. He was a walking, talking reconnaissance unit. But nothing Uncle Sam had offered prepared him for what he saw when he arrived.

The first thing he encountered was thick smoke that made it hard to breathe and an odor unlike anything he'd known; a mixture of metal, wires, and human flesh. He showed his badge as he moved past men with their hands up to bar his way, and watched his step. Dust and debris everywhere; large pieces of steel, concrete, paper, checks someone had written, glass, body parts; complete and utter chaos. Cars and trucks were mangled and crushed; an emergency vehicle stood still, its light flashing.

Someone handed him a mask and directed him to make-shift command center. He shook hands with guys, not even hearing their names. He had one mission.

"I'm here to help look for survivors. I believe my sister and my niece are in there somewhere. They've got to be." Almost without warning, he began to sob like a kid.

"We're doing the best we can, sir," a fireman said. "Come on we'll show you where we've been working. We're taking it slow because from the looks of it, World Trade Center 7, the American Express Building, is going to come down soon."

Felton glanced towards the structure the fireman pointed out. Fire was raging in the building and it sounded as if it was groaning. They had it closed off.

"Have you found any survivors yet?"

"No, we haven't. We're just trying to figure out the next best thing to do."

Felton never made it to the site where the Twin Towers had once stood, because a few minutes later, World Trade Center 7 collapsed. Every man ran for dear life.

Chapter Twelve

Orella Bookings turned the key to the door of her garden condominium on 3rd Avenue, Upper East Side Manhattan. The large clock in the corner of the room chimed eleven times as she entered and kicked her shoes off, pulled her black knit skirt down over her hips, her matching knit top over her head, and unhooked her bra. She was tired. It had been a long day. She walked across the thick white wool rug that covered the center of the room. Her stocking feet touched the cold hardwood floor as she reached the well- stocked bar. A full brandy decanter and a snifter accompanied her back to the newly upholstered cerulean couch that had belonged to her grandmother.

The whole place had belonged to her grandmother, who had nursed a wealthy widow for years, changing her diapers and bedpans, spoon feeding, and coddling her during her last few years. When the woman died, she left the apartment and everything in it to Orella's grandmother.

"Rellie, I want you to have it. I got no use for a city apartment. I need a big yard and trees," her grandmother had said the day she handed Orella the keys.

Orella had thrown her arms around the woman who had raised her and hugged and kissed her.

"You need a better place. You got a good job, you need to live like you've got money," her grandmother had continued.

Orella had moved from her tiny one bedroom into this sixteen hundred square feet condominium in 1991. The place had three bedrooms, two and a half baths, a living room, a dining room, and a kitchen. She'd washed windows, cleaned the floors, polished the antique furniture, and planted a few flowers in the garden. When her grandmother died, the little money she left to Orella allowed her to make a few improvements, but it was the generous gift of an interior decorator, hired and paid by a friend, that had turned her home into a showcase of taste. The few times she'd had guests over, they'd marveled at how beautiful the place was, but all of the questions were ridiculous.

"How did you afford this place on your salary?" was the most popular.

"Who is your Sugar Daddy?" was another.

"None of your b-i-z," was Orella's stock answer to all cross examinations.

The condo was now worth more than $2,000,000 after all the renovations. Kathy Woods, her friend, had hired a gardener, too, who kept the garden in tip top shape. She loved sitting out there, drinking cocktails, and listening to a CD of birds chirping with crickets and frogs chiming in.

She sat down, poured herself a nice big drink and slid the stack of color coded books that she would never read over to make room for her feet. She switched on the compact stereo on the end table beside her at the same time that she clicked the remote to turn on the television. Taking a swig from her glass while moving the shaggy calypso pillows to fit behind her back, she leaned back and closed her eyes; listening to Luther Vandross croon about how he didn't want to be a fool.

Forty-two years old and counting, Orella was an attractive African American woman. She was in good shape considering she didn't exercise on a regular basis. Her eyes were hazel and her hair was thick with some shade of auburn that only her beautician knew for sure. Her full lips were never without red lipstick or her ears without earrings.

She had made a promise to God and she intended to keep it. If she would get away with leaving the scene of the accident earlier this morning, this would be her last night of drinking. She had an hour to go before midnight so she might as well use her time wisely. She threw back the snifter and swallowed the mellow liquid. Humming along with the music, she sensed the burn as the brandy moved down her esophagus and began to warmly attack the knot that forever dwelt in her belly. The second drink was almost poured to capacity when she glanced at the television that was perpetually muted. What she saw caused her to spill the valuable liquid onto her glass top table.

"Oh hell no!" She exclaimed.

She watched as one of the twin towers collapsed. She scrambled for the remote. Realizing that it was soaked with brandy, she rushed to the kitchen and grabbed a towel from the drawer to mop away the liquor that she was tempted to lap with her tongue. Back in the living room, she turned up the volume. For the next few hours, she had drink after drink while she watched what most of America had been watching all day: the attack on the World Trade Center.

Chapter Thirteen
September 12, 2001

Kathy was at the hospital when Jessica woke up, hoping against hope that her memory had returned. According to Dr. Ford, the best way to handle the whole situation was to act normal and carry on a conversation in an effort to spark a memory. Someone had attacked Jessica and Kathy wanted to know who was responsible. The perpetrator had not touched the five hundred dollars in cash in her purse nor had he stolen her American Express card, Visa, or her wedding rings—a huge diamond of at least six carats, and a band encrusted with smaller diamonds weighing at least three more.

"Good morning, Jessica, how are you today?"

"Physically I'm a little better, but…I still don't know…anything," Jessica answered carefully.

"Well, I can help you with some facts," Kathy said. She was quiet for a beat wondering how to say what had to be said. She didn't want to upset Jessica, but it was best to get straight to the point. "Your full name is Jessica Woods and you were married to my brother, Troy," she said. "You live in Texas."

Jessica kept her eyes on Kathy's face, digesting the information she had just received. She swallowed and then posed a logical question.

"Where is my husband?"

"He died a few days ago and you came to New York for his memorial service."

Jessica closed her eyes. "How did he die?" she asked.

Kathy pulled a chair next to Jessica's bed and sat down. "He was in an accident at a job site he was overseeing. You telephoned me and gave me most of the details over the phone. It was bad. You had him cremated immediately." Kathy's voice cracked and her bottom lip trembled.

"I'm sorry to hear that. I have to be honest and tell you that I don't feel anything about what you just told me other than it must be bad for you, since he was your brother."

"Troy and I weren't close. In fact, I hadn't seen or talked to him in years. Not until he called to tell me about you. You were married just over two weeks ago."

"Oh," was all Jessica managed. She tried to move and winced with pain. "What kind of accident did you say I had?" she asked.

"You were not in an accident, you witnessed an accident. A woman was killed and you collapsed and hit your head on the street curb. The doctor thinks that's the reason for your amnesia."

"I'm hurting all over, especially my stomach. Are you sure I wasn't in an accident?"

"No, you were not; the pain you're experiencing could be from the fall or something else."

"I must have fallen pretty hard."

Kathy wondered if it was a good time to tell her about the abuse the doctor suspected. Would it be too much? Or could hearing about it cause her to remember? She decided to tread the water lightly and then dive under.

"You know that you can get something for the pain if you need to," Kathy suggested.

"That's okay, it makes me sleepy. I want to watch TV. All that stuff about the World Trade Center is horrible. I feel so sorry for all of those people."

"It's just awful. I'm trying not to watch it anymore." Overcome with pity, Kathy took Jessica's hand. "You've been through a lot. You need to rest and try to remember, not fill your head with worry and sadness. Why don't I turn the TV off for a while?"

"If you'd like. Maybe it's all this news about terrorists that's making me feel afraid. It's like I should be somewhere doing something and I don't have a clue what it is."

Kathy decided to put all the cards on the table. "Sweetheart, the doctor believes you were beaten by someone."

Jessica's eyes widened. "Beaten?"

"Yes. And it wasn't the first time. The doctor suspects repeated abuse. That's why you're in so much pain."

"Abuse? By whom? The only thing I remember is seeing the doctor for a short time and then waking up and seeing you and the nurse."

"I don't think my brother was responsible, but we'll know for sure when your memory comes back." Kathy was disappointed. She had hoped that the information would spark a memory.

"I wish I could remember."

"We all want to know what happened to you. The doctor says your memory could come back anytime. I brought along some pictures of Troy. Perhaps they'll jog your memory."

Kathy pulled a small photo album from her large purse and handed it to Jessica, who immediately began to flip through the pages. Her face showed no signs of recognition. She gave the album back to Kathy.

"I don't recognize him. You know what else? Why do I know how to talk and how to think? I thought victims of amnesia had to be taught everything all over again."

"Well, you didn't have a brain injury. You've got the kind of amnesia that is induced by trauma. It doesn't affect your language skills or your cognitive ability. You just can't remember anything. As I understand it, the mind does that to protect you. You've gone through something that was so painful that your mind has repressed it."

"Gosh. Maybe I don't want to remember anything."

Kathy smiled sadly. "When it's time, when your body is ready, you will. In the meantime, you're going to come home with me. I have plenty of room at my house and it is an excellent place to recuperate. The doctor ordered bed rest, and he's given the okay for you to attend the memorial service. When you're ready, you can select the urn for Troy's remains. I felt that was too personal for me to do."

"Kathy, I appreciate your offer and I don't mean to be rude, but how can you be sure about this? I mean you said we don't know each other."

"I've never been more certain of anything in my life as I am that you and I will get along just fine. Before you know it, we'll be like old friends. You and I are family; you need my help and I want to give it to you. I don't want any more objections—you're coming and that's that."

Chapter Fourteen
September 12, 2001

The call woke Orella. An automated voice announced that her workplace was closed until the following Monday due to circumstances resulting from the 9/11 attacks. Whatever circumstance the voice referred to was good news because she was in no shape to get up. She had a hangover to beat the band. Around noon, she showered, dressed quickly in a pair of jeans, a pink tee shirt, her sneakers, and a floppy hat with the intentions of getting breakfast and a bottle of wine. But when she got outside to her normal parking spot her car was not there.

What the hell? She immediately returned to her condo. Things like this had happened to her before, but if she put her mind to it she could usually remember something, and then follow the clues. She was miffed with herself. She'd gotten a lot better about losing her car when she'd decided to do her heavy drinking at home.

She glanced over at the brandy decanter. It was empty, which meant she'd been at home drinking. So where was her car? She took a deep breath. She needed a drink. She went over to the bar and selected a bottle of cognac, opened it, and poured herself half a snifter. She sat down in an armchair that was upholstered in a pattern of cerulean and beige, trying to recall her actions the day before.

She remembered getting dressed on Tuesday morning. She'd had an appointment for a pap smear, so she'd taken the morning off. She remembered having an omelet and a glass of wine. She remembered walking to her car, sipping from her flask of vodka. After that, she didn't remember anything. Nothing. The best place to start was with the OB/GYN.

Humiliated, she called the doctor's office and went through banal greetings with the receptionist before she got to the point. She had to have kept that appointment; she'd already cancelled it three times.

"Did I leave a book at your office yesterday?" Orella asked casually.

"You didn't show up for your appointment—yet again," the receptionist said coolly.

"Oh my goodness something came up. Let me get back to you and reschedule." Orella hung up.

So she didn't go to the doctor's office? Then where did she go? She took a sip and closed her eyes. Then she saw a flash of her grandmother's house, and herself walking through the leaves. Was that yesterday? She needed noise. She could think more clearly with sound.

She clicked the remote to turn on the television. And there it was! The World Trade Center attack. She'd been on the sofa watching the news last night, drinking. Suddenly the local news came on.

"An unidentified woman was killed in a hit-and-run car accident just after the first plane flew into the North Tower yesterday morning. Witnesses reported seeing a red sports car fleeing the scene. Anyone having any information about this incident is asked to call the number at the bottom of the screen," the anchorwoman reported.

Bam! That's why she had been at her grandparents' home. She had driven her car there to hide it. She had killed that woman. And then she remembered her promise. She got up and poured the cognac from her snifter and the cognac in the bottle down the drain. She immediately called her insurance company and reported her car stolen. She'd go down to the precinct later and file a report. She had to get it on record.

She poured out every drop of liquor and beer in the place; and there was plenty. But she wanted a drink badly. Was she sure that she could do this? How long had it been since she'd gone one day without a drink? Not since senior year in college. She was becoming increasingly restless. Feeling nervous was foreign to her. Paranoia about being handcuffed and hauled away to jail set in. It would not look good to be drinking if they came to arrest her. But no one had knocked on her door yet. Should she wait around until they came? Should she leave town? No. There was no way she was leaving New York City. This was her home. Her castle. She sat down to think.

The victim was a woman. The victim died. Orella was a murderer—an accidental killer. She hadn't meant to do it. It wasn't like she took a gun and blew the woman's brains out. That happened every weekend somewhere in the city. She felt bad about it, but what was she supposed to do? Turn herself in? Go to jail voluntarily? Ruin her career? Orella had not prayed in a long time but now she began petitioning God to keep her out of prison. She had a nice home, a good job, a spotless reputation, and respect in the community. People liked her. She had been blessed. Her grandparents had worked hard all of their lives to take care of her and educate her, leaving everything they'd owned to her. She couldn't let that come to naught because a woman wasn't watching where she was going. She couldn't think about it. If she thought about it too long, she'd need another drink. And that was what had gotten her in this mess in the first place. She needed help. She found the number to Alcoholics Anonymous, dialed it twice and hung up both times when someone answered, because another thought had occurred to her.

If no one saw her, no one could blame her. Thank God for those tinted windows! The main reason she had them was for privacy. She sometimes liked a drink on the way home from work. A cop driving up beside her while she drank from her flask would be bad news. Funny that no one had reported seeing her. A woman had looked right into her eyes and screamed, "Stop!"— just before she'd felt the bump and knew that she'd hit something. The face of that woman was seared into Orella's brain—she would never forget it. She could swear that the woman had seen her, too. Why didn't she report it to the police?

She stood up suddenly. She had to keep busy. Keep her mind off things. She went into her bedroom. Her closet needed straightening! She could take out some things she didn't wear anymore and give them to charity. That would be a good deed. Didn't the bible say something about blessed is he who gives? A blessing was what she needed.

Chapter Fifteen
September 12, 2001

Port Liberté, a European styled community of condominiums and townhomes, offered its residents an awesome view of the Statue of Liberty as well as the manmade canals and gardens throughout the property. Designed by a French architect, the luxury homes were located on the western side of Upper New York Bay on what was originally known as Caven Point, a natural sand beach.

Foley Brogdon woke up in a pink bedroom. He rolled over and stared into the glassy eyes of a giant teddy bear wearing a red dress and a big white bow on her head. *What the hell?* He kicked off the pink comforter and sat up on the full sized bed. There were dolls everywhere; big ones, baby sized ones, Barbie and her friends, and of course, Ken in his swimming trunks. He stood up and almost tripped over a cage containing two hamsters; one white, one black. He shuddered at the sight of them as he regained his equilibrium. Everything came rushing back to him. The plane crash, the smoke, the dust, the people, the mad scramble to the docks, arriving in New Jersey, and Anissa was missing.

He was in the bedroom of little Tabitha Laferty, a seven-year-old, high spirited, young lady who'd cheerfully shared her space.

"You can sleep in my bed, Mr. Doctor Brogdon," she'd declared.

"Thank you very much," Foley had responded, trying to match her eagerness.

As he dressed in the new clothes he'd purchased, the view from the window permitted no view of the smoldering remains of the World Trade Center, but his sooty clothing lying in a heap confirmed the nightmare of the day before.

"Good Morning," he greeted everyone minutes later as he entered the breakfast area to join the family seated at the table, staring at a television on the counter.

"How did you sleep?" Janet Laferty asked, rising to get the coffee pot.

"Fine. Thank you again for sharing your bed, Tabitha," Foley addressed the pretty little girl.

"You're welcome," she beamed.

"Thank you very much for welcoming me into your home," Foley addressed the adults.

"Glad to do it," Paul Laferty replied, handing Foley a plate with pancakes and sausage while his wife poured coffee into a cup in front of an empty place setting.

Foley sat and drank the hot liquid quickly. The pancakes were delicious, but he had no appetite. After expressing his gratitude for their hospitality, he left the Laferty home and took a ferry to Manhattan. He needed to look for his wife. According to the news, there was a trauma center set up near the site.

Chapter Sixteen
September 13, 2001

The memorial services for Troy Woods were over in an hour. Kathy sat on the front pew next to Jessica. They were both dressed in black. Kathy had purchased black flats, hose, underwear, and a dress for Jessica who was now surrounded by relatives and friends of the family, all of whom were complete strangers to her. Kathy could tell that she was uneasy.

"How are you feeling, Jessica?" she asked, knowing that it was a silly question, but wanting to communicate with her all the same.

"I'm beginning to feel a little calmer. I've been so nervous and anxious; but today, in this quiet room, listening to the eulogy was good for me. He said some good things about life and death."

"Yes, it was good," Kathy agreed.

Victims from the World Trade Center were being eulogized as well, filling all the chapels with funerals; most for public servants. The Mayor appeared in the vestibule to greet mourners and extend his condolences. The families of the victims seemed to welcome him as one of their own as he appeared to share their pain.

Back at Kathy's house for the repast, Jessica mingled, accepting condolences and wishes for a speedy recovery. One uncle, who always told jokes no matter what the occasion, was busy with an anecdote. He had Jessica laughing in no time at all. The food was plentiful, served buffet style. Additional chairs and tables placed in the large family room accommodated most of the family. Others spilled into the kitchen and the dining room. By 9:00 p.m., everyone had left. Jessica was exhausted and excused herself, leaving Kathy alone with Geoffrey Winston.

"Are you going to be alright?" Geoffrey asked.

"Yes, I will. Thank you so much for being here with me," Kathy replied.

"I wouldn't have it any other way. I'll always be here for you. It was good to finally meet your friends and family."

Kathy sat down in an oversized burgundy armchair and admired the swift clean-up by the staff. The room was back to normal. Kathy loved this huge room. It served as a family room, but had enough space to entertain. Someone had turned on the gas log burner. The fireplace was warm and, despite the somber occasion, the flames were inviting and set an atmosphere for romance. Geoffrey was seated on the large burgundy sofa that was the focal point of the room. The end tables and the sofa table were dark wood, polished to a shine. Fresh cut flowers on the low cocktail table added pleasant aroma. The sand colored rug on the floor provided sharp contrast, making the burgundy colors of the upholstered seating pop. A large burnished urn containing a huge peace plant sat in an alcove. The sight of the plant was comforting because it had been in the house since Kathy's father died.

She leaned back and considered the day's event. As far as remembering the dead goes, it had been a nice occasion. Sadly Jessica still didn't remember anything, and had no family of her own to help stir her past. On the other hand, being an orphan protected Jessica from the grief that revisits most people as they lose family members. She and Jessica were in the same boat now, without immediate family.

Geoffrey came and knelt in front of her. He was a kind man with shrewd intelligence, and she trusted him with her life. He was fifty but did not look a day over forty. Six feet tall, with warm brown eyes and dark brown hair that was beginning to turn grey around the edges—he was a very handsome man. She wasn't sure if she loved him yet, but he was definitely growing on her. He took her hands into his as he looked deep into her eyes.

"I think everything went well. I'm sorry about your loss and it's a shame that the widow can't remember her husband, but you remember him, and for now that's got to be enough to try to help Jessica get her memory back. I'm available to do anything you need me to do," he added with a suggestive lift of his eyebrows. He kissed her hands and smiled.

"Maybe it's a blessing that you and your brother were not close; like you've said yourself what you're feeling is more grief for the lack of closeness," he continued.

"Thank you, Geoffrey. I appreciate that," Kathy replied sadly. "I feel so badly about Troy; the way he died and how sudden it was. But honestly, it seems like he's been gone a long time because we just never talked. We were rarely in the same place long enough to discover if we had anything in common besides our parents. When they died, it got worse. I got married and went to live in Georgia and he went to Europe for a while and then lived in Texas. He hasn't stepped foot in this house since mom and dad passed and now he never will. But maybe I can make amends by helping Jessica. Her world has been smashed and she doesn't even know it. They were in love, and when her memory comes back, she's going to have to go through mourning all over again. I can be here for her. That gives me consolation."

"Good girl. And once she gets her memory back we can find out who attacked her," Geoffrey added, standing to his feet.

She smiled up at him, the desire in her eyes matching his, as he pulled her to her feet and wrapped her into his strong arms. She felt at home there, like she belonged. She sighed with pleasure as she pressed her body against his. He grabbed her hips on either side and lifted her until their private parts were flush. She squealed as she felt his hardness.

"Once again you put it right there," she giggled.

"Let's go put it *in* there," he whispered in her ear. She took him by the hand and led him to her bedroom, where he promptly made her forget about everything except her body and his. He was a passionate lover and knew just what to do with his hands and mouth to drive her crazy. When he entered her and ground his pelvis against hers, he set her clitoris on fire, plunging in and out until she lost herself. She floated on a cloud for hours after their lovemaking. Just the thought of him when they were apart left her wet and filled with longing.

They lay back breathless and spent. A few minutes later, she was asleep breathing softly against his chest. She had no idea how much time had passed when she was awakened by a soft kiss on her forehead. She opened her eyes and saw that Geoffrey was fully clothed.

"Where are you going?" she asked softly.

"I've got to get back to Atlanta. Retirement has not slowed me down. I've got some urgent matters to attend to, with bomb threats emptying buildings all over the country. I've got a long drive ahead of me so I'd better get going. You get some rest. I'll call you later. I love you."

"I know," she managed before drifting off to sleep again.

Chapter Seventeen
September 13, 2001

Canvassing hospital emergency rooms all day Wednesday searching for his sister Clementine and his niece Sherry had been futile. Felton's friends on the force had helped, making it possible to cover more territory. He'd heard that a lot of the victims were either out cold in hospital rooms or lacked identification. Every instinct told him that unless they left the building before the plane hit, his relatives could not have survived. Nonetheless, he operated as if they were still alive.

Tina, as he'd called his sister all of his life, was a survivor. She'd had to be because she'd married a guy that their parents strongly disapproved of and ran off to New York when she was seventeen. Widowed at the age of twenty-three, she'd been devastated. Her husband, a U.S. Army soldier, had been killed in action in Cambodia during the Viet Nam War. One year after his death, a brief affair left her pregnant with Sherry. The veteran's benefits had helped, but it was not enough to provide a decent lifestyle. After years of night school, she'd earned a degree and been hired by a business firm that paid a decent salary.

Six months ago, the company had relocated to the World Trade Center and Tina had been promoted to director of risk management with a hefty increase in salary. The move had created job vacancies, so she was able to get a position for Sherry in another department. Felton's eyes were brimming with tears when he'd left the boys with a sitter again because all schools were closed. He didn't know how to tell them that their mother and grandmother might not be coming home that night either.

Fliers for both Tina and Sherry were now taped on glass windows, brick walls, and telephone booths. He left them with hospital emergency room personnel, in police precincts, and any empty space on subway walls he could find. Friends had helped get them up on Staten Island, Brooklyn, and Jersey City in hopes that the two women could have taken a ferry and were somehow lost in a different borough of New York.

He gazed longingly at their faces as he put the last two in place at the 42nd street subway. Tina was still attractive at 58 with a constant twinkle in her eyes that the camera had captured perfectly. She had begun to grey a little and was always talking about dying her hair blond, like Sherry. He looked at Sherry, her long blond hair, brown eyes, pretty smile; she was too beautiful and young a girl to die. She had a crush on someone who worked in the Twin Towers as well, and she came up with new excuses to drop by his office every day. He worked on the 16th floor. Felton hoped that she'd found a reason to be in his office when that airplane crashed into the building. If so, there was a possibility that she got out in time. He willed her to still be alive. Her sons needed her.

Determined, he made his way toward Ground Zero as quickly as he could. Felton shook his head as he thought of the true meaning of ground zero—the point directly above, below, or at which a nuclear explosion occurs. An airplane crash was a nuclear explosion? He didn't think so, but nobody had asked him.

Police radios had crackled all morning about bomb threats, and all available bomb squads were out in full force. Grand Central terminal had been evacuated as well as Macy's Department Store, and the Port Authority Bus Terminal. All Broadway theaters were closed. Felton thought that was just as well, because he didn't know anybody who'd be planning dinner and a play right now. People were worried that there would be another attack.

Felton was dressed to work. He wore a heavy long sleeved shirt, heavy denim jeans, and hard soled, high topped khaki suede boots from his days in the military, a baseball cap, and carried a thermos filled with coffee. If Tina and Sherry were anywhere in that rubble he wanted to be there when they were found.

Arriving at the scene, he became nauseated. The pictures on television could not portray the damage and carnage before him.

Almost six stories of tangled steel, stuck out at all angles from the pile of dust and concrete. One lone steel beam stood erect in the midst of the rubble. How could anyone be alive under all of that? The street was still filled with dust and smoke still lingered in the air. And the stench! It had intensified a thousand times over. If Sherry and Tina were trapped under all that mess they were in bad shape. He leaned over to vomit, as a gaunt fireman approached him.

"You need some help there?" he asked.

"Nah, man." Felton wiped the spittle from his mouth with the back of his hand and produced his badge.

"We found one survivor yesterday," the fireman announced.

"Male or female?" Felton asked holding his breath.

"Male. We had to dig him out. You should have seen it, man. These guys passed that guy about 200 feet, from one man to the other, until we got him where the ET guys could work on him."

Felton released his breath and turned away. He wanted to hit something. He wanted to tear something apart. He was so angry he began to cry. Was there any use? Should he just give up and go sit the boys down and tell them the awful truth? Suddenly, he felt the strong arms of the fireman enveloping him. He pulled himself together, thanked the guy for his sympathy, and strode into the mountain, ready to move steel and concrete. His heart ached as he ground his teeth together. Jaws clenched and fists balled into hard weapons he stumbled through the wreckage. Firemen were still fighting the blazes that seemed to continually break out.

He began to work side by side with volunteers, using five gallon buckets to gather debris and pass it down an assembly line of other brave men who were determined to make a difference. He felt depression setting in as he worked until dark without finding a single sign of life. What he did find was a shoe—a single black pump he could have sworn he'd seen Sherry wear before.

Chapter Eighteen
September 14, 2001

Jessica woke up in that lazy state where sleep has gone, but thoughts still drift and eyelids remain closed. She saw herself standing in a beautiful room with gold draperies and white sheers at the windows. There was a four-poster bed in the center of the room with a gilded framed picture of a French chateau above the headboard. From out of nowhere, a fist crashed into her jaw. The blow knocked her against a table, the sharp edge cutting into her shoulder, as she slumped to the floor. Her face stung, she tasted blood and felt her ears ringing.

Quickly she scrambled to her feet, trying to fight back. This time her attacker slammed his fist into her stomach. She doubled over from the pain. The man placed his hands around her neck and began to squeeze. She began to claw at his hands, struggling to breathe. She couldn't see his face. With her last ounce of strength she yanked his hands away, as she opened her eyes and sat up, gasping for air. Relief flooded her body when she saw that she was in one of Kathy's guest bedrooms. *Was that a memory?*

She was in a beautiful bedroom, her bed flanked by two windows with green and beige striped draperies. Light streamed into the room, danced off the heavy beige brocade comforter onto the plush white robe draped over the high backed bench at the foot of the bed. Two bedside tables of dark polished wood, with brass lamps covered by ivory pleated lampshades, stood at attention next to the bed. Fresh cut flowers were positioned on the corner of each table, their soft scent drifting past her nose. The room was large, the walls painted pale green. Prints of green leaved plants on beige backgrounds decorated the walls. The massive bed sat in the middle of a white rug with green and beige patterns on the border that made the bed appear as if it were floating. An armless green chair to the left and two large beige armchairs in the sitting area with a glass topped table between them completed the picture. It was a very pretty and modern room. Kathy either had good taste or had used a fantastic decorator.

Jessica took a deep breath. Did her husband really beat her? Or was it someone else? She put one hand on each side of her head and closed her eyes, concentrating, trying to force the face of the man to come into view; trying to remember something, anything. After a few minutes she realized that it was useless. She picked up the remote to the television and clicked.

The CNN Newsroom was broadcasting the World Trade Center attacks. The newscaster began by giving the time line of the assault by air.

"On September 11, 2001, American Airlines Flight 11 departs late from Logan International Airport in Boston at 7:59 a.m.; destination, Los Angeles. It's a Boeing 767 carrying 81 passengers and 11 crew-members. Hijackers immediately rise from their seats and stab two flight attendants with box cutters. Within minutes, one of them takes control of the airplane. At 8:14 a.m., United Airlines Flight 175, a Boeing 767, also departs from Logan International Airport, destined to land in Los Angeles also. This flight is carrying 56 passengers and 9 crew-members. Moments later, hijackers take over the plane. A flight attendant aboard Flight 11 calls out via air phone to alert authorities that the plane has been hijacked. At 8:20 a.m., American Airlines Flight 77 departs from Washington Dulles International Airport en route to Los Angeles. It's a Boeing 757 with 58 passengers and 6 crew-members. In minutes, this flight is hijacked, too. At 8:26 a.m., Flight 11 makes a 100 degree turn to the south and heads towards New York City. With a 40-minute delay, United Airlines Flight 93, a Boeing 757, takes off from Newark International Airport bound for San Francisco, carrying 37 passengers and 7 crew-members. Minutes later, hijackers control this plane as well. At 8:46 a.m., two F-15 fighter jets leave Otis Air National Guard Base, intending to intercept Flight 11, but thirty seconds later Flight 11 crashes into the north side of the North Tower between the 93rd and 99th floors."

Scenes of each crash appeared on the screen as the timeline continued. The video of the World Trade Center was attributed to a French documentary filmmaker who was working at a firehouse when the call came in about the crash. The newscaster continued:

"At 9:03 a.m., Flight 175 crashes into the South Tower between the 77th and 85th floors. From 8:48 a.m. till approximately 10:28 a.m., at least one hundred people jump or fall to their deaths from both towers. At 9:37 a.m., Flight 77 crashes into the western side of the Pentagon and fire breaks out. At 9:45 a.m., United States airspace is shut down, all civilian aircraft are grounded, and all aircraft in the air are ordered to land immediately at the nearest airport. At 9:58 a.m., the South Tower of the World Trade Center collapses. The Marriot Hotel located at the base of the two towers is destroyed. At 10:03 a.m., passengers aboard Flight 93 try to stop the hijackers on board, but the plane crashes into a field in Shanksville, Pennsylvania. At 10:28 a.m., the North Tower collapses."

"Oh…my…God!" Jessica said aloud as she watched the huge cloud of smoke and dust spread down the streets of lower Manhattan, engulfing buildings and people as they frantically tried to outrun the gargantuan pall. It was unbelievable; debris fell, papers flew through the air, and then blackness engulfed the camera lens. Jessica felt the panic and the fear, her stomach knotting with anxiety.

A knock at the door drew her attention away from the television, but not from the anguished feelings over all the death and destruction. "Come in," she said.

"Good morning," Kathy breezed into the room carrying a tray with an array of breakfast foods. She seemed momentarily taken aback as she regarded Jessica warily. She glanced towards the television and saw the CNN headline, *World Trade Center Disaster*.

"I brought you something to eat. I didn't know what you'd like so I took the liberty of choosing several things," she said as she put the tray down on the foot of the bed. She reached for the remote and switched off the television.

"Enough. You need to rest and think happy thoughts…and try to remember."

Kathy busied herself placing the tray across Jessica's lap and opening the napkin. She handed it to Jessica as she leaned in and gently guided her forward. After fluffing the pillows, she moved the tray in closer as Jessica sat back.

“Thank you, Kathy.” Jessica suddenly felt torn. She wanted to share the brief flash of memory that she’d had, but she didn’t see the man’s face. Kathy would want to know who it was. She’d want to know if it was Troy. Jessica decided to keep it to herself.

Chapter Nineteen
September 14, 2001

Dr. Jennings Ford went home to Brooklyn and collapsed on the bed, fully dressed, not even bothering to turn on a light. He had worked long and hard since September 11th. He was not a young man and he was long overdue for some time off. He stayed in bed until morning.

When he finally woke up, he noticed the dust in his bedroom for the first time. It was so thick he could write in it. The window had been open since Monday night. He liked sleeping with a window open. *My God,* he thought, *will I ever get away from the destruction?* He called his cleaning lady, Sophia, who lamented with him about the dust. Her apartment had to be dusted and cleaned from top to bottom. She arranged to be at his place within the hour.

He picked up his dog from the sitter and walked far enough to see that a lot of debris was scattered on the streets. He stopped along the way and chatted with other dog owners about the horror of it all. Later he went grocery shopping, paid bills, and read the latest medical journals. He opened the morning paper, immediately turning to read the obituaries like many people once they reach a certain age, looking for the names of old friends and acquaintances. The last name, Troy Woods, seemed familiar. He began to read the brief obituary, his memory stirring. He could not quite put his finger on it, but he knew he had come across the name before. He removed his reading glasses and stretched. He was tired.

Widowed for eleven years, he still missed his wife. She had died the same way she'd come into his life—suddenly. He'd come home from work and found her sitting at the kitchen table—dead from an aneurysm. A few years later he sold their house and bought the apartment. It was small; just two bedrooms and one bath. The kitchen was rather large compared to the other rooms. Ironically, it was the least used room in the house because he didn't cook.

He hired Sophia, a middle-aged woman with grown children, to clean and walk the dog. His was a lonely life most days, but he stayed busy. He spent time with his daughter and his grandchildren whenever he could. They lived in Manhattan, not too far from the hospital where he worked.

The frantic pace of the emergency room provided distraction; it did not allow time for dwelling on the past. He usually rendezvoused with his memories right before he drifted off into a deep coma-like sleep induced by long hours on his feet at the hospital.

He put his glasses back on and continued reading. “He leaves to mourn his wife, Jessica Woods, and a sister, Kathy Stockton.” Jessica Woods! The beautiful young woman with the bruised body. He had not thought much about her since Tuesday, but her appearance had deeply disturbed him. It was obvious that someone had been abusing her for a long time. He shook his head. He had never been able to understand how any woman could tolerate abuse. Nor did he have any sympathy for a man who resigned himself to using his fists on a woman. It was the cowardly way.

He sighed as he thought of the protests from the woman’s sister-in-law. She was so certain that her brother was not responsible. She had to be right, because some of the woman’s injuries were too recent for the husband, who had died a few days earlier, to be responsible. At least that’s what the sister-in-law had said. And yet, someone had abused her— but who? The young woman couldn’t tell because she couldn’t remember anything. It was probably for the best: she would probably never press charges.

Nonetheless, he was glad that he had reported it.

Chapter Twenty
September 14, 2001

Foley Brogdon and his parents had come to the crowded Manhattan precinct to file an official missing persons report, hoping that police expertise would produce results. Foley had not had any luck locating his wife, Anissa. None of his father's efforts had produced any clues about her whereabouts. He'd been as close to Ground Zero as regular people were allowed to go and the sight of the destruction had made him sick. He had not been able to stay. Volunteers were working as fast as they could to locate survivors. Foley wanted to go back there every day but the officials discouraged it. They promised to let him know if they found Anissa's body. He'd gathered as many phone numbers as he could and let them know without reservation that he would be calling them. Surprisingly one small corner of the Marriott had remained, but everyone who'd been trapped there was rescued.

A rather serious looking police officer came toward them.

"Good morning folks, I'm Jeff Evers. Come with me please, I'll be taking down your information."

Foley, Lacy, and Foley, Sr. followed the officer down a hallway to a room with a sea of desks. The officer led them to his desk and indicated chairs for them to sit down. Foley glanced around the room as the officer got himself together. Desks were littered with file folders, papers, empty Styrofoam cups doubling as pen and pencil holders, and phone books. A large American flag stood in the corner. The Stars and Stripes seemed omnipresent, as people displayed them everywhere since 9/11, determined to show unity and patriotism. There was an old refrigerator against one wall and a table with a large coffeemaker and a box of donuts. This officer had recently spilled something all over his desk. It was still wet; soaked paper towels that had been used to mop up whatever liquid it had been sat on the corner of the desk. Foley was losing confidence in his competency by the minute.

"Can you give me your wife's name and description, please, sir?" Officer Evers asked, preparing to fill out a missing person's report form.

"Certainly," Foley handed the officer a flier. "Will this help?"

Jeff glanced at the pretty face of the woman on the flier and smiled sadly. "It certainly will. Thank you." The officer read the descriptive information briefly. "Can you tell me what she was wearing the last time you saw her?"

Foley looked embarrassed for a second. "I don't know, something green," he snapped. "She was not dressed the last time I saw her, but I'm positive she didn't leave the hotel that way," he explained.

"Which hotel?"

"The Marriot World Trade Center."

Jeff put his pen down and looked at Foley, obviously struggling before he spoke.

"Have you checked the hospitals?" he inquired somberly.

"Yes, I have. Both the morgues and admissions. I asked for Anissa Brogdon and Jane Doe." Foley hesitated as he thought of Anissa's wallet. Every piece of identification she owned was in that wallet; the wallet that was inside his briefcase.

"You're thinking that maybe she didn't have any identification, that she left the hotel in such a rush that she didn't grab her purse?"

"Yes," Foley responded, hiding his relief. With pandemonium everywhere, it was plausible that a woman would save her life first.

"Any birthmarks or other distinguishing features?"

"No."

"We'll do our best, Dr. Brogdon. We've got our hands full, as I'm sure you can imagine," he added in a monotone as he stood, extended his hand to Foley's parents, shaking each one firmly. He turned to Foley to offer the same courtesy, his hand reaching out.

"May I have your card please? I'll be contacting you," Foley offered, ignoring the officer's hand. "I'd hate to be the last one to know when you find her."

The young officer looked as if he'd been slapped, but placed his card in Foley's hand and then turned to lead them back the way they'd come.

His parents' presence in the city made everything less complicated for Foley. His father used his influence to get into places that ordinarily were closed to the public. He was allowed to walk through the makeshift trauma centers set up near the wreckage of the towers. He was allowed to make an appeal on camera because of his father's friends. He stood there beside a group of mourners who were also searching for loved ones. They each faced the world and made their entreaties to the public on air, unable to hold back the tears. But so far nothing. All he could do was wait and hope. Each night he stared at her photo and silently pledged his love to her.

"Anissa, I love you so much. Please come back to me. I promise I will love you until the day that I die," he whispered softly to the face staring back at him.

He meant those words. When he had first met her, he knew that she would be his wife and the mother of his children. It took longer than he thought to convince her to marry him, but he had finally won her hand. They had been happy together for three years; their relationship worked because they were polar opposites. He was strong where she was weak; she would do anything to please him while he only wanted to do things that were in the best interest for both of them; she had been born poor and he entered the world as the son of a very wealthy man. They were compatible in every way beneath the sheets. Life without her was unfathomable. He had to find her.

He and his parents began the arduous task of putting up fliers. Rumors claimed that thousands of victims lay unconscious in hospitals or were wandering the streets in a daze. Fliers were everywhere; walls, storefronts, lampposts, subway stops, and phone booths. Foley and his parents taped or stapled Anissa's face beside the others. Foley's mother slowed to read some of them. She became more and more distressed as she perused the faces of the lost; compassion for their families causing tears to flow.

“These poor people—so many of them,” she said disconsolately.

Foley thought it best that they finish as quickly as possible; he didn’t like to see his mother upset.

Chapter Twenty-One
September 17, 2001

Having dropped the boys off early at school, Felton Dade had time to stroll toward Wall Street, heading towards Bowling Green Park. The New York Stock Exchange had re-opened this morning. Not usually superstitious, he crossed the street and rubbed the bull.

Often referred to as the Charging Bull, this bronze sculpture with its head lowered, nostrils flaring, horns ready to gore, was a popular tourist attraction, as well as an icon, representing the power and strength of the American people. Stroking its back was believed to bring luck. Felton needed all the luck he could get and then some. Technically, the bull did not belong to the city of New York, the copyright being held by the sculptor who himself trucked and installed it in the middle of Broad Street in December of 1989. The police impounded it, but the public protested to such an extent that the New York Parks and Recreation Department had installed it where it presently stood.

He looked at his watch. He had a good thirty-five minutes before he was due in the office. His captain had told him to take all the time he needed.

"I don't expect to see you here. You've been through a lot and every man here supports you. If you need anything, let us know."

"Thank you, sir. I appreciate that, but I need to work. I need to keep busy," Felton had responded.

He took a deep breath, remembering the past Sunday morning, when he'd finally sat down with his nephews and told them the truth.

"Both of you know that your mom worked at the World Trade Center, right?"

The two boys held his gaze. Nathan, the elder of the two, swallowed and nodded his head.

"Well, I've been looking for her and Grandma Tina since Tuesday, the day everything happened, and I'm afraid that they're not coming back."

Justin began to cry outright, while only a single tear fell from Nathan's left eye as he held Felton's gaze.

"You're afraid they're not coming back or do you mean they're not coming back?" Nathan asked bluntly.

"They're not coming back. They were on one of the floors above the plane crash, and there was just no way for them to get out," Felton continued, his voice cracking with emotion.

"Are they dead?" Nathan whispered with disbelief.

"Yes, son," Felton replied.

"Do you think Mama and Grandma Tina went to heaven?" Justin sobbed.

"Yes I do," Felton said, pulling both boys into his arms. Nathan wrenched himself away and stood up with his fists balled. "Why did the terrorists do this? Mama and Grandma Tina didn't do anything to them." Tears began to stream down his face as he finally asked what burdened his heart. "What's going to happen to us?"

"I love you guys and I'm going to take care of you," Felton promised. "We're all going to stay here and be a family." He reached out for Nathan and this time the boy came to him willingly. Felton closed his eyes as he held them to his chest. He cried with them, all the while wondering how in the hell he was supposed to become a parent overnight.

Chapter Twenty-Two
September 19, 2001

New York City officials were still conducting a rescue and recovery mission at the World Trade Center site. More than an estimated 5,000 people were still missing. Orella had taken the subway down to the west end as far as she could and then walked over to Maiden Lane, one block away from Ground Zero, looked through her binoculars and saw the devastation with her own eyes. She was overwhelmed by what she saw. The magnitude of the attack hit her like the clichéd ton of bricks. She could only imagine what the people who lived in the area were going through. Even from this distance, the odor permeated the air. The smell of death. She began to cry as she thought about the woman lying dead in the street because of her. She was no better than a terrorist herself. She should go to the police station right now and tell the truth.

No. I can't go to jail. I can't live the rest of my life as a common criminal. If they come for me I have no choice but to go and I will. But until then...

Many curious onlookers stood with her, some taking pictures. Orella hadn't brought a camera. She didn't want to view this as a tourist attraction. She wanted to see the harsh reality of an event depicting the depravity of mankind. The sight of all of it would remain with her. There would be plenty of pictures for the public to view. She had no desire to have any of her own. The memory would be far more powerful than anything a camera could capture.

She bowed her head and prayed for everybody whose lives had been touched by this act of terror. She murmured words of thanks and beseeched God's mercy on his children. She was getting good at this prayer thing. It was the first thing she did every morning and the last thing she did every night. If she was going to jail, she might as well get in the habit of pleading with God.

There was going to be another candlelight vigil in Union Square that night. She would be there with two candles. That's the least she could do. One for the person whose life she had snuffed out with the wheels of her car and one for all the victims of the mass destruction a few blocks away.

"Amen," she said quietly.

She smiled sadly at a few people as she turned to head back home. She was proud of herself. She'd passed several liquor stores and had no desire to go in; well maybe she had a desire, but she'd resisted. *Please God, don't let me go to jail,* she prayed.

Orella nearly had a heart attack when a blond woman near the front of the crowd began to make her way toward her. For some reason the woman's face was familiar. *Good Lord was that the woman who'd looked into her face at the accident scene*? Orella ducked down and pretended to tie her shoes that didn't even have shoelaces. As the woman walked by, Orella realized that it wasn't her. Orella prayed that the one woman who could put her away was a tourist and had gone back to Kalamazoo or Tarzana, or some other lost city. She hoped all of the news of the terrorist attack had erased Orella's image behind the wheel of a red car from her memory.

Chapter Twenty-Three
September 20, 2001

Jessica Woods looked at photos of her late husband every day hoping that something would jar her memory. He remained a complete stranger to her and so was his sister, Kathy, even though each day they grew closer. Kathy had mentioned that she and Troy were not pen pals or chatty on the phone. Jessica had learned that her late husband owned a construction company in Texas and that he was very wealthy. Kathy had been in contact with the general manager, informing him of Jessica's condition, and asking him to take authority until further notice.

Her body was healing and the pain was subsiding. The bruises were mostly purple now. The first few days when she had looked at herself in the mirror, she could not believe the discolored blotches that covered every ounce of flesh on her abdomen and her back. She cried more from her appearance than from pain. Who could have done such a thing to her? And why? She and Kathy had eliminated Troy. Even though she could not remember him, based on what Kathy told her and the time line of meeting and marrying Troy, she knew that there was no way that he could be responsible for the continued beatings.

He had been dead already when the last beating occurred; the doctor's examination had proved that. Could she have had a relationship with an abusive man before she met Troy? That brief flash of memory placed her in a room with a man who was hitting her. Could this man have been overcome with jealousy and have followed her to New York? Could she have agreed to meet him somewhere, and that was why she chose not to have Kathy meet her at the airport? Could this mystery man have become angry with her and beat her somewhere on the streets of Manhattan? Or had it simply been a random act of cruelty? An attempted robbery gone wrong? No, a robbery didn't fit the memory and the memory of the man's hands on her throat was real. And besides, nothing was missing from her purse.

The oddest thing was the constant yearning in her groin. She and her late husband must have made love often and hard because that part of her body ached to be filled. She resorted to masturbation to get release.

She put the photo album down, dressed in her white robe, and started downstairs. The guest bedroom was on the second floor. Across from her room were another bedroom and a library. From the landing, she could look down into the foyer. The walls were covered with peach colored damask wallpaper—the slanted ceiling seemed to soar up to the third floor. A huge chandelier hung just above the entry door. The stairway curved with an ornate wrought iron railing. The stairs, covered with a runner and a peach colored artisan rug, felt cool to her still sore bare feet. Downstairs she walked to the bay windows, where a large bouquet of yellow roses sat on a shiny mahogany table. She'd intended to look out and check on the weather, but the sight of the roses caused her to shiver as she leaned over to smell them. The instant the scent hit her nose; she felt transported back in time as memories began to rush back like a feature film in her head.

She was in a school, walking down the hallway beside a line of tiny people that were clearly elementary students. She led them to a cafeteria where little children were seated at long tables chattering away while they ate their lunch.

"There you are!" said a petite woman wearing glasses and a very severe grey skirt suit. Jessica knew her name immediately: Mrs. Jones.

"Lunch time," Jessica said.

"We have something in the office for you!" She beckoned to Jessica to come with her.

Jessica fell into step beside her.

"Voila!" announced Mrs. Jones, opening the door to the main office and spreading an arm toward the counter where a large vase with four dozen yellow roses and an envelope attached stood.

"They're for you! When are we going to meet this man?" asked Mrs. Jones.

"I have no idea," Jessica answered.

"Mr. Oscar will bring those down to your classroom. They look heavy."

"Thanks," Jessica said as she pulled the white envelope from the roses and took out the card. It read: *Please have dinner with me. I think about you all the time. You have bewitched me.*

Another memory. Did Troy give her these yellow roses? Had she been a teacher? Should she tell Kathy?

Chapter Twenty-Four
September 20, 2001

The boroughs of New York saw countless funerals and memorial services. Today was the service that Felton had dreaded. As a rule, he didn't go to funerals. He hated them and their cause: death. Necessity brought him to the front pew of his sister's place of worship, the Right Divine Methodist Church. To his left sat nine-year-old Nathan and to his right sat seven-year-old Justin, both wearing their Sunday best and a stoic demeanor. It was their turn to follow the ritual of publicly acknowledging the death of their loved ones.

The church was filled with people, expressing sympathy, especially for the two boys who would grow up without their mother.

A large photograph of Sherry stood on an easel on the right of the pulpit; Tina's photo stood on the left. The floor was covered with flowers—in pots, on stands, and some in vases. Felton felt the tears before they actually streamed down his cheeks. He wanted to be strong for the boys, but he knew that if he let lose the tears, the boys might let go a little too. They needed that.

As the pastor delivered the eulogy, the boys finally started crying when they heard their mother's name. Felton allowed his mind to wander, remembering the last conversation he'd had with Sherry.

They had been at home. It was after midnight and Felton had just acted as referee for a brawl between Sherry and Justin's father, Chase Reynolds.

"You need to get rid of that chump and find yourself a good man. Get married and settle down," Felton had said.

Chase, the chump he referred to, was a low-life who liked to hit women. He'd knocked Sherry around earlier that evening. Felton had clocked him upside the head with the butt of his pistol and then arrested him for trespassing. Sherry refused to file charges against him. The dude was scum. He didn't pay child support; in fact, he hadn't been in Justin's life at all. He'd just show up in the middle of the night for a booty call, and as unbelievable that Felton thought it was, Sherry went along with it. Chase had control issues. He didn't want Sherry, but he didn't want her to be with anyone else.

"Uncle Fell, you don't tell me how to live my life. I appreciate you helping to get him out of here, but you can't tell me who to love," Sherry had replied.

"You're too smart for this, Sherry. You lost your teaching job because of this dude. You gonna let him keep beating on you until he kills you?"

"No, Uncle Fell. I got this. I…got...this!"

Tina grabbed Felton by the arm and pulled him into the kitchen. The boys were upstairs in their room and were told not to come out during the ruckus.

"Let grown folks alone, Felton. Some people have to learn the hard way," his sister had chastised him.

"Tina, you know me. You know I can't put up with this shit and I don't see how Sherry does!"

"She loves that sorry boy and there's nothing you or I can do until she sees the light."

That was the last time he'd spoken to either of them. All of them had been angry that night; Tina at Sherry, Sherry at Felton, and Felton at both of them.

The emotion was still with him— anger. Righteous anger. But this was neither the time nor the place for wrath. This was a time for sadness, a time for remorse. He had attended four funerals in the last few days—two for fellow officers, one for a fireman, who'd perished with his whole squad, and one for a friend.

Next on his agenda was getting custody of his two nephews. Nathan's father was long gone; he never even met his son. It was Justin's father, Chase, who would be a problem. He was making noise about 'raising his son.' Felton wasn't having it.

"Let us remember that our loved ones live forever in our memories," the pastor said as he ended his sermon. Felton breathed a sigh of relief. One down. One to go.

On Sunday, September 23rd, the three of them would go to Yankee Stadium for a memorial service in honor of all of the families who had lost loved ones. Then they would begin the long journey of putting their lives back together.

Chapter Twenty-Five
September 24, 2001

Breakfast had always been Kathy's favorite meal to prepare. Options were so limited that it didn't take a lot of thinking or prep time. She took out whatever was the choice of the day and went from there. Today it was wheat toast, eggs, one half grapefruit, tea for Jessica and coffee for herself. She hummed as she flipped over the eggs.

She loved her kitchen. The Bertazzoni appliances added style—a side by side refrigerator- freezer, two wall ovens, a warmer, a dishwasher, and a Master Series 36 inch gas range in sterling silver made it easy to concoct any meal. Her cook, who was in charge of lunch, dinner, all snacks, and baking, raved about all the counter space.

"Good morning!" Jessica said cheerfully as she entered.

"Good morning to you."

Kathy noticed that Jessica seemed more excited than usual.

"I remembered something!" She said excitedly.

Kathy quickly placed one egg on each plate and turned to give Jessica her full attention. Finally a breakthrough.

"I think I was a teacher. I had this clear memory of being at a school, with a class and the school secretary, a woman named Mrs. Jones, came to the cafeteria to tell me that I had roses in the office. Am I right? Was I a teacher? Did Troy tell you about that?" Kathy could hear the hope in Jessica's voice.

"No, dear," Kathy answered slowly, careful not to crush Jessica's hope. "He was somewhat tightlipped about who you were and what you did for a living. All I know is that he loved you and was about to introduce you to his family."

"Yellow roses. The roses he sent were yellow," Jessica's voice trailed off as she continued; "The yellow roses in your foyer brought the memory to me."

"Yellow roses huh? I'll have to keep them all the time. They're a trigger. Do you remember who the roses were from? Were they from Troy?" Kathy asked.

"I didn't see a name on the card, just an invitation to dinner."

Kathy knew that yellow roses had been their mother's favorite. Troy would have remembered too. He would have also remembered that his mother kept fresh cut flowers in the house.

"Mrs. Jones wanted to know when she was going to meet the man that sent them," Jessica added.

"So a mystery suitor? A romantic? I hope they were from Troy, I honestly cannot tell you if he was a romantic though," Kathy again considered how little she knew about her brother.

"I can't tell you either," Jessica sighed as she scooped up her grapefruit.

"Perhaps we can somehow find this Mrs. Jones. She may be able to help us find other people who know you," Kathy suggested.

"Yes, but Jones is such a common name. I don't even know if this is a recent memory, so I wouldn't even know where to begin to look for her." Jessica put the spoon on the table and glanced at the television on the kitchen counter as if she could find an answer there.

Kathy had been watching the news reports that were still preoccupied with information about the 9/11 attack. Many of the passengers on the hijacked planes had made frantic last minute phone calls to relatives, friends, employers, or coworkers. Those last words were seared in the minds of those left behind. Apparently those last words had spread quickly, because the passengers on Flight 93 had learned of the attacks on the World Trade Center and the Pentagon from such phone calls.

They fought to save their lives and brought down the plane in Shanksville, Pennsylvania, averting another major catastrophe; likely in Washington, D.C. President George W. Bush had called them heroes. The terrorists were cowards, and Bush promised that those responsible for the attacks would pay. Kathy wasn't so sure that revenge would help heal the wounds of those who mourned their lost loved ones.

"On a brighter note," the newswoman reported, "One of the world's largest retail stores, Wal-Mart, reportedly sold over 100,000 American flags on September 11th."

Chapter Twenty-Six
September 25, 2001

It was morning. Jessica sat freshly showered in Kathy's library in a very comfortable chair, wearing the same fluffy white robe that she'd worn every day since she'd arrived. She'd tossed the pillow onto the cocoa colored brown suede couch that sat in the center of the room to her left. Her glass of milk sat on a coaster on the end table, joined by framed pictures of Kathy and Troy when they were teenagers, and a polished silver lamp. She had just finished eating a delicious piece of pound cake, as she sat admiring the sheer beauty of the room—all the furnishings complimented each other perfectly.

On the square shaped white coffee table in front of her were two large candles ensconced inside two very large and unique candle holders made of glass and wood. A very healthy rubber plant sat in the center between them.

The shelves behind the sofa were lined with books of all genres. Jessica loved books, and the library was her favorite place in the house. Kathy had so many old volumes like *Gone with the Wind, Pride and Prejudice, Anna Karenina, A Tale of Two Cities, The Three Musketeers,* and many more brown or navy blue leather volumes.

A matching chair covered in brown swirls, dots, and stripes on a white background with blue trim at the bottom sat across from her. Jessica opened the book she'd selected today. It was about French art. The first chapter was entitled "The Renaissance." Suddenly memories came flooding back.

Chapter Twenty-Seven
December 1997

She was standing in a courtyard in front of Eckhart Elementary School, surprised to see the man who sat on a bench. Her eyes traveled up a brown pin striped pant leg to a neat waistline to broad shoulders held captive by a matching brown pin striped suit coat to a blue shirt and white tie to the well-tanned, handsome, aquiline face with the beauty mark on the right cheek just below a pair of the bluest eyes that she'd ever seen. Blond and gorgeous, his long legs indicating that he was at least six feet tall, he flashed a smile at her.

"Hi," he said.

"Hi."

"I'm hungry, let's have dinner."

He dazzled her with that smile again.

"I don't date," she answered.

"I'm not asking you for a date. You eat don't you? Can we share a meal?"

"How many times have I heard that line? A guy thinking that asking a lady to eat with him is not a date is old school." Surely he could do better than that.

"That's me. Mr. Old School. Will you have a bite to eat with me?"

"Why?"

"Because I want to get to know you better."

"Maybe some other time." She started towards the parking lot to her car as he fell in beside her.

"You're not making this easy."

"That's because I'm not."

"Not what? Easy? Of course not. But I am!"

She laughed. He was so handsome and he looked so innocent standing there. She felt herself being overpowered by his maleness. It had been a long time since she'd been in a relationship and the last one had soured her opinion of men. Other faculty and staff were exiting the building and naturally, their attention was drawn toward the two of them. The one thing she tried to avoid was putting her business in the street, so she took a deep breath and accepted his invitation. After all, she was hungry and the only thing waiting at home was a frozen Weight Watchers meal. She offered to follow him in her own car, so that she could leave when she was ready.

Reminding herself to not take anything too seriously was the first step, as she was not in the mood for a one-night stand, or wasting her time trying to win over a Prince Charming with less than honorable intentions. Polite, but not too forthcoming about anything would be her modus operandi, not accepting a second invitation if one came.

"How long have you been teaching?"

"Two years at Eckhart. Before that, I taught eight years at a middle school in South Carolina. That's my home, and I wanted to give back."

"So while you breathe, you hope?" He smiled at her. He went up fifty points in her opinion poll. He was the first man she'd ever met who knew South Carolina's state motto.

"Why do you know that?" She giggled.

"I memorized all sorts of stuff about these United States. I know, for instance, that South Carolina was named for King Charles 1, your state flower is yellow jasmine, your state bird is the wren, and your state tree is Palmetto, hence the Palmetto State. That's why the yellow roses; jasmine is not easy to find, except maybe in South Carolina."

"Wow! I'm impressed."

"Then I have succeeded," he grinned.

"And where did you get such a fine education?"

"Princeton of course. How about you? Where did you learn to teach?"

"Well, I learned to teach in the classroom. See, they didn't tell me what to do when confronted by thirty middle school children for seven class periods a day at Tennessee State University. I had to find out the hard way; on the job. Sink or swim."

"Like me. I learned by doing as well."

"I know what kind of work you do."

"Do you? So you checked me out?"

"Of course. I need to know who's been around my students."

"And here I thought you did it because you found me irresistibly handsome and debonair. Silly me!"

She did find him irresistible. She couldn't keep her eyes off his mouth when he spoke, in spite of the fact that she prided herself on her ability to look people in the eyes. But his mouth was delicious; he actually had a fully defined top lip; quite rare for a WASP. She found that he knew a lot about African American history, Hip Hop and R & B, soul food, and he swore that he could dance. The more he talked, the more she liked him. When they parted for the evening, she wanted to kiss him badly, but he only offered his hand and an invitation to a private screening of a new movie which she graciously accepted without thinking. Dating a white man was a first for her, but she had always been curious. Now was as good a time as any to indulge those curiosities.

Her father had been white and her mother had told the horror story of their relationship so many times that she'd made her daughter almost afraid of white men. Her mother had loved her father and believed that he loved her—until his parents forbade him to see her when they found out she was pregnant. They threatened to disinherit him when Nedra was conceived. That was the end of the romance between her mother and the father whom she'd never met.

"I want you to know that this will not develop into anything serious," she told him. "I am not looking for romance, but I don't mind having an escort once in a while."

"Okay then. I'll be your escort for a while but I'm expensive," he winked at her.

"I didn't mean it that way; I just want things to be clear from the start."

"I get it. You're not looking for love. So we'll just hang out."

Ignoring all her own objections, she decided that dating him was a cultural learning experience.

On the third date, they made love. It started with a kiss. Kissing was her favorite part of the sex dance. And could he ever kiss! He began by touching his lips to hers lightly and then pulling away. When their lips touched for the first time, she lost her breath. It came back when he touched his lips to hers a second time, lingering for a few seconds. The third time his lips pressed slightly harder as he tenderly coaxed her mouth open with his tongue, gently sucking her tongue into his mouth. He was alternately circling and sucking her tongue with his, each time a little more intense. She felt waterworks letting loose between her legs. He moved from her mouth to her neck with light nipping kisses and then back up to her mouth to molest her tongue again as he slowly unbuttoned her sheer blouse.

She gave him back as good as he gave, settling herself in to thoroughly enjoy whatever came next as he skillfully unhooked her bra and removed it. The real action began when he gently took one of her nipples into his mouth and then nursed it aggressively. He continued to undress her as he moved down, stopping at her belly button while he slid off her skirt and her panties. She had never considered her navel particularly sexy or erotic. It was just there; it was an 'inny' instead of an 'outie' so he had to plunge his tongue inside of it. When he finished his ravishing, she would forever be turned on by attention to it.

She steeled herself as he moved lower, stopping just above her labia. She was not a real fan of cunnilingus, because the few men that she'd allowed to attempt it in the past were terribly awkward and clueless as to what the whole thing was about: stimulation of the clitoris. They were slobbering, lick and spit, hit and run artists who kept asking 'Is that it?' This lack of savoir-faire left her wet with their drool instead of her own body juices; completely aggravated and frustrated to the point that she wanted to scream "Enough already!" She automatically tried to close her legs, but he was having none of that. He put his tongue on the right spot immediately. Almost involuntarily her legs opened wider as wave after wave of orgasmic pleasure caused her body to tremble as he skillfully nipped and teased with his tongue; culminating with hungry suckling. He aroused her to a frenzy; she moaned and cried out with passionate desire for more.

She thrust her body upward and moved her hips with the rhythm of his mouth until her insides erupted and exploded. And just when she thought she could not take anymore, he plunged into her and began the erotic dance that men and women have danced with their bodies thrashing together through the ages. If he had charged her money for the satisfaction and fulfillment he gave to her she would have gladly paid.

When it was over he locked his blue eyes with hers and whispered "I—love—you. I cannot bear the thought of you being with someone else. I want you to be mine, Anissa."

Chapter Twenty-Eight
September 25, 2001

Anissa! Her name was Anissa, not Jessica, and she was married to Foley Brogdon, not Kathy's brother Troy. Fear began in her belly and rose to her throat; she muffled a scream. *Oh my God! Foley! Where was Foley?* He would be looking for her. *So much time has passed!*

She frantically rushed to the bedroom to look for clothes, something to wear. She had to get out of here. She had to get to a phone to call him, to explain about the accident, the amnesia, everything. She reached the top of the landing just as Kathy came down the stairs, dressed for the day wearing a lavender silk blouse and grey trousers.

"Hi, Jessica! Where are you going? You're supposed to be resting remember?"

"Kathy, I remember everything and I have to call my husband. It is urgent that I let him know where I am. Please, I must have a phone."

"Don't you remember that your husband is dead? Just let me get you back in the bed and we'll talk," Kathy coaxed, guiding Anissa toward the bedroom.

"My husband is not dead," Anissa began. "My name is Anissa Brogdon and I'm married to Dr. Foley Brogdon, a cosmetic surgeon from Brentwood, Tennessee."

Anissa hesitated to gauge Kathy's response as they looked at each other. Kathy folded her arms across her chest and raised her eyebrows, giving Anissa the impetus to continue.

"We are here in New York because he was a speaker at a medical conference at the World Trade Center. We were staying overnight at the Marriott, the one between the two towers. My husband was at the conference and I was alone in the room when a woman knocked on my door and screamed for me to get out of the building. Instead of staying near the hotel, I kept walking until I got to a dead end at a traffic light. There, a woman started talking to me and then she stepped off the curb right into the path of a car. I screamed for the driver to stop and tried to pull her back by the strap of her purse, but it was too late. Her purse came off in my hands and then she was under the car. It was the worst thing I've ever seen in my life." Anissa began to cry, tears streaming at first and then she began to sob uncontrollably.

Kathy led her over to one of two black and white, striped chairs that sat on either side of a black lacquered table and sat her down. She offered Anissa a tissue, staring at her with a look of incredulity on her face. Finally she spoke.

"Do go on."

Anissa blew her nose, took a deep breath and continued. "My husband is probably going crazy wondering where I am. I have to call him. He's going to be angry, but maybe he'll understand when I explain that I was hurt and that I couldn't remember who I was."

Kathy pulled the second chair away from the wall so that it faced Anissa. She sat down and crossed her legs.

"So you're telling me that you are not my brother's widow, Jessica Woods?"

"Yes, I mean no, I'm not his widow. But why do you think I am?"

Kathy let out a sigh of exasperation.

"They went through your purse! And I went through your purse."

"What purse? I didn't have a purse, my husband won't ever…" Anissa's voice trailed off, wringing the tissue with her hands. There was no way that she was going to tell this stranger that Foley had taken away her wallet and her purse and her shoes to keep her in that hotel room until he returned. Anissa suddenly realized how lucky she was that he had not left her bound and gagged. She shuddered at the thought. She'd actually felt no need to grab anything before she left the hotel room. She looked down at her hands and then back at Kathy. This had to sound crazy to her.

"I thought you were my brother's wife because you had her purse. You are telling me that you tried pulling my sister-in-law out of harm's way by her purse, ended up with that purse in your hand and that's where the mix-up began? Let me ask you, if you were me, would you believe that?"

Anissa was impressed by Kathy's composure. Faced with the same set of circumstances she wondered if she could have remained calm. Of course, Foley would have; calm was his middle name.

"No, I wouldn't believe it, not without proof. Why don't you google the words Foley and Anissa Brogdon, Wedding on your computer. You'll see pictures of me and Foley. I don't have anything else to prove that I am who I say I am."

Kathy didn't move. She seemed to be thinking now, as she focused her eyes on the wallpaper above Anissa's head. Anissa waited.

"And if what you're telling me is true it means that the real Jessica, my Jessica, was hit by a car and is dead? You know what? You'd better hope I find you on the Internet because if not, I'm calling the police!"

"I'm telling you the truth. I can see her just as clearly lying there not moving, her face all smashed in. I just went out like a light after it happened."

Kathy stood, pushed the chair back into place, and went upstairs to her office. Anissa followed. Once there, she sat down at the computer and typed in the words that Anissa had suggested while Anissa watched over her shoulders. She clicked on a link and there, smiling gaily, stood Anissa beside her new husband, Foley Brogdon. Kathy tried a few more links and was able to gain enough information to know that what Anissa was telling her was true.

"So who is beating you up?" Kathy asked.

Anissa had expected that question, but was emotionally unprepared to answer. She burst into tears and turned away to hide her shame. "I just need a phone please," was all she could say.

"Forget about the phone. You're not calling anybody until I hear or see something that makes sense of all this. And you need to calm down. You're making me nervous and I don't like to be nervous."

Anissa made a decision. There was no need to tell Kathy anything else. She was going to leave this house by force if necessary, because her life depended on contacting her husband as soon as possible. She knew who she was now. She knew who had beaten her. And she knew that as Mrs. Brogdon, her allegiance was to her spouse and his family name.

"I wasn't beaten. I'm very clumsy. I fall down a lot."

Kathy came around and stood in front of her.

"Where is your purse with your own ID? And you know what else is weird? You didn't have any shoes! What happened to your shoes?" Kathy demanded, changing the subject.

"I left them in the hotel room. We had to evacuate so quickly, I didn't stop to get my purse or my shoes, I just left the room," Anissa lied.

"The doctor said you were beaten. You were covered with bruises and you know it. Who did it?"

"I must have gotten bruised when I fell, after I fainted."

"No, you didn't. Some of those bruises were old. Now you tell me the truth or else I'm going to turn you over to the authorities and let them sort this mess out. For all I know, you could have faked that amnesia. How did you get those bruises?" Kathy was losing some of her composure.

Anissa looked down at her feet that were still sore from cuts and bruises. Time was being wasted here, precious time. The sooner she contacted Foley the better. He would be crazy with worry. He would think that she had left him. What if he'd already taken drastic action? It was clear that she wasn't getting away from Kathy without physically moving her out of the way or answering her questions. Kathy had been kind to her, kinder than anyone had been in a long time. She owed her the truth. She locked eyes with her and began to explain.

"Sometimes my husband loses his temper and hits me. He doesn't mean anything by it, but he gets these crazy ideas in his head that I might leave him, so he does things to ensure that I won't. Like take my shoes and my purse so I won't have any money. If I decided to run, I would have to do it barefoot and penniless." She shrugged her shoulders, her face covered with shame, willing Kathy to accept this truth. It was humiliating to have to share the cruelty she had endured.

Kathy looked into her eyes a long time with an indiscernible look on her face.

"Your husband beat you like that and you want to go back to him? Why in the world would you want to do something like that?" Kathy laughed.

Anissa was startled at first and then she became angry. This was no laughing matter.

"I'm glad this amuses you, Mrs. Stockton, but it's not funny to me. I have to go. Do you have the clothes that I wore to the hospital?"

"So it's Mrs. Stockton now? Are we no longer friends, Mrs. Brogdon?" Kathy still had a smile on her face, but it softened as she began to unbutton her blouse. Anissa became alarmed. What was this woman doing? Kathy removed her blouse and turned so that Anissa could see her back. Stretching from the middle of her left shoulder blade all the way down just below her waistline on her right side was an angry looking scar. Kathy looked triumphantly at Anissa over her shoulder.

"That beautiful scar is a gift from my husband. He got mad because I couldn't carve a turkey so he took the knife and demonstrated on my back. Of course, the doctors and nurses at the hospital believed that I did this to myself trying to commit suicide. I'm such a silly fool you know, and very clumsy." She put her blouse back on and turned to face Anissa.

"I left the hospital and went back to him. Imagine that!" She laughed again, a deep throaty laugh.

"Your husband did that to you?"

"Yeah, sometimes he got angry, but he didn't mean anything by it. He had this crazy idea that I might leave him so he did things to ensure that I wouldn't."

"Are you mocking me?" Anissa was indignant.

"Yes, and myself, too. Look, lady, what I'm telling you is that I've been there and done that and I learned a lesson that I'll share with you: if you really intend to go back to him you might as well kill yourself right now to save him the trouble, because that's where you're headed: to an untimely violent death. You can't go back. Haven't you tried to leave him before?"

"Yes, I did. When he finds me, there's no telling what he will do. He promised to hurt my sister if I left him and he'll do it. He may have already done it."

Anissa knew that she was talking too much. She had to stop talking. There were rules that she lived by; rules she obeyed.

"But he doesn't have to know where you are or that you're even alive does he?" Kathy asked.

"What are you talking about?" Anissa asked.

"You could be dead for all he knows! The Marriot Hotel has been reduced to rubble."

Kathy paused. It seemed as if she were trying to give Jessica time to absorb what she'd just said.

"*He* could be dead! He was in the World Trade Center during the attack; God knows how many people were killed there. If you ask me, this is perfect timing," Kathy continued.

Anissa wasn't listening to her. The anxiety she felt was almost overwhelming. She had to do something. She wasn't dead. And she didn't know if Foley was dead or not. It had never occurred to her that he could be dead. All she could think about was what he'd do to her for not letting him know her whereabouts.

"I'll call his parents. They will know where he is."

Kathy put her hands on Anissa's shoulders and shook her gently.

"Listen to me," she said. "And think about it as I go along. You were beaten very badly; the doctor feared that you had an injured spleen and a back injury. Thank God you didn't, but Anissa, that's no way for a lady to be treated. When did it start?"

"I don't understand what you're asking me."

"I'm asking you when your husband began to beat you." Kathy's voice was insistent.

"On our honeymoon."

Chapter Twenty-Nine
June 1998

The June wedding befitted a royal couple. Anissa was the proverbial blushing bride, dressed in flowing lace, pearls, and sequins. She and Foley's mom had gone on a shopping trip to Italy to buy her gown. Her Maid of Honor was Carlie Harper, a friend since high school, who looked regal. She had five bridesmaids, one of them her only sibling, Nedra Wilkins, who was married with three children. The wedding was held at Brentwood Heavenly Home Baptist Church, with a reception following at the Opryland Hotel.

"I am so glad you picked this purple honey. I look good," Nedra declared.

"Indeed you do!" Anissa responded.

"Someone has outdone themselves with this get-together! Your wedding qualifies for lifestyles of the rich and famous! I feel honored to be a part of something like this!" Carlie, her best friend and maid of honor, said.

Anissa loved Carlie. Brash and unsympathetic, she was Anissa's complete opposite, but that's what had drawn them to each other. Both of them had been track runners in high school.

"You got it going on in every way, sister girl, and I wish you years of happiness," Carlie saluted with a glass of champagne.

"And remember what I told you about taking half if this doesn't work out!" Nedra whispered into Anissa's ear. Nedra was a taker and not a giver, but Anissa loved her sister anyway, although she felt that Nedra had never returned the sentiment.

They'd all hugged each other and when they came apart Foley was standing beside her, asked for her arm, and gently led her to the dance floor for the first dance. How lucky was she! Foley was the catch of the century.

"I love you, Mrs. Brogdon," he whispered as he held her tightly against him.

"I love you, Mr. Brogdon," she whispered back.

The rest of the evening was a blur. Anissa only remembered that Carlie caught her bouquet when she threw it into the crowd just before she climbed into the limousine with Foley on the way to their honeymoon and the beginning of her happily ever after. Soon they were whisked away in a private jet.

Their destination was Paris, a long flight during which Foley was relatively quiet. He was polite to the flight attendant and was affectionate to Anissa, but said very little. They were served champagne and strawberries to celebrate their wedding.

She was tired but happy and so excited to be going to France for the first time after studying about the country and visiting it vicariously through her textbooks, travel shows, and videotapes. It was dark when they arrived at Charles de Gaulle, but there was a car waiting to take them to the hotel.

"Get ready, sweetheart. I have a surprise for you. Ahh, the things I am going to do to you. You are mine completely now," he whispered to her once they were settled in the back seat. Anissa shivered with anticipation of what was to come. He had already done everything so well; the thought that he had something else up his sexual sleeve excited her.

"Bring it on, big boy!" She winked.

Their penthouse suite was in the Georges V, Four Seasons Hotel. It was beautiful. Anissa took in the lavish furnishings. The sitting room had a blue sofa with coordinated toss pillows. There were two blue and white upholstered armchairs arranged at an angle with a table between them. On the table were yellow roses and an ice bucket filled with champagne. She headed through the bedroom, winked at the king sized bed that was covered with a white down comforter, to the bathroom to change into the lingerie she'd splurged on for their wedding night. It was lacy, frilly, pink, and so sexy. A little tipsy, she undressed carefully, leaving her clothing on the floor, giggling with excitement as she admired herself in the mirror.

The bathroom made a statement too. A loud one. A huge whirlpool tub sat in marble in the middle of the floor. There were separate walk in showers, his and her lavatories and commodes, and a bidet. It was done up in shades of blue with everything one needed to refresh oneself.

She stuck her leg out of the bedroom first and then let herself slither erotically around the corner, into the sitting room. Her hair was loose and hanging in her eyes the way Foley liked it. She was ready for whatever he had for her.

"Take that off and put this on," he said quietly, standing beside the bed.

The stillness of his voice was the first thing that signaled to her that something was different, and then she saw what he held in his hand. It was a black sheer apron. She laughed aloud before she could stop herself.

"Are you serious?" She asked.

These were the last words she'd speak that fateful wedding night. What happened then ruined her honeymoon and her future. From out of nowhere, Foley's fist crashed into her jaw. She hit the wall behind her with such force that one of the lamps toppled off the table.

"Timing is everything, Anissa. Let that be the last time you laugh at me or question anything I do. Things have changed. You are my wife now, you belong to me. I am the king of my castle and what I say goes. Do you understand? I don't want you to speak I just want you to nod your head. Do you understand?" His voice was soft, but his eyes were like ice water.

Anissa's face stung, she tasted blood, and felt her ears ringing. He had hit her hard. She lunged at him with her fists balled up, but learned quickly that she had made a mistake. He punched her in her stomach, blindsiding her so that she was weakened and at a definite disadvantage. She doubled over from the pain.

"I asked if you understood what I said. You didn't answer me. Don't ever try to fight me, Anissa—I'm better than you," he said, his voice hard as steel.

He moved in closer and placed both hands around her neck and began to squeeze. Her instincts caused her to begin to flail with her fists at his head and shoulders. He continued to squeeze, not hard enough to choke her to death, but enough to cause loss of consciousness.

When she came to, she was on the bed, spread-eagled with her wrists and ankles tied to the bedposts. She pulled hard but could not free herself. Her neck was sore and her jaw ached. Her stomach was like a painful abyss. She was naked except for the black apron that was raised, exposing her genitals. He stood at the foot of the bed staring at her. She opened her mouth to protest, but found resistance, abruptly realizing that she was gagged with a hard ball-like object that was attached to some type of binding that pulled at the sides of her mouth and wrapped behind her head. Terror filled every fiber of her being. What was happening? What was wrong with Foley?

"I love you, Anissa, but you have to learn something about me very quickly. Until I know which way you are going to go with this you will remain in the position that you presently find yourself in. Make no mistake: I am in control. I am a very good customer at this hotel and my every wish is their command. I wish not to be disturbed, so we will not be disturbed. You and I are going to get reacquainted so that our lives as husband and wife get off to a good start. What happens to you in the next few days may seem cruel to you at first, but in the end, you will understand that all is for your own good. Now, lesson number one. When I give you something to wear, it is my wish that you thank me and wear it. Do you understand? Nod your head if you do."

Anissa nodded her head, watching as he undressed. He put on a nice pair of silk pajamas and pulled a chair over to the bed. Anissa was becoming more afraid as time ticked by. She kept trying to make eye contact with him, but his eyes were on her body. He started at her feet and moved slowly up to her breasts and then down again.

"You know, Anissa, you are a very selfish person. You are very beautiful; I have to give you that, but I think that I've spoiled you. No more sex for you. I can control your passion by withholding mine."

He stood, leaned over, and kissed her on the cheek.

"We will spend this time together making progress. I will talk and you will listen. And when it's time to go back to the States, you will be ready to assume your place in Nashville society as my wife. Know this: I don't take 'no' for an answer. Do you understand?"

She nodded her head.

"Good. Now, let's begin."

Chapter Thirty
June 1998

Anissa had often criticized women for staying with men who beat them. She'd never thought that she would become one of them, but she wasn't going to stay in that situation. She made up her mind to get away from Foley as soon as she was back on American soil.

At Atlanta Hartsfield International Airport, they made their way from the gate into the flow of traffic heading towards the baggage claim and connections to other flights. Foley gripped Anissa's arm firmly, but she was on high alert, looking for an opportunity to escape. But how? The bathroom?

"Foley, I need to go to the restroom," she said abruptly.

"No. You're not leaving my sight."

"I'm getting my period and if I don't do something, I'm going to be walking along with blood running down my legs all over these Jimmy Choo shoes and you wouldn't like that, would you?" She couldn't keep the sarcasm from her voice as she looked at him defiantly. The flash of anger that she had come to recognize appeared in his blue eyes, but just as quickly disappeared.

"Anissa, I've taken note of your cycle and it's not time for it so that ruse will not work."

"Have you heard of irregular cycles? Or bleeding brought on by stress? I'd say I've been under a lot of stress lately, wouldn't you? And you can believe me or not. When I leave a blood trail behind me, somebody's going to start asking questions and we wouldn't want that, would we?"

"Be careful," Foley said quietly, his eyes darkening. "You know I won't hit you in public, or do you? We don't really know that do we? Don't let your mouth write a check drawn on an account that I can close." He kissed her on the cheek.

"I'm sorry, Foley. My period makes me moody. I just don't want to embarrass you or myself. May I please go to the restroom and get a few pads from the machine?" She looked at him pitifully, all the time hating herself for what she had become in the short three weeks since the wedding.

"That's much better. Go ahead, Anissa, but please know that I'll be waiting for you right here. Don't try anything foolish, there's only one way in and one way out and I'm watching. You know the saying wherever you go, there you are?"

Anissa wondered what brought that question out of left field. "Yes, Foley."

"Here's a new twist, just in case you're thinking about running from me: wherever you go, there I am." She didn't miss his meaning.

She walked away from him into the restroom, her mind whirling. Now that she was free how would she stay free? There was only one way in or out. How was she going to get away?

The first person she saw was a member of the janitorial staff, a middle-aged, tired looking, African-American woman leaning against her cleaning cart. She smiled at Anissa.

"How you doing?" she asked.

The kind words and the smile were more than Anissa could take. She began to cry as she entered a restroom stall, sat on the toilet, and began to think. If she could only change her appearance or if there was some way out he could not see. She was beginning to panic. There was no solution; she had to go back to him. Even if she broke into a run, he would surely catch her wouldn't he? She was fast; she held the record for the two hundred meter dash at her high school. Maybe she could outrun him. But not in the heels he had forced her to wear. She would have to run barefoot. She came out of the stall, washed her hands, looked in the mirror, and stared right into the eyes of the cleaning lady.

"Are you alright?" she asked.

Anissa broke down, capturing the attention of every woman in the bathroom. They showered her with sympathy and before she realized what she was doing, she lifted her blouse and revealed the purple, yellow, and blue bruises on her body. The words tumbled out as she described her ordeal of the last three weeks. Everyone in hearing range agreed that for her own safety, she'd better get far away from Foley and never go back to him again.

"He's waiting for me outside. There's no place that I can hide, and if I don't come out of here, he will come in for me."

"You know it's almost one-thirty," the cleaning woman said.

All eyes turned in her direction.

"At one-thirty things happen around here."

Chapter Thirty-One
June 1998

Just over an hour later, Anissa sat in the passenger seat of a Kia Sephia as Ilene Watson, the cleaning woman from the restroom, steered into the flow of traffic on I-285 from the Atlanta airport.

"There's a Fifth-Third Bank at the next exit. They close at six on Fridays. We should get there in plenty of time," she said to Anissa.

It was just pure good fortune that Ilene had a nephew who also worked at the airport, who drove a motorized cart that pulled several large trash receptacles on wheels like a train. At one thirty every day, he stopped at the restroom Anissa had used. Ilene had locked her inside the utility closet just inside the entrance to the restroom and out of sight of anyone outside in the main passageway. Ilene had talked to her nephew on his cell phone while he was en route, explaining the situation and the need for his discreet cooperation. The young man had lined one of the receptacles as best he could with empty garbage bags. He stopped, unhooked a trash container, and rolled it into the restroom, stopping in front of the utility door. He looked around and then opened the utility closet and entered, closing the door behind him quickly. Anissa slipped inside the receptacle he had pushed in, he then rolled it back out, linked it to his mini train, and drove away.

When the trash train finally stopped and Anissa heard a short tap from the outside she lifted the lid and climbed out. She was near a door marked 'Airline Employees Only.' Ilene, just finishing up her shift, was coming out of the door just as Anissa straightened her clothes. Ilene invited her into a nearby restroom, where she handed her a cap, an extra shirt, and oversized jeans. They could hear the announcement and knew that the airport employees were on alert and looking for her. But they were looking for a blond woman in a green pants suit wearing Jimmy Choos and carrying a Jimmy Choo bag. The Jimmy Choo purse and shoes as well as her green pants suit were now in the big bag Ilene always carried into the airport.

The shoes and the suit were going to the wife of the young man who had smuggled her out of the restroom; the purse was a gift to Ilene. Ilene was thrilled to have the oversized leather Jimmy Choo bag and Anissa was glad to part with it. The purse had been a part of traveling attire given to her by Foley just before they left Paris.

"I bought you something in my favorite color to wear home sweetheart," he'd told her. "I'm sorry for having to visit prostitutes while you lay here bound and gagged. French whores are the best; and I met one that I became rather attached to." He'd smiled at her, focusing those clear blue eyes on hers.

"You just weren't that appealing, darling," he continued. "And besides, that little whore did things that you don't have the imagination for, not yet anyway. But don't worry, I'm protecting us. I would never be as thoughtless and cruel to contract some type of venereal disease or God forbid AIDS." He looked so sincere, speaking as if using protection while committing adultery were as simple as covering his mouth when he coughed to keep from spreading germs.

Together Ilene and Anissa walked out, Anissa in her stocking feet and her blond tresses stuffed inside the cap. They'd wished Ilene's workmates a nice evening along the way. Some were curious, but no one said a word; the silent code among underpaid, overworked, and unappreciated workers.

Ilene agreed to drive her to the bank so that she could withdraw some cash from an account Anissa had opened when she got her first job years ago. Regular deposits were made each month by automatic debit from her checking account for the past eight years. She'd never mentioned the account to Foley, who had insisted on knowing about her money. "My money is your money and your money is mine," he'd said. Anissa believed that a woman should always have a little stash of mad money. She was mad now, along with a host of other emotions simmering inside of her.

It was her plan to get all the money from her secret savings account, about $11,000.00, and get an inexpensive motel room to lay low until she had a plan. She was free and she intended to stay that way. She dared not go home to her mother in Chester, South Carolina. She knew that Foley would come after her, expecting her to go to there.

From this moment forward she would have to be very careful. He had proven that he was a very dangerous man. Soon she would learn just how dangerous he really was.

Chapter Thirty-Two
June 1998

When Anissa locked the door of the motel room on Camp Creek Parkway, she pushed a chair behind the doorknob. The room smelled, the carpet was stained, and the bedding felt like it would disintegrate if pulled too hard. Four hours had passed since she'd seen Foley, and she was feeling stronger. Ilene had taken her to K-Mart where she'd bought toiletries, pajamas, a few pairs of jeans and some tops, underwear, socks and sneakers, and snacks. In a sales bin, she'd found a piece of luggage.

She took the time to pack everything, except what she'd need for the next day. She was taking a Greyhound bus to Texas where she planned to spend one night. Her plan was to keep moving until she'd put thousands of miles between herself and Foley. Thank God, she'd insisted on keeping her purse. He had wanted to keep it for her while she went into the bathroom at the airport. She was exhausted and her body ached. She took a long hot shower, brushed her teeth, and took a nap.

A dream about Foley woke her after an hour. She looked around the room, remembering where she was and what she had done. She could only imagine the trouble she was in should Foley ever catch up with her. She needed to let her mother know that she was okay. Foley had probably called her by now, upsetting her—she dialed the number.

"Hello," her mother answered after one ring.

Anissa's eyes filled with tears at the sound of her voice.

"Mama, this is Niss. Listen very carefully. I've left Foley. If he hasn't contacted you already, he will soon. Please don't tell him that you've heard from me. Something terrible has happened and I can't live with him anymore. I'll tell you all about it when I see you, but I don't know when that will be."

"Niss, what are you talking about?" Her mother was clearly upset. "You just got married! You're on your honeymoon for goodness sake!" her mother exclaimed. And then, there was silence.

"Mama?" Anissa could hear her mother breathing.

"Hello, Mrs. Brogdon," Foley's voice came on the other end of the line, sending a chill up her spine. He was at her mother's house in South Carolina. How had he gotten there so quickly? "How rude of you to leave your husband alone at the airport. Is that any way for a new bride to behave?"

Anissa's heart was beating so fast and loud that she thought it would burst. She looked frantically around her hotel room as she tried to think. She had to get out of here; she had to find someplace to hide, just long enough to file for a divorce.

"Mary Sue, do you think I could get a glass of water?" Foley called out. After a second or two, he spoke to Anissa again.

"You have to come back to me. Otherwise, I don't know how long she'll live. Your mother, I mean. You see, if you don't come back I'll be forced to hurt her and I can't leave her suffering, so she'll have to die. And then I'm going to visit your sister and her family. You didn't seriously think I'd let you leave me? Haven't you learned the lesson I tried to teach you in Paris? You don't leave me. You don't do anything without my permission. You're my wife and that means that you belong to me. Do you hear me? Do you understand?" He was calm and cool, sure that his wish was her command.

Anissa shivered at the memory of his fists and his hands around her throat. She should hang up at once and call the police to report his threats and the abuse. His next words seemed as if he'd read her mind.

"Don't think about telling the authorities. In fact, don't think about telling anyone. Ever. It won't help. It will be your word against mine and you're the one who deserted her husband, taking all the money and our traveling documents and doing God knows what with them."

"And you're the one who made me a prisoner and beat me like a dog. You're the crazy one. I have bruises on my body to prove what I've gone through!" Anissa shouted.

"You're accident prone and you've become irrational. You're not yourself, but I love you and I'm willing to forgive you, just come back to me, sweetheart. I need you. Your mother needs you. I don't think she's ready to die yet. Do you? Now tell me where you are."

Would the police believe him? Filing charges against him would prove whether or not he was right. And he wouldn't dare hurt her mother! Or would he?

"Anissa, I'm warning you. I hate to do it, but I will kill your mother and I'll make it look like a natural death. It will be your fault because you're so selfish." His voice was soft and still, just like when he'd sat at the foot of the bed and talked about her shortcomings and the changes she needed to make. She really didn't know what he would do, how far he would go. The man she thought she knew was gone, the boogey man had taken his place. She couldn't risk her mother's life. This was her fight. She would find another way. She'd kill him. That's what she'd do. She would find a way to kill him.

"I'm at a motel on Camp Creek Parkway in Atlanta," she said quietly.

"Thank you, sweetheart. I need the address so I can send a car to drive you back to the airport."

Chapter Thirty-Three
July 1998

Back at home in Brentwood, Foley became the man she'd met and fallen in love with again. He waited on her hand and foot, constantly inquiring into her well-being. He made no more threats and he did not speak about the terror in Paris or her running away. Nothing.

When he made love to her the first time after they returned home, she willed herself not to respond, but her body betrayed her. She welcomed his kisses, and matched them with her own yearning. It had been so long and he laid all of the things she liked on her. He lingered on her neck and shoulders until she wanted to scream. He circled his tongue around her areola, abruptly pausing mid center to suck her nipple into his mouth with such urgency that her secret place began to melt, readying itself for the inevitable.

He continued down, stopping to tease her navel, and then on to the Promised Land. He brought her to orgasm over and over as his mouth possessed her. When she thought she would go into spasms from sheer pleasure, he gently turned her over on her stomach and lifted her hips. He thrust himself inside her so deep that he hit a spot that sent her into an orgasmic tremor radiating all over her body. He pounded away as she arched her back and opened her legs wide, meeting each thrust with her own motion. It was beautiful, and when it was over she felt light as air. He lay beside her, caressing her body until he was overcome with passion again and their lovemaking began anew. She hated her wantonness, but lost complete control whenever he came near her.

They had been home for four days when the phone call came. Foley always answered the only telephone they owned that sat on the desk in his study. He came to the door of the family room to tell her that the call was for her.

Anissa hurried to his office. "Hello?" She heard sniffles on the other end.

"Niss?" It was Nedra, her sister.

"What's wrong?" Anissa intuitively knew that something bad had happened.

"It's mama. They found her dead a few hours ago," Nedra sobbed.

Anissa froze. Dead? How could that be true?

"What happened?" she asked desperately.

"The doctor says it looks like a heart attack. She's been dead at least four days, Niss. I went over there, but I couldn't stay in the room it smelled so badly."

Anissa felt rather than saw Foley. She turned slowly to find him standing in the doorway, watching her with a look of triumph on his face. And then she knew. Foley had killed her, just like he said he would. He had killed her mother to punish her for running away, for trying to leave him. She told Nedra that she would take the next flight out and hung up.

She was furious. The total helplessness she felt as she thought of her mother lying dead in her own home for days was unbearable. Without thinking, she picked up the paperweight from his desk and threw it at his head. It missed him, but hit the window behind him shattering it into a million pieces. She looked frantically for something else to throw.

He moved so fast she barely saw him coming. He shoved her backwards so hard that she fell over one of the armchairs onto the floor. He straddled her as she flailed her fists wildly at him, hitting any place she could. He pinned her shoulders down with his knees as she tried to kick him. He placed both hands around her throat and began to squeeze.

When she came to, she was in a room with concrete walls and what appeared to be a steel door. There were no windows. She sat in a wooden chair with a soft leather seat. Her arms were strapped to the arms of the chair and her ankles were strapped to the chair legs. She tried to move and saw that the chair was bolted to the floor. A leather band around her neck strapped her head to the chair and wires connected her chest to a machine that beeped in the corner of the room. She was also hooked to an IV. She realized that she was wearing a hospital gown that was open in the back and that the seat she sat on had an opening like a toilet. What in the world was going on? She turned her head to see Foley standing in a corner watching her.

"Hi, sweetheart! I had this room equipped with all of the latest conveniences just for you." He opened his arms wide in a sweeping motion to pan the room. "How do you like it? I had it built as my man cave, but it's perfect for you to be alone for a while to think."

Is he planning to leave me here? Anissa thought. He had to be insane.

"I can monitor your vital signs and you don't have to get up to go to the bathroom. I had to choke you again. I really hoped I wouldn't ever have to do that again—but, Anissa, what am I going to do with you? You tried to hit me and that's unacceptable."

He walked over and checked the machine beside her. He nodded with satisfaction.

"Looking good," he said cheerfully.

Anissa was about to speak when suddenly he punched her in her abdomen so hard that she couldn't catch her breath. The pain was white and hot, sweeping through her body as she struggled for air.

"What happened to your mother could have been avoided. I warned you didn't I? Don't worry, she didn't suffer."

His face was pleasant and mildly concerned, as if he were telling her to remember to take an umbrella because the weather forecast predicted scattered showers.

"She just couldn't move while she suffocated. I gave her a dose of succinylcholine; it works like a charm. The trick is choosing an injection site that's hard to detect. I chose her scalp at the back of her neck. I can confess this to you now, because when you're finally permitted to leave this room you won't remember a word I've said."

He stopped pacing and stood in front of her. "Learn to do what I tell you to do and stop fighting me. Or else I'll get to your sister Nedra and her little family. And then, who knows? Maybe Carlie will have an accident on her way to wherever she likes to go. It's not just about you anymore."

He punched his palms with his fist and then walked over to open a cabinet.

"You're in no shape to travel to South Carolina," he said with his back to her. She couldn't see what he was doing. "But don't worry I'll send your regrets. You can sit here and recuperate peacefully or end up in the hospital as a result of a terrible accident. Do you understand?" He walked towards her with a hypodermic needle in his hand.

"Did you know that if a medical professional did not first clear the needle with a short squirt that air could be injected into your veins? An air bubble that would disappear, but of course not before it stopped your heart from beating. Isn't it good that I'm careful?"

She nodded her head as she felt a prick in her arm. As she drifted off she realized that she would never see her mother again.

Chapter Thirty-Four
1998 to present

By the time she was allowed to come out of the concrete dungeon, her mother had been buried, but contrary to what he'd indicated, she remembered everything that Foley had said and done to her. He wasn't as smart as he thought. He would not allow her to contact Nedra or anyone else and no one contacted her.

"No one loves you like I do, Anissa," Foley said confidently. "You see how none of your friends or your sister ever call or come to see you? I'll always be here for you."

He was right. Except for Foley's parents and his friends, she seemed completely cut off from the rest of the world. While she was on her 'sabbatical,' as he'd called it, he'd had bars placed on all of the windows, a high wall built around the property with a heavy gate installed, and more deadbolt locks than she'd ever seen in her life. When he left for work, he locked everything.

"You've got books, a television, music, and the housekeeper. She has orders to only follow my instructions or else," he told her solemnly.

Over the next three years, Anissa learned to read Foley's moods and respond accordingly in order to avoid conflict. She was afraid and tense all of the time. The only time she relaxed was when she slept, because Foley gave her a little something to help her sleep every night. The lovemaking didn't calm her anymore; it just eased her body's need.

"I know you know better by now, Niss, but I can't take the chance that you might slip away into the night while I'm asleep, and I have to sleep. I've got to make a living for us." He'd gently pushed her hair back as he plunged a needle into her arm.

As long as she behaved like a Stepford wife, he was kind to her. He had yellow roses delivered every day. He was affectionate towards her when guests were in the house and when they went out together as a couple. He showered her with expensive clothes; most of them in various shades of green, his preferred color. Shoes, purses, and jewelry galore. Naturally she was not permitted to work.

"No wife of mine is going to work outside of the home," he'd said.

He came home from work one evening and proudly made an announcement.

"I want you to stop taking birth control, Anissa. It's time for us to begin our family. I want at least two girls and two boys. A baby would complete us."

The last thing she wanted was a baby. Foley was self-centered and impulsive. She never knew when he would hit her; she did not want to take the chance that he'd hurt her child. But what could she do? She couldn't tell him no, instead she said what he wanted to hear.

"You're right, Foley, a baby would complete us. He or she would make us a family."

"No time like the present to get started," he said softly, pulling her up from the chair and away from the novel that she'd been engrossed in.

"I'm ready for round one," he whispered.

But she continued taking contraceptives until he discovered them.

"Anissa, when are you going to get it? Okay, remember what our cave is for? To give you time out."

True to his word, he dragged her kicking and screaming back to that dungeon for three days. When she came out, they had sex three or four times a night. Six weeks later, she knew she was pregnant. She was sad and happy at the same time; sad because she didn't want Foley's child, and happy because a new life was growing inside of her. She shared the news with him over dinner one evening.

"I think I'm pregnant. I've missed my cycle," she said nervously.

"I'm so happy for you, my darling. Let's fix up the nursery," Foley was delighted.

In spite of everything, once her pregnancy was confirmed, Anissa allowed the happiness to overrule her sadness as she began to choose things for the room that would house her baby. Eight weeks into her pregnancy, the room was complete. She'd chosen yellow and green as her colors and often found herself standing in the doorway to the nursery, imagining that a baby would change things. Maybe Foley would not want his child to witness violence.

At the end of ten weeks, he came in one evening with that vacant look in his eyes. She instantly felt dread.

"I've decided that I don't want a baby now. You still have so much to learn and I don't want to have to discipline a child and my wife, so let's forget about it."

Anissa cringed, preparing herself for a gut punch.

"I've made an appointment for you to have an abortion tomorrow morning. Afterwards we'll go shopping, and get you something pretty to wear. How does that sound?"

She felt as if her heart shattered like glass, breaking into sharp pieces, each piece piercing her insides. It was all over. Now this child would die before ever having had a chance to live. She refused to show him how much he'd hurt her.

"That's fine with me, Foley. I'd better go to bed now; I'll need rest for the procedure." He gave her sleeping pills to help her and the baby to have a peaceful last night. When they left the hospital after the abortion he invited her to join him on a business trip to New York in September to celebrate.

Chapter Thirty-Five
September 25, 2001

To learn that Anissa was not Jessica Woods was a shock, but finding out about her louse of a husband was more information than Kathy needed in one chunk. She had to do something useful with it. The real Jessica, her brother's wife, had died in that hit-and-run, so there was nothing to be done about that. The most pressing thing now was to convince Anissa not to go back to her abuser.

"I should have followed my instincts the first time my husband hit me," Kathy announced.

She knew that Anissa had to feel like a weight had been lifted off her shoulders. The first time Kathy talked about what went on behind her own closed doors she was ashamed, but the more she told the easier it became. Kathy would never judge Anissa for staying with Foley; she'd stayed with her own husband for seven years.

"Did he hit you before you married him?" Anissa asked, surprised.

"Of course not! Why would he give himself away like that? Did Foley hit you before you tied the knot?"

"No."

"You had no clue that he might turn out to be the controlling son of bitch that he is?"

Anissa tilted her head to the side in thought. "Well he told me what to wear; he ordered for me when we ate out; and he always made plans to do something with my facial structure one day when I saw nothing wrong with the way I look. He didn't like my friends, and he insisted that I lose ten pounds before the wedding. Things like that."

Kathy recognized all the signs. "And you didn't think that was odd?" she asked.

"I just ignored it, I guess. I didn't like it, but I saw no point in making a big deal out of it," Anissa responded.

"You thought he'd change, right?"

Anissa blushed. "I did think that. And he changed alright, but not like I expected."

"And so did mine." Kathy smiled bitterly, remembering those fists and that ugly angry face. If she'd only known then what she knew now.

"He always apologized after a beating. And fool that I was, I believed him. Things just got worse and worse. How about you? Has anything been good since the first beating?"

"No," Anissa answered quickly. And then: "Except the sex," she added with her head down.

"Don't feel badly. Your story is my story. Well almost. My husband was not a red-hot lover. Fortunately for you though, I know how this saga ends."

Anissa looked at Kathy strangely. "What happened to your husband?"

"He died," Kathy shrugged.

"Did you kill him?" Anissa asked quietly.

"I wanted to. But his heart gave out. And if your husband is dead, too, it is a blessing that is not in disguise." The death of her husband had saved Kathy's life; she knew it as well as she knew that raisins were dried grapes.

"I need to find out. I can't just stay away from him," Anissa added.

Kathy could find out for her. She had friends that knew other friends who knew that information is the only real currency.

"I'll find out. In the meantime, you pull yourself together and consider the opportunity that has been handed to you. He can't hurt you right now, and now is all we really have. Anyway, you're sort of part of my family now, and nobody messes with my family," Kathy said defiantly. She watched as Anissa began to pace back and forth. It was obvious that she was thinking. Finally she spoke.

"Kathy, what you're saying makes sense, but you don't know him. The longer it takes for me to let him know I'm okay, the worse it will be for me. He's probably worried about me. I have to go back to him. What else can I do?" Anissa was wringing her hands now.

Kathy was getting annoyed. Was she herself ever this obtuse? She sat down at her father's desk and waved her hand toward the mauve armless chair to her right.

"Sit down, Anissa. Pacing makes me jumpy."

Kathy considered for a brief moment the possibility that her father's ghost could be roaming this house. If so, he had learned something he never knew about his daughter, who had always gotten into fights with boys when she was younger—and won. And then, she considered the gravity of the situation before her.

"Yes, I do know him," she snapped. "Not personally, but I know his kind, and I know his lack of remorse for the pain he's caused you. I guarantee you, he's worried. Scared that he's lost his punching bag. You've got to ask yourself if you want to continue to live like that. Do you?"

Anissa looked confused and angry. "No I don't and you know I don't. But staying away will be suicide. He'll find me. He's rich and powerful," she retorted.

"Well guess what? So—am—I!"

"And how does that help me?" Anissa began to cry.

"Now is not the time for tears. Now is the time to make a decision. Do you realize that they thought you had a ruptured spleen? That you were bleeding internally? There are bruises on the back of your head for goodness sake! If you go back now, he's ten times more likely to kill you!"

Kathy's mind was racing like a thoroughbred in a high stakes competition. She'd watched the news so often that she could make her own newscast and be ninety eight percent accurate. According to reports, there were many victims who had not been found and were believed dead. Foley could be among the dead. By the same token, Anissa could be deceased, too.

"If Foley is as cockamamie as my husband was he will blame you because he couldn't find you. If he's still alive, you better believe he's looking for you. Let's get real here; your husband is a savage person and civilized people do not cohabitate well with savages."

Anissa smiled for the first time all morning. "I don't know, Kathy, I mean we've been together for three years now, and I've learned his moods and how to avoid an attack."

"Have you now? So I guess you saw that last beating coming?" Kathy asked bluntly.

Anissa's face showed the effect of Kathy's words. "I have to go back to him," she declared.

"You don't have to do anything but die black," Kathy said. She saw Anissa raise her eyebrows and giggle. "Forgive me, I've got an African-American friend here in the city and that's her mantra," Kathy added.

"Well, I hope she does a better job with that old saying than you just did," Anissa giggled again, her body language no longer as tense.

"You could be dead for all Foley knows."

"I'm standing here alive," Anissa declared.

"Please promise me that you'll stay here and consider what I'm proposing while I go out for a while. When I come back, I'll know more than I know now. Or do I have to threaten to call the police again? I don't want to do it; I want you to save yourself." Kathy held her breath.

Anissa looked pitifully at Kathy for a beat and then nodded her assent. "Okay, I'll wait until you come back," she said.

"Good! I've got enough money to help you live without him as long as necessary." Kathy exhaled as she took Anissa by the hand and led her out of her office down to the kitchen, at the same time making a mental note to disconnect all the phones and lock them in her bedroom when she left. Anissa was very fragile and subject to change her mind once left alone with her memories.

Chapter Thirty-Six
September 25, 2001

The New York Mayoral Primary Election that was supposed to have been held on September 11th was postponed. When the polls opened, two weeks later than originally planned, Felton did his civic duty.

He felt the ache inside that had become like comfortable old clothes. He knew that it would not leave him anytime soon. He hadn't driven much since the attack because he was shaky behind the wheel. Every morning he took the kids to school via the Path train. Sherry had found some loophole that allowed her to enroll the boys in public school on the upper west side. Now that they were his responsibility he was determined to do a good job. He didn't know the hows or the wherefores of parenting, but he would learn.

The kids were having a hard time. Justin woke up every night crying, and Nathan was withdrawing more each day. Once he got custody worked out, Felton planned for all three of them to get professional help. He hated to admit that he needed it, but he did. He needed to talk to someone about the anger, about his thoughts, and about a plan. For a plan he would need, and soon. Their world had been turned upside down in a single day. Justin and Nathan would be orphans, were it not for him. Was he ready? Could he do what needed to be done to raise those boys?

He walked from the school to his precinct, the three-two. The 32nd and the 28th precincts served Central Harlem. In the 1920s and 1930s, a flood of exemplary artistic work by African Americans known as the Harlem Renaissance, had taken place in Central and West Harlem. At that time Harlem had been a center of African-American businesses and places of entertainment that included bars, grills, lounges, cafés, rib joints, supper clubs, speakeasies, cellars, taverns, theaters, nightclubs and jazz clubs, flourished. The most famous, Connie's Inn and the Cotton Club, where Duke Ellington played, were restricted to whites only while the Savoy Ballroom was integrated and was popular for swing dancing. Most of those places were long gone. The Apollo Theater, formerly a burlesque house, opened in 1934 on 125th Street and was still a banging joint.

When Felton first moved to New York, he and Tina had lived in Harlem. They would probably still be there if their uncle Percy had not fallen in love with a white guy and moved in with him to 'the gate,' as it was fondly referred to. Its official name was Seagate. Located on the far end of Coney Island, on the southwestern tip of Brooklyn, Seagate was a gated and exclusive community. When James, Percy's white lover, died he left his home to Percy, who at his death eighteen years ago left the home to Felton's mom, who then gave it to him and Tina because she wasn't leaving the South. The house was large enough for two families. Now it would be home to only three people; Felton, Nathan, and Justin.

As he walked along, he passed a phone booth that was covered with fliers picturing missing persons. He backed up for a minute to read some of them. He paused at one and read it twice, studying the woman's face. He was certain he'd seen her some place before, but could couldn't remember where. It was her name that disturbed him: *Anissa Brogdon*. And the other name on the flier was the one name he'd never wanted to hear or see again as long as he lived: *Foley Brogdon*. And then it came back to him. A note from his mother and a newspaper clipping of a newly married Mr. Brogdon with his blushing bride—the same woman staring back at him from that flier.

"Well, well," he thought. "Foley is in New York."

Chapter Thirty-Seven
September 25, 2001

Foley entered the emergency room of New York Presbyterian Hospital, his eighth ER visit of the day, with a handful of fliers that asked if anyone had seen Anissa. He and his parents had already put them up in every hospital reported to have received victims of the WTC attack, but Foley was running out of patience. He'd decided to retrace his steps. At each hospital there was only one person that he desperately needed to talk to—the doctor assigned to triage on 9/11.

He approached the receptionist, who was on the phone. He instantly became irritated. He stood, staring her down, willing her to hang up. She must have felt his vibe—seconds later she directed her attention toward him.

"Sign in please," she said, indicating a clipboard on the counter.

"I'd like to see Ford Jennings," he said calmly.

"Sir, you need to sign in first," she said impatiently, looking down at her fingernails.

"Young lady, I don't know how long you've had this job, but if you want to keep it, you'll get Ford Jennings for me."

She looked at him impudently. "Well, the last time I checked, the chief of staff at this hospital wasn't you. So sign in like everybody else or I can get security to help you make a decision or an exit," she snapped, glaring at him.

Foley chuckled to himself as he quickly sized her up. Early forties, overweight, stringy blond hair, and too many long hard days at work. Calling her a young lady had been a stretch of the imagination. But she was not timid. And she had no idea who he was. He could let her know, but why waste precious time?

"Get security," he said—his blue eyes boring into hers.

"My pleasure," she said as she picked up a two-way radio.

Foley walked toward the entrance to the inner sanctum of the emergency room and leaned against the wall to wait. A few minutes later two very able looking gentlemen in their nicely pressed uniforms arrived. He watched as they approached the receptionist. She gave them an earful and then pointed in his direction.

The two men, one looking too stupid to understand English, and the other just slightly more capable, strolled over and stood directly in front of Foley.

"Sir, do you need some help?" the stupid one asked.

"Yes, gentlemen. I am looking for Ford Jennings. I'm a doctor from out of town and he is an old colleague of mine. I just wanted to say hello," Foley answered disingenuously.

"Dr. *Jennings Ford* is not in. Is there something else we can help you with?" the more capable one asked.

"When will he return? As I understand it he's been gone for several days. Shouldn't he be here?"

"Sir, it's not our job to question the comings and goings of the doctors on staff here. It's our job to protect them." The stupid one put his hand on his gun. Cool, Foley thought.

"Thanks, guys. I guess you don't mind if I put a flier up for my missing wife do you?"

The more capable one looked at the fliers in Foley's hands and then back at Foley with a sad look in his eyes.

"We'll be more than happy to do that for you, sir. The bulletin board is on the other side of those doors. Sorry to hear about your loss."

Against his better judgment Foley left a few fliers with them. Dr. Ford or whatever his name was, had evidently gone on vacation immediately after the influx of patients. On 9/11 he'd been on duty. He would know if Anissa had come in—whether or not she'd been delirious, not knowing who she was. Foley had shown her picture to almost everyone else and they'd not recalled seeing her. What kind of doctor takes a vacation in the middle of all this turmoil?

Foley was so busy fretting over the absence of the doctor that he didn't see the squat, unhurried, elderly gentleman without a strand of grey hair until it was too late. As they collided, the man went sprawling, landing on his back. He got up almost as quickly as he had fallen. Foley placed both hands on the man's shoulders to steady him.

"Are you alright?" Foley asked.

"I'm fine," the man said, as he gained his balance and moved around Foley to enter the ER.

“Are you sure? I’m a doctor, I’ll be more than happy to help you,” Foley said to the retreating man who looked angrily back over his shoulders.

“An apology would be good for starters. I don’t think they teach you that in medical school though,” he said brusquely.

“Okay, I apologize,” Foley said as the automatic doors closed. New Yorkers! Why did they have to be so rude? He continued down the street with thoughts of Anissa churning in his head. That’s exactly how he’d met her—he’d opened a door and accidentally knocked her off her feet. He had no idea that he’d just collided with Dr. Jennings Ford.

Chapter Thirty-Eight
September 25, 2001

Anissa sat in an alcove on the second floor in a chair made of sturdy black lacquered wood. The arm pads, back, and seat were covered in a heavy fabric splashed with black hexagons on a white background. The chair was centered in front of a wall covered with black and white striped wallpaper.

Not knowing who she was had been a blessing. It had given her time to experience peace and not fear. The constant pain in her body had subsided a great deal and she was so glad that she didn't have any damaged organs or a ruptured spleen. But now fear was back. How had it come to this?

She had been in love with Foley, desired him still, and yet was terrified of him. Whenever he hit her, it was with so much force that it felt like he was pounding away her very essence of being; that she was dying inch by inch. Living in constant dread of the next attack left no room for happiness and yet she found herself forcing a smile whenever he was around.

Was it twisted to think that if she smiled he would forget about being cruel to her? She thought back to how she roamed from room to room in that huge well-furnished house like a zombie, feeling so alone with no one to talk to.

She had required emergency room treatment after one of his beatings, but it was kept all hush–hush. The doctors had feared that she had internal bleeding. Foley had told them that she'd fallen down the stairs in their home; leaving out the part about kicking her and punching her with his fists before he shoved her to the bottom of the stairs. His mother, Lacy, had been so sympathetic; seeming to genuinely care that Anissa was hurt so badly. She was at Anissa's bedside in the hospital.

"Sweetheart, you have got to be careful. Foley told us that this is not the first time you fell like that," she'd said with a worried expression on her face.

"Mrs. Brogdon, may I tell you something?" Anissa had asked softly.

"Of course you may, my dear. What is it?"

"I didn't fall, Foley pushed me. He kicked me and hit me in the stomach with his fists." Anissa began to cry.

"Honey, why would he do something like that? What did you do to him?"

"What did I do to him?"

"Listen to me, Anissa, married women have to learn to take a lot of adversity," Lacy continued. "Men are delicate creatures; we are much stronger than they are. Just learn to do what he asks and try to be the best wife you can be. You have to help him, support him. When you've never had anything you aren't used to anything. Marriage to Foley guarantees that you will never want a single thing. It will pay off in the end, you wait and see."

Lacy had sat there with her immaculate nails, her hair perfectly coifed, and a Louis Vuitton Purse on her lap, looking smug and confident. She had continued giving absurd advice.

"Just remember this scripture: '*And we know that all things work together for good to them who love God, to them who are the called according to his purpose.*' That's Romans chapter 8, verse 10 and that scripture has been my lifeline. I know what I'm talking about." She'd beamed with pride, totally ignoring the news that her son had beaten his wife so severely that she had to be hospitalized.

Anissa turned away. She could no longer look at Lacy. For good? What good could come from being beaten? How could she believe in a God who let a man treat a woman this way? And to what purpose was Lacy called? What kind of mother was she? Fear suddenly took over, as she realized that Foley could find out that she'd told his mother. So, she begged Mrs. Brogdon not to tell Foley and apologized profusely for making accusations against him. She put on a pleasant face, and made this incident the first and last time that she ever mentioned anything about Foley to his mother.

For a while after that beating, Lacy had called their house every morning to ask how they were getting along. But she had a hidden agenda: Foley.

"What are you planning for dinner tonight? You know Foley loves lamb. Or did you try that roasted chicken with herbs, and the green beans? If you don't like your cook you can always borrow mine. Foley loves her cooking. She's been with us for years." Lacy Brogdon could care less about her daughter-in-law, she clearly loved her son.

Anissa's thoughts came back to the present as she considered the possibility of never seeing Foley Brogdon again. She would never feel his arms around her or feel his luscious kisses—she loved him when they made love.

Now she was considering dying with a stranger as an ally. Maybe this was God answering her prayers and cries for help at last. If she looked at it without bias, she would have to admit that it seemed like a miracle—trying to save a woman from stepping in front of a car led to meeting Kathy Stockton who seemed to have a heart of gold and a purse overflowing with it, offering her a chance to leave Foley without him knowing about it. How often does that happen? Maybe pretending to be dead would work. On the other hand, if she was going to pretend to be dead, how was she going to live? It was kind of Kathy to offer to help her, but she could not allow herself to be supported by a woman she had just met. Or could she? She'd been supported by a man who abused her, deprived her of love and affection, placated her with sex, and who enjoyed demeaning her. Where was the dignity in that?

If she agreed to this plan, she could never go near anyone she knew again. Foley would have to believe without a doubt that she was dead; she couldn't take the chance that someone could discover the truth.

But staying dead when you're alive is not easy. Could she do it? Could she stay hidden from Foley for the rest of her life? The good thing was that when you're dead, the only place people look for you is in the cemetery.

No one would believe that kind, charming, professional, and philanthropic Foley would do anything to hurt his wife, or anyone else, for that matter. As long as she lived with him, she was doomed to live by his rules. She would never be able to get away from him as long as he was alive.

She took a deep breath, summoning courage. Yes, she could do it. She could hide forever if it meant never having to be hit or mistreated by him again. The attack on the World Trade Center was a tragedy, but perhaps one good thing could come from it; her life could be saved.

Chapter Thirty-Nine
September 26, 2001

Kathy served Eggs Benedict for breakfast on fine pink china that she called Well-pleased Wedgewood ware. She was dressed for the day wearing a simple grey dress with a purple scarf. Looking very chic, wearing her grandmother's pearl earrings and necklace, she sat opposite Anissa at the table.

"I am well-pleased with myself this morning," she quipped.

"As well you should be," Anissa replied, pulling the collar of her fluffy white robe together as she put a bite of egg in her mouth.

"Okay, here's where we are," Kathy said, putting down her fork and clasping her hands beneath her chin.

"The Jane Doe in the morgue at New York Presbyterian that was killed by a hit-and-run driver could be my sister-in-law. I don't know what she looks like. The good news is that we can arrange for you to leave Foley by just staying gone. Let him believe that you are dead."

Kathy felt the momentary panic that she'd felt yesterday when she saw that flier with Anissa's face staring back at her with Foley's name and phone number as contact information.

"And we know that Foley is alive and well and looking for you."

"Yes," Anissa agreed.

"Are you ready to escape ass whippings for the rest of your life?"

Anissa stared at the prints on the wall behind Kathy, her face non-committal.

"I'm serious. I went through seven years of hell until my husband dropped dead at the ripe old age of 42 after breaking my nose the night before. Go figure!"

Kathy reached out and took Anissa's hands. She was convinced that she was doing the right thing. She knew nothing about this woman other than the fact that she had been abused by her husband, but that was enough. She recognized that look of fear and hopelessness in Anissa's eyes; she had seen it looking back at herself from the mirror often enough.

Her husband had been a wealthy man, and now she was a wealthy widow with no chance of spending all the money she had even if she lived to be two hundred years old. She could use some of that money and all that she had learned to save this woman's life.

"If you're going through with this, we have to get you out of New York. We'll go to my home in Georgia," Kathy continued, hoping that Anissa would agree to the plan.

"I thought this was your home," Anissa offered, changing the subject.

"This is where I grew up."

"Kathy, I'm scared. Every time I think about Foley finding out that I'm alive I get physically ill."

"I understand. That's why we're leaving New York. Contrary to popular belief, New York is really a small town. This island is less than fifteen miles long and three miles wide. There's just a lot crammed in together to make it look big. So it's not safe to stay here. You need to be able to go outside and feel the freedom of sunshine on your face without worrying about someone recognizing you. You need to stretch your wings, girl!"

"I guess the sooner the better. If he were to find me now I just don't know what I'd do."

Kathy did not want to give her time to re-think. She had to keep adding fuel to the fire.

"You're going to get well. You're going to heal," she declared as Anissa put her hands on the table, staring at her eggs. Kathy could almost see the wheels turning in her head—trying to rationalize staying with the man.

"That man has almost taken your soul and you have to get it back," Kathy admonished. She had a look of determination on her face as she continued talking.

"Don't worry about anything. My husband left me enough money to buy a few countries if I wanted to. Do you know much I'm going to enjoy helping you? You have to enjoy the irony that an abuser's fortune will help a victim of abuse get away. I surely am. And you're helping me as well. If you weren't here, I'd be alone and sad and lost in the doldrums. You give me something to do!"

"I'll do it," Anissa said looking directly into Kathy's eyes.

"Thank you, Anissa." Kathy let out a long sigh of relief. "You don't know how much this means to me. When we get this all sorted out, I have a story to tell you and hopefully it will explain why I am so adamant." Kathy smiled at her.

At that moment, the doorbell rang. Kathy excused herself and answered the door to a courier with an express delivery from Woods Construction Company, Troy's business in Texas. She signed for it and without the least bit of hesitation opened it. She gasped when she realized that it was a custom photo album done by a professional wedding photographer. Kathy opened it and looked into the smiling faces of her brother Troy and his new bride, Jessica.

"It's very fortuitous that your memory came back. Look what just came for me," Kathy said to Anissa as she placed the open wedding album on the table in front of her.

"That's her!" Anissa exclaimed. "That's the woman who stepped in front of that car."

"She was a cute little thing," Kathy noted as she turned the pages of the photo album.

"I'm so sorry, Kathy. This must be hard for you," Anissa offered.

"True, but I'm going to accept this as fate. It's sad about Jessica, but if there really is an afterlife, she and Troy are together again."

Kathy studied the pictures as she considered carefully the risks involved in identifying Jessica's body. If her plan to get Anissa away from Foley was going to work, her sister-in-law would have to remain unknown for now.

"I now pronounce you dead. Anissa Brogdon is dead. I know that's hard to swallow, but you understand don't you?"

Anissa's eyes blazed. "Never ask me that question again. If I don't understand something I'll tell you."

"Yes, ma'am!" Kathy said, raising her hand to mockingly salute Anissa. She put her feet together and clicked her heels playfully. The moment passed quickly as Kathy recalled the flier taped near the emergency room at New York Presbyterian. It was just a matter of time before the staff put two and two together. It was time to get out of Dodge.

The plan was to leave that night. Kathy had decided to drive, because Anissa would not be able to take any type of commercial conveyance without identification. The incident of 9/11 had turned all modes of transportation into a nightmare for all travelers.

"It will be fun to drive. Just think of it as best friends on a road trip. We are driving out of here tonight and unless we have to, we're not stopping until we hit D.C. I don't mind driving and I've got a comfortable car," Kathy declared, ignoring the look of confusion and uncertainty on Anissa's face. Someday she'd look back on all of this and remember that the events of 9/11 had created a catalyst to change her life—to set her free from Foley's abuse.

Chapter Forty
September 27, 2001

A few days after September 11, President Bush had warned the Taliban government to turn over Osama bin Laden and Al-Qaeda leaders operating in Afghanistan, or face attack. Al-Qaeda had been blamed for carrying out the attack on the World Trade Center, the Pentagon, and Flight 93. American intelligence had learned that Bin Laden had declared war on the United States in 1996, because he believed the continued presence of U.S. forces in Saudi Arabia five years after the first Gulf War morally obligated him to retaliate.

Al-Qaeda was a large organization that extended throughout the Middle East, Africa, Europe, and Central Asia. Some of their associates had ties to the United States. The group was not large, containing less than 100 members, but it was part of a much greater radical movement that was expanding through the Arab world. This contagious collection of battle-hardened men was well-trained and willing to sacrifice their lives, taking as many people as possible with them. Their faith led them to believe that God would reward them in the afterlife. The world was awaiting their response to President Bush's warning.

Dr. Jennings Ford had decided that it was time to go back to work. He rarely took a lot of time off, because he felt that things fell apart when he was absent. He had not planned to be away for so long, but he had been so exhausted that he had no other choice. Now, well rested, he was ready to get back into the fray. He rubbed his lower back again. It had been sore since he'd been knocked to the ground by that arrogant whippersnapper calling himself a doctor.

His desk was as he had expected: overloaded. He was on staff as an emergency room doctor, but he was one of the few who had an office; one of the fringe benefits that persuaded him to come back to work after his wife had passed away. He had fallen apart after his wife's death and could no longer keep up his thus far flourishing private practice. It was a dear friend who pulled him back to humanity by offering this job temporarily. Working was good. It kept him sane. And the three years he had been at the hospital had passed more quickly than he ever imagined.

He liked to keep the bulletin board current. It seemed like paper sprouted roots and grew in his absence. Yesterday's news and notices did nothing for him, nor for the people he worked with. How many times had someone gone looking for a person with a couch for sale only to find that it had been sold days before? He found that today was no different. A variety of fliers had been tacked on top of each other.

He carefully began to remove them, taking care to read them first. He chuckled to himself as he thought of the many times that he had insisted that persons placing fliers put a date on them so that he would know how long they'd been up. He was near the middle of the bulletin board when the face staring back at him caused him to pause. A lovely young woman with the heading *"Have You Seen this Woman?"* Of course he had seen her. At least he thought so. She looked like the pretty young lady who'd been savagely beaten.

He had only seen a woman beaten that severely once in his career and he never wanted to see it again. What had been her name? Jessica. Jessica Woods, whose tests had shown that she was out of the woods. He chuckled at the pun. Based on the name alone, the woman looking back at him could not have been under his care. Her name was Anissa Brogdon.

He had a strong feeling that he was missing something. Without thinking, he folded the flier and placed it in his pocket—further investigation might be needed.

Jessica Woods had been released to a sister-in-law. Kathy Stockton. Mrs. Stockton had told him herself that his patient was recuperating. He didn't believe in coincidences. As much as he hated to pry, he was going to have to somehow make sense of this. Mrs. Stockton was the best person to ask, but he got no answer when he dialed her number.

Chapter Forty-One
September 27, 2001

Kathy and Anissa were in a black Mercedes-Benz ML 320 Sport Utility Vehicle heading south on I-95. Anissa wore jeans and a white sweater with sneakers. Kathy wore black sweat pants and an *I Love New York* tee-shirt. Neither of them had spoken for the last hundred miles. Kathy wanted to keep a conversation going because she knew the mind frame of an abused woman. They had one thing in common: they had fallen head over heels in love with the wrong man. None of them paid any attention to early warning signs that the man of their dreams would soon turn into a gargoyle with cruel hands, a grating, hurtful, and demeaning tone of voice, and a temperament more vicious than any wild animal. They never wanted to talk about it and given too much time to think, they'd return to the abuser.

Kathy's therapist taught her that her husband's beatings had nothing to do with her and everything to do with him. Nothing that she could have done would have changed him. He was who he was. The odds were almost one hundred percent that he would have eventually killed her had he lived and had she stayed with him. He had cut all her hair off, broken her right pinkie, locked her in the trunk of a car overnight, and raped her whenever he felt like it. And those were only some of the highlights.

"It's amazing to find out that a woman really has the freedom to walk away from an abusive situation, if she leaves the moment it begins," Kathy pointed out, breaking the silence.

"I left Foley once, Kathy," Anissa responded. "And I tried to leave a second time, but he stopped me before I could get away. After that I didn't try anymore. I was too afraid."

Kathy glanced at Anissa. She saw the shame. She recognized the same defeat and denigration that had stolen her own self-confidence. Eyes back on the road, Kathy continued to talk.

"I know. I was scared of my husband too. But I want it to be my life's mission to help any woman that I can to get away. I've tried this before you know. Twice."

From the corner of her eye she saw Anissa turn toward her.

"The first woman was called Rochelle; I'm not giving last names. She had three children, and the bastard she married had started beating them, too. I was able to talk her into leaving the state and starting over. I bought her a house in Phoenix, got her a job, a new name, the works. The day we were supposed to begin her new life, she left my house just after dawn with her children going back to her house to get one of the kid's favorite teddy bears. She thought her husband was at work and that it would be safe. But he wasn't at work. He was at the house and shot her and the three kids, killing them all instantly. Then he turned the gun on himself."

She heard Anissa's sharp intake of breath. Kathy nodded her head several times to indicate that what she'd said was unbelievable but true.

"Then there was Carol," Kathy resumed. "A beautiful woman, married to a man with tons of money. He beat the living crap out of her even in public. She went on and on about her jewelry and her furs. She couldn't believe that I'd provide for her until she was on her feet. She loved material things so much that she went back to him. She's missing now and he swears she left on a vacation. I can't tell you how badly that hurts me. All she had to do was get on an airplane bound for freedom. I know he killed her and he's getting away with it. So far, the vengeance fairies haven't visited him, but they've been dispatched. I promise you he will not be the first man to be convicted for murder without a body." Kathy glanced at Anissa again and winked.

"Now here you are. You, my friend, have to be my success story. Whatever you need, I will get it for you. Just please don't leave in the middle of the night to go back to him. Don't get soft and try to contact him. Your story will only end badly if you do."

Anissa exhaled loudly and leaned her head back on the headrest.

"If you decide to go back to him, by all means, tell me first so I can have you committed to a mental hospital. At least you'll be safe until you come to your senses," Kathy pleaded. "You're doing the right thing for you. Trust me."

"I do trust you, Kathy, and you have to trust me enough to believe that I don't want to go back. You're giving me a chance and I'm taking it. I never thought I'd ever break those chains."

"Better late than never! You are going to have to stay beneath the radar. Let that be your new mantra 'I am beneath the radar.' And no men! No men for a long time. You've got to get to know yourself. Another man will only complicate things."

"Are you serious?" Anissa asked indignantly.

"No, but I'm just saying."

"And I'm just saying that what I want to do is get on with my life. I don't know if I'll ever trust another man, Kathy."

Kathy laughed, shaking her head as she thought of her lover.

"Sweetie, it can happen. Geoffrey is good to me and my body. I tried for a long time to avoid men myself, but I have needs and you do too. My late husband wasn't worth a flip in bed. Maybe yours knew how to knock your boots; if so he's left an ache that's going to have to be soothed sooner or later, if you know what I mean."

"Indeed I do. Foley was a good lover and I got wrapped up in the sex from the beginning. I don't want that to happen to me again."

"I understand. But, believe it or not, the time will come. You are a beautiful woman and men will be attracted to you."

Kathy realized she was doing all the talking. Preaching was not her calling. Concentrating on the road and the cars around her would be time better spent while Anissa was lost in thought. Smoothly moving over to the middle lane, Kathy set her cruise control, tuned to a classical music station on the radio, and continued to put distance between the two of them and New York, where she imagined Foley was still roaming the streets looking for his wife.

Chapter Forty-Two
September 27, 2001

The time had come for Foley and his parents to return home. For the last sixteen days, they had done everything possible to find Anissa. No success. Each day it became more apparent that he would never see her again. He'd heard the stories of the casualties, the exact number still unknown. Predictions were that anyone still left in the Marriott when the South Tower collapsed was gone, except for those lucky ones who got out or were trapped in the one corner that remained standing.

Foley had not been able to sleep. His eyes were framed by dark circles, and his usual well-groomed façade seemed to have crumbled. He looked in the mirror and almost didn't recognize himself. Food was tasteless, but his mother fussed over him so that he'd eat at least some of what was placed in front of him.

They were not alone as they searched all the places where a disoriented person might be found—hospitals, shelters, churches, parks, subway stations...so many people were searching, so many people were lost.

His eyes brimmed with tears as a heavy lump crowded his chest. This was not how he had planned to leave New York. He wanted his wife by his side. His parents had done all they could to comfort him. His mother was great at quoting scriptures. *"Blessed are they that mourn for they shall be comforted."* That was one of her favorites. But Foley was not comforted. He was heartbroken. He loved Anissa. It seemed like only yesterday that he saw her for the first time. He'd opened a door and literally knocked her off her feet.

She was on the floor. Her marvelous figure was somewhat exposed as the fall had caused her pink silk blouse to ride up, exposing her midriff, and the black skirt to come up around her thighs, showing off her shapely legs that were byproducts of a long track career. Her hair was disheveled around her lovely face. Her skin was perfect and so were her cheekbones. All things put together made her a well wrapped-package waiting to be opened by someone worthy of receiving it. She sat there, obviously getting angrier by the second, staring up at the stranger that had sent her sprawling.

"I am so sorry. Here let me help you up," Foley said with concern. He'd dropped his briefcase and lifted her to her feet. The strong sensual scent of her cologne almost overpowered him.

"Thank you," was all she had managed as she straightened her clothes.

"Are you alright?"

"Yes, I'm fine, just a little embarrassed."

"Please forgive me. I don't usually make an entrance like that. Are you sure you're alright?"

"Yes, I'm fine. Just fine," she'd repeated.

"I'm Foley Brogdon," he'd smiled, extending his hand. Her hand had been soft and warm, fitting perfectly inside his.

The police had informed him that there was no hope of finding more survivors; it was time to begin a massive cleanup. Those still missing were considered casualties. Anissa was a casualty. The woman that he'd held in his arms, whose smile could light up his world, whose hand fit perfectly inside his, was reduced to a casualty, a mere statistic, a footnote to a catastrophe of historic proportion. He tried to stifle the sobs that began to come from a place deep inside of him. How was he supposed to live without her?

He and his parents had attended a memorial service at Yankee Stadium the day before. "A Prayer for America," as the service was called, was the first formal program held in memory of those lost. James Earl Jones, the actor, opened the services, Bette Midler sang "The Wind Beneath My Wings," and Placido Domingo sang "Ave Maria." Oprah Winfrey was the host. That almost broke Foley's heart—Anissa loved Oprah. Mayor Giuliani stepped to the podium to deliver his message, and the huge crowd stood up applauding him. Archbishop Demetrious of the Greek Orthodox Church of America gave the benediction. Designed to initiate healing and bring hope, the program had been peaceful and inspiring.

Now it was time to hold a memorial for Anissa in their hometown.

Chapter Forty-Three
September 28, 2001

Dr. Jennings Ford ate lunch with the coroner, Earl Bost, in the hospital cafeteria. Contrary to most hospitals, the meals were actually very good, especially the lasagna.

"How are things going, Jennings?"

"Couldn't be better. I'm back in the swing of things. I took a few days off and got some rest because I needed a little break. The whole World Trade Center attacks got to me."

"Yeah, I know what you mean. I've never seen anything like it in my life," Dr. Bost replied soberly as he chewed his salad.

"It's hard to believe that anything like that could happen in the United States," Dr. Ford said as he sipped his coffee. It was strong, just as he liked it.

"You're telling me. There still are so many missing people, although I guess it's more appropriate to call them casualties after all this time. I'm still getting people trickling in searching for lost loved ones. It breaks my heart."

"I've been a little depressed myself. Have you been down there yet? To Ground Zero?"

"No." Dr. Bost put his fork down and crossed his hands underneath his chin.

Dr. Ford took a bite of his lasagna. It was the seasoning and the meat that made it so good. The cook used beef and sausage.

"I had one doctor from Tennessee who came in like clockwork for a while. He wouldn't accept that his wife was dead," Dr. Bost continued, taking a sip of his lemonade. "He wanted to see the body."

"You know, I can't blame him. Sometimes it's hard to believe your loved one is dead when you see the body. I can't imagine the difficulty accepting if you don't see."

"He introduced himself to all of the medical examiners on staff. It's like he went behind my back and questioned them to double check what I told him. He was an arrogant prick."

"Is he still coming around?"

"I haven't seen him lately. But I remember his name. Dr. Foley Brogdon. He's a plastic surgeon; supposed to be the doctor for the country stars down in Nashville. I told him I'd keep him in mind if I ever felt like a new look." Dr. Bost laughed.

"Man, please, plastic surgery won't be much of an improvement for you. You're just plain ugly and nothing can fix that!" Dr. Ford teased. Earl was a good friend and he had a good sense of humor.

"He must have gone back to hillbilly country," Earl added.

"I guess he gave up."

"Yep. You gonna eat your other roll?"

Dr. Ford gave the roll to his friend. He was getting that uneasy feeling again. Brogdon—now where had he heard that name before? A flier. He felt his lab jacket. It was still there in his pocket. He pulled it out and unfolded it.

"Take a look at this," he insisted.

"That's the doctor's wife, Mrs. Brogdon!" exclaimed Earl as he glanced at the flier.

"Are you certain?"

"I told you that man was here nearly every day showing that picture to everybody."

Dr. Ford finished his lunch lost in thought. Something was not adding up. The woman he had treated was Jessica Woods, but she looked exactly like Anissa Brogdon, the doctor's missing wife. But what had Kathy Stockton said? Something about never having met her sister-in-law? Could Anissa Brogdon have pretended to be Jessica Woods? No. She had been identified by documents in her purse. She had never said who she was, because the poor thing had amnesia. Or did she? He sat staring at the flier. The woman in the picture could definitely be the woman that he treated and released.

Could she have been some kind of criminal? No. The flier had been dropped off by a man looking for his wife. So she wasn't a criminal. And yet she couldn't be Jessica Woods either unless they were twins. He didn't understand it at all but he had an obligation to do something.

He was a doctor and a man who had lost his wife. He knew what it felt like to lose the woman you love. Should he contact Dr. Brogdon? No. Dr. Brogdon could be the man who had beaten his wife. When you see a woman beaten like that, more often than not the man she lives with is responsible. If Brogdon beat his wife, then Jennings, as a doctor, had an obligation to protect the woman. His experience had taught him that most abused women will not report the abuse. The woman could very well be back at home with her husband, and if so, out of his reach. There was one sure way to find out.

He quickly said goodbye to his old friend. When he reached his desk Dr. Ford dialed the number at the bottom of the flier.

"Hello," answered a female voice.

"Yes, I'm trying to reach Dr. Foley Brogdon."

"He's not available. Is there a message?"

"Is this Mrs. Brogdon?"

"Yes, can I help you?"

Dr. Ford was suddenly embarrassed. "I'm sorry to disturb you, ma'am." He hung up abruptly and tore the flier in half. Mrs. Brogdon was home. There was no need to interfere.

Chapter Forty-Four
September 28, 2001

What a strange call, Lacy Brogdon thought, fingering her long braid, a habit whenever she deliberated. She'd asked the man politely if he wanted to leave a message; usually people did. Anyone knowing Foley would expect a prompt return call; that's the way Foley operated. He was meticulous and thorough, just like his father. She was indeed Mrs. Brogdon, but maybe she should have explained that she was his mother and not his wife. Oh well, no use crying over spilled milk.

She flicked her braid off her shoulder and admired herself in the bronze mirror on the wall to the left of Foley's desk. She liked her hair. It was her best feature—thick and long, hanging down her back. She would not cut it, no matter how many times the hairdresser tried to tell her that women her age looked younger with short hair. She didn't care about looking younger. She just wanted to look nice and respectable. She was sixty-two years old after all, and she wasn't getting any younger. She might as well look her age.

Lacy was a beautiful woman. Foley had definitely inherited his good looks from his mother. She had the true blue eyes and the thick naturally arched eyebrows. Her long blond hair was mixed with only seven strands of grey. She'd counted them. The elegantly narrow face with the aquiline features showed no wrinkles. Her perfectly tulip shaped lips were unlined and the beauty mark under her right eye had been mimeographed to Foley's face. They both had the same petite cleft in their chins. She had always been pleased with Foley's looks, knowing that he would have been just as beautiful as a woman. When she looked at him, she saw herself and that always called her to arms. She lived to protect him. She wanted to be a better mother to him than her own mother had been to her. Lacy's young life had been hard.

She was the oldest child of six children and when they were younger, her mother had to work all the time. Their father died when the youngest child was only a baby. Lacy had been fourteen and was forced to quit school to help out, because they had been so poor. Somebody had to clean the house, cook, and take care of the little ones. Her mother worked in the kitchen at school during the day and was a waitress at the town café at night.

Foley Brogdon, Sr. had come into her life purely by accident when she was eighteen. He was lost and stopped to ask for directions. They lived in the country just outside of Pigeon Forge and he was trying to get to somebody's house in Gatlinburg. She'd been unable to help him. When he asked to use the phone, she was embarrassed that she had to tell him that they didn't have one. He'd lifted one eyebrow in surprise, looked around at the condition of the house, the little children, and she could see sympathy in his eyes. He found his way somehow that day, but he came back a few days later, and brought flowers for her and a bag of goodies for the kids.

That's how their relationship began. He visited her off and on for two years before he finally asked her to marry him. She'd jumped at his offer and left her mother's house with her belongings in a brown paper bag. Foley was not a rich man at the time, but he worked hard. And he was smart. Soon he owned property in the Smoky Mountains where he built eighteen cabins and sold them all in no time at all. That was the beginning of a real estate empire almost rivaling that of his father who'd left and gone north when he was a boy. It wasn't long before they moved to northern Kentucky where Foley was born.

Her son changed her life. She wanted to keep him safe as long as it was in her power to do so. She was heartbroken to learn that she'd never have more children, so he became her whole world. He was such a good baby, not fretful or whiny. And she loved him so much.

Life in Kentucky did not suit Foley Sr. He bought twenty acres of land in Brentwood and built their current estate. Lacy had decorated every room in the house lovingly, without the aid of an interior designer; she had chosen the paint colors, window treatments, flooring, cabinetry, and furnishings. Her husband gave her free hand to make the house look just like she wanted it to look. The house was huge—over 25,000 square feet on four levels.

The top level contained the master suite complete with a kitchenette and a laundry room. Her walk-in closet was efficiently organized and immense, and approximating the size of half a regulation sized basketball court. She had separate sections for pants, skirts, blouses and tops, long dresses, short dresses, suits, jeans, and sweaters. Her shoes were kept in compartments in the center of the huge closet. She also had shelves for her Sunday hats and her purses. Lacy never had nice clothes as a young girl, so she more than made up for it now. She bought clothes and accessories with complete abandon and every time she put something new in her closet, she took something out to donate.

Three other bedrooms with full baths were in the west wing of the top floor. The second floor had five more bedrooms with full baths and balconies, a sitting room, a recreation room, and a kitchen. The main floor had two living rooms, a gallery sized kitchen, a library, a study, an office for her husband, and a full dining room. The bottom floor or basement had an indoor pool, a game room and a theater. There were adjoining five car garages. To Foley Sr. the house stood as a symbol for all of his wealth and power. Lacy loved the house because she'd made it a home.

However, Foley Sr. was a hard man to love. She thought back to the first time she objected to his working hours. She'd been crying and turned her back for a moment to get a tissue, when out of nowhere something hard slammed into the back of her head. She literally saw stars. She turned to meet a fist pounding into her jaw. That night marked the beginning of years of cruel and unmerciful beatings, until the day they suddenly stopped.

Chapter Forty-Five
October 3, 2001

Foley sat on the front pew alone. His mother and father were seated behind him. He couldn't stop crying because he missed his wife so much.

"Anissa Brogdon will be missed by her family. No one can deny that her death was tragic, but we must go on. Anissa would want you to go on." The reverend came down from the platform and extended his hand to Foley, signaling that his eulogy was over.

The church was filled with friends of the Brogdon family. Anissa's sister, Nedra, and her family had made the drive to Brentwood for the ceremony. Carlie Harper, Anissa's best friend had flown in from Seattle. Most of the faculty and staff from Eckhart Elementary attended as well. Foley thought to himself how unfortunate it was that Anissa's mother was unable to attend.

Lacy provided the only floral arrangement on the floor beneath the portrait of Anissa that was draped with white sheer fabric, intertwined with white roses. The family had requested that donations be made to charities in Anissa's name in lieu of flowers. A single candle burned to represent Anissa's spirit. That was his mother's idea. He looked at the image of his wife, grateful that he'd commissioned an artist to portray her beautiful face. He'd never see her again. He'd never hold her again; never again express his love to her. He was angry at himself. He never should have taken her to New York with him.

He took a deep breath and struggled to compose himself. It was time for him to face the grim reality that Anissa was dead and life as he knew it was over. It was of no consolation to him that many people were unaccounted for. The only thing that brought a little relief for him was knowing that she had died doing what he had told her to do: wait for him in their hotel room.

"I'm so sorry, Foley," Carlie said behind him. He turned to look at her.

"Thank you for coming, Carlie. It's so kind of you. I know it was last minute," he added. He had not expected to see her at all. He'd waited purposely until yesterday afternoon to tell her about the memorial service. He didn't care for Carlie. She could have become a powerful influence against him with her outspokenness.

"Foley, do you need help with Niss's things?" Nedra asked. He wanted to laugh in her face. If she had any designs on Anissa's clothes and jewelry, she'd better get over it.

"I can't bear the thought of going through her things right now, Nedra. But I'm sure she would have wanted you to have something. As soon as I'm up to it, I'll send for you."

"Just let me know, I'll stay in touch," she offered saccharinely, trying to conceal her greed. Nedra had been a thorn in his flesh as well, because she'd been a type of insurance policy that required timely premiums. But she was cancelled now. Anissa's death had cancelled everything.

Chapter Forty-Six
October 26, 2001

"All Rise!" the bailiff announced. Everyone in the courtroom stood.

"Kings County Family Court of the state of New York is now in session, the Honorable Judge Orella Bookings presiding."

Orella entered the courtroom and sat on her throne. As was her custom, she took a sip of water from her personal glass, which was filled from her personal container of water laced with vodka, while gazing at the faces looking back at her. As a family court judge, it was her duty to hear matters involving children and families, including adoption, guardianship, foster care approval and review, child abuse and neglect, family violence, and child custody and visitation. All decisions were at her discretion, unless a jury was involved. There was no jury today.

Contrary to popular rhetoric about a person who imbibes regularly, her memory for names and faces was excellent, at least when first contact was made when she was sober. Some people who appeared regularly in her courtroom were like old friends. Or enemies, depending on the circumstances.

Ashley McHenry was back. She'd been before Orella three other times. The first two cases were dismissed because Ashley dropped the charges. Last month she had requested and been granted a restraining order. Two weeks ago, Mr. McHenry had nearly beaten her to death. Today she was filing formal charges and his ass was going to jail. Orella would ask the bailiff to discreetly give Ashley a business card that contained the name and phone number of a self-proclaimed domestic abuse fixer. Maybe she was ready for fixing.

Benny Wise was back: one of the most notorious juvenile delinquents in Brooklyn and by far the most charming. Orella believed that the boy could have a future, if only he'd get out of his own way.

Leila Swain was seeking to adopt yet another child. That lump sum of money paid by the state to adopt a foster child was spurring her on to motherhood, repeatedly.

Marie Turner was seeking child support for her newest baby. One of these days, this bitch was going to add the word contraception to her vocabulary. And abstinence. Maybe today would be the day that Orella told her that keeping her legs closed would solve her child support problem.

Felton Dade, a new face in the crowd, was seeking custody of his niece's two sons, Nathan and Justin Long. Justin's illegitimate father, Chase Reynolds, wanted custody of the boy as well.

Chase Reynolds was not good father material. Orella knew his claim to fame. She hoped Mr. Dade had all his ducks in a row.

"Bailiff, call the first case," she ordered.

Chapter Forty-Seven
October 26, 2001

Dr. Jennings Ford sat in a chair near a window that faced Park Avenue, looking at a book about healthy foods. Pictures of various grains that he had absolutely no interest in glared at him from the page. He sighed, closed the book, looked at his watch and then at the clock on the wall. He had been waiting five minutes. If five more minutes passed, that would be his cue to exit. He didn't want to be here anyway. An orthopedist had examined him thoroughly. There was nothing physically wrong with his back, but the pain was there. Time would have to heal it.

"Why don't you see a chiropractor?" Earl Bost had suggested at lunch a few days ago.

"I don't believe in chiropractors," Dr. Ford had answered.

"You believe in pain though?" Earl asked impudently.

"Good God, man! I don't talk about my aches and pains just so you can jest!"

"I'm not jesting. See my chiropractor. One visit. If the pain gets better you can tell me what you believe then. I didn't believe in all that rigmarole either, but since I've been going I feel like a new man," Earl insisted.

"Jennings Ford?" said a pretty young lady wearing a floral jacket commonly worn by women who work in medical offices.

"Yes?" Dr. Ford answered.

"You can come on back now," she said.

He stood and followed her down a hallway, where he passed several patient rooms, each containing a patient on a narrow cot in the middle of the room. From the waist, the cot swayed up and down. The young lady led him into a room identical to the ones he had just passed. Upon closer inspection he discovered that the cot was not a normal cot. It was covered in leather, and broken into three segments. One for the head obviously, then a break for the upper torso and another break at the midsection. At the end was an adjustable section for the feet. Dr. Ford sat in one of the chairs.

"The doctor will be in to see you in just a minute. He's going to go over a few things with you and if you decide to try our program I'll be back to get X-rays." She smiled and left the room.

Dr. Ford stood and read all the medical certificates on the wall. Most showed the doctor having completed different studies at various universities. The thing that caused concern was the length of time of the curriculum. Some were eight hours, some twelve, the longest time period was three days. How in the world do you learn to tamper with someone's spine in that short period of time. He'd about made his mind up to leave when a man breezed in, full of cheer.

"Hello there young man! Will Mashburn. How did you hear about me? One of my seminars, on television, on the radio?"

"A friend told me about you."

"Good," he said as he extended his hand. He was taller than Dr. Ford, and younger—somewhere over forty. He had a strong grip. After the handshake he rattled off a spiel that was so laced with facts that Dr. Ford had a hard time doubting that he knew what he was talking about. A quick demonstration indicated that Dr. Ford's equilibrium was off. Will Mashburn was convinced that he could get rid of the back pain. The pain that had nagged at Dr. Ford since that fall in front of the hospital the day he'd dropped by the hospital and been knocked down by that so-called doctor.

Forty-five minutes later, after a series of X-rays and an 'adjustment' that felt like he was being worked over by a bully, Dr. Ford left the office, determined to never return.

"This is not an in-and-out place of business. We need to get to know you—you need to get to know your body and know that it can heal itself," Dr. Mashburn said.

He wanted to see Dr. Ford again for a second visit to go over the X-rays and to prescribe a wellness program, tailored just for Dr. Ford, to get rid of the pain in his lower back.

"People get well when they do what I tell them to do," Dr. Mashburn declared. It was more than obvious that Mashburn considered himself the be-all and know-all of the health profession. As if chiropractors were taken seriously by real doctors.

Dr. Ford had made it clear that he was a medical doctor. That in itself should have been ample notice he had a working knowledge of the body and of his own health. He'd had quite enough of that rough treatment. In his younger days he would have resorted to blunt force trauma with a man who manhandled him the way that 'wellness specialist' had done. He crossed over Park Avenue, heading towards his car. He had a few words for Earl Bost. One visit indeed!

Chapter Forty-Eight
November 2001

The President of the United States had declared war. Osama Bin Laden, the leader of Al-Qaeda, the terrorist group assumed to be responsible for the attack on September 11th, was thought to be in the mountains of Afghanistan. The President had demanded that Bin Laden be handed over, but the Taliban refused to do so without proof of his involvement. The United States had been joined by the United Kingdom in an attack in Afghanistan on October 7th.

Anissa had been in Powder Springs, Georgia for two months, and she loved it. It was a small town that was incorporated in 1838 on the lands of two Indian Chiefs, Chief Nose and Chief Ana Kanasta. The first settlers in the area had come to find gold, because gold had been discovered in Georgia in 1828. The city was originally called Springville, due to seven springs in the city limits with water containing at least 26 minerals that turned the surrounding sand black like gun powder. Hence the name (gun) Powder Springs became the official name in 1859.

The 2000 census reported 12,481 people residing in the city, most of them Caucasian. Kathy's sprawling mansion was not within the city limits. It was located in Cobb County, which had been created in December of 1832. It was one of five core counties of Metropolitan Atlanta. They were just a few miles away from the bustling metropolis which was home to the fabulous Fox Theater, the Phillips Arena, CNN, Lenox Mall, and fine restaurants. Atlanta was also the birthplace of Julia Roberts, who later moved to Smyrna, Georgia, also in Cobb County.

Anissa and Kathy had become very close. True to her word, Kathy had friends everywhere, and thanks to an anonymous benefactor, Anissa's new identity had been validated. She was introduced to everyone as Kathy's sister-in-law, Lynn Stockton, a recent widow from Kansas. Her 'late husband,' Tom Stockton, a fictional half-brother to Kathy's late husband, had on his death bed made his wife, Lynn, promise to find his brother.

"Why do we have to tell this ridiculous story?" Anissa asked Kathy. They were seated on wicker furniture in Kathy's sun room.

"We have to cover our trail," Kathy had responded. "One of these days I'm going to have to do something about Jessica Woods. My late sister-in-law? And when I do, you have to be somebody besides my brother's wife!"

"You're right, as usual."

Kathy read the story to her and then they practiced different scenarios, where Anissa would be called upon to explain her presence in Powder Springs.

"This is a small town with a lot of nosy people. And you are an African-American living in my house. We have to get our story straight. From now on your life is a lie, but we've got to make it true to you."

"My life is a lie for sure," Anissa repeated sadly, "has been for a long time. My marriage was a lie—everybody thought we were a happily married couple."

"I know. This new lie will suit you much better. So what's your name? Where are you from?" Kathy inquired.

They practiced until they had it together. Lynn Stockton graduated from Howard University with a BA in French education and a Masters from Duke. She was a former French teacher at a middle school in Wichita, Kansas. She never had any children. She and her husband were married one year; he died from cancer. He and Kathy's husband had the same father; a lie that could never be refuted because both of the elder Mr. and Mrs. Stockton were dead. Kathy's husband had one sister who lived in Asia and had not been to the United States for years.

Lynn Stockton had a new social security number, a new Georgia driver's license, and a Visa with an undisclosed credit limit. When Anissa first saw the documents that established her new identity, she was mystified.

"How did you do this? Do you know someone who works with the witness relocation program? This is the kind of stuff that they do."

"Like I said, I've got friends, honey. Amazing doors open for you once you no longer have to claim you walked into one to explain a black eye."

Kathy laughed aloud. She laughed a lot. She said she'd cried for so many days and nights from pain caused by her abusive husband that she deserved to laugh for the rest of her life. She was a fountain of wisdom with boundless energy and an immense capacity for love. They had spent many nights talking, and Anissa had trusted her with things about Foley that she thought she'd never tell anyone. It seemed that for each atrocity visited upon Anissa, Kathy countered with one that not only visited, but stayed a while.

"You know it was like he didn't understand that pain hurt. I dreamed of killing him. I would imagine myself doing it and then get scared to death for even thinking about it," Kathy stated, her face showing anger and frustration.

Anissa knew exactly what she meant. She had felt the same. It was hard to talk about it, but Kathy was relentless. She continually encouraged her to communicate.

"You'd be amazed at how many times I cooked grits with the intentions of pouring them over him while he slept," she'd declare in the middle of rehearsing Anissa's new life. "The only thing that kept me from doing it is that I knew he would get better and when he did I was a dead woman. None of my friends knew about the abuse. I isolated myself." Kathy would begin to cry when she talked like that, but not for long. Once tears escaped her eyes, she seemed to use them as fodder for the laughter that would follow. She shrugged and looked expectantly at Anissa.

Recalling how isolated she too had been, Anissa empathized with her "sister-in-law." She'd spent days anticipating Carlie showing up and demanding why Anissa hadn't called. But she never did. Nor did Nedra. The whole time Anissa had lived in Nashville she had never come to visit Anissa.

"I claimed that I'd found a new religion or some new cause to keep me too busy to see anyone," Kathy continued. "I finally stopped looking for excuses and just became a hermit. Once I did that, he stayed on me. It was a slap or two in the morning, a kick or a gut punch when he got home, and if dinner wasn't just right, it was a fist pummeling for the rest of the night unless he went out. He wouldn't allow the maid, the cooks, or the gardener near me. He paid them well and convinced them that I wanted to be left alone. In the midst of all of this cruelty, he still insisted on having sex with me. That man believed in showing his woman a good time." She'd throw her head back and laugh that wonderful lilting laughter and then look at Anissa with deep knowing.

Most of the time, they sat in Kathy's sun room. A large room surrounded by windows set into white cedar plank walls. Everything was white and yellow—a white couch and chairs accented with yellow pillows, white end tables with yellow lamps, a white coffee table with white cut flowers and a huge yellow sculpture. The furniture was centered on a large yellow and white wavy striped rug on shiny hardwood floors.

"I had a nickname for him," Kathy said.

"What nickname?"

"Pisspot!"

"Pisspot?" Anissa giggled.

"Yes. That grown assed man would pee in the bed. He said he dreamed that he was in the bathroom whenever it happened and of course he got mad at me because I knew."

Kathy also talked about her family. They had old money, and with both parents deceased, and now her only sibling as well, she was the sole heir to a fortune. It turned out that her husband had also been very rich, and as his widow she'd gained everything that he owned, leaving her sitting pretty for the rest of her life.

"I have so much money it's not even funny. And I swear, I will use every penny of it to help women escape from abusive situations. And after that I'm going after these parents who abuse and neglect their children. I'm going to establish a village all over the world if I have to. And you are going to be my first successful candidate. I'm just beside myself with joy, girlfriend."

Anissa appreciated Kathy's enthusiasm, but did not share it. She was still afraid most days and sad on others. She didn't want to admit that she still loved Foley, that she missed his touch. She hated herself for those feelings. Why would she still care about him? And then she'd get a flash of his fist coming toward her. And his cold blue eyes as he looked at her.

"Kathy you will never know how much I appreciate all that you've done for me," she said, snapping herself out of her reverie.

"It's my pleasure! Now, where'd you teach last year? And how did your husband Tom make his money?"

Chapter Forty-Nine
November 2001

Felton Dade had gained full custody of his two nephews in October. His next step would be adoption in a year or so. Nathan's custody hearing had been a piece of cake compared to Justin's. Chase, Justin's father, had nearly frightened both boys out of their wits by threatening to take Justin away, severing the only remaining immediate family ties for each of them.

Judge Orella Bookings had done what most family court judges would not be inclined to do. According to the law, a biological parent had a superior right to custody of his or her child. Judge Bookings begged to differ. She nipped it all in the bud.

Chase Reynolds had come to court prepared with the birth certificate that proved he was Justin's biological father. His mother came to court and lied about how much she loved her only grandson and had not been permitted to see him while Sherry was alive. She claimed to have sent money to Justin by Chase. She was very credible, though Felton had never seen her before. Chase had to have parents, of course, but Felton had always assumed that he had been spawned from wolves.

Felton had also prepared his petition well. He'd shown that Sherry had taken care of Justin all of his life, not even bothering with giving Justin his father's last name nor asking him for child support. He had no way to prove that Chase did not want the boy; he only knew that he'd never behaved like a father who loved his son.

When the bailiff called his case, Felton was nervous, wondering if his decision not to bring an attorney had been a mistake. He'd read up on custody battles and felt like he could handle it himself.

"Are both parties present and ready to proceed in this matter before the court?" Judge Bookings asked.

Chase answered first. "I am."

He was so clean that Felton almost didn't recognize him. He had a new haircut, wore a nice navy suit with a white shirt and striped tie. He had papers in his hands. He looked like a responsible person.

"I am also," Felton replied.

"Please approach the bench."

Felton and Chase walked up to the judge's bench.

"And you are?" the Judge nodded toward Felton.

"Felton Dade, your Honor, I am the petitioner."

The judge looked at Chase. "And who might you be?" she asked.

"Chase Reynolds, your Honor, I am the bi-loshical parent."

Judge Bookings never changed her expression at the mispronunciation. Instead, she looked down at the papers in front of her.

"Are all the facts stated in this petition and your responses true?" She looked at first one man and then the other.

"Yes, your Honor," Felton answered.

"Yes ma'am, your Honor," Chase replied.

"And at the time this petition was filed, both of you had resided in the state of New York for at least six months?"

"Your Honor, I been in New York all my life," Chase blurted.

"A simple yes or no will suffice," Judge Bookings replied without looking at Chase.

"Yes," Felton stated.

"Gentlemen I have reviewed your case. I would like to call a recess at this time so that I may speak with the child, Justin Long, in my chambers."

Two hours later, Felton and Chase stood before the judge again for her decision. Felton was a little upset because he had not been asked any questions about his suitability to raise a child, nor had he been able to provide evidence that Chase wasn't fit to raise a puppy. He had not had a chance to talk to Justin to find out what went on in the judge's chambers.

"Mr. Reynolds, based on the fact that Justin is currently living in the family home he is used to with his biological sibling, I am denying your custody request based on the fact that you relinquished parental rights through surrender, abandonment, persistent neglect, unfitness, and other like extraordinary circumstances."

"But your honor…" Chase began to argue, but was interrupted mid-sentence.

"Mr. Reynolds I know your history. And you know that I know it. Don't interrupt me."

Judge Bookings directed her attention to Felton.

"Mr. Dade, I am basing my decision to grant full custody of Justin Long to you on these factors: I believe that siblings should be kept together and Justin has unequivocally stated that he wants to remain with you. He says that he doesn't know his father. I'm inclined to believe him. Your history is excellent; you have not been accused of crimes involving drugs, alcohol abuse, or fathering and then deserting multiple children. You have a steady job as a police detective and an income that will allow provision for the child's needs. The child is familiar with the existing family home and school. Furthermore the child does not wish to see his father after today, and based on some of the things he has shared with me I can understand why."

Felton was so happy he could have hugged her. She'd subtly let him know that she'd known all about Chase—he was not even granted visitation rights. However, his mother, Justin's biological grandmother, was. But Felton doubted he'd ever see her again, especially since he'd never laid eyes on her before that day.

Chapter Fifty
November 2001

Kathy had decided that it was time for Anissa to see her therapist, Dr. Dylun Forat, to begin her road to recovery. Although Kathy seemed to be absorbed in her own conversation most of the time, she carefully observed Anissa's reactions or lack thereof. She recognized every facial expression, every body movement that indicated self-loathing and shame, and the difficulty in talking about her feelings. Dr. Forat had pulled Kathy out of a slump and helped her regain self-confidence.

Kathy also needed to figure out what she was going to do about Troy's wife, Jessica. There was no way that she could allow Anissa to continue living as Jessica Woods, because some well-meaning friend or business associate of Troy's might stop by to express their condolences. She knew for a fact that one of Troy's main distributors was in the Atlanta area. One look at Anissa and the cat would be out of the bag. Southern people are known for their hospitality, but they also have a tendency to dip their noses where they don't belong.

Identifying Jessica's body now was not a good idea, because she'd allowed Anissa to come home from the hospital in New York as her brother's wife. But until Jessica was declared legally dead, Troy's estate remained in limbo. It was not a question of money because God knew that Kathy didn't need it, but she couldn't leave her brother's business in the hands of the general foreman forever. There had to be a way to get it done without leaving an open trail for Foley Brogdon to pick up. She had been so wrapped up with Anissa and her problems that she'd totally neglected her own. Geoffrey was a good problem solver. Eventually she would elicit his help.

Geoffrey Winston had come into her life and made all the difference. She'd met him at a fund-raiser for the Governor of Georgia at the seafood table. He'd been loading his plate with shrimp while she'd selected the smoked salmon, cream cheese, capers, and onions. When he'd reached over her to get at the stuffed crab, one of his shrimp fell on top of Kathy's smoked salmon. She'd inadvertently let out a little shriek.

"My goodness, did I forget to wear deodorant?" he asked, jumping slightly, causing three more shrimp to fall, hitting the side of Kathy's hand.

"I'm allergic to shrimp," Kathy wailed. She rushed immediately to the serving staff, handed them her plate, and headed for the nearest restroom to thoroughly wash her hands. Merely touching shrimp could cause an allergic reaction. When she came out of the restroom he was standing there, looking very tall and forlorn.

"I apologize. I'm so clumsy," he said simply.

"That's okay. You couldn't have known."

"You're absolutely right, I couldn't have known. But I could have watched my manners and waited until you finished. I just haven't eaten all day," he replied sheepishly.

"You're fine. No harm done," Kathy said over her shoulder, walking back to her table.

"I'm Geoffrey Winston, by the way, you know in case you'd like to know who just put your life in danger." He took two steps to get beside her. He smiled, and for the first time, Kathy noticed how handsome he was.

"I'm Kathy Stockton, nice to meet you," Kathy extended her hand.

"May I call you Shrimpy?" he laughed, taking her hand into his just long enough to feel the sparks.

Kathy laughed as she walked on. "Not if you expect me to answer."

"I'm kidding. Do you come here often?"

Kathy stopped walking and put her hands on her hips. "Seriously? Is that your best move?" she asked.

"No, I've got great moves. You want to get out of here and go someplace quieter so I can really impress you."

"I know just the place." Kathy led him outside to the gardens where they both sat in folding chairs they'd grabbed, and Geoffrey Winston made his move.

He was a retired member of the Office of United States Marshals, the oldest federal law enforcement office in the country. Created in 1789 by the first United States Congress in a Judiciary Act, the office specified that a U.S. Marshal's primary duty was to execute "all lawful precepts directed to and issued him under the authority of the United States," even though the Act did not refer to the marshal as a law enforcement officer. A marshal was able to command all necessary assistance in the performance of his duties.

Kathy was tickled to death at the irony. If she'd met this man a few years ago, he might have helped her escape from her husband.

"I'm wondering where you've been all my life," she teased.

"Have you been looking for me?"

Their eyes met for a beat before Kathy changed the subject.

"Have you ever killed anyone?"

"Of course not, although the opportunity has presented itself on several occasions. We do a lot of protective custody and not too much gun fighting nowadays."

Kathy was genuinely fascinated when he shared a little of history with her. The second marshal to die in the line of duty did so trying to prevent injury to a fugitive slave in Boston in 1854. In the 1960's, the marshals were on the front lines of the Civil Rights Movement, and they were also involved with the witness security program that began in 1971.

"Who was the first marshal killed in the line of duty?" Kathy asked.

"Robert Forsyth, the first U.S. Marshal for the state of Georgia."

"Wow. Did he die trying to save a slave too?"

"No, he was trying to serve papers. He knocked, and the man shot him through the door."

Kathy laughed out loud. "I'm so sorry," she giggled. "I don't mean to be insensitive; it's just so funny the way you said that."

He laughed too. "I didn't know I was a funny guy."

She and Geoffrey had made a dinner date that night, five years ago, and the rest was history, as they say. She knew that he had strong feelings for her and would do anything she asked. He was the one who contacted old friends to get new identification for Anissa after checking her out thoroughly and conceding that she was sane and rational. He learned that no official reports of abuse were on record, but Anissa had been hospitalized once for severe injuries caused from a fall on the stairs. She'd also been seen at home by a doctor for injuries from an automobile accident that was never reported to authorities.

Foley had a stellar reputation in his hometown, but Geoffrey had discovered a sealed record that suggested otherwise. Kathy didn't know if Geoffrey had found out why the record was sealed, because he'd never told her and she had not pressed the issue. The important thing was that Anissa was no longer with him, and that once he realized that Anissa's husband was a son of a bitch, Geoffrey was more than willing to help her.

Chapter Fifty-One
November 2001

Foley Brogdon was trying to adjust to life as a widower. He felt like a zombie most days. He returned to work, but wasn't very productive, performing his duties perfunctorily. He wanted to be left alone to grieve for his wife. The outpouring of sympathy from his co-workers and patients was so great that he felt like he'd choke. The fact that Anissa's body had never been recovered helped to fuel his belief that she would return to him some day. Every night he prayed that when the morning came he'd have news that Anissa had been found.

He knew his parents were worried about him, but that was too bad. They did not understand his love for her.

"Son, you've got to do something with Anissa's things. Donate them to charity. There are people out there who could be wearing these beautiful clothes," his mother said every time she was in his home.

"Yes, mother. I will. Just give me time."

Back at work, he did consultations and caught up with his surgery schedule. He shared his practice with another surgeon, but Foley's clients were loyal. They'd waited for his return, especially those seeking breast augmentation and tummy tucks, as those were his specialties. He'd completed his residency at UCLA and worked in Beverly Hills for a short time. His education had prepared him well and he reaped the benefits. After a full day at work, he returned to his home to be alone.

His mother brought food or some other ridiculous thing to cheer him up, but nothing helped. He settled into a routine—work, home, a drink, dinner, and then bed. The sooner he went to bed, the sooner he could close his eyes and be with Anissa. He dreamed of her often, and sometimes in his dreams she was smiling at him, telling him that she had forgiven him and that she loved him, only him. He knew that some of the things that he'd done to her were a little extreme, but it was for her own good. It was imperative that she fully accepted and understood that life with him on his terms was as good as it gets.

He had always kept in shape but now he exercised relentlessly. He had more gym equipment added to his already full sized fitness center. He hired a personal trainer. He opted for a female first, but later changed his mind and hired a male. He wanted no entanglements anytime soon. He felt that his heart belonged to only one woman, and now that she had been snatched from him, he dared not love another. He ate meals on Sundays at his parents' home and attended church with his mother occasionally.

There was a golf course in the neighborhood, and he played at least twice a week, usually alone or with someone in need of a twosome or a foursome; never did he play with close friends because he didn't have any. He'd not had a close friend since high school. That had been Shon, an African American guy who had a way with the girls. Foley smiled to himself as he remembered wanting to get next to Shon so that he could meet some African American girls. He ended up liking Shon. But all that had ended almost overnight. Since then he'd had many acquaintances, but no one got close enough to him to become a pal. Nevertheless, he was going to have to make some decisions soon about the house, about all of Anissa's things, about whether he even wanted to remain in Brentwood.

Some nights the images of the last day they shared haunted him. He felt positive that he had taught her a lesson, one that she would not forget. In his heart, he knew that she had waited for him in the hotel. That explained why she was never found. But he allowed his imagination to wander, to envision her roaming the streets of New York, destitute and homeless.

Maybe, in spite of everything, she'd obeyed the evacuation order and the shock of the whole attack had disoriented and confused her. She had no identification, no shoes, and no means to live by. Soon she would call him and let him know where to come for her. He just hoped she hadn't wandered into Harlem; the thought of that evoked apprehension and dread.

Like everyone, Foley had enemies. One of them lived in Harlem and wished him ill. An enemy that would surely do him harm if given the opportunity. Finding his wife alone in the streets would provide such an occasion. And Foley couldn't blame him.

"Vengeance is mine, saith the Lord," was another of his mother's favorite bible verses. Revenge is a strange thing. Most people got pay-back and thought about the Lord getting his later—if they thought about him at all. Foley's enemies were not Christians. Especially this one. He had to hate Foley with a passion—a hatred that was well deserved.

No, he decided. Odds were that she had not shown up in Harlem, or else Foley would have received a phone call. Or Anissa's ring finger in the mail.

Chapter Fifty-Two
November 2001

Orella enjoyed cooking. It gave her an opportunity to drink wine, turn the music up, and dance in the kitchen. She was preparing her favorite meal, spaghetti with meatballs. Her grandmother had taught her how to season the meat, adding just the right amount of spices, and rolling perfectly formed orbs of ground flesh. And the sauce!

"Never tell anyone how we make the sauce, sweetie. Womenfolk need some secrets, and a good recipe is one of them," her grandmother had said as she stirred the bubbling brew.

Orella's eyes filled with tears at the memory. She had spent many days with her grandmother in that old kitchen, helping prepare meals. She looked around at her modern kitchen, with all the latest gadgets and appliances. Kathy had insisted on Bertazzoni, while Orella chose the color—black. She opened the refrigerator to take out tomatoes when she heard the doorbell.

It could be one of two people she thought, ignoring the buzzing sound. Either her neighbor, Olonzo, wanting to have a drink, or a Jehovah's Witness. No one else ever came to her door uninvited. She was in no mood for company. She was feeling good and soon she'd have a hot delicious meal.

Aretha Franklin sang about getting respect. Orella sang along with her until a loud banging on the door interrupted her. *Who in the world?* She put her glass on the counter, moved the pot from the eye—she didn't want burned sauce—removed her apron, and went to the door. She took a deep breath before opening it—preparing herself.

Her heart almost stopped beating at the sight of two police officers, one stocky, one thin as a rail. *They've finally come for me,* she thought. Just as quickly she decided to go down with dignity. If she was going to jail, she'd go proudly.

"Orella Bookings? Judge Orella Bookings?" the thin one asked.

"Yes," Orella answered, not breaking eye contact.

“We’re investigating a hit-and-run that occurred on September 11th,” he continued.

“The day of the attacks?” The only thing that came to Orella’s mind.

“Yes,” this time Stocky answered.

“How can I help you?” Orella asked.

“Well, witnesses reported seeing a red sports car driving away from the scene,” the thin man spoke this time.

Orella could sense that they were as nervous as she was, but she didn’t understand why. All they had to do was pull out handcuffs; she was the one who’d have to wear them. She looked at first one and then the other. She would not be the next person to speak.

“Paul Bookings registered a red BMW with the state of New York and gave this address,” Tall and Slim continued.

“He was my grandfather,” Orella replied. “He died a few months ago. He bought the car for me as a birthday gift, but it was stolen on September 11th.”

“Really? Did you report it?”

“Yes, I did,” Orella answered. *They didn’t know that?* Maybe she was safe after all.

“Was the car ever found?” The stocky one this time.

“Not to my knowledge. The insurance company is handling it as a loss.” Orella’s pulse was moving back into the normal range.

“We should have checked that before we came out. Sorry to bother you, Judge, we’ve been backed up with work.”

“I can imagine. That was a tragic day for everyone,” Orella smiled sadly as she pasted a look of compassion on her face to mask the relief reverberating through her body.

“Have a nice evening.” The two men turned away from the door. Orella quickly decided to show concern.

“Was the accident serious?” she asked, placing her hand on her heart.

“A woman died at the scene,” the thin man answered.

“That’s a shame. Well, good luck with your investigation.”

“Thanks, Judge.”

Orella closed the door behind them and stood with her back against the door, taking deep breaths. Had she escaped?

For the moment, yes. She was still free. She straightened, walked back to the kitchen, and put the pot of sauce back on. James Brown was singing about getting even—payback. Orella drained her wineglass, twirled around, and slid down into a graceful split—her best ever imitation of James Brown. Her payback had definitely been delayed another day.

Chapter Fifty-Three
December 2001

On December 3, 2001, the United States Special Forces and Marines were on the ground in Afghanistan; British, French, and German forces joined as well. Heavy bombing by the U.S. destroyed Taliban trenches and killed many people, and yet Osama Bin Laden had not been captured. Kathy had briefly spoken with her husband's sister in Asia, and learned about an article in the BBC News that claimed a foreign official from Pakistan had leaked information to the BBC, about American officials predicting military action in Afghanistan in July 2001, well before September 11th. Kathy was astounded at the implication of such news, and even more so at hearing from her sister-in-law. They chatted for over an hour, and Kathy was relieved to hear that no visits were planned to the United States.

Kathy stayed in contact with many of her friends and most were in favor of the war. American flags were still dominant in yards, on cars, in front of businesses, and the bonds of patriotism were strong. Kathy vowed to only take in an hour of news per day.

Anissa was doing well. She was attending therapy on a regular basis. One evening, the two of them sat in Kathy's family room, a comfortable space with antique white walls, large windows draped in lime green fabric and French doors leading out to a cedar deck. Kathy had already begun decorating for the holidays. The one thing still lacking was the Christmas tree. To the right of the white camelback sofa a warm fire blazed in the fireplace. Kathy sat in a wing backed chair to the left and Anissa reclined on a beige chaise a few feet away, engrossed in a novel.

The phone rang. Kathy answered and carried on a brief conversation that consisted of 'That's right,' 'Really?' and 'I really appreciate you.' Seconds later she hung up.

"I've got a job interview lined up for you!" she announced.

"A job?" Anissa looked up from her book.

"Yes. Teaching French at the new middle school. The current teacher will not return after the holidays. She's having a baby."

"How do you know that?" Anissa was amazed at the information Kathy was able to acquire without leaving her home.

"A friend works in human resources. She just called. I'd mentioned you to her and asked her to be on the lookout. I didn't expect anything until next school year, but there you have it. You've always said that you enjoyed teaching."

"I did. I do," Anissa sputtered.

Kathy felt that working could be a good change. Anissa's mind would be occupied with something other than therapy sessions, listening to Kathy, reading, and gaining weight.

"Your interview is day after tomorrow. We'll go shopping tomorrow morning to get you some nice professional outfits. I know just the place—Lenox Mall in Atlanta. They have a huge Macy's Department store, your favorite place to shop."

Chapter Fifty-Four
December 2001

Opened in 1959, Lenox Square Mall was located in the heart of Buckhead, a ritzy area in northwest Atlanta. Kathy, driving south, exited Interstate 75 at West Paces Ferry Road, where mansions lined both sides of the street, including that of the Governor of Georgia. Buckhead was originally called Irbyville to honor Irby's General Store and Tavern, which had become a stopping place for rich and not so rich travelers after its opening in 1837. The story goes that the tavern owner went hunting and killed a big deer. He had the 'buck's head' mounted so that travelers could see it, some say intending to mock European noblemen whose walls were filled with hunting trophies. At the time, it was a thinly populated wilderness, but a wealthy community began to grow and thrive around it. A late 19th century campaign to change the community name to Northside Park failed.

Lenox, as the locals called it, was located on Peachtree Road, the main street in Atlanta that starts at Peachtree Street at Five-Points—a point where five streets intersected downtown. The mall was originally a 74-acre estate last occupied by a banker and his family. The estate was purchased by a foundation that wanted the site to be turned into a shopping center. The grand opening was held in August 1959, with two department stores, Davison's and Rich's, becoming anchors. A landscaped plaza and mall surrounded by specialty stores, a bowling alley, a Colonial grocery store and a movie theater, Atlanta newspapers referred to it as the largest shopping center south of New York. Its slogan was "Everything's there at Lenox Square." Davison's was renovated and became Macy's in 1986. Neiman Marcus opened its only Georgia location there in 1972. Anissa had to agree that everything was there, indeed.

In addition to gaining weight, Anissa had cut her hair and dyed it auburn. She almost looked like a different person from a distance. Kathy spared no expense, insisting that Anissa needed professional suits and dresses to wear in the classroom.

"How many times do I have to tell you that I hope my dead husband is turning over in his grave every time I swipe this credit card?" she laughed.

"Kathy, I don't even have a job yet!" Anissa argued.

"That's a mere technicality. This time tomorrow you will be employed."

"And you know this how?"

"I'm a genie," Kathy laughed.

Anissa tilted her head and laughed. They were standing just beyond Macy's, when suddenly she heard someone call her name—Anissa Brogdon. She instinctively reacted by turning her head toward the sound and then froze instantly and whispered to Kathy.

"Did you hear that?'

"What?'

"Someone just called out my name. Someone has seen me."

"Someone thinks that they have seen you. You keep walking and ignore whatever you heard."

Anissa felt herself trembling all over. She could not do it. She had to get out. What if the person caught up with them? This new life would be all over. Everything would be ruined.

"We have to leave, now."

"Fine, Lynn. You follow me. You need to remember that your name isn't Anissa anymore, but I guess it's going to take time, huh? We'll go through this store and then down the escalator and out the back. Quick like a bunny."

They hurried to the car. Anissa was not able to stop shaking until they were back on Interstate 75 headed north. Someone had seen her. It was someone she knew, because the voice had been eerily familiar but she couldn't put a name or a face to it. What if whoever it was told Foley? He would come looking for her, and when he found her he would surely hurt her, probably even kill her. He had no reason not to, because the rest of the world thought she was already dead.

"I can't stay here," she gasped.

"Why not? No one knows where you live or who you are today. Even if someone really saw you, what can they say? They can't give an address, a phone number, or a post office box. If they wanted to look you up, how could they find you?

You are no longer Anissa Brogdon. You are safe. Now calm down. Haven't you heard that old saying that there's nothing to fear but fear itself?" Kathy asked defiantly.

"In my vocabulary fear has a name. It's Foley Brogdon. If he believes that I am alive he won't stop looking until he finds me."

"Was it a man's voice that called out to you? Because what I heard sounded very female. Unless Foley has had a sex change it wasn't him." Kathy looked at Anissa with eyebrows raised.

"You heard it? You stinker! Of course, it was female and it sounded familiar. I just can't place the voice right now. Whoever it was knew me on sight even with my red hair."

"They thought they saw Anissa Brogdon. But that's impossible, because she's dead. Are you with me?"

"Yes. But, Kathy…"

"I know," Kathy interrupted, "I know what you are feeling, but I also know that there is no way in the world that he can track you down just from one sighting. So what do you want to do now, shop from a catalog or shall I hire a personal shopper for the both of us?"

Anissa laughed halfheartedly. She was nervous and scared, but nothing seemed to upset Kathy. She had an answer for everything; she was so sure of herself and so fearless—and she was right. To the world and to Foley, she was dead. There was no way that he could find her here. He shouldn't even be looking for her after all this time. It was best to forget all about it and concentrate on practicing for her interview. And then the light bulb flickered. It was Carlie! The voice that called out her name belonged to her friend Carlie.

Chapter Fifty-Five
December 2001

Orella had cleared her calendar for the afternoon to do some early Christmas shopping. Normally she waited two to three days before, but all of the destruction caused by 9/11 made her begin to value the lives of others. Her list included her friend Kathy, co-workers, neighbors in her building, the drycleaner, and the folks who owned the liquor store that she frequented the most. She'd gotten her drinking under control, and for that she was grateful. She'd had lunch at a nice restaurant on Fifth Avenue that had included only one bottle of wine and a cognac. The few shots of vodka that she'd had during the morning had actually worn off by noon. The buzz was completely gone.

It was a nice day for shopping she decided as she entered Bergdorf Goodman Department Store—founded in 1899 by Herman Bergdorf and later owned by Edwin Goodman.

"Good Afternoon, may I help you?" asked a saleslady who was rapidly approaching Orella.

"No, thank you," Orella replied pleasantly, glancing toward the jewelry department.

"Are we looking for anything particular today?" the saleslady asked.

Orella looked directly at the woman this time. She was young, slim, and quite pretty. "I don't know about you, but *I'm* looking for whatever catches my fancy. Thank you," Orella said in a dismissive tone.

She continued to the jewelry counter to the big pair of gold earrings that had caught her eye. In her peripheral vision she saw the saleslady looming just slightly to the left of her. There were people working in the jewelry department. There was no reason for that woman's attention to still be focused on Orella. This store seemed to hire people who operated under the assumption that people of color needed heavy monitoring. Orella did not like to be bird-dogged. Oh well, she thought to herself. Time to pull out her American Express card and prove she could afford to shop here.

"May I help you?" asked the woman behind the counter.

"I'll take these earrings," Orella said, pointing to a pair of huge gold dangly spheres.

"Those Van Der Straetens?"

"Those are the ones," Orella answered gaily, handing over her credit card.

The lady wrapped them in tissue, completed the sale, and wished Orella a nice evening.

Orella went next to the dress department where she walked away with a cute black Halston with beads on the front and a little red number with gold sequins by Givenchy. Naturally she couldn't leave without shoes so she bought a pair of black satin Oscar de la Renta pumps. The fact that she'd just spent over $5,000 did not spoil her mood. She felt so good that she stopped at the next bar and grill and ordered herself a cocktail.

Chapter Fifty-Six
January 2002

Foley was in one of the guest bedrooms preparing for bed. He'd decided that there were too many memories in the room he'd shared with Anissa, yet he was not ready to call in a decorator or get rid of her things. This particular room was painted dark grey with light grey horizontal stripes spaced about four feet apart. There was a print of breaking waves on a beach done in muted shades of grey giving the sense of an impending storm on the wall over a bow front chest. The floor was covered with a textured pale blue carpet with grey splotches. He placed his shirt on one of the two oversized grey velvet chairs with brass tacks on the arms that flanked the chest. He switched on one of the chrome shaded floor lamps that stood beside each chair, sat down on the orange striped stool that provided the only splash of color in the room, and kicked off his shoes.

He had an early surgery the next morning. He needed to sleep and felt that perhaps tonight his thoughts would not keep him awake in this dark room. The ringing of the phone on the night table disturbed his thoughts. Perhaps he should go back to having only one in the house. He snatched it up.

"May I help you?" he asked whoever was calling.

"Hello, Foley! Carlie Harper. How are you?"

"I'm fine, Carlie, how are you? I haven't seen you since the memorial," Foley replied plastically.

"Yes, I know. Did I catch you at a bad time?"

Foley considered the question. Having to talk to Carlie was always bad timing. He didn't like her. But he would be polite.

"I'm getting ready for bed. Early surgery. Is there anything I can do for you?" he asked caustically. He would make this conversation short and sour.

"You know how the memorial was because Nissa's body was never found?"

"Yes," he answered quietly. His reason for being in this room with a white four-poster bed had been not to think about Anissa. Was there no escaping the memory of her?

"Well I was wondering…" Carlie paused. "Did they ever find her?"

Foley's heart skipped a beat as he glanced at the sunburst mirror above the bed. "Of course not. Why do you ask?"

"Well I thought… I mean… I don't know how to say this…" Carlie muttered.

Use your words, Foley thought, but he remained silent.

"I guess I'll just say it. I thought I saw Nissa in Atlanta. I tried to let it go, but I just kept thinking about her. I guess it must have been someone who looks like her," Carlie's voice faded away to almost a whisper.

"Anissa is gone, Carlie. I'm having a hard time believing it myself, but you're right, it had to be someone who looks like her." The sadness combined with impatience in his voice was almost palpable.

"And laughs like her and tilts her head to the left just like her? I actually called out to her. But the woman ignored me. Oh goodness, I'm rambling. I'm so sorry to bother you, Foley. I agonized over making this call. I probably sound like I'm crazy, but I just wanted to be sure."

"I've got an urn filled with ashes that represent her remains on my mantle. I've got a death certificate and we memorialized her." Foley felt himself getting angry. He ran his hands through his hair, took a sip from the bottle of Perrier he'd placed on the nightstand, and sighed. Yes, Carlie was crazy. Who else but a demented person would call the husband of a dead woman and tell him that they saw her? No one, that's who.

"I'm going to bed. You have a nice evening, Carlie," he said calmly.

"Again, I'm sorry, Foley. Goodbye." He heard the dial tone.

Carlie had been mistaken. Anissa did not have a dime to her name. He'd made certain of that after that incident at the Atlanta airport. He'd made her close every account that she'd had and he'd never put cash in her hand. How would she get to Atlanta or anywhere else without money? If Carlie said she saw her in Manhattan, he might have believed her. He would have accepted it as truth just as a thirsty man dying on the desert would eagerly grab at water. But not in Atlanta. There was no way that she could be in Atlanta, Georgia.

He finished undressing and lay down on top of the quilt, staring at the ceiling. He'd done everything he could think of to insure that Carlie would be absent from his life. Under pretense of getting a signature stamp made, he'd asked Anissa to sign several pieces of blank stationery; then he'd composed a short universal note:

Greetings,
I have a new life and a future filled with new friends and family. I don't want to bring anything from my past along. I know that you will understand and abide by my wishes when I say to you that I am severing all ties of days long gone. I will always cherish our memories.
For Auld Lang Syne
Anissa S. Brogdon

He'd mailed this declaration to Carlie, Nedra, and every other person that Anissa had known. He'd not included a return address. Some people, like Carlie, Nedra, and Anissa's personal trainer, had been stubborn. They had called and tried to talk to her. He was the sole person permitted to answer the phone and he'd always given the same response:

I'm sorry, Anissa does not wish to speak to you.

He took a deep breath, wishing he'd taken a yoga class or knew some other relaxing technique. He'd never needed them before because he controlled his own destiny, therefore nothing upset him. He closed his eyes, drifted off to sleep and once again, the dream that had haunted him since Anissa's death returned.

They were on the plane en route to New York. A young man was seated across from Anissa, who'd introduced himself immediately.

"I'm Richard," he'd said, extending his hand to Anissa.

“Hi, Richard, this is my husband, Foley.” She turned to Foley with a smile on her face. He nodded and extended his hand. “Nice to meet you, Richard.”

He thought that would be the end of it. Foley always had a way of discouraging conversation. He simply ignored people. But not Anissa. The boy talked the entire flight. He’d not been home to New York in years. His mother was sick and he was going to visit her. He didn’t get on well with his brothers and sisters. Blah blah blah blah blah.

Foley felt himself getting angry at the sound of the man’s voice. Not to mention the fact that he was totally monopolizing Anissa’s time. Not once did she turn away or ignore him. Had she learned nothing?

When they got to the door of their hotel room on the concierge floor of the Marriott, Foley tipped the bellhop and closed the door behind him. Anissa was going on and on about the view.

Whop!

He made contact at the center of her back with his fist. Her knees buckled. He dragged her by her hair and threw her savagely onto the bed, face down. He straddled her, pummeling her with his fists on her shoulders, her upper and lower back, and the back of her head. God how it felt good! Her face was wedged into the mattress. She tried to turn her head to get some air, but each time she moved he grabbed her hair, yanked her head back around, and pushed her face into the mattress as he continued hitting her on the back of the head with an open hand.

“It was so nice to meet you! I hope everything goes okay for you and your family,” he ranted, mimicking her voice. “How many times have I warned you not to talk to strangers?” His voice was cool and calm again. He moved away from her, satisfied.

She rolled over onto her back, gasping for air, sobbing with each breath.

“I’m sorry. I’m so sor...sor...ry,” she sobbed. “I didn’t mean anything. I...I was trying to be polite.”

Whop! Whop!

He double punched her in her stomach and listened as the air in her lungs came out. He followed this by placing his hands around her throat; beginning to squeeze until she slipped into darkness. Choking just enough not to kill the person was an art that he'd perfected. He'd been practicing since high school. Erotic asphyxiation was how it had begun. Now it was a great control tool.

He sat down in a chair and watched until she slowly came to, opened her eyes, looked around the room until her eyes came to rest on his.

"Why do you make me do these things to you?" he asked.

Chapter Fifty-Seven
January 2002

Anissa began her new job as Lynn Stockton, eighth grade French teacher at Valeria Middle School in Cobb County, on January 2, 2002 with three days of pre-planning. She was amazed at how smoothly everything had fallen into place. It was a miracle that her fingerprints did not expose her true identity. Every teacher across the country has to be fingerprinted and she had done so in Nashville, before she ever met Foley, and yet, no blips came up on the radar when she used her false name. Kathy's friends in high and low places really knew their stuff. Kathy would answer no questions, she merely reassured Anissa that everything would be alright.

She would be teaching on a provisional certificate until she had the state teacher's certification. She had already taken the test in December, when she was hired, and was waiting for the results. The one question on the certification test that still haunted her was the identity of the composer of Bolero, a French ballet. How could she forget that it was Maurice Ravel? It was his most famous musical composition, one that he always claimed to have written without music. She knew that she'd missed other questions, but that one nagged at her. Once she received notification that she had passed the test, she would become fully certified with a T-5 certificate based on a master's degree in French literature from Duke University.

Valeria Middle was a mere twenty-minute drive from Kathy's house. Anissa had been assigned a classroom on the seventh grade hall near the Spanish teachers and the German teacher, who was also the foreign language contact for the school. Anissa was relaxed and happy for the first time in years. She had settled in to her new name and her new hometown. She'd also insisted on having her own place, and within the next two months, she would probably be moving to a lovely home in a new subdivision. Kathy had purchased it as investment property, but Anissa was emphatic about making the monthly mortgage payments.

"My dream is to relocate battered women all over this country, to get them started with new lives. That means I'm going to have to buy a lot of houses so I might as well start with you," Kathy contested. After a lengthy discussion, she finally agreed to payment terms for the house. Anissa also had a new Lexus, a Christmas gift from Kathy.

"You need a way to get to work," she smiled as she placed the keys in Anissa's hand.

Anissa laughed to herself when she thought about how close she had come to giving it all up a month earlier, when she'd heard Carlie calling out her name. She had struggled with fear and the urge to call her husband and let him know she was alive, but nothing more had happened. Foley had not shown up in the middle of the night and now she had her job to occupy her mind.

Today she planned to decorate her classroom. She'd dressed casually in a pair of jeans and a low cut red cashmere sweater. She'd tied a red and blue scarf around her neck.

"Good morning, Miss Stockton, are you ready for a new school year? Well, for you; it's the middle of the school year," said Meike (pronounced my-kah) Schmidt, the German teacher. She stood in the hallway near their classrooms.

Meike Schmidt was a big woman, both tall and wide. She was almost six feet tall and had to weigh at least 250. She had blond hair styled in a bob cut and piercing blue eyes. She wore khaki pants with a white shirt tucked inside. On her feet were sensible shoes.

She'd immigrated to the United States from Germany when she was twenty-five, with two years teaching experience and a Master's degree in German literature. None of her education had counted for much in this country. She'd had to attend an American university to get yet another degree to obtain a teaching position. Now, at age forty, she was hard at work trying to earn a third Master's degree so that her pay would increase. She'd given all of this information to Anissa within fifteen minutes of meeting three days ago.

Jake Tyler, the principal, had invited her to the school to show her around. She had not expected anyone else to be there because of the holiday break. Meike seemed to have appeared out of nowhere. And she let Anissa know in no uncertain terms that she'd wanted another teacher to be hired.

"You're not my choice for this position," she'd announced.

"I beg your pardon," Anissa replied, taken aback. Who greets someone for the first time like that?

"I interviewed another teacher who had middle school experience; a young American girl. I wanted to hire her and so did Mr. Tyler. Point of fact, he did hire her. But he said the decision to hire you came from Human Resources." The resentment in Meike's voice was unmistakable.

"I'm sorry; I didn't realize that another teacher had been hired before me. I can't imagine what happened. I just applied for the job, interviewed, and was hired." Anissa was annoyed by Meike's obvious rudeness.

"She came here with all of her things last Friday to get her classroom ready, and Mr. Tyler had to send her away. It was such a shame, she was so well qualified for this job," Meike continued.

"I'll do a good job. I love to teach," Anissa said.

"Are you from the Islands or Africa?"

"No, I'm American," Anissa replied.

"So how is that you speak French?" Meike asked, showing her skepticism.

"We have schools in America that have excellent foreign language programs." Anissa couldn't help but be sarcastic. "Good to meet you, Meike. I'll talk to you later," Anissa had hurried away from her to find the principal who'd conveniently disappeared.

Now, as Anissa was getting ready to make her classroom hers, Meike had arranged to be the first person Anissa saw yet again.

"Good Morning, Frau Schmidt," Anissa replied politely. Maybe she needed to show courtesy in order to receive it from this woman. She would have shaken hands, but hers were gripping the sides of a box filled with things to decorate her room.

"That sweater you have on is too revealing. We don't wear things like that here; there are boys here, you know," Meike stated, looking disapprovingly at Anissa's chest.

Really Meike? Anissa thought. "There're no students here today so I guess I'm safe," she responded.

Meike gave a curt little smile.

"I'm having a meeting in my classroom in ten minutes. You need to be there, so I can go over what I've already told the other teachers at the beginning of the school year."

"Okay," Anissa agreed, going into her classroom to put the box down.

"You don't have time to do any decorating. We have certain procedures at this school, and an elementary teacher would not be aware of them. I imagine you're going to have your hands full for the rest of the year. Besides being bigger, middle school students are quite different," Meike snapped as she walked back toward her classroom.

Anissa had decided that she needed to avoid Meike as much as possible until she got her feet wet. Whatever she needed, she would ask from someone else. The one thing that Anissa knew was how to evade people; her husband and his beatings had taught her skills like averting her eyes to keep her secret safe or pretending not to see others when they were in her midst. It was an acquired aloofness. She could tell that Ms. Schmidt did not like her and that was fine; plus being friendly would invite confidences and she had no desire to share, lest she make a slip and reveal her true identity.

There was nothing extremely important about being the Foreign Language Contact Person in a middle school. It was not like a department chair at a college or university or even a high school, for that matter. These people were paid for their efforts; a middle school contact was not. Meike had no authority as far as hiring people or telling other teachers what to do. Her main duty was to inform the other foreign language teachers at the school of news from the county supervisor of foreign languages.

The amount of paperwork the woman had given her so far was ridiculous! There were classroom procedures, lunch procedures, lunch line procedures, walking in the hall procedures, textbook issuance procedures, going to the library procedures, being absent procedures, substitute teacher procedures, bus duty procedures, meeting procedures, procedure lists procedures, etc. etc. etc.

Anissa was not new to the teaching profession, just new to this particular school. And she had taught middle school before. Someone had forgotten to tell Meike, but Anissa certainly wasn't going to tell her. Like any reputable school district, a procedures and policies manual was provided to all teachers. If one could read, there was no need for instructions from someone. She knew how to teach, and she knew that, as a teacher, she had a right to establish her own procedures as long as she kept them within the guidelines of her local school and district policies. Meike Schmidt was a German teacher. Lynn Stockton was a French teacher, whose immediate supervisor was the principal of the school. Not Meike.

Going into a classroom in the middle of the school year was difficult enough. Working with someone who was all in a huff because another teacher didn't get the job would not be easy.

Chapter Fifty-Eight
January 2002

Orella Bookings sat at the desk in her chambers, relaxing. It was the end of the day; she'd completed all of her paperwork. Her chambers contained dark paneled walls, leather furnishings, and bookshelves filled with law books. She'd added a few personal touches to put color in the room. She took off her robe and hung it in place. She slid her comfortable black flats underneath her desk and stuck her feet into her red heels. She stood, tucked in her red blouse, and adjusted her navy straight skirt. A quick glance in the mirror above her credenza verified that her lipstick was still good to go. Grabbing her purse, she headed out to the parking lot, continuing the silent debate going on in her head.

She'd received her credit card statement the day before and saw charges made at Bergdorf Goodman that totaled almost $6000. Shocked, she'd poured a drink and sat down to think, to remember. The charges were dated back in December when she'd taken that afternoon off to do some holiday shopping. But she didn't buy anything. The next day there were no bags, no boxes, no gift cards—nothing to indicate that she had in fact gone shopping. She'd shrugged it off as another of those days when she'd overdone the drinking. She remembered that she'd drank steadily all morning, but those were sips. She remembered going into that restaurant and ordering her meal and a cognac. She saw herself taking the first sip. After that—a blank.

Things like that had happened before, but she'd always gone home once she knew she'd had too much. That would explain why she didn't do any shopping. She clearly remembered being puzzled about it the next day. Could she have lost her American Express card? She checked her purse, found it, and dialed the number on the back of the card. She followed several automated prompts until a human being answered. Orella explained the situation.

"I do see those charges, Ms. Bookings. And you say your card has not been out of your possession?" the representative asked.

"No, it has not. I'm looking at it as we speak."

"Have you had any break-ins?"

"No. I haven't had any break-ins and my purse is with me all of the time," Orella responded. She knew that no one at the courthouse would go into her chambers and take anything from her purse. So she thought.

"Ms. Bookings, I'm setting up a dispute, but first I need you to tell me the last two charges that you remember making."

Orella racked her brain. Where was she the last time she used her card? And then it hit her. A gift shop on Broadway last month. She shared the information with the representative.

"Thank you. We will remove the charges pending an investigation. I'm going to go ahead and issue you a new card," the representative replied.

"Thank you," Orella graciously responded.

She'd breathed a sigh of relief, but she'd been confused all morning. How did someone get her card? Maybe they stole the information from online and ordered all of that stuff. Anyway, the charges were gone and she could count on the credit card company to get to the bottom of it. Yet she kept getting the nagging thought that maybe she should stop drinking.

Every alcoholic Orella had known drank every single day from the time the sun came up until they passed out; in other words if they were awake, they were drinking. Ordinarily nice, smart people until the booze turned them into belligerent, stupid, angry, and violent persons, they could never hold a job, were irresponsible, and had countless arrests for public drunkenness or driving while intoxicated. They stank— breath and body. All of their friends were drunks.

Orella was always nice and non-violent, very intelligent and she used hand-made soaps to bathe every day. After her bath, she doused herself with dusting powder, deodorant, and Chanel No.5 body cream, lotion, and cologne. She always had breath mints or peppermint candy in her purse. None of her friends had drinking problems. She had held a job with the court system for twenty years, and she had an excellent memory. She paid all of her bills on time, and she was fanatical about justice—except when it came to herself. That hit-and-run was the only blip on her list. It was the first thing she thought about every morning and the last thing at night, which was one reason why she'd had to start drinking again.

The only thing she had in common with an alcoholic was that she enjoyed several drinks every day. Cocktails. Snifters of brandy. Glasses of wine. Several mugs of beer; the expensive kind. But she needed it to calm her nerves. She felt that drinking was much better than taking pills. She'd never turned up a bottle of alcohol and drank from it. She had class. One check on the list did not make her an alcoholic.

It was a good thing she had a good memory. If she'd been an alcoholic, she never would have remembered hitting that woman with her car. Was it really her fault that the woman died? Could it have been all the commotion on September 11th that delayed medical help for the poor lady? And if she were an alcoholic, she certainly would not have remembered to report her car as stolen. She had told the truth when she said that her car was not in her regular parking place one morning and that the last time she saw it was the morning of the attack on the World Trade Center.

She'd meant the promise to stop drinking as long as she was free. So far, God had honored her request. But she had failed to keep her vow. Why couldn't she stop and stay stopped?

She'd been certain all of her life that she could do anything she wanted to do once she put her mind to it. Born in Kosciusko, Mississippi, December 2, 1959, to a single mother who'd died shortly after she was born, Orella was taken to Connecticut with her grandparents when she was still a baby. They'd raised her.

After an episode of Perry Mason when she was a little girl, she'd announced to her grandmother that she wanted to go to law school. An excellent student, she'd done her undergraduate study at Columbia and law school at NYU. She clerked for a judge in the family court until she passed the bar. That judge recognized Orella's brilliance. When he moved on to a higher court, he recommended her as his successor. Once behind the bench, she mimicked his approach until she got her feet on solid ground. She had been there since, having never stepped into a courtroom as a lawyer.

She had gone without drinking for over a month after 9/11. Not even one sip when everybody was freaking out about Anthrax. She was a high ranking public official, and it was conceivable that she could have received a letter or a package containing white powder. Just because she didn't live in D.C. didn't make her safe. A ninety-something woman in Connecticut had gotten one. People were scared. Probably drinking more, but not Orella. She took it on the chin like a big girl, Anthrax be damned!

Then one day in her chambers, before entering the courtroom to hear the case involving Chase Reynolds, she reached for the bottle of vodka that she'd brought in as a courtesy for visitors. She needed a drink to look at Chase. She poured herself a shot and threw it back before she realized what she'd done. She was completely fed up with that lazy, whorish boy's behind. How many baby mamas did the fool have? Several of them had stood before her crying because he refused to pay child support. His ass had been in jail so many times. She'd made up her mind then and there to deny his petition, wishing she could lock him up again.

And his mama! She deserved an Oscar for that performance: crying with no tears to show for all that noise. There was no way that Orella would have allowed Chase to have custody of a child. For what? To pimp the youngster out as a drug mule? Teach him how to have sex without a condom? No. She'd made a good decision. It was fortunate that she had that much authority and that Chase was stupid. She believed that Felton Dade would do right by those boys, losing their mother like that. Such a shame.

She guided her new black Mitsubishi Montero into traffic. The city was gradually recovering; a feeling of brotherhood and patriotism had unified New Yorkers. American Flags were everywhere— homes, courthouses, restaurants, nightclubs, parks, food trucks, and storefronts—symbolizing the strength of the American people. Even months later, the main topic of discussion in almost every meeting or after-hours gathering of the legal community was the 9/11 attacks, and particularly the collapse of the twin towers. One judge in particular had to emphasize the same point every time:

"When they questioned witnesses, many of them responded that they heard an explosion and *then* saw the plane hit the building! Pay attention people!"

Most people agreed that it appeared more like a demolition. Orella had learned from her grandfather years ago that steel can lose its strength at 1100 degrees Fahrenheit. She knew that those planes had to have hit with extreme force when they burst into flames. Parts of the building had been found six blocks away near Church and Murray. All that fuel, running down the sides of the building, plus all the carpet, furniture, computers, and printers had been enough to ignite an inferno hotter than 1100 degrees. That was her two cents worth, but she never gave her opinion. She listened and sipped her drinks.

She braked as the traffic light turned red. A dump truck pulled up in the lane beside her. The City Department of Design and Construction had split the Ground Zero site into quadrants for massive cleanup. Construction companies, environmental specialists, and engineers were each assigned a quadrant to manage. More than seventy-five trucks a day left the site carrying rubble. Press releases reported construction workers saying that they'd never seen steel pulverized to such a degree.

There were reports of molten steel in hot spots throughout the site. Large concrete barriers were put into place to prevent contamination of the entire subway line as workers used super vacuums to remove the dust and debris from the lines closest to the site.

Orella had not been back to Ground Zero. News Reports stated that the air was not safe. Plus she'd decided that once was enough for her.

All these depressing thoughts made her thirsty. It was cocktail hour!

Chapter Fifty-Nine
January 2002

Felton and the boys had begun therapy two days after the New Year. After two weeks the boys showed signs of improvement. The doctor had told him that it would be a long time before things were back to normal, but they were definitely on the mend.

Felton was struggling with his grief—and with parenthood. It had been rough for the first months. Nathan had started getting into fights at school, and Justin's grades had begun to drop. Things really started to turn sour right after Sunday, October, 28th, when another memorial service was held for the families of 9/11 victims. After the ceremony, everyone gathered at Pier 94, the Family Assistance Center. Felton and the boys had visited the center on one other occasion. A wall plastered with fliers of the missing had been covered with plastic for protection, and anyone headed to the center had to pass it.

The first time the center was flooded with police, firemen, people wearing FEMA jackets, the army, and the National Guard. The boys had been given teddy bears with notes attached that read, "I hope this bear will comfort you." All sorts of dogs in one area of the huge warehouse proved to be a diversion for the kids while Felton filled out papers. Adults and kids alike were drawn to the area to pet the dogs.

The purpose for the October 28th trip to the pier was the presentation of the urns. Booths were set up with volunteers who each read a short note of condolences to each family and presented them with an urn containing ashes that represented the victim along with a small flag.

"I need two," Felton had said, trying to keep his emotions in check.

"I'm sorry, sir, but we're only allowed to give one per family," the young man replied.

"I need two," Felton repeated, this time a bit forcefully.

"Only one to a family, sir," the young man stood firm.

There were more urns than people at the pier. Felton didn't want to make a scene, but he'd decided that he was not leaving with only one urn.

"Listen, my sister and my niece, the mother of these two boys, perished at Ground Zero. If you're going to do this, then do it right," Felton was angry by then and the young man picked up on that right away. He called a supervisor who graciously agreed to make an exception in Felton's case.

Back at home, Felton had placed both urns on the sofa table in the family room. All three stood there in silence. None of them had spoken much since they'd left the pier.

"It's so little," Nathan said, finally breaking the silence. "How can mama be in there?"

Felton knelt before the two boys and pulled them into his arms. "She can't. Nor can Grandma Tina. The city government wanted to show that they understand how sad we feel. We've got your mom and Tina in our hearts. They'll always be just like they were when we saw them the last time."

Felton persuaded the boys to flip a coin to see which one would sleep with their mom's urn and which one with Grandma Tina. That was a very difficult day.

December brought the news that President Bush had declared September 11th a new holiday, calling it Patriot Day. It was also in December that the rubble at Ground Zero finally stopped smoking.

And then came Christmas. In the past, all he'd ever done for the holidays was give money. He'd stuff it in an envelope or a card and he was good to go. But he couldn't let two kids get up on Christmas morning without a tree and presents. He'd sat in the family room of the house that he'd shared with Tina, Sherry, and the boys for almost eleven years, and cried like a baby. He didn't even know where to begin to plan a good holiday. He chose to begin with a thorough house cleaning from top to bottom.

Over five thousand square feet, the brick house that he and the boys called home had been built in 1901. Over the years, houses the same size up and down Neptune Street had been converted to two family homes. The house had three floors. The top floor had originally had two bedrooms, but when Felton moved in, he'd knocked down walls and converted it into a huge suite. He'd had a new bathroom put in and the floors stripped and refinished.

He'd found a fabulous rug on the curb one night that someone had put out for the garbage people to collect. He took it to a rug cleaning specialty shop and paid almost four hundred dollars to have it deodorized, scrubbed and immaculately done up. It was beautiful when he laid it down on those hardwood floors. It was burgundy with splotches of grey, navy, and beige. Tina had bought him a Grey comforter and bed skirt. Sherry had the windows done with beige curtains, and grey sheers. His uncle's four poster bed sat right in the middle of the room. He had an oversized beige chair—the women tried to put pillows on it, but he wasn't having it—and a chest of drawers on one wall next to his television and console. He had a nice room.

The boys and Sherry had rooms on the second floor, each with their own bathroom. Nathan's room was football land and Justin's basketball kingdom. The bottom floor had one bedroom where Tina had slept, a bath and a half, a family room, a dining room, and the kitchen. There was a new porch on the back— all three adults had put their pennies together to pay for it as well as a sizeable yard for the boys to play. There was a basketball goal and a gym set.

Felton had taken the boys with him to shop for a live tree. They'd brought it home, pulled out decorations, and made the tree sparkle. Each day Felton would sneak gifts under the tree. His big surprise was three new bikes. He bought a turkey, green beans, potatoes, onions, pickles and mayonnaise for potato salad, cornmeal, eggs, vegetable oil and milk for cornbread dressing, and a chocolate cake for dessert. Felton's mother had taught all of her children to cook.

"You need to know how to fix yourself something to eat," she'd said. "Don't wait on nobody to cook for you, do it yourself."

The heartbreak had come Christmas morning when the boys brought the urns for Tina and Sherry into the family room before they opened gifts.

"It's like they're having Christmas with us," Justin said.

Nathan cried. Felton cried. And soon Justin was crying too. They got through it, and that's when Felton made the decision to get professional help for all of them. The first visit all three of them sat together and talked to the doctor. On the second and third respectively, only the boys went in and Felton waited.

This week on Wednesday Justin would go in alone and Friday would be Nathan's solo day.

"It's cool," Nathan said, when Felton asked how he felt about the whole thing.

"I like him," Justin said. "He's nice."

"When are you going in without us?" Nathan asked.

"Um, maybe later," Felton answered. He felt that saying never would have been too harsh.

Chapter Sixty
March 2002

Anissa felt like she was in hot water, being cooked to a frazzle. She had tried every trick in her bag to establish a working relationship with Meike and the principal, but both openly resented her presence in the school. She brought donuts, cups of coffee, brownies, and flowers. In spite of all of her efforts, she still met with resistance. Once a month, Meike held her morning meeting with the foreign language teachers.

"Well, look who decided to join us, our elementary teacher just can't seem to tell time. That's a lesson taught in first grade, I believe," she'd taunt looking at her watch. She'd told Anissa that the meeting began at 8:00 a.m., but asked the other teachers to be there at 7:30 a.m. So, when Anissa walked in at 7:45 a.m., thinking herself early, she was in fact late for the meeting.

"Ms. Stockton needs some help in classroom management. She's writing up students every day. I need someone to give her a few pointers," Meike announced at one meeting.

"Excuse me, but I taught middle school for eight years. I hardly need classroom management lessons, "Anissa snapped. "And I write referrals because I will not tolerate disrespect or class disruption." She was getting more and more tired of Meike's rude and spiteful behavior. She'd mentioned it to Kathy once over dinner.

Anissa had invited Kathy to her house, a nice two story in a new subdivision about ten miles from where Kathy lived. Anissa paid fifteen days ahead of the due date each month and always added an extra $300 payment at the end of the month. She was whittling away at that principal balance little by little. The house had two bedrooms, a large kitchen, a living room, family room, dining room, and two and a half baths. It was red brick, with white columns.

She'd prepared grilled halibut, salad, and steamed broccoli. They were seated at a beautiful oak dining table that Anissa had found at a thrift store. It was nearly new, without a scratch, with seating for six. In the center of the table was a vase of fresh cut flowers.

"She's making it so hard for me, Kathy. She's blaming me because the teacher she wanted did not get the job. She's rude and unpleasant most of time. She reported to the principal that I'm late for meetings and that I'm argumentative. He called me into his office for a conference where he also made a point to tell me that he doesn't like it that I write so many administrative referrals," she shared, her voice dripping with exasperation.

"I can fix that. Meike and the principal can be transferred to another school by the end of this week," Kathy replied, as she took a bite of halibut.

Anissa's mouth fell open in shock. She didn't want that. She wasn't vindictive. She just wanted them to like her, to give her a fair chance. She'd come to learn that Kathy could do everything that she said she would do. Anissa was going to have to learn to fight her own battles, and now would be a good time to start. She made a decision to handle it on her own. She had the job thanks to Kathy and her friend in human resources; if it got so bad that she couldn't stand it she would request a transfer.

"No, Kathy. Don't do that. I can handle it."

"Are you sure? Because you don't have to. Remember all you *have* to do is..."

"Be black when I die," Anissa interrupted, laughing out loud.

"Right!" Kathy chimed in.

Anissa had made friends with one of the Spanish teachers, who was also new to the school. Maria Lamb, married to a restaurant owner, was an attractive lady with short auburn hair. Anissa started double-checking any information from Meike with her, and made sure she'd know the correct times for meetings.

Maria was from Spain and loved to talk about her country. She talked about the Mediterranean Sea, and family vacations in the summer. Bordering Spain on the south and the east, the vast sea connected to the Atlantic Ocean. For years, the sea served as a route for colonization, trade, and war. It also provided seafood, Maria's favorite protein. France was

Spain's neighbor on the north and northeast. She and Anissa talked about Paris once, Anissa having to admit that she'd not seen much of the city. Maria was an etymology buff—immensely enjoying researching the origin of names.

"The word Mediterranean comes from the Latin word *mediterraneous* and it means 'in the middle of the land.' Aptly named, don't you think?" Maria asked over lunch one day.

"I do," Anissa agreed.

"My mother chose my name because there are many Roman Catholic saints with the name Maria. It means star of the sea. Where did your mother get your name?"

Anissa laughed. No one had ever asked her that question. "From the liqueur anisette," she answered.

"Anisette? What does that have to do with Lynn?" Maria asked with a puzzled look on her face.

Anissa recovered immediately. "My grandmother, Lynn, loved to drink anisette. My mother named me for her," Anissa said, counting on the noise from the kids to distract Maria. She wanted to kick herself. How could she have let that slip out? Hopefully, Maria would forget about it.

That was not the first mistake that she'd made about her past. Meike had come to the supply room one evening and was quite friendly. She talked about her family, her dogs, and her plans for spring break.

"I have a chocolate and a black cocker spaniel," Meike had beamed. "They are my babies. They are spoiled rotten."

"I used to have two chocolate cocker spaniels," Anissa offered.

"Really? Aren't they the smartest dogs?"

"Indeed they are. I have a Rottweiler now. His name is Joey and he's pretty smart."

"I can't stand big dogs. Too hard to pick them up. Maybe you're stronger than I am," Meike added.

Anissa felt Meike's hatefulness coming so she turned back to getting the things she'd come into the room for—construction paper, glue, and copy paper. She was not interested in talking any more.

"I'm going to visit my sister next month for spring break. She lives in Nashville and they just bought a new house. I'm going to help her unpack. She's such a packrat and a talker! I guess I'll have to hear about her latest crush—being married to a homely man makes her daydream about good looking men. But it's such a boring city," Meike continued.

"Enjoy yourself," Anissa answered absently. There was no blue or yellow construction paper.

"Enjoy? Have you ever *been* to Nashville?" Meike asked derisively.

"I used to live there," Anissa answered. Just as quickly, she wished she could have put the words back into her mouth. Her story was that she was from Kansas.

"Sort of, anyway. When I was a little girl I visited relatives for the summer," Anissa added. "Well, have a good evening," she said as she quickly left the supply room. What was wrong with her? She had rehearsed that back story so many times. She had to keep her distance from Meike. She was not Anissa's friend no matter how often she feigned affability. She decided that the time to leave for the day had suddenly come. She normally liked to stay after school to write her plans for the next day on the board and do grade updates on the computer, but not today. Today she was going home to spend time with Joey. Joey loved her and was always glad to see her.

Joey was one year old. She and Kathy had rescued him from the pound. Anissa felt like she needed company in her new home. She smiled as she considered that it was a far cry from the house she'd shared with Foley in Brentwood. But it was home to her now and she loved it. Joey was an extra added touch to truly make it her home sweet home.

He was so adorable. After having had two bad experiences with dogs, Jessica had vowed to never own another. She had a dog when she was twelve and loved him dearly. He was hit by a car, dying instantly, and she had been so hurt that she never wanted to have another dog again. Meike had reminded her of the two chocolate cocker spaniel puppies she'd seen one day in a pet shop. Foley had allowed her to get them.

Such precious and such loyal friends until Foley became jealous of them and accused her of paying more attention to the dogs than she did to him. He started kicking them and wouldn't allow her to feed them because he felt they were getting too fat. One morning when she came down for breakfast, they were gone. Foley told her he'd taken them to the pound; he was tired of smelling dogs. She was heartbroken, but she had to hide it. She cried many times over those little dogs. She'd loved them so much.

But now she had Joey who was playful, and so strong. She took him out for a romp in the neighborhood as soon as she was out of her dress clothes and into something more comfortable. He liked to play with a ball and the fact that she had a nice size back yard made it easy to accommodate his desire to chase the ball and return it to her, panting in anticipation of the next toss. She planned to have the yard fenced in on her upcoming pay period at the end of the month. Her next-door neighbors had agreed to allow Joey to stay in their fenced yard during the day when they were out of town and they traveled a lot.

He was a good dog. At first she did not allow him on the bed, but he always looked so sad and forlorn that she finally gave in one night and patted the empty side of the bed. He jumped up immediately and much to her chagrin, he snored for most of the night. She remedied that right away by buying him a pillow. He would wake up at times, barking, and she always got up to investigate, because in spite of the fact that she was miles away from Foley with a new identity and a new look, she still wouldn't allow herself to get too comfortable.

Joey seemed to understand her concern, because he watched as she looked out of windows, checked door locks, and turned on lights. They usually discovered whatever caused him to bark: a neighbor's cat meowing, another dog barking, or the paper carrier when he missed the yard and had to get out of the car and toss it where it belonged. Joey was her pal, and true to form, he was standing right in front of the gate to the neighbor's back yard when she arrived.

"Hey Joey! How's mama's baby? How's mama's big boy Joe? You ready for a walk? Okay give mama a minute and we'll go."

By this time he was wagging his whole behind, jumping—and smiling (she insisted that he smiled) eager to hit the road.

Chapter Sixty-One
March 2002

The death toll of the 9/11 attacks had been lowered to 2789, from early estimates of 6,000. Grieving families struggled with blame, some citing the building as defective, others claiming that the planes should have withstood the crashes. Felton had no opinion. Not about that. He was too busy trying to mend his family.

The city was on the mend too. On March 1, eighty-eight searchlights had been placed next to the site of the World Trade Center to create twin vertical towers of light. An architect had come up with the idea, and Consolidated Edison, the electric utility company for New York, brought the idea to fruition. They officially named it "The Tribute in Light." On clear days the lights could be seen from miles away. The only snag was the birds. For days, during migration, they had become trapped in the beams. The lights had to be turned off for twenty-minute periods each day to allow them to escape.

The country was still at war in Afghanistan, but the city of New York was coming back to life. Missing and lost persons' fliers could still be seen in some places, but everyone knew that all survivors had been found. Felton pulled down the fliers for Sherry and Tina anytime he passed one. He'd also taken down one other. It was for Anissa Brogdon.

Felton had recently followed up on a report of an abused woman being admitted to New York Presbyterian on 9/11. To say the department was behind in business as usual would be putting it mildly. At the hospital he'd spoken with the doctor who'd filed the report.

"Dr. Ford, I'm Detective Felton Dade. I'm following up on a report you made about an abuse victim? Jessica Woods?"

Felton produced his badge. The doctor ran his hand through his hair and wrinkled his brow. He looked confused—as if he was hearing the news for the first time.

"Yes, I did report the abuse. The strange thing is that the victim had amnesia and couldn't remember anything, not even her name. Her sister-in-law claimed that the husband was dead, so I have no idea who was responsible."

"I need to talk to her. Maybe she's remembered something by now."

"Well, I wish I could tell you where she is. I've tried to contact her myself because the strangest thing has happened."

"What strange thing?" Felton asked. He was beginning to feel like this case was coming to a dead end before he even got started with an investigation.

"There was a flier for a missing woman by the name of Anissa Brogdon on our bulletin board. She and my patient, the abuse victim, could have passed for twins. Identical twins." Dr. Ford looked at Felton, his face a mask of conflicting emotions.

Felton felt himself beginning to get angry at the sound of the name Brogdon. He'd gone for years forcing himself to not even think about it and now all of a sudden he was running into it everywhere he turned.

"Her husband was a doctor from Nashville, a Dr. Foley Brogdon, who came here to the morgue regularly looking for her. When I saw the flier, I called him. His wife answered the phone. Anissa Brogdon, if she was indeed the victim of abuse, is back at home in Tennessee. And that's out of your jurisdiction."

Felton had to agree—they were not in good old Tennessee. And for that he was grateful. It was time to go. He felt like he'd gag if he heard Foley Brogdon's name one more time. As he turned to leave the doctor's office a thought occurred to him. "By the way, did you ever find out what happened to Jessica Woods?"

"I have no idea. I haven't had any success trying to contact her. She left here to go home with her sister-in-law. Like I said, the two women could have passed for twins. You can have what little information I have for Jessica Woods. Maybe you can locate her."

Dr. Ford went to his desk, typed a few keys on his computer, waited a beat, and then wrote Kathy Stockton's address and a phone number on a pad. He tore the sheet off and handed it to Felton.

"Thanks again, Dr. Ford." Felton said as he left the doctor.

A brilliant detective who had a good feel for human nature, Felton was positive that Foley Brogdon was a bastard who enjoyed beating women. If Jessica Woods and Anissa Brogdon were one and the same, and Jessica Woods had been beaten, then there was a good chance that Foley was behind it. But one thing was for certain, he'd never contact Foley. Not that sadistic freak. If Felton ever saw him again, he was fairly convinced that he would beat the hell out of him. He threw the paper that the doctor had just given him into the first trash receptacle he passed. This had been a waste of time.

If Anissa was Jessica and had somehow escaped from Foley, the woman who answered the phone when the doctor called could have been Foley's mother. If anyone was capable of lying and covering for her son, Lacy Brogdon was. She'd done it before.

Chapter Sixty-Two
March, 2002

In the grand scheme of things, Lacy Brogdon had come a long way— from rags to riches and from heathen to saint. She had never been to church nor even considered God until she went to church with Foley, Sr. for the first time. There she learned of a supernatural being that had created the world and everything in it. Not only that, this being supposedly loved everything that he'd created because it was good. That was news to Lacy. She'd never known love. She thought she loved Foley until he hit her, and that feeling quickly turned to hate.

She enjoyed church so much that she got dressed and went back. Again and again until she learned the protocol— hypocrisy is what Jesus Christ called it. To be a good hypocrite one had to possess great acting skills. Her husband, Foley, was a great actor, but Lacy was better.

Foley Sr. considered himself benevolence personified. Lacy helped him. It wasn't long before she volunteered for every need in the church and her generous husband gave whatever the church needed.

"Foley, the food pantry at the church is low. We're just not getting enough donations. We had a family come in yesterday and all we had was a few cans of chili and some dry goods," she'd said to him one evening.

He looked up from his newspaper.

"The pastor said that it would really be a blessing if the Lord touched the hearts of people to bring food in," Lacy added. Their pastor had a habit of praising the gifts of benefactors in front of the congregation. How wonderful it would be for him to mention Foley's name. Lacy could almost see the wheels turning in her husband's head.

"Well, go shopping, Lacy. Get everything you think would make a decent meal, as much as you feel is necessary."

Lacy convinced her husband that tithing was the right thing to do, so every Sunday he sent her to church with a whopping big check. And the pastor did his job of telling most of the members that the Brogdons were philanthropic.

Then Lacy got herself elected treasurer. For the past twenty-five years she had held back a little each Sunday and diverted it to a personal account that contained more than $300,000. It was for a rainy day. Her husband gave more than any other church member, so she felt that some of that money was rightfully hers. The initial plan was to save enough to get away from Foley and his fists and feet that kicked swift and sure. But then, she'd found redemption.

Sitting in church Sunday after Sunday learning about a God who loved her, gave Lacy faith, especially the story of Abigail and Nabal in the book of 1st Samuel. Nabal was a fool, a wicked fool, and Abigail, his wife, devised a plan without telling him and prevented their certain deaths at the hands of King David. Abigail's resourcefulness inspired Lacy to make a plan.

One evening, Foley came into the kitchen in a sour mood, the type of mood that always led to violence. Lacy, her back to the sink, prepared herself for what was coming.

"What in the hell did you buy shoes for?" he accosted her, with his credit card statement in his hand.

"For church, honey," she answered sweetly. Before she could blink, he punched her in the stomach. She doubled over from the pain, gasping for air. She was hurt, but not so bad that she couldn't move. She stumbled toward the island in the center of the large kitchen. She knew he'd follow her. He enjoyed making her run from him. She staggered over to where she kept her new cast iron skillet on a back eye of the stove and stopped, facing him. He stalked her, reaching towards her throat. Choking was always a part of the ritual.

Lacy had read somewhere that a man who choked his wife or girlfriend was ten times more likely to kill her. She'd never forgotten that detail. Foley was so intent on getting his hands around her neck that he didn't see the iron skillet until it was too late. With all the strength she had left, she clobbered him upside the head. He groaned—his eyes stretched in disbelief as she came up with an upper slam to the chin. He went down for the count.

Lacy crumbled to the floor beside him to pull herself together. Skillet still in hand, she made ready to pummel him again if he came to. But he didn't. She checked his pulse and saw that he was still alive. After a few long minutes, she stood, gathered all her strength, and dragged him to the elevator, chanting "I can do all things through Christ who strengthens me." She had faith in God that she'd have the strength to do what needed to be done.

Down they went to the bottom floor, where no one else was allowed. His secret chamber, where he'd tortured her many times. She strapped him into the special chair. She was hurting all over but adrenalin had kicked in. She took the skillet and pounded his bound right hand, breaking three fingers on contact. He screamed in agony. She stretched his pinkie and his thumb out as he cursed and struggled against his bonds. She whacked those two digits. And then, she stretched the other hand as he clawed, scratched, and howled from the pain. She broke all five fingers with one blow, nipping her own hand in the process. His ankles were next, each one strapped to the chair made it convenient for her to hobble him. She stood back, scrutinized her work, saw that it was good and said two words to him: *Never again*.

When all of his anger and rage was gone, she let him out of that room. He became a new person. An invalid, whose hands and feet could no longer deliver blows, but a new human being nonetheless. It took several surgeries for him to get back some semblance of hands, but all vestiges were useless. Mobility required a walking cane. She had to force herself not to chuckle aloud as he manufactured lies to explain his injuries.

She promised him that if he ever touched her again, she'd kill him. She read scriptures to him while he recuperated. She chose the ones that promised death to anyone who touched God's anointed ones. After that she had complete serenity. She no longer feared him and he knew it. Never again would she have to submit to his cruelty. It was too late to save her son, however. He had witnessed her black eyes, bloody noses, and a few trips to the hospital as a child and learned from them.

When Anissa told her that FJ was responsible for the 'accident' that had sent her to the hospital, Lacy knew it was true. He was his father's son, and when he got married, she was devastated. Anissa was all wrong. She was a pretty woman, but the wrong color. Not that Lacy was a racist; she was a realist. Marriage to a black woman would cripple FJ's standing in their Southern high society. She knew that Foley Sr. wouldn't like it, and true to her expectations he voiced his opinion the first time he met the child.

He preached about all people being equal regardless of race, creed, or skin color, but it became a different matter when it involved his home and his family. But FJ had threatened to leave forever and that could not happen. So, Anissa had become a part of the family and several times she noticed her husband almost falling over his own feet trying to impress his new daughter-in-law. He learned to love the girl, in spite of her skin color.

And now Anissa was gone. Her son was heartbroken, but life had to go on. It was a shame the way her daughter-in-law had died, but it was much better than having FJ beat her to death. And that would have happened eventually. Anissa was weak. She would not have boded well from years of abuse. Lacy was strong now that she'd found God. She had endured and not been found wanting. She loved her home, her fine clothes and jewelry, and her status in Nashville society and the church. There was no way she'd give that up because of a beating. Time healed her bruises and scars, and once it was over she still had a mink coat for every day of the week and Sunday, too.

With Anissa's demise, once again she had to manage her son. He had always needed managing. He was a child of privilege and felt as if he could do no wrong. He did mean things as a little boy—kicking dogs, setting animal traps, or 'finding' the neighbor's pets mysteriously burned or poisoned. Houses in the neighborhood were broken into and valuable mementos stolen. She'd always come to his rescue.

When that slut, Stacy Smith, accused him of raping and beating her his senior year, it was Lacy who had gone to the girl in the dead of the night and convinced her to blame someone else. The girl was flustered and confused. FJ couldn't have done it, he was home with his parents at the time; Lacy would swear to it.

Lacy knew that FJ and his best friends, Felton Dade and Shon Glenn, both African-American, had been together on the night in question. Stacy claimed that FJ and Shon had drugged her and Shon held her down while FJ raped her. Shon had stood by and watched FJ beat and kick her and then left her on the side of the road. Her story was that FJ had threatened to kill her parents if she told. The little strumpet went to the police anyway with her parents in tow. Imagine everyone's surprise when she changed her story and accused Felton Dade. It was easy for the poor girl to get confused because of the drugs and both boys' names began with the letter "F".

Lacy was sorry that Felton had to go to a juvenile facility until his eighteenth birthday. Stacy swore that he'd had nothing to do with it, that he was a nice guy. He had been fifteen at the time and smart as a whip. He was already a junior in high school when he went away. Lacy used some of her stolen money to pay for Stacy's medical bills, and her abortion. She also paid for Shon to attend Morehouse University, where he'd met his wife. Stacy had wanted to become a nurse; Lacy footed the bill for her education at Vanderbilt. Both of Stacy's parents died in a fire before they saw the success their daughter achieved. So unfortunate.

Both Shon and Stacy signed confidentiality agreements. Stacy eventually had a nervous breakdown and ended up strung out on drugs. Shon and his wife lived in Savannah, Georgia with their three children, and seemed to be doing okay. Felton got away. But not before Lacy hired an attorney to get his record expunged. And she made certain that he was sent to a facility where he could study for his GED. The boy didn't deserve to be punished for the rest of his life. It was the decent thing to do—he had done his time. Shortly after his release, he enlisted in the Air Force. The last she'd heard from him he was living in Harlem with his sister, Tina.

She sighed as she realized it was time to take dinner to her son. The poor boy was not taking care of himself at all. She often wondered if he'd ever marry again. She hoped that he wouldn't. He hadn't learned anything from being married to Anissa because she died before he beat her to death. Marriage to another woman would only create another victim. Unless he chose a good Christian girl who'd learn how to use the word of God to exact revenge. Lacy didn't want to see that happen to her son. For his sake, it was better to remain a widower.

Roasted lamb—and a salad with broccoli and cornbread. He was always partial to cornbread. She checked the huge grandfather's clock in the hallway as she headed towards the kitchen. She had time to whip up a dessert.

Chapter Sixty-Three
March 2002

Dr. Will Mashburn had become one of Dr. Ford's favorite people. He'd gone back to him for that second visit and since then saw him once a week—Fridays.

It had taken only twenty-four hours for Jennings to notice a change. After that fall, sudden movements would send hot flashes of pain across his lower back. As the doctor had warned him, a little soreness occurred, but he used the ice as suggested, and by morning he was fully mobile and without pain.

Improper posture or seating would sometimes cause a flare-up, but he'd fixed that by buying an ergonomic chair for both home and the office, although he didn't usually sit a lot at work.

Not only had he softened to the chiropractor's spinal adjustments, he'd also taken some of his suggestions for more healthy eating. He ate lasagna only once a month now at lunchtime. Most days he had a salad and fruit. He'd started buying organic fruit and vegetables like carrots and celery to snack on at home. He didn't cook, so he didn't need much else.

His daughter had been trying since his wife died to get him to lose some weight and to eat better. He was at her house some weekends and she'd always send him home with plastic containers of food.

He was down fifteen pounds since he'd started seeing Dr. Mashburn. He'd considered joining a health club, but he let that thought pass.

"So, looks like you might not be too old to change!" Earl Bost laughed.

"Maybe not. But seriously, thanks, Earl. I'd never have considered going to a chiropractor had it not been for you," Dr. Ford said.

"Well if you ever see that doctor that knocked you flat you can thank him," Earl said.

Dr. Ford thought back to that day. The doctor, as he claimed to be, had been tall, blond and arrogant. There was a look of hatefulness in his eyes. And he'd not had the wherewithal to even apologize for knocking him down. No, he'd never forget the man's face, down to the mole on his cheek, but he'd never thank him if he saw him again.

"I don't believe I'd have much to say to the man, Earl. Did I tell you he didn't even apologize?"

"Do you want to know how many times?" Earl almost doubled over from laughter. Jennings guessed that he needed a sense of humor considering that he worked with the dead. Not too much to laugh about in the morgue.

"No. Are you still coming by to get a view of the "Tribute in Lights" from Brooklyn tonight?"

"I'll be there. And then I'll beat you in a game of checkers."

"In your dreams, old man. I told you, you're never winning another game."

Chapter Sixty-Four
April 2002

Foley undressed in the bedroom that he had shared with Anissa. He'd had a particularly hectic day and was exhausted. He flung his shirt on top of the off-white frilly comforter that he'd given his approval for. He glanced around the room that he'd permitted Anissa to decorate shortly after they'd returned from their honeymoon.

"The room has to be blue. Blue is a male color. I will not sleep in a room that's pink or purple or any other color of the rainbow," he'd said to her firmly.

"Yes, Foley," she'd responded meekly.

"If you want to mix in color, use white. Do you understand?"

"Yes, Foley."

He had to admit that he'd gotten a tad upset when he saw the walls the first time. She'd used blue and off white as the colors but the room was definitely feminine.

"What have you done to the walls, Anissa?" he'd asked quietly. "I said blue and white but I didn't mean flowers on…what is that? Is that fabric?" He'd touched the wall and what he felt was definitely not paper.

"It's chintz. Your mother suggested it," she'd answered.

He had already begun to make a fist when she mentioned his mother. It occurred to him that there was no need to punish Anissa for doing what Lacy said; he would have done the same. He decided he could live with, as he later learned from his mother, the blue roses and hydrangeas. The room had two large double windows on each side of French doors that led out to a patio from the sitting area. Directly in front of the doors, about five feet away, was a blue chaise. To the right was an armless chair covered in the same god-awful fabric as the walls. On the left was a white wood framed chair with the same blue upholstered back and seat as the chaise. There were toss pillows in the wall fabric scattered from the bed to the chairs.

The windows had been done with off-white curtains that began just below the ceiling molding, high above the actual windows. There were flower pedestals in front of each window that contained white peonies while Anissa was alive. Now they each supported a pot of ferns. The floor was covered with pale beige carpeting. He kicked his shoes off, pulled back the covers, and got in bed. In a few minutes he was asleep.

The ringing of the telephone jarred him awake. He decided to let the answering machine pick up because he had no desire to be civil. He glanced at the clock. It was 6:30 a.m. He'd slept all night without dreaming.

"Mr. Brogdon, you may be interested to know that your wife, Anissa Brogdon, is teaching French at a middle school in Georgia. I'm sure you will be willing to pay a substantial reward for what I can tell you. I will call…"

"Hello!" Foley snapped, interrupting the guttural German accent.

"Mr. Brogdon?"

"Yes, who is this? You mentioned my wife, Anissa?'

"Yes I did. I'm the foreign language chair at my school. I believe your wife is one of my teachers."

"And what makes you think that? My wife died a year ago."

"You think she died. She is alive and well."

"Who is this?" Foley demanded.

"That's not important. A woman at my school is the spitting image of your wife. She has red hair, but I am positive that it is Mrs. Brogdon. She has revealed all sorts of tidbits about her past without meaning to; she actually told one of the teachers that she was named for the liqueur anisette and she told me herself that she used to live in Nashville. She's using another name, but I thought you deserved to know."

"And how is it possible that a dead woman is teaching at your school? Who are you and why would you choose this God awful way to tell me about it?"

"Listen, I'm sorry to have bothered you. Goodbye."

"Wait! You didn't give me your name. You didn't give me the name of the school. You really haven't given me very much information at all," Foley said forcefully.

"Like I said, I thought you might be interested enough to pay a reward."

"Number one, I can have the police trace this call because it is now a part of my telephone records. Number two, I can have you arrested for harassment. And number three, extortion comes to mind."

"Well, you do that, Mr. Brogdon, and when they get here they'll be happy to know that the little woman is still alive and that you've probably collected a hefty insurance payout."

"Don't threaten me. Why don't we talk about this? I can arrange to pay you something if what you're telling me is the truth. But if not, you have just put your career and all that you hold dear in peril," Foley warned her.

"And don't you threaten me! I didn't have to call you. She's still going to lose her teaching license!" And with that the woman hung up.

But she'd said Georgia and anisette. Anissa had told him that story about the liqueur, too.

Chapter Sixty-Five
April 2002

Orella was completely mystified. She was in the back of her walk-in closet looking for the mate to a shoe when she found a dress bag hanging with two brand new dresses from Bergdorf Goodman and a shopping bag with a pair of earrings and a pair of shoes. All of it stuffed so far back that she wouldn't have seen it until it was time for summer clothes.

Back in January, she'd received a letter informing her that the charges had been removed and her claim was being investigated. It would be resolved within the next thirty days. It was the last paragraph that gave her concern. "If we find that the charges are valid, the full amount will be credited back to your account."

She certainly did not need that. She called them and asked to speak to a supervisor, after supervisor to make sure that the charges would stay reversed and was told the same thing:

"Ms. Bookings, you do not have to worry. If you did not make these charges we will take care of everything. Don't you worry."

And she hadn't worried. Not until she opened her March statement and saw the charges back on her new account. $5,763. 87! It had been too much for her. She'd bought a big bottle of cognac and drank until she passed out. All she could do was make a minimum payment and pray that somehow she'd figure out what had happened. She couldn't just refuse to pay the bill. And she didn't dare call them again. The only other alternative was to consult with an attorney. She just hadn't done it yet.

And now, in her hands was the evidence. She found receipts in the bottom of the shopping bag. She sat down on the floor of her closet and tried to think. She had to have done this because no one else would have brought them into her home. What kind of stupid thief would do that? She ran her fingers through her hair as she looked at the date on the receipt. She got up and checked her calendar. That's the day she cleared the afternoon for shopping for holiday gifts, after drinking all day in the office.

She only remembered going into that restaurant and ordering a drink. Nothing after that. After not finding bags, gifts—nothing in obvious places to show that she'd actually made any purchases, she'd just finally chalked it up as one of those days of too much drinking. She didn't even drive downtown that day. She took a taxi.

Good Lord! Was she losing her mind? Now she had to return these purchases. And she had to explain to the credit card company. They were going to think she was crazy as hell. And then it hit her. She'd have a cousin who visited for the weekend and somehow got Orella's wallet by mistake. If they asked why it had taken so long to find out she'd make up something at that time. All was well. She'd return everything, they'd have their money, and she'd be debt free.

Her next plan was to go to a meeting of Alcoholics Anonymous. This thing was getting out of control.

Chapter Sixty-Six
April 2002

Hartsfield International Airport, formerly the Atlanta Speedway, was initially called Candler Field, after the then mayor and Coca Cola tycoon, Asa Candler, in 1925. More than fifty years later, on September 21, 1980, William B. Hartsfield Atlanta International Airport opened, and by 1998, had become the world's busiest airport with passenger traffic. Foley Brogdon, one of the many passengers, had landed. He'd walked away from the Avis Rental counter with keys to a Ford Taurus in his hands. He had not bothered to pack any luggage, not even a toothbrush. He was here to see if his wife was alive.

At first, he was inclined to ignore the call from the anonymous woman. And then, the conversation with Carlie replayed in his head. Carlie thought she had seen Anissa in Atlanta. Immediately, he got to work to find out the missing information that he so desperately needed in order to know if what the woman told him was true. He called the telephone company and had the call traced. The trace led him to one Meike Schmidt residing in Kennesaw, Georgia, a suburb of Atlanta. Typing her name into a search engine eventually led him to an article about Valeria Middle School. This information led him to the county school system where he was eventually led to the school web page. There he was able to see the faculty list where one French teacher's name appeared, Lynn Stockton.

After a call to one of his father's friends in the governor's office and a short wait he was provided with an address in Powder Springs, Georgia for one Lynn Stockton, the new French teacher at Valeria Middle School. Powder Springs was twenty-five miles west of Atlanta. He'd chartered a private jet.

Now he was in Atlanta, maneuvering the car onto I-285 via Camp Creek Parkway. He took the ramp to I-20 West and drove to the Thornton Road exit. The residence was ten miles from the interstate. It was his plan to wait at the home until she arrived. He checked his Rolex. School was dismissed at 4 p.m.; it was now 10:45 a.m.

If the woman calling herself Lynn Stockton was really Anissa, he planned to overpower her, weaken her with a few carefully aimed blows, and then get her into the trunk of the car. He had to be careful not to shed any blood, because he didn't want any evidence of violence left in the car. He wanted to kick himself for being so impulsive. He'd come here without any weapons and no rope.

Her fear of him would be his greatest advantage. Once she saw him and he gave her a little pounding, she'd be like putty in his hands once again. He had dreamed of what he'd do to her if she'd pulled a fast one on him. The last thing she'd think about before she took her last breath was how good she'd had it and what a fool she had been to throw it all away.

Committing murder was nothing new for him. Once before a woman in his life had dared to defy him and he'd been forced to burn her house down with her parents in it. He saw nothing wrong with taking a life as long as one could be assured of getting away with it. Death was an unpleasant fact for everybody; not like a freak occurrence for only a few.

There was just no other way to teach Anissa that leaving him was a mistake, short of amputating all of her limbs, and he wouldn't want to live with her like that. Everyone had accepted her death, so killing her was the only way. He turned right from Thornton Road onto Bankhead Highway. He followed this road all the way into the little hamlet of Austell and then turned left and crossed over the railroad track. He followed this road to Powder Springs where he turned right on New Macland Road, and then took Macland Road to the first right onto Ben Hur Drive.

It was a relatively new subdivision and the house across the street from the Stockton address was vacant. He could see that there was still construction going on at the lower end of the street. This was perfect. He would blend in like an interested buyer. He drove right into the driveway of the empty house, looking across at 1647 Hur Majesty Lane—Lynn Stockton's address.

Now where in the hell had she gotten money to buy a house? It was two story, brick, white columns, nice lawn, with a two-car garage. He craned his neck, but could not see into the back yard. He looked around and observed that most of the houses seemed as if no one was home. When he lowered his windows, he could hear the sounds of men hammering, sawing, and talking. He did not want to raise the alarm of any well-meaning soul who could be watching from a window, so he got out and pretended to look at the vacant house.

No signs advertising for a neighborhood watch were posted, but in these days of children getting snatched and women being raped in their own homes, he knew that he had better stick to his plan and behave purposefully, as if he had a right to be there. He checked his watch. It was 12:20. He made a decision. He would cross the street and get into the house and look around. There was no security system; at least there were no signs in the yard advertising one.

As he made his way down the driveway toward the back of the house, he passed a fenced-in yard, where a big Rottweiler came toward him snarling and barking. He kicked at the fence and gave the dog the finger. "Go to hell!" he snarled back at the mangy fleabag. He hated dogs. With a passion.

He kept walking, to the backyard, up the stairs to the sun deck and to the back door. The one useful item that he did have was his pocket sized breaking and entering tool that he kept with him at all times. One never knew when a locked door could impede progress. He knew a few tricks. He'd learned them from some of his young buddies on long evenings after school when they had nothing better to do.

They were all rich kids who felt like none of their parents would even notice if anything was missing from their homes. They'd each taken turns burglarizing each other's houses. It was fun. He quickly opened the door and stepped inside. He was in the kitchen. He whistled to himself. Nice house. He hoped to find some proof that Anissa lived here. The last thing he wanted to do was waste his time with the wrong person.

The kitchen was all white, good flooring, nice cabinetry—an inviting place to prepare meals. He walked into the hallway that led to the living room. It was tastefully furnished in shades of orange and white. He moved upstairs to the master bedroom, where he checked the closets for signs of a man's clothing. Nothing but ladies' clothes. He was glad of that. The clothes were off the rack and a lot cheaper than what Anissa was used to wearing.

But it wasn't clothes he was interested in. He wanted to know if Anissa lived here—or rather, Lynn Stockton. It was early. He had plenty of time to find a utility bill or something to let him know who lived there. The logical place was the office he'd just passed. He went in and opened a desk drawer. He had the element of surprise. If someone came home and it wasn't Anissa, he'd just have to knock the hell out of whoever came through the door and then worry about it later. He'd come too far.

Chapter Sixty-Seven
April 2002

When Anissa pushed open the door to the teacher's lounge on Wednesday morning and spotted the only occupant, Meike Schmidt, standing in front of her mailbox, she'd immediately pulled herself together for a round of ignoring a person. She'd directed her attention towards her own mailbox. Meike never spoke in the morning, not even when spoken to directly.

"Guten Morgen. It's a fine morning isn't it, Mrs. Foley Brogdon?"

Anissa froze. Her mouth turned dry in an instant. Her heart raced. Did she really hear what she thought she heard or did she imagine it? How did this woman know her real name? How should she respond? Once she was able to focus, she spoke.

"Who are you talking to, Meike?" Anissa demanded, trying very hard to compose herself.

"I'm talking to you, Missy. Your name is not Lynn Stockton. Look what I found at my sister's house in Nashville," Meike announced triumphantly as she produced two newspaper clippings from behind her back.

Anissa looked and saw herself and Foley, in wedding garb, announcing their wedding. The other clipping announced a memorial service for Anissa Brogdon, a local victim of the World Trade Center attack.

"My sister was a fan of your husband, Dr. Brogdon. She's kept everything she could find in print about him. She's had a sort of crush on him; thinks he's handsome," Meike sneered.

Swallowing the bile that had just rushed to her throat, Anissa turned to leave the room.

"Not so fast, Madame Stockton. I knew you didn't belong here and now you're never going to be able to teach anywhere once I report this. The Professional Standards Commission will not take this lightly."

Anissa pulled the door open. All she could think of was getting away.

"I called your husband last night. He was very keen on finding you, and now he knows exactly where you work!"

Anissa turned to look at Meike.

"Meike, what have you done? Why couldn't you leave it alone? Leave me alone?"

She ran blindly down the hallway to her classroom. Foley knew she was alive. He knew where she was. She had to get out of there. Should she run out of the building now? Get in her car and start driving? What to do? Before she could ask herself a second time the bell rang and her sense of responsibility for her students took over. She couldn't walk out without a substitute teacher. She would need to arrange for one immediately. She went to homeroom and jotted a quick note, and sent it by a student to the eighth grade administrator, requesting to leave due to an out-of-town family emergency.

For the next hour, she struggled through her classes, imagining the worst. Foley bursting into her classroom. Foley standing in the door of the lunchroom. Foley waiting outside the school. All these visions danced through her head. She calmed down when she got a note back saying that no substitute could be found, but the 8th grade administrator would come to take over her classes after lunch if she could wait that long. Even if Foley knew she was alive he couldn't possibly know where she lived could he? Meike said she told him where she worked, so it was possible that he could come to the school. If he followed correct protocol and went into the office first, they would notify her that she had a visitor and then she could run. But what if he came looking in every classroom for her without stopping at the office? Surely, Officer Brown, the police officer who worked at the school, would see him before he got too far. But parents walked into classrooms during class all of the time unannounced—Foley's presence would not seem out of the ordinary. She stood near the door so that if she spotted him she could quickly lock her door.

When the bell rang to dismiss first period she called Kathy.

"Hello?" Kathy answered.

"Kathy! Listen, Meike Schmidt knows who I am. She says she called Foley and told him where I am. I've got to get out of here! I need your help."

"Are you serious? How did she find out? Oh, that doesn't matter now. You're right you have to get out as soon as you can."

"I've got someone coming to take my classes at 4th period. I have to stay here until then. I can't just desert my students."

"Tell them it's an emergency. What if you had a heart attack? Just like that your students would be left to fend for themselves."

"I said it was an emergency. An out-of-town family emergency. They all move to the beat of their own drummers here. I have to wait until someone comes to relieve me."

"You won't be going back to that school or that job, so act crazy. Push that button and tell them you have to go immediately. It's really a matter of life and death; yours."

Anissa hung up just as the bell to begin second period rang. She walked into her classroom and pushed the white button.

"Front office," answered the secretary.

"Someone needs to come to my classroom immediately. The situation has worsened and I have to leave now!" Anissa blurted out.

"Just a minute, Miss Stockton."

Anissa turned her attention to her students, giving them instructions on the assignment for the day. The class had settled down when Jake Tyler, the principal, opened the door. Anissa could tell by the look on his face that he was not happy.

"Miss Stockton, may I see you for a minute?" he asked.

Anissa already had her purse and all of her personal belongings in a tote bag in her hand. She looked around frantically to make sure she wasn't leaving anything else. Satisfied she walked towards the door.

"I'm sorry, Mr. Tyler, but I have to go." She walked past him. He quickly turned on his heels and followed her.

"Miss Stockton, where do you think you're going? You can't just walk out and leave your students unattended."

"I'm not. I'm leaving them with you. You are, after all, the bottom line when it comes to safety and the welfare of these students at Valeria Middle, are you not?" She kept walking. She knew he was furious and she was glad that she no longer had to make a choice between her job and the right thing to do. She was leaving this political arena. She was going to pack a few things, get Joey, and then head to Kathy's house.

Chapter Sixty-Eight
April 2002

Anissa arrived at her house in less than twenty minutes. She got out of the car and went over to her neighbor's fence, where Joey stood wagging his behind more than his tail. He was always so happy to see her. She really appreciated being able to put Joey in the fence when the neighbors were out of town. She'd contracted to have her own yard fenced in the next three weeks. Alas, she wouldn't need it now, because she was about to be in the wind.

"Hey, Joey! How's mama's boy? How's mama's big boy, Joe? You ready to get out of that fence? Let's go, boy!" She unlatched the gate to the fence, and Joey came bounding out, heading towards his own back yard. She followed him nervously. It was unlike him to run off without greeting her first.

"Joey? What are you doing, silly boy?"

She rounded the corner of the house and saw that he was up on the sundeck, scratching at the door and barking like crazy. Why was he so eager to get into the house? Her instincts told her to run. Forget about her plans to get a few things. Get Joey. Get in the car and go.

"Joey, come here!"

The dog trotted over slowly, but continued to bark, looking back towards the door as he did so. She ruffled his head as she reached for the door that led into the garage from the deck, noting that the fur on his neck was standing straight up. Something was wrong. Joey was in stealth mode.

Could someone be in the house? Foley? Had Meike told him where she lived as well? She'd noticed a car in the driveway across the street, but there was always someone over there looking at that house. Joey was still barking. She grabbed him by his collar and pulled.

The very instant her hands touched the doorknob she got a strong sense of foreboding, like none she had ever experienced. She hesitated as the words from Meike Schmidt rang in her ears again "Guten Morgen, Mrs. Foley Brogdon."

Joey looked up, desperately trying to tell her something as the door was suddenly snatched open from the inside.

"Hello, Anissa, or is it Lynn Stockton?" Foley's frame seemed to fill the doorway as he glared at her triumphantly. For a minute, everything went into slow motion. There stood Foley looking cool as a cucumber. The next second Joey lunged forward, his weight knocking Foley off balance to the floor. Joey bit into the side of Foley's face. Anissa screamed and scrambled back to her car.

She quickly turned the ignition, threw the gear into reverse. She heard Joey howling in pain, and her heart almost tore in half because she knew she had to leave him there. She backed out with such speed that she nearly rammed the mailbox of the house across the street. She was still able to turn and head out of the subdivision as fast as she could. In her rear view mirror, she saw Foley running across the street holding onto the side of his face, blood running down his cheek, but she kept moving.

She didn't stop at the stop sign and barely missed a green truck approaching from her left. She pressed the gas pedal to the floor and watched her speed climb, 40, 50, 60, 70 miles per hour and she was up the road approaching a sharp curve. She knew she had to slow down or else she would lose control of the car.

As she took the curve, she glanced back and saw a car in the distance behind her. It had to be Foley. She accelerated again and climbed the hill, racing to the stop sign at the end of Ben Hur Drive. Macland Road was a busy divided thoroughfare with a concrete divider and three lanes on each side, and it was lunch time. As she approached, she could see that traffic was beginning to back up. She couldn't stop and she couldn't go across. She slowed enough to turn out into the far right lane and then merged. Horns were blaring. She maneuvered to the left lane, glancing back into the rear view mirror.

Foley's car had merged into traffic as well. What to do now? *Left turn. Left turn.* The words kept repeating inside her head. What good was a left turn going to do? He could turn left too. She couldn't go over the concrete median without destroying her car or causing a wreck. And then she knew.

She was approaching a traffic light and she could see that Foley was behind her now. She could clearly see his face in the mirror, so clearly that she could imagine the hard line of his jaw clenching. The light was yellow. She had to get back on the other side heading in the opposite direction where the traffic was moving faster but she needed to be able to do it so quickly that he could not follow.

If she could time it right, just when the light turned red, she could do it. She couldn't get in the left turning lane or else he would know what she was going to do. She would have to turn from the center lane. She would have to cross in front of the car in the turning lane, but if she put the pedal to the metal she just might make it without causing a collision. She slowed and the light switched to red. She braced herself, said a quick prayer, and turned the wheel as hard as she could to make the wide U-turn smoothly with one fluid motion just as the cars in the oncoming lane began to move across the intersection.

She did it! Her back end fishtailed, but she was headed back in the direction she had just come from. She hit the gas pedal and glanced back. Foley was stuck at the traffic light. Just for an instant their eyes locked. She increased her speed and then turned right at Pilgrim Road. She made two more left turns and drove until she reached Dallas Highway. This was a straight shot into the city of Marietta. She kept an eye on her rear view mirror. Foley's car was nowhere in sight.

She took a deep breath to calm herself and slowed down to the speed limit. The last thing she needed was a traffic ticket for speeding. Every fiber of her being screamed at her to back-track to the house and get Joey. She loved that dog. She hated leaving him like that, but her rational mind told her that going back was too dangerous. Kathy could get Joey later. He was so brave, attacking Foley like that. She'd have to give him a doggie treat when she saw him again.

Chapter Sixty-Nine
April 2002

Foley cursed. Anissa had just successfully done something he would never have believed she'd even try in a million years. When he saw her pull into traffic, he thought she was a goner, but the cars braked long enough to allow her to straighten up and keep going. Their horns were blaring in protest, but she had escaped without incident. He sat there and pounded on the steering wheel trying to keep her in sight in his rear view mirror, but she disappeared in no time. The light changed. He made the U turn, sped down the hill. He saw a street to his right. Did she go that way or did she keep going straight? He didn't have a clue so he kept going straight. It was easier to move faster on a two-lane road so he decided that she would have taken the easy way and kept going straight.

She would count on speed to get away. He increased his speed until he had a good view of the few cars ahead. Three white cars. One could be Anissa. He began to maneuver in traffic to get close enough to see. Two were SUV's and the third a Town Car. Hers had been a Lexus; he remembered the L on the back. No more white cars in sight. He looked down each street that he passed, but there was no white car. Where did she go? He could see down the road a long way. What now? What to do now?

He had lost her. She had been so close to him, he could almost touch her and now she was gone again. He slammed his fist into the steering wheel again and then caught himself. He didn't want to draw any attention, because he was now bleeding profusely. Blood was on the steering wheel and on the seat. The front of his shirt was covered with blood. Damn dog! All this blood had to be a mixture of his and the dog's blood. He needed to get to a hospital, get a rabies shot, and clean himself up. But that would mean questions and he didn't like questions unless he was doing the asking.

The bite on his face needed medical attention, but he was a doctor. A few things from a drug store would fix him right up. There had to be one nearby. The only things that he could think to do were to clean his wound and bandage it. He'd take off the bloody shirt until he could get somewhere to get a new one and then hope that Anissa would go back looking for that damn dog!

Where else would she go? She had to know that he was out of his element in this strange city. He knew nothing about tracking people and even less about this town. He took a deep breath and made a left turn at the next street, because he saw the familiar blue H that meant a hospital was near. And where there were hospitals, drugstores were scattered close by. He knew how sappy Anissa was about dogs. He'd get himself patched up, go back to her house, and wait until she returned.

Chapter Seventy
April 2002

Anissa was familiar with her surroundings and Foley was not—that was her advantage. He would not know where she was if he was not able to stay right behind her. She had lost him, she was certain of that. "I might as well get used to calling myself Anissa again," she said aloud to herself.

When she reached Marietta Square, she parked her car and just sat until she was able to move without shaking. Then she got out of the car and began to walk. People were everywhere, some heading home from work, others shopping, others going into the various restaurants on the square. She waited on the corner for the light to change and then walked toward the park. She remembered the first time that Kathy had told her the story of why it was called Marietta Square. It was mainly because of the park that was constructed squarely in the center of town. The land was donated to the county on the condition that it remained a park or else it would return to the heirs of the donor. It was officially named Glover Park and was a very peaceful place to sit and while away the time, except for today. Anissa sat down on a bench, pulled out her cell phone and called Kathy.

"Hello?"

"Kathy, he's here!" she blurted into the receiver.

"Who's here? Foley?"

"Yes. He was in my house when I got home today. Joey attacked him and gave me enough time to run, but I think Foley hurt him. I heard him cry out as I backed out of the garage." Anissa was crying now.

"Where are you now? Are you sure he didn't follow you?"

"He tried, but I out ran him. I'm on the square in Marietta."

"Are you still in your car?"

"No, I'm in the park."

"Out in the open? You've got to get inside someplace where you can see him coming if he followed you. Get up and walk across the street to that little restaurant on the corner. Sit back from the window, but make sure that you can see the door and the street. Leave your car right where you parked it. Do not go back to it. You understand?"

"Yes. But Kathy, I need you to get Joey!"

"I'll get him. You get inside that restaurant and don't draw attention to yourself by blubbering. I'm sending a taxi for you, the driver is a friend of mine and he's radical. He wears a red wide brimmed hat and he has long dread locks, so you'll know him when you see him. He'll get there pretty quickly. When you see him, I want you to come out fast and get in the cab. If anybody is following him, he knows how to lose them. He'll bring you here. I'll see you soon. And cheer up, you're about to leave Mr. Brogdon in the wind again." With that Kathy hung up.

Fifty minutes later, Anissa walked into Kathy's living room and hugged her. She was still shaking and the cab ride had only increased her anxiety. She felt like her world was coming to an end yet again, and that this time her life was in danger as it had never been before. She was scared. And then she remembered her dog.

"Where's Joey?"

"Okay, lady, the first thing we're going to do is get you changed and then we'll talk about Joey." Kathy, ever the optimist, led the way into her bedroom.

"Change completely," Kathy demanded.

Anissa looked at the things laid out on Kathy's bed.

"All of that?' she asked incredulously.

"Yes. And put on lots of make-up— eye shadow, blush, lipstick, mascara, eyeliner. You know, the works—I want you to look nothing like yourself," Kathy ordered.

There was a pair of jeans, a white shirt, a black vest, a long yellow scarf, large gold earrings, about six bangle bracelets, a full curly platinum wig, a black cloche hat, large, brown sunglasses, and a pair of low cut black boots with 3 inch heels. Anissa dressed carefully and thirty-five minutes later, took a long look in the mirror.

"You've come a long way, baby," she said to herself as she applied another layer of red lipstick. She took one last look and decided that, indeed, she looked nothing like herself. She joined Kathy in the living room again.

"Let's go," Kathy said, moving towards the door.

They walked out and got into the back seat of a stretch limousine. The limo was soon headed south down I-75 towards the airport. Kathy began to rattle off instructions.

"Here's the plan. You're flying into Logan International Airport in Boston. Here's your new purse. Inside you have some cash, a credit card, a new social security card, a Massachusetts driver's license, and the address and key to an apartment on Commonwealth Avenue. You are now a new woman with a new name and hopefully a new attitude. There is also a cell phone; you will use it to talk to me and only me. Do you understand? It's important that you understand."

"I hate those words. Foley used to ask me if I understood all of the time."

"Okay, I won't use them. How about *comprenez-vous*?

For the first time since she'd known her, Kathy seemed upset.

"Yes, Kathy, I understand what you're telling me."

"Good. We cannot underestimate Foley Brogdon. I don't know how he found you, but he is good."

"Meike told him!"

"She couldn't have given him your address. She doesn't know where you live."

"Yes, she could. You know we have a phone list with addresses for all teachers."

"Meike Schmidt has really gone and done it now." Kathy sat back in the seat.

Anissa suddenly burst into tears. The weight of the day finally dropped with its entire heavy load and she buckled under the strain. She could see Foley's eyes and almost feel the anger coming from him now. It was so unlike him to display anger. She knew without a doubt that if he had gotten his hands on her, she would be in a lot of physical pain now.

"He came so close, Kathy. I had forgotten how much I was afraid of him. He almost paralyzed me with that fear until Joey jumped at him. Where's Joey? If it had not been for him Foley would have me now."

"Well, he does not. You have you. And you have me. So, chin up, sugar ball. I want you to take a taxi from the airport to the apartment. Go inside and take a nice hot bath, drink some wine, order up some Chinese, and wait until you hear from me. There's a menu on the fridge. I've got to go over and see what's going on at your house. I contacted your neighbors and they went over to your house." Kathy paused. "Joey's dead…"

"Dead? He killed him?" Anissa blurted, interrupting Kathy in midsentence. "Oh no! He died trying to protect me!" She began to sob uncontrollably. Kathy continued.

"He was on the kitchen floor. His throat had been sliced open. Foley must have used one of your knives. It's a bloody mess, they tell me. I told them to close the door, go home, call the police, and say that they'd heard a disturbance. They know not to talk to anyone but me about you. And apparently, there's a Ford Taurus parked down the street that's been there much too long. It's my guess that it's Foley waiting for you to come back. He's got a wait in store for himself. He's relentless, but so am I, and the good thing is that I knew a man just like him, so it will be hard for him to get around me. I'm his new worst enemy."

She put her arms around Anissa and held her.

"Listen, I know you loved that dog, but thanks to him you're still alive. Now go ahead and cry, but you've got to pull yourself together by the time we get to the airport. And believe me, this time next week, Meike Schmidt is going to wish she'd minded her own business. I hear there are some schools in this district where the kids make the teachers cry, and they're always looking for new hires or transfers. Just can't seem to keep them."

Chapter Seventy-One
April 2002

Foley sat in his rental car, his cheek burning from the bite Anissa's dog had inflicted. Damn stupid dog! He chose not to even worry about how his face looked because he was a cosmetic surgeon with the knowledge to guide one of his colleagues into giving him a new look. He found a Walgreen's where he'd purchased a sweatshirt with a big lion on the front and the words E.A. Version High School, some medical supplies, and some razor blades. The checkout girl was totally preoccupied with his chest peeking underneath his jacket and the blood all over his face.

"I cut myself shaving. But I'm going to keep practicing until I get it right," he winked at her and smiled.

He could feel his charm oozing through his blood as the checkout girl smiled back. He made a quick stop at a gas station and put on the sweatshirt, washed his face, and cleaned and bandaged the wound as best he could. He opened the razor blades and slipped them in his pocket. Excellent weapons in a pinch. Every fiber of his being was on high alert. He directed his attention towards Anissa's expensive new home as he willed her to return. She had to return. No way would she just keep going without coming back for that dog. She had not expected Foley to be there, so she was not prepared. If it had not been for that mangy mutt, he would have her and all of his troubles and worries would be over.

He had to admit that she looked good. She was heavier and she had a sexier look about her with the red hair. She was in front of him for only a few seconds, but that was long enough for him to smell her. He smiled as he realized she was still wearing one of his favorite scents, a fragrance of gardenias. He insisted that she wear it on all of her sensuous places—behind her ears, at her neck, between her breasts, her thighs, and the bend in her legs. The thought of her body made his warm all over. He loved the feel of her flesh next to his, the way she'd moan, and the way it felt when she reached orgasm, her wetness and softness engulfing him from the tip of his penis to the base as she trembled so hard sometimes it shook him as well. It was going to be nice to screw her one last time. No woman had ever satisfied him like Anissa. She responded to his slightest touch, and the more urgent he became the more she seemed to melt. God how he had loved her!

Inside that pantry, he'd known it was Anissa when he'd heard her talking to that mutt. She sounded so happy. But that wouldn't last. If he couldn't be happy, she certainly would not be. He would never be able to live with her again, not after this deception. He had his pride, after all. How could he face society again with a wife that was dead and now alive? He'd placed her on a pedestal, gave her anything that she wanted or needed, and this is how she chose to repay him? The ungrateful little skank! He chuckled to himself as that unfamiliar word crossed his mind. Skank? Well she was! All she cared about was herself. He would never have called her that to her face. He knew that she would have taken it as a racial slur and he was not a bigot.

The color of Anissa's skin was what made her so beautiful. He hated looking at a white woman, seeing veins beneath pale skin. He truly wished that there was a way to permanently add pigment to a white person's skin, just enough to give them a permanent tan. He would have made so much money. He shook his head to clear his thoughts. He didn't like the direction they were taking. He didn't need to think about money or white women; he needed to keep his mind on the injustice he'd suffered.

The couple living next door to Anissa had already been over to the house. He'd watched as they'd unlocked the front door and gone in. He marveled at how trusting his wife had become. He would never have allowed a neighbor to have a key to their house in Brentwood. They were inside about twenty minutes, and when they came out they looked up and down the street. He knew that they saw his car, but he didn't care. Let them see it.

He laid his head back on the headrest of the car and looked around the interior. He'd cleaned up the blood very well but what a crappy vehicle. Here he was, used to driving a Bentley, and now he sat in a Ford trying to track down a wife who didn't have enough sense to realize that he was the best thing that ever happened to her and that no one else would ever love her like he did. He had time to repent for some of the things that he'd done to her, he'd even been angry with himself for being so possessive and wanting to ensure that she'd never be with another man. It didn't do any good, she'd still left him. And now, he'd rolled up all of that anger that he'd felt at himself into a huge ball of fury that sat in his chest, directed at Anissa.

The sound of an approaching car snapped him back to attention as he looked up eagerly to see if it was Anissa's white Lexus. It was not. It was a police car. Foley could care less about the police. He made more money in a day than they made in several years. He watched the car slowly pass him as his thoughts went back to Anissa.

How did she get money to buy a Lexus? What had she gotten herself into? Was she some man's whore? There was no way she earned that kind of money teaching. She had a Master's degree, but she didn't earn enough to afford this house and that car. Had to be a sugar daddy. His blood was literally boiling he was so angry.

The police car made a U-turn and headed back towards Foley. He stopped directly in front of him with the lights shining brightly in Foley's face, even though it was daylight. Foley had to chuckle because he recognized this tactic for what it was—an attempt to intimidate. *Well I don't get intimidated, boy*! The officer got out and walked towards Foley. He seemed young, mid to late twenties, average height, well-built, displaying a red neck swagger. He had a flashlight in his hand and when he reached the door, he aimed the beam of light right at Foley's eyes. He stood there in all of his redneck majesty with his too tight uniform and oversized head.

"Do you have some identification, sir?"

"Yes, sir, if I can see how to find it. You've almost blinded me with that spot light." Foley pulled out his wallet and handed over his Tennessee driver's license.

The officer took a quick glance and then looked back at Foley. "You're a long way from home, Dr. Brogdon. What are you doing here?"

"This is a public street. I stopped to rest my eyes and it looks like I'm going to need to stay even longer now that you've dilated my pupils. I don't want to make myself a danger to others on the streets by driving with tired eyes."

"Well, if you're tired, I'd be more than happy to give you a ride down to our station. You're welcome to rest there if you feel like you're unable to drive. You haven't been drinking have you?"

"Only on holidays and special occasions, and unless you have a reason to arrest me, I'm not going to your station or anywhere else with you. You know I could consider this harassment. My attorney hasn't sued anyone on my behalf in a long time." Foley glared at the officer. He'd never had much respect for the police.

"Sir, this is a residential area. We received a call about you sitting here in your car in a neighborhood watch area, so I would advise you to move on before one of these neighborly men feels threatened by your presence and accosts you. I'd have to take you in, then. And by the way, we don't worry too much about getting sued around here. I work for one of the richest counties in Georgia."

"No problem, Officer. Had I known about the neighborhood watch I would never have stopped. We put up signs to warn people in my neighborhood. May I have my license back? I'll be on my way." The cop was lying. There were no neighborhood watch signs anywhere.

"Certainly, sir. One more thing: what happened to your face?"

"I cut myself shaving."

"Interesting. You have yourself a nice evening. And drive carefully."

Foley turned on the ignition and pulled away from the curb. The police officer waited for him to turn around and head out of the neighborhood. Foley watched from his rear view mirror as the officer pulled right behind him. It only took a short distance for Foley to realize that he was going to follow him, so he headed towards the airport. The police followed until he entered Fulton County. Foley had never been so humiliated in his life. Anissa had better enjoy her freedom. It wasn't going to last long.

Chapter Seventy-Two
April 2002

Felton Dade looked at his watch. He was going to be thirty minutes early. That would not be kosher. He would have to waste enough time in order not to arrive at her house no earlier than five minutes before eight. Most women made a man wait anyway. He was nervous. The guys were right—he'd been out of the game too long. Suddenly becoming a parent had taken all thoughts of women out of his mind.

He'd only known Karen about two months before the tragedy wrecked his family. They'd been on one date. She was cute—nice figure, her own hair and nails, and she was smart. She'd been calling, checking up on him, and dropping hints about wanting to see him again. Plus he'd thought about her once or twice and really didn't see any harm in trying to get to know her better. Marriage was out—she knew that already. His mother had prepared him well.

"Felton, don't you waste no woman's time. If you know you don't want to get married, tell her. No point in going around breaking hearts. Women want a husband," she'd told him over and over during those days just before he left for the military. He actually got tired of hearing it, because he wasn't thinking about getting married at the time.

Maturity had caused him to appreciate that advice. He made a point of letting any woman he dated know from jump street that he wasn't ready for a serious relationship. Karen had been so advised. And if she thought he'd changed his mind because of Nathan and Justin, well, she had another thought coming. He had a very full life in his future caring for his nephews.

He stopped off at a coffee shop near Karen's apartment, opting for a cup of hot chocolate. He'd left the boys with a sitter and a list of tasks—homework completed, one hour of playing or television, kitchen neat, bath or shower, teeth brushed, and in bed no later than 8:30 p.m. In that order. He was strict and he knew it, but they were going to grow up to be men and he wanted them to know how to accept responsibility.

He'd always been fond of the little guys, but now he could honestly say that he loved them. A lot. And they loved him. He looked forward to the weekends as much as they did. They'd go to Manhattan and just ride the subway sometimes. Other times he took them to the park, to the museum, he was teaching them to bowl, and they'd even caught a Knicks game. It was good to see them laughing—they'd shed enough tears.

Dr. Brown, the therapist, was a great go-to-guy. Felton also had female friends on the force with children. And advice from books—he'd done more reading in the past three months than he'd done all his life. He sipped his hot chocolate and glanced at his watch. He frowned at the thought of conversational topics. She worked for the New York Department of Health and she'd mentioned that the department had done an investigation to determine the composition of the airborne dust and indoor and outdoor settled surfaces around the World Trade Center site and nearby residential areas. Everybody knew by now that the air had to have been filled with all kinds of microscopic debris. And he'd been in the middle of it. He would make every effort to change the subject if she mentioned it tonight. He didn't want any more bad news.

He rang the doorbell at exactly 7:57. The door opened and Karen stood there dressed and ready to go.

"Hi," she said.

"Hi," Felton responded. He was impressed.

Chapter Seventy-Three
April 2002

In 1952, Logan International Airport, originally known as Boston Airport, became the first United States airport to have an indirect connection to rapid transit. Named for General Edward Lawrence Logan, a Spanish-American War veteran, the airport was built on at least 1800 acres of landfill in the Boston Harbor, and surrounded by water.

Anissa's flight arrived at 9:30 p.m. She followed the signs to the exit, went to the taxi area, got into the first one, and directed him to the address on Commonwealth Avenue.

She sat back in her seat, took a deep breath, and began to cry. Once again, she was running for her life, and without her best friend. Poor Joey. He had given his life for her. She had never allowed herself to hate Foley; she feared him, was repulsed by him, and disliked him terribly, but she would never sink to hating. She truly despised him now, because he had killed a helpless animal. Joey would never have attacked him if he had not sensed the evil that permeated every fiber of Foley's being. The man's decisions made no sense. He could have wounded the animal, better yet; he could have stayed out of her life. She was gone. It had been almost a year. Why couldn't he just go on living and find some other victim?

She knew that hate was not constructive because it hurt the hater more than the hatee, but she was going to sit here for a while and hate him. He destroyed everything she valued. Every time she thought about her relationship with Foley, she felt sore inside. She had never been able to understand how someone could profess love and then hurt you. She could see his eyes and the cold lifeless look that they would take on just before his fist made contact with her body. She thought of the beginning, when they'd first begun their love affair. The open display of affection, the sudden way that he would grab her up against him, sometimes swinging her off the ground and gazing into her eyes with what she thought was pure love. The impromptu kisses, the way he would reach for her hand, the way he would casually put his arms around her waist, the way her body would tingle with excitement just being near him.

She spotted a slight tear in the lining at the top of the taxi. A weak spot. A blemish. Just like her life. She'd been a successful woman. A great athlete in high school and college. She'd only had one false start and that had been enough to teach her to move only when she heard the signal. Her marriage to Foley was yet another false start, and what had she learned from that? To move only when Foley gave her a signal. He had just signaled that it was time to run— for her life. Would she be able to outrun him? It was true that Kathy had money and resources, but so did Foley.

Foley's father had lots of money and lots of friends and she was certain that there was no limit to the amount of time, energy, and money they would invest to track her down. She would appear as the ungrateful, deceptive, selfish wife who'd tricked her innocent husband into believing that she was dead. She could almost hear the Foleys. Their son had married someone from the wrong side of the tracks who had disgraced the family name.

Chapter Seventy-Four
April 2002

Brentwood, Tennessee, an affluent suburb of Nashville, was located in Williamson County, which ranked among the wealthiest counties in the United States. Lacy and Foley, Sr. had called it home for twenty-nine years. The couple sat side by side on what Lacy fondly referred to as a settee in their entry hall. Their son, FJ, sat in an armchair directly across from them, having just returned from his trip to Atlanta.

"You're telling us that Anissa is alive? Have you lost your mind son? And what happened to your face?" Foley Sr. was incredulous.

Lacy stared at her only child, watched his reflexes, the way he held his head. He was telling the truth. Somehow, by some miracle, Anissa was still alive.

"Yes, she is alive," FJ said adamantly. "She was living in Powder Springs teaching French at a middle school. She has a new name. She's calling herself Lynn Stockton. She doesn't look the same either."

"A new name? Why in God's earth would she have a new name, son? And where in the hell is Powder whatever? This doesn't make any sense!" His dad was staring at him like he was from outer space.

"Georgia. Powder Springs is in Georgia."

"Well where is she now? And why would she pretend to be dead all of this time?" Lacy Brogdon asked thoughtfully. It seemed that she had underestimated Anissa. Had she developed the nerve to leave her husband? To pretend like she'd died on 9/11? That was a clever move.

"I don't know. I don't know where she is. One minute I'm looking at her going into her front door, and a few minutes later I'm banging on the door trying to get in. The next thing I know she is gone out the back door. She got into her car and drove away. I tried to follow her, but she was familiar with the area and I wasn't. She was gone, just gone, like she disappeared into thin air. I've got to find her, Dad. I want my wife back. I love her!"

"How did you find her?" Lacy asked. She was curious. It was such a great escape plan. How did she ever slip up and get caught?

Foley, Sr. looked at Lacy, his eyes pleading for help in understanding what was going on.

"Talk to us. There's something that you're not telling us. And for God's sake, what happened to your face?" Foley Sr. asked.

Lacy regarded her son carefully. His left cheek was covered with gauze and antiseptic tape, with dried blood matted to what appeared to be a wound. He was wearing a high school sweatshirt and his pants were stained. In short, he looked a mess. And he'd not answered her question about how he'd located his wife.

"I got into it with a dog, but don't worry about that. I'm fine. Let me try to explain." He took a deep breath and as he did, Lacy noticed the subtle way that his eyes shifted to the marble floor. He was lying now. "Anissa was unfaithful to me. She no longer supported me. When I found out, I confronted her. She was using drugs. The trip to New York was supposed to be a fresh start. Somehow, she made it out of the Marriott and I guess she contacted the man that she was seeing. She couldn't face what she'd done, so she ran."

"How do you know what happened if you didn't have a chance to talk to her?" Lacy asked. When was this boy going to tell the truth?

"Anyway, she ended up in Powder Springs, Georgia, and got a job teaching," he continued. "One of the teachers at the school recognized her and called me. I was so happy that I took the first flight to get her. But she wasn't happy to see me. She ran. I love her and I want her back. I forgive what she's done. We can work through this, our marriage can work..."

He stopped abruptly and looked helplessly at his father. Lacy turned to her husband as well. He was completely snowed. His son could tell him that the sky was orange and he'd find a way to make it so.

"Georgia? Do you hear yourself, son? If all of this is true, it sounds like she doesn't want to be a part of this family anymore. If she doesn't want to be with you, then let her go. There's no reason for you to go chasing after her. She's been gone a long time and we've all gotten used to her not being around. It's time for you to go on with your life. There are many other women who would love to be your wife. Let it go, son," Foley Sr. tried to placate his son.

"You can't help it if you love her, FJ," Lacy said softly. She believed that he did love Anissa, as much as his ego would permit him to love anyone besides himself. Anissa had loved him as well. Too much. She had to have loved him to blind herself to what was right in front of her eyes. Lacy knew her son. He was cruel, and had never learned to be any other way. His wife had escaped. He might as well get used to it. She would never come back to him. Why would she? Lacy decided that the best way to handle this situation was to coddle him. Turn his attention towards himself, otherwise he would be hell bent on vengeance. No woman had ever walked away from him.

"I do love her, mother. I love her so much and I want to work this out if I can just find her," Foley lamented.

"And how do you presume to do that?" his father demanded. "You don't know where she went, do you? If someone does not want to be found, you can't find them. That's a fact of life, my boy. Why don't you just call the police? And why would you want an adulteress and a drug addict for a wife?"

"Because I love her. The police won't help and I don't want them involved. They may try to convict Anissa of some crime and I just want her home with me. We can use a private investigator."

Foley, Sr. rested his useless hands on the top of his cane, his face dismayed.

"Son, think about this. Are you sure that she'll come with you even if we find her? Women make up their minds about a thing and it's hard to change it."

"Yes, I'm positive that she'll come with me this time. Don't you know people? You know how to find people! What about that man who swindled you? You found him. And it only took you three months. So help me, dad! Help me find her!"

"That was different. That man made all kinds of mistakes. He was easy to find. It sounds to me like Anissa is a lot smarter than any of us gave her credit for. It's easy to find a stupid person, but not so easy to find a smart one. I just don't know son. I think it best to let it go."

Lacy watched her husband propel his body upward, using his cane. He stood unsteadily a moment.

"I will not let it go," FJ towered over his father, glaring down at him. "I can't let it go. If you won't help me, I'll do it myself. I'll quit my job, sell my home, and hit the road searching for her until I see her again or until I die."

FJ knew that any talk of leaving always brought his father around to his way of thinking. Lacy continued to watch the show.

"That's crazy! And you're being overly dramatic! You're going to give up a lucrative career for her? Don't do that, son. Think! Think about what you're saying, you have to think!"

"Dad I am thinking...with my heart," FJ whined.

"Look, son, get a good night's rest, let me make some calls and we'll take care of this. Just don't do anything crazy yet. I'll help you all I can." His father began to hobble down the hallway towards his study where he spent most of his time these days.

"Thanks, dad. I can't rest, but I do appreciate your help. We need to get on this fast, like right now." FJ took a few steps behind his father.

"Alright, go with your mother and eat something or drink something, or talk. Just give me a few minutes okay?" His father made a gesture with his distorted hand, indicating that he was done talking.

"Okay, dad. Mother may I have a cup of hot chocolate?' FJ turned toward Lacy with his killer smile in place. He played both of his parents like violins. She was very much aware of that but she loved him.

"Of course you can, my love, let's leave your father alone for a while." She took her son's hand and led him to the kitchen just like she did when he was a young boy.

Chapter Seventy-Five
April 2002

Anissa unlocked the door to apartment 3127 Commonwealth Avenue, switched on the light, and stepped inside another residential paradise by Kathy. Anissa had always had an appreciation for lovely home décor. A brass chandelier that had to be 17th century Italian was suspended from a very high ceiling in the center of the room. It was hanging by chains and the lights appeared at first glance to be tapered candles. The floor was hardwood parquet, and even though she was obviously standing in the living room, there was no rug on the floor. A large armoire stood against the wall straight in front of her, flanked on either side by floor to ceiling windows, that upon closer inspection, were actually doors. She opened one of them and peered out onto the street, the neighboring buildings, and the traffic below.

Turning again she noted the beige sofa with a baby blue ottoman in front of it. There were two comfortable brown armchairs and two comfortable baby blue chairs on either side of a fireplace. The painting on the wall behind the sofa consisted of contemporary paint splotches arranged in block patterns of brown, blue, celery green, tan, and beige. The kind of painting that made you believe that you could paint if art was that simple. A large bouquet of white flowers graced an end table. It was a very warm and inviting room.

The kitchen was true to Kathy's state of the art preferences. An island sat in the middle with three suspended lights overhead. The counter tops were honed marble. It was a sizeable kitchen and seemed to have everything you needed to prepare a gourmet feast. To her delight a door led straight from the kitchen to the hallway. The one reason she had never wanted to live in a high-rise apartment was that there was typically only one way in and one way out. She'd be trapped. But not here. From the kitchen she walked into the simple yet elegant dining room. She switched on the elaborate iron and crystal chandelier.

An arched opening led from the dining room into a hallway that led to a half bath on the right, a lovely bedroom of peach, plum, and pale green on the left and then directly ahead to the master bedroom that was resplendent with a large dark mahogany four poster bed. From the bedroom, she glimpsed a vintage freestanding claw foot tub in the master bathroom. It was a beautiful home. Anissa appreciated beauty. As a child, she'd dreamed of one day owning a lovely home. Never in her wildest dreams did she imagine living in the opulence that Foley had provided. But his beneficence came with a price. Once again, she was overwhelmed with Kathy's generosity.

She lay on the bed and pulled the colorful quilt of purple hearts and red, blue, and yellow flowers and lavender watering cans up around her and began to cry. Again. Joey had been her friend. No matter what time of day she returned home he was always glad to see her. And now, he was dead, and she was no longer dead to Foley. How long before she opened this door and found him standing there, ready to unleash his fury?

What had she done to deserve a life like this? She'd gone to Sunday school and church as a young girl but found the 'dos and don'ts' of the Church of God in Christ frustrating. Don't wear make-up, shorts, sleeveless blouses, or nail polish. Don't dance, don't play cards, don't go to clubs or parties, and never listen to the devil's music. When she went to college, she'd attended a Baptist church and felt more comfortable.

Marriage to Foley and his brutal treatment changed her view of God. She'd strayed away from her faith because she couldn't believe that a loving creator would allow such cruelty. Lately, she had begun to pray again, thankful that deliverance had finally come. Until now. *Where are you now God? What do I do now?*

She could pick up the phone and call Foley to get it over with. She could go back and hope that time away from him had softened him some and that perhaps he would be happy to have her back. She could. But she'd rather die than go back to him. She'd learned enough from therapy to know that he would never change. All she was to him was a possession, a human punching bag. She saw that dead emptiness in his eyes and his facial features twisted in rage for just a moment when he stepped from behind that door. That was enough to let her know that she had to keep running.

The knot in her stomach was back and it was roiling inside her stomach. It was fear. She felt herself tensing all over as she relived the past twelve hours. Her heartbeat quickened, her palms were wet, she felt that doom was upon her, and she could not stop crying. She rolled over onto her back and began to wail out loud. This apartment was so old and so well built, the neighbors surely couldn't hear her; and if they could she didn't care. She had to lie here until she summoned enough courage to live for another day.

For a brief moment, she considered killing herself to save Foley the trouble. Then she remembered that she had not yet had a child and she hadn't been to Africa. These were two things she intended to do before she died. Certainly, she had a new name and some new credentials, but her face was the same. She was still almost the same size. Plastic surgery! She could have her face altered so that he'd never recognize her, even if he saw her again up close. But she couldn't alter her walk, or that habit of tilting her head, or her laughter. And, why should she? He'd taken her soul. Why should he take her looks too?

The telephone rang and snapped her out of contemplating her impossible situation.

"Hello?" she answered.

"Hey, girl!" It was Kathy.

"Hi."

"Don't sound so forlorn! Cheer up! You're in Beantown, home of the Boston Celtics and the world famous Duck Tour."

"Kathy, what am I going to do? He thought I was dead, yet he found me. You know he'll find me again now that he knows I'm alive!"

"Well, I think we should cross that proverbial bridge when we get to it. There is absolutely no way that he could know where you are at this very moment. So relax. I know it's hard, but try it anyway. Live in the now. Now!"

"Okay, but I can't keep living off of your kindness."

"Haven't we been through this before? I can afford it. Plus, you're helping me to train for the next woman who needs my help. We're a team."

"Kathy, I just love you and I know that I'll never be able to pay you back."

"No need to. Listen, there is a woman who works for me, her name is Josefina. She keeps the place clean and she cooks and shops for me when I'm there. I know I sound bourgeois, but sometimes I don't feel like going to the grocery store because I'm always hungry and I go in and buy hundreds of dollars' worth of food that I don't need and that will only contribute to my waistline. So she goes for me. She'll be there in the morning, but she dropped off some stuff for you tonight: juice, eggs, bacon, sandwich meat, and bread. I didn't tell her about those god awful grits."

"Kathy, thank you so much. You know I was seriously considering just calling Foley and telling him where I am to save him the time and me the drama."

"You do that and I might kill you myself! That man means you no good. Telling him where you are just shortens your time on earth! Have you learned nothing in therapy?" Kathy's voice was filled with impetuosity.

"I said considering, I didn't say I was going to do it. I'm just scared, Kathy. I had almost forgotten what it felt like to be scared like this. I don't like it—I don't know how to get over it."

"A little fear is good. It will keep you from dropping your guard. But the big fear? Let it go and let me worry about Foley. I could hire a hit man to take care of him for you."

Anissa sat up abruptly, summoning all the authority at her disposal to her voice.

"No, you will not. That will make you no different than he is. You're better than that."

"Actually, it will make me very different, because unlike him, I will succeed. I've got some very good friends and they're all good at what they do."

"I believe you, but you're not going to commit murder for me. We'll just have to keep me hidden."

"That's the ticket! Hidden like an Easter egg it is!" Kathy laughed.

Anissa was beginning to relax a little. The sound of Kathy's laughter added warmth to the room. Maybe she was giving Foley too much credit. He wasn't Superman.

"You will be safe there as long as you don't do anything silly. Get some sleep. Josefina will be there in the morning and we'll talk about your new job that's waiting for you whenever you're ready to go back to work"

"What new job?"

"I got you a job in the foreign language lab at Boston University. There was a vacancy."

How did she get a job for her so fast? It hadn't even been twenty-four hours. The woman was amazing. Maybe she was Superman.

"Doing what?" Anissa asked.

"Language lab stuff," Kathy quipped.

"Thanks, lady, but I think if I stay in this apartment I'll be safe. It was working with a loud-mouthed co-worker that led him to me."

"Okay, so you're going to do the hermit thing, huh?"

"Yes. The hermit thing. Goodnight, Kathy."

"Goodnight, Anissa, I mean Ansasha. How do you like your new little ghetto name?"

"It's not a name I would have ever chosen for myself, but a rose by any other name is still what? Anyway what are you trying to say? That I'm ghetto? I look ghetto today. If names and dress code could hide a person, I'd never be found. You know, you're the only white person that can get away with calling me ghetto, don't you? Talk to you later." Anissa felt herself cheering up a little.

"Oh, one other thing," Kathy added. "Watch out for the hag across the hall. Lucille Doud, from Texas. She's a bigot—rude, nosy, and bossy. She's the kind of woman to plan a party, mail everybody a detailed list of how things are to be done, and then get mad if someone deviates from the plan. Control should be her middle name. Avoid her like the plague!"

"Okay. I will, and thanks again, Kathy. Bye."

"I get it. You want to hang up, don't you? Bye, girl. I love you!"

"I love you, too!" Anissa hung up and pulled the covers over her head.

Chapter Seventy-Six
April 2002

The last therapy session had been one on one—just Felton and the shrink, Dr. Eli Brown. A harmless guy, shorter than Felton, in his fifties, with wire-framed glasses. He was sharp. Felton had to give it to him. He was also a snazzy dresser. He always wore suits and ties and shiny shoes.

The first time they met, Felton made a quality decision that he would not be doing much talking. He had come for the boys' sake. They needed help. Felton was a grown man. He was not going to lay his soul out for another man to see. Not again. He'd been there, done that, with a couch doctor in the Air Force. But Dr. Brown had insisted that the two of them talk, without the boys.

"Aw-ight, man," Felton had agreed. "But don't expect no revelations from me. You'll just be wasting your time."

"In my case, Felton, time is money," Dr. Brown winked at him.

"Yeah, my money," Felton replied.

So after an hour of his life that he would never get back, Dr. Brown informed him that he needed to forgive. Somehow, the doctor had made him to talk about his past. While the United States was at war thousands of miles away, Felton surrendered to the war that had raged inside of him for years and shared the night that changed his future.

He had been a junior in high school, in his hometown, Nashville, Tennessee. His best friend, Shon, had taken up with Foley Brogdon, a rich kid with no manners and not too much home training. He was arrogant and didn't know how to treat animals. Felton's family had always had a dog of some kind running around, and there was one cat that stayed outside all of the time. Felton liked animals.

Shon had brought Foley to a football game one Friday night.

"What's up, Dade?" Shon asked. Felton looked from one to the other, wondering what Shon was doing with a white boy.

"Ain't nothing to it. What you up to?"

“This is my friend, Foley Brogdon. Foley, meet my best friend, Felton Dade,” Shon said gesturing toward Felton.

“Hi Felton Dade,” Foley said, smiling, raising his hand to slap palms. Felton didn’t like him on contact. But he loved Shon. They’d been friends since first grade.

“Hello,” Felton responded, keeping his hands in his pockets. Felton didn’t slap hands, he shook hands like a man, like his father had taught him.

Shon, a good looking star athlete, was a ladies’ man. He’d met Foley at some party where Stacy Smith, a classmate of Shon’s, introduced them. Stacy was a hot mama every day and Sunday too. But she didn’t date white boys. Foley started sucking up to Shon to get next to Stacy. The three boys went to the movies once or twice and hung out at the school gym playing basketball. Felton got his first indication of Foley’s mean streak one night as they were leaving, after a scrimmage.

An old hound dog often hung around outside waiting for somebody to drop a few scraps of food. Felton usually had potato chips or cookies. He did that night too. He dropped a few chips on the ground, but before the dog could get to them, Foley had kicked him in the side. Hard. The dog got away as fast as he could while Foley laughed.

“I can’t stand damn dogs! The only thing they’re good for is lighting them up and watching what they’ll do,” he grinned. Shon grinned too, but not Felton—he recognized a sociopath in the making.

“I like dogs, and if you do that again to a dog while I’m around, it might be the last time you use that foot,” Felton said. He was a few inches taller than Foley, and bigger. He was a lineman on the football team and he didn’t mind taking a body down. Foley must have seen something in Felton’s eyes, because he’d wiped that silly grin off of his face.

Shon was all impressed that Foley had money and a nice car. One night they all went to Stacy’s house for a party. Stacy liked to party when her folks weren’t home. Soon after they’d arrived Stacy was dancing all over Shon. A little later, Felton noticed that she was wrapped up in a corner with Foley. He’d found that odd, but he’d been kind of busy himself. A bunch of the guys from the football team were there, and Felton had gravitated towards them at first and then a chick he'd thought was cute.

Two hours later, Stacy had been raped, beaten, and sodomized, and Felton had not been able to do a thing to stop it, because he didn't know it at the time.

Shon came out of nowhere, running up to Felton.

"Hey, man, we gotta go," his face had looked scared.

"What's wrong with you, dude?' Felton asked.

"Nothing, it's just time to go. You coming or not?" Shon looked nervous.

"Nah, man, I got this chick sweatin' me. Ya'll go head. I'll catch a ride."

A few days later Felton found out everything when he was arrested for beating and raping Stacy.

"How did you feel about that, knowing that you were innocent?" Dr. Brown asked.

"That's a stupid question, Doc. I was asked that dumb question by a shrink in the military. I'll tell you like I told him: How the hell do you think I felt?" Felton had felt betrayed.

He had been hurt and angry. He was only fifteen years old. He'd had good grades, his coach had promised to help him get a scholarship when the time came—his future had been bright. And then, Stacy and Shon had ruined everything. Shon was supposed to be his friend. He could have told the truth.

"Did you ever find out why Stacy lied and Shon held back the truth?" the doctor asked.

"Shon came to see me at Mindsend Facility. He told me that Foley had threatened to kill his parents if he told the truth—and Stacy's parents, too. Shon was scared of Foley after that night. And Foley's mom went to see Stacy and threatened her and made all kinds of promises about money to Stacy's parents. She went to see Shon, too. As it turned out, because they went along with the lie, she paid for both Shon and Stacy to get an education, while I rotted away in that detention center."

"Did you ever hear from Foley again?"

"Nah, man. And it's good I didn't. I'd be in jail for murder. I got out, enlisted in the Air Force, thanks to some encouragement from the ROTC instructor at my school. He'd been a colonel and had a lot of friends. When I was discharged, I headed straight to my sister's apartment in Harlem, and I've been here ever since. I hadn't thought about none of this crap until recently. I worked it all out with that shrink back at Nellis Air Force Base."

Felton shrugged his shoulders. He was tired of talking about it. He hadn't meant to bring it up. It's just that he'd seen that picture of Foley's wife, Anissa, with her beautiful smile and sad eyes. The name Brogdon had brought everything back.

"It looks like you're still holding some resentment. You need to let it go. Forgive Foley and his mother. And Stacy and Shon, too. They've probably forgotten you and the incident and you're still holding on to it, allowing it to still anger you."

"I'll forgive them. But I'll never forget about it. I lied on my application to the Police Academy. I never mentioned this mess. My record was supposedly expunged when I turned eighteen and I believe Foley's mother was responsible for that. Somebody paid for that lawyer I had, too."

"Forgiving does not mean forgetting. It means letting go. Let it go, Felton."

Felton left the good doctor's office, stating in no uncertain terms that the remaining sessions would include the boys. He was done. Talking about the Brogdons had left a bad taste in his mouth.

Chapter Seventy-Seven
April 2002

The ringing of the doorbell jarred Anissa from her sleep. She was groggy and felt sourness in her stomach as she tumbled from the bed. She stumbled towards the door, pulling at her hair and rubbing her eyes as she went.

"Who is it?" she called out.

"It is Josefina, Señora Stockton's maid. I am here to help you," answered a female voice with a heavy Spanish accent.

Anissa opened the door. Josefina was a lovely Hispanic woman, about fifty years old. She was not overly heavy, just definitely full figured. She had a warm smile.

"Come in, Josefina. It's nice to meet you." Anissa had to think for a minute to remember her name of the day. "I'm Ansasha," she said, stepping aside to allow Josefina to enter. As she did, she noticed that the door to the apartment across the hall was ajar. She could see the top of a head with brown hair sprinkled with grey. Lucille Doud, presumably.

"It is nice to meet you too, Miss Ansasha. Señora Stockton say I am to help you in any way that I can. I do what she tells me and I don't ask no questions," Josefina said as she crossed the threshold. The door across the hall closed quietly. Anissa had to smile. Lucille really was nosy.

"Would you like breakfast?" Josefina called over her shoulder as she bustled toward the kitchen.

"No, thank you, and I really don't need anything, Josefina." Anissa followed her.

"Yes, you do. I've got some things for you."

Josefina produced a large tote bag that she reached into and pulled out a map.

"Here is a map to the 'T.' That is what we call our subway system. Señora Stockton say that you should get out and ride it, get familiar with your new town. Boston is a beautiful and safe city, so do not be frightened to go out alone."

Josefina handed the map to Anissa. She reached into her big bag again. "Here is a list of some good restaurants. She say that you like Italian food. Also, she sent you the names of some salesladies in some of the boutiques on Newberry Street. She said you should go there today and get a few things to wear."

Anissa took the list from her. Josefina walked over to the cabinets near the refrigerator and opened the top drawer.

"Here are some brochures for some of our best attractions, like the Duck Tour, the Science Museum, the aquarium, and a map of Little Italy."

She pointed to a magnet on the refrigerator that held a laminated sheet of paper.

"That is a telephone list for all the places that pick up and deliver, like the dry cleaners and the laundry. I don't do laundry. I clean and I will cook sometimes. I am a definite Spanish cook, I do not do Mexican. I am not from Mexico, I am from Madrid," she said proudly.

Josefina walked to another cabinet in the island and opened a drawer. Anissa wondered how much more there was to know.

"Also here is a map of Boston University. That is where you will be working. My daughter works there, too. Her name is Juanita and she will meet you Friday morning. She will show you around and introduce you to everyone. She is a Spanish professor there and the Director of the foreign language lab. Do you have any questions for me?"

Finally. The information had stopped.

"Well, no. You've just said a mouthful and I thank you. I don't think I'll be going anywhere so I don't need all this stuff and I don't think I'll be starting to work on Friday," Anissa said politely.

"Whenever you are ready, she will be there. Señora Stockton asked me, and like I say, I do what she asks me to do. I'm going to do a little cleaning in the bathrooms and I don't know if you have a soap preference, but Señora Stockton likes the soaps from l'Occitane. I also need to dust."

Josefina disappeared around the corner and returned with a bucket full of cleaning supplies. She also had a notepad. She placed it on the counter with a pen.

"You write down what kinds of things you like to eat and that's what I will buy. We have excellent seafood here and a wonderful vegetable market near Little Italy. I shop for food one day a week so if you will make me a list I would appreciate that very much."

She started towards the living room, stopping suddenly. "Oh, I have my own key that I will use from now on. I will come in twice a week to clean. I didn't want to startle you this morning since you had not met me, that is why I ring doorbell."

Josefina bustled on into the living room and Anissa sat down on a bar stool and pulled the pad toward her. She began to make the list for grocery shopping. The thought occurred to her that perhaps she should go out and pick up a few things. She didn't even have a change of underwear. Josefina had mentioned boutiques, but what she needed was Macy's. She'd have to find out if there was one nearby. She most certainly did not intend to have Josefina shopping for her underwear. She finished the food list and headed back to her bedroom to take a shower with the l'Occitane soap.

She had cried and tossed and turned for most of the night until she made a list of pros and cons as to Foley's ability to know where she was or find her at this very moment. The cons had far outweighed the pros. The only thing that she wrote on the pro side was that he knew that she was alive. That's all he knew. So, for the time being she was safe. She wondered what his parents were thinking because it was a natural course of events that he would tell them. He'd leave out the details of his cruelty, of course, and blame everything on her. Naturally they would believe what he told them—especially his father.

Chapter Seventy-Eight
May 2002

Winston Merlot Candy was an African-American male, born to a father who played professional basketball in Europe and a mother who was a psychologist. He was the only child to this union, which lasted for five years. He grew up with his mother, but his father was a definite presence in his life. He had his mother's eyes, which changed colors from brown to almost green, depending on the light. He was fair skinned, had 'good hair', perfect teeth, and a beautiful smile that had a tendency to make his handsome face glow.

Like his dad, he was tall—six feet four inches, but he'd only played basketball well enough to make the team. He was no stand-out player. He made his stellar moves in academics; holding a Harvard degree in criminal law, graduating top of his class. He had a black belt in karate and kickboxing, numerous certificates that lauded his ability as an excellent marksman, and a PhD in street smarts thanks to his father and all of his father's buddies.

After graduation, he went to work at a prestigious Boston law firm. That was long enough for him to meet and work with a man who introduced him to the District Attorney for Fulton County in Atlanta, Georgia. He made such a good impression that the DA asked him to come to Atlanta and work full time as an investigator. Merlot was ready for a change. It wasn't that he didn't like all of the white men he worked with, it was just that he didn't like feeling that he needed to respond with 'yessuh, massah.' He had studied the law so that no one would tell him what to do.

He knew what *not* to do, and the laws he didn't need to break. It wasn't long before he'd established a reputation in the ATL, a.k.a. Atlanta, Georgia. He was an excellent investigator, specializing in hunting down a person and finding them wherever they'd chosen to hide. The money was good. So good that he was soon able to hang out his own shingle, and then business started rolling in almost immediately. He was amazed at how many people chose to disappear and then sit back and relax in the false belief that they could not be found.

At age thirty-eight he also was a bit of a secret weapon. He looked like Ivy League. Talked like Ivy League. Thought methodically and shrewdly like an Ivy League graduate. But he was a straight up street thug when he had to be. He was a definite believer in the 'don't-start-none-'cause- if-you-do-it's-definitely-gone-be-some' theory. The first time he went into the hood looking for someone, a brother got in his face and started talking trash about Merlot being the white man's boy. Merlot had him on the ground with his foot placed squarely on his neck in an instant.

"Don't talk to me like I'm stupid. I graduated from Harvard and I will kick your ass intelligently. And good. Look at me close, man; I'm just as black as you are. My last name is Candy. Do you know what I had to prove to dudes like you with a name like Candy?"

Merlot had spoken these words with an unmistakable threat and a ring of truth in his voice. When looking directly into Merlot Candy's eyes you knew that he meant what he said and would do what he said. He got the information he needed, and before long word got around and he earned the respect from most of the brothers. When he was looking, they were eager to help him—everywhere, all over town, and any day all the time. He was careful not to push his luck too far. He didn't want to have to kill or be killed.

He'd received a call the night before from a very good client, Stan Mobley.

"Merlot, I'm sending you someone. I know you make your own decisions, and I know you like money," Stan said.

"You know I appreciate the business, Stan, but money has lost its flavor a little. I've made enough so that I can just say no if I feel like it."

"And that's a good place to be, Merlot. He'll be there in the morning. His name is Foley Brogdon. His dad's an old friend of mine. Talk to him and see what you think. Good talking to you."

"You, too." Merlot looked at the phone a long time, deciding whether or not to call back and tell Stan to tell this potential client to keep stepping. But he owed Stan a favor.

Chapter Seventy-Nine
May 2002

Foley was the only occupant who sat in the office of Merlot Candy, anticipating being summoned to his presence soon. He had been waiting fifteen minutes. Foley didn't like to wait. Having money had taught him that he could have anything his way; all he had to do was pay what it took to get it done. He was willing to pay, but not willing to wait too much longer.

"Mr. Brogdon?" the receptionist addressed him. "Mr. Candy will see you now."

Foley stood and followed the middle-aged woman in the red suit. She led him down a short hallway to an office and opened the door, standing aside to allow Foley to enter. He was not prepared for the size of the man who walked up to him and extended his hand. Merlot Candy looked like an NBA player, dressed in an expensive white three-piece suit with a pink shirt, tie, and pocket kerchief. The shirt was silk and the bling-bling coming from his cuff links looked like two-carat diamonds.

He had light brown skin and was very handsome. Some men would have been intimidated by Merlot Candy. Not Foley. He had nothing to fear from an African-American because there was not an ounce of racist blood in his body. He always saw people first, not the color of their skin. His parents had taught him that to think less of another human being because of the color of his skin was wrong and foolhardy. His dad had to swallow his own words when he'd balked at Anissa, but the old guy came around. Foley believed that his parents had grown to love her.

No, he was not afraid at all to be in the company of this man. As a matter of fact, he was going to enjoy getting to know if he was as good as his father believed he was. If so, Anissa would be home soon.

"Mr. Brogdon, Merlot Candy. Come on in and let's talk," Merlot waved his hand toward an overstuffed orange leather chair in front of his desk.

Foley sat down and looked around as Merlot positioned himself behind an ornate oversized table that acted as his desk.

The only thing on it was a notepad and an expensive gold pen. A fantastic view of the city faced Foley.

The office was large and surprisingly well furnished. To the right of the desk was a wall lined with shelves that held volumes of law books. A matching armchair sat to the right of Foley. On the left side of the room were a cream colored leather sofa and two orange leather side chairs. A large table in the middle of this grouping held copies of the Law Review and some magazines. The art was subtle, but definitely made a statement and gave the office a welcoming atmosphere. Foley noted the lack of diplomas on the wall. He knew that Merlot was a Harvard grad, and found it odd that he didn't flaunt it.

"What I can do for you, Mr. Brogdon?"

"I want you to find my wife," Foley said.

Merlot sat back in his chair and looked at Foley for so long that it made him uncomfortable. Finally Merlot spoke.

"And why do I need to find your wife?"

"Because I don't know where she is."

"Why?"

Now it was Foley's turn to look hard at the other man. He considered the question of why. He didn't want to tell him the truth. Actually, he wanted to tell him as little as possible, because he was going to kill Anissa whenever he got his hands on her again. That part was of no importance to him.

"Anissa, that's my wife, and I have had some problems in the past. She was in the wrong about most of it, and she feels like I won't forgive her. She doesn't understand that I love her and I am willing to work things out, if she will just give me the chance. I don't want to get into all of the details, because I don't want you to judge her. So just let me say that she and I need to talk this out. I want to tell her that I am willing to forgive and to go on with our marriage."

"Tell you what, Mr. Brogdon; tell me a little about your wife. Not what she's done, but about her, as a person," Merlot said. His eyes had not moved from Foley's the whole time he'd been speaking.

"Well, as I said, her name is Anissa. She's African American, so that should tell you something about me."

"What should it tell me?" Merlot's eyebrows went up a notch.

"That I'm not a racist."

"Oh."

"I don't mean to sound condescending, Mr. Candy."

Merlot smiled. "Then don't. Now about your wife?"

"Well, she's beautiful. I've got a picture of her." Foley took out his wallet and pulled out the photo of Anissa that he still carried in spite of having an urn of ashes on his mantle. He handed it to Merlot.

"She looks different now. Her hair is red and shorter and she's about five pounds heavier. She calls herself Lynn Stockton. She was teaching at Valeria Middle School in Powder Springs, Georgia, but I don't believe that she is there anymore. I've tried calling her and was told that she was no longer with them."

Merlot took the photograph, still looking at Foley. Finally, he glanced down.

"Interesting. Where do you think she is?" Merlot asked as he studied the photo.

"I have absolutely no idea. She has a sister in Chester, South Carolina, who has not seen her since…" Foley hesitated. Should he tell him that Anissa faked her death? It would be a good test of the man's skills to see if he would uncover that on his own. But not telling him would only waste time and destroy some of Foley's credibility.

"My wife and I were in New York on September 11th. We stayed at the Marriott Hotel at the World Trade Center."

"Really? And you were not hurt?" Merlot interrupted.

"Well, if you'll allow me to finish. May I?" Foley asked.

Merlot spread his hands wide. "By all means," he smiled strangely.

"As I was about to say, I left my wife in the room in bed and went to the South Tower of the Trade Center for a medical conference. As you know, the towers and the hotel went down. I thought she was dead. Her body was never found. I held a memorial service for her. I've got ashes from the state of New York in an urn in my home. A few days ago I found out that Anissa was working at the Valeria Middle School, and living in Powder Springs. I came looking for her, but when she saw me she ran."

"That's quite a story, Mr. Brogdon. It looks like she went through a lot of trouble to keep you from knowing her whereabouts. And you've heard nothing from her since 9/11?"

"Nothing. Like I said, I thought she was dead."

"And you think she went through all of this because of your marital problems? You didn't beat her did you?"

Foley didn't flinch. "Of course not, and I resent you asking me that. Like I told you, she felt badly. She used drugs and had an affair. She knows the kind of husband I've been to her. She hated that she'd hurt me. She is a very private person. A very public divorce, which is what she feared, was more than she could deal with. I'm a very rich man, Mr. Candy. Perhaps she feared retribution, but there is no need for her to feel that way. I love her and I would never harm a hair on her head. I don't want a divorce. Will you help me find her?"

Merlot handed Anissa's photo to Foley and stood up. He walked from behind his desk towards the door.

"Mr. Brogdon, I'm going to decline. It's not easy to find a person who does not want to be found, and it sounds like your wife does not want you to find her. Have you talked to the police at all?"

Foley was flabbergasted. Didn't this detective know who the Brogdons were? How dare he dismiss him! When he spoke his voice was calm.

"No, I have not. And it is unacceptable for you to turn me down without trying. Money is no object as far as I am concerned. I want my wife back, and I don't have time to waste running from one private investigator to the next. I need your help right now. I need you to start looking yesterday. Please forgive me if I sound rude or demanding," Foley protested quietly.

"It's not about money, Mr. Brogdon; some things in life are just what they are. I don't know if I can find your wife. I like to deliver when I'm hired. So in your best interest, I think you should find someone else. You have a good day." He extended his hand towards Foley.

"If you don't mind, I'd like to make a phone call," Foley said, ignoring the hand.

"Take your time. Now if you'll excuse me, I need to make some calls myself."

Merlot closed the door to his office as Foley punched in a number on his cell phone. Ordinarily a stunt like that would have cost Merlot his career, but Foley was desperate.

Chapter Eighty
May 2002

Merlot liked that most people underestimated his intelligence. He had learned a lot from his mother and her love of psychology. He had an instinctive grasp of why people behaved the way they did. Take this man, Foley Brogdon, for example. He was not telling the truth, the whole truth, and nothing but the truth. He didn't have the vibes of a bigot, but something was amiss. He was hiding something, and not because he feared Merlot would judge his wife. What it was he did not know and he didn't care. He didn't like playing hide and seek. Not in the first meeting.

He could tell by looking at him that Brogdon had money. Lots of it—that explained his arrogance. But if money was what Merlot wanted there was no reason not to take the case. However, lately he had started to take his cases based on merit rather than money.

Anissa Brogdon was indeed a good looking ' hammer,' as his great uncle used to call fine women. Her smile was a killer. There was sadness in her eyes though. Her head was tilted to the side, her blonde hair falling into her face and giving her a sassy look.

Merlot had felt the hairs on the back of his neck tingling the whole time Foley talked, and he didn't have much hair back there. That sensation was a foolproof indication that something was not kosher. He was being handed a full-fledged baloney sandwich without mayo or lettuce and tomato. None of what he'd heard made sense to him and he didn't want to take the time to try to sift through untruth.

At that moment, Merlot's intercom buzzed.

"Mr. Mobley on line one," his secretary informed him. Stan Mobley had done many favors for Merlot. He knew what was coming.

"Put the call through," he responded to his secretary.

Fifteen minutes later Merlot placed the receiver back into its cradle and buzzed his secretary to see if Foley was in the reception area. The man had never left. He abruptly opened the door and stood there, a noncommittal look on his face that Merlot could not read.

"Am I your client?" he asked confidently.

"Alright, Mr. Brogdon, it looks like I'm your man. But there is certain information that I have to have in order to get started. I need a detailed description and background information on your wife's habits, favorite foods, restaurants, friends and family, old boyfriends, pets, tree house locations, anything that might help me get inside her head. I'd also like current information like name and location of that school and the most recent known address," Merlot said.

"Do you want me to write it down or tell you?" Foley asked, heading for one of the orange chairs. Merlot did not want him sitting down again. So, he stood and walked to the door. Again, using the oldest, most obvious trick in the book to get someone to leave.

"My secretary will get you started. Don't skimp on details. The more I know about your wife, the better are my chances of finding her. I must say that it would be a lot easier to find her if she had committed some type of crime. Then we could involve the police. They have resources that I don't have. She hasn't committed some criminal act, has she?"

"Does faking your own death count?" Foley didn't move.

"She didn't tell anybody that she was dead. She just never came home right?"

"Right."

"Have you collected an insurance settlement?"

"Mr. Candy, I don't need insurance money. The answer to that question is no."

"I don't think there's any law against not coming home. You know what I'm saying, homeboy?" Merlot laughed at Foley's semi-shocked face. "Forgive me for that, I like to throw in a little something ethnic now and then to see if my clients are paying attention. I see that you are, and I like that," he continued all the while continuing to size up Mr. Foley Brogdon. He was certain that he did not like him.

"I'll pay you two hundred and fifty thousand dollars today to begin the search, Mr. Candy. I'll give you an additional five thousand daily for expenses. I want her found. When she is, I will pay you two million dollars."

"That's very generous of you, Mr. Brogdon, but that's way more than I normally charge."

Merlot was tempted to tell the man what he could do with his money. The things one did when one owed a friend favors! But money was an even better friend. He directed Foley to the conference table, where he sat down and wrote out a check and handed it to Merlot.

"As I said, money is no object to me. I believe that if you pay a person well for services rendered, then you get more than what you pay for. In this case, I'm expecting to be holding my wife in my arms very soon. Do you understand, Mr. Candy?"

"I do. And I'm not going to argue about the money, but what I will not do is guarantee results. I will do my best, and in the past my best has been good enough to find whomever I've searched for, but there's a first time for everything. What I don't want is for you to think that just because you pay me exceedingly and abundantly above my usual fee that I will instantly produce your wife from whatever rabbit hole she's run into. Do you understand?" Merlot folded the check and slipped it inside the inner pocket of his jacket.

"Yes, I do. We understand each other."

Merlot buzzed his secretary.

When Foley left his office, Merlot summoned his best investigator and security specialist, Glenn Baush.

"You wanted to see me?" Glenn asked, standing in the doorway.

Glenn was like that. He had no personality, was one of those drab kinds of people who melted in a crowd unnoticed. He wore brown pants, always. He alternated between a white shirt and a yellow polo. He didn't wear a tie, and prided himself on wearing sensible shoes that Merlot called ugly. He was a man of few words, but he was brilliant. He was the main reason that Merlot had so much success, because he was a whiz at research. Merlot paid him well for his expertise.

"Yes, I've got a job for you. I want you to dig up everything you can find out about Dr. Foley Brogdon and his wife. He's a plastic surgeon practicing in Nashville. I need a full report."

"Will do," Glenn answered. Merlot knew that he would.

Glenn had graduated with honors from MIT and had become a legend with computers. He had a reputation for snooping and finding the dirt on most people he encountered. He was quiet and kept to himself, often referred to as the weirdo. Merlot had sat beside him at a basketball game and found out that he had incredible knowledge about the game. They became friends, and when Merlot hung out his shingle and needed someone to help him pry into the private business of other people, he made Glenn an offer that he could not refuse. Glenn would put together a two hundred page report with more details on Foley than Foley himself knew. The man was thorough to say the least.

Chapter Eighty-One
May 2002

Orella parked her car and turned off the ignition. Holy Wonderful Hearts United Methodist Church had not been difficult to find. She was twenty minutes early for a meeting that began at eight o'clock. She took a deep breath and sat back as a car pulled into a parking space near the side entrance to the church. She watched as a man got out, carrying a can of coffee and a bag filled with Styrofoam cups. He went inside. Now she no longer had to wonder where the entrance was.

She'd dreaded this all day. It took her a long time to decide on a place that she'd be certain not to see anyone that she knew. The Bronx seemed the best choice. For as long as she'd lived in New York she'd had no idea that all of these AA meetings were going on. They were everywhere! A church setting would be more conducive to privacy, and the people would probably all be Christians. Surely they'd never tell anyone that they'd seen her here.

She'd dressed down for the occasion—green sweat pants and matching jacket, with sneakers. She'd pulled her hair back and put on a cap with the brim cocked to the side. She'd appraised herself in the mirror before leaving home and decided that she didn't look like a judge. She really would never have come at all if the woman who'd answered the phone at the office of Alcoholics Anonymous had not been so friendly and offered to mail her a meeting schedule.

This morning had been another one of those days when she woke up and couldn't remember very much about the day before—not even how she got into bed fully dressed. She'd put it off long enough—now it was time to go to a meeting—if she could find the meeting schedule

After thinking hard she called the AA office again. This time the woman asked her one question.

"Can you *not* drink today?"

Orella looked at her decanter. Certainly she could not drink today. She'd done it before.

"Is that all I have to do?" Orella asked.

"And go to a meeting," the woman replied.

A noon meeting would have been out of the question, so Orella promised to attend the one tonight. She would treat this meeting like an information session. They would give all of the info while she gave none. No need to tell anybody anything. She wanted to learn how to drink without overdoing it. She'd pay attention and take any classes they offered.

At 7:55 p.m. Orella locked her car and went into the building, not knowing what to expect. A rather thin, handsome gentleman greeted her as she entered.

"Hi there! Welcome!" he said.

That was a good sign. She relaxed a little. Once she sat, several people came over to introduce themselves. Promptly at 8:00 the meeting began with an announcement and introduction of a speaker. Orella was immediately excited. Surely this speaker would give tips about not drinking to excess.

A very attractive woman stood up and walked to the front of the room. She was casually dressed, but the clothes were expensive. She had long mousy brown hair pulled back into a ponytail. Her make-up was immaculate.

"Hi everybody, my name is Culina and I'm an alcoholic," she stated.

The group chimed in with "Hi Culina!"

After that she started talking and the more she said the more Orella felt herself becoming nervous. This woman was talking about her. How did she know those things about her? It took a moment for it to soak in that the woman was talking about herself, but the experiences she'd had with alcohol sounded just like Orella's. Listening intently, Orella was disappointed when the woman began to draw to a close by sharing that she'd not had a drink in fifteen years. *Fifteen Years!!!* Orella exclaimed to herself. How in the world did she stay sober fifteen years? She sounded like she enjoyed partaking of the vine as much as Orella did. When several people went toward Culina to thank her, Orella stood, took one last glance and started towards the door.

"Did you enjoy her story?" asked a woman behind her.

Orella turned. "Yes, I did," she replied, turning away again.

“My name is Nana,” the woman offered. “Is this your first meeting?”

“Yes,” Orella answered, simultaneously thinking that it was also her last.

“Do you have a drinking problem?”

Was that Nana’s business? “No, I drink socially,” Orella told her, but the question made her think about the fact that she drank every day.

“Talking with other alcoholics will get you through it, and you have to go to meetings!” The woman’s face glowed; she looked like she’d never been drunk a day in her life.

“I don’t have to do anything but stay black and die,” Orella replied. That was one thing she didn’t stand for—people telling her what she had to do.

“You just haven’t hit your bottom yet,” Nana said.

Orella didn’t believe Nana or Culina had been sober for years. Who drinks that much and then just stops? For years?

“It was a pleasure meeting you, Nana,” Orella smiled and made her exit. She had not planned to stop drinking for years. As soon as she got home the first thing she planned to do was drink.

Chapter Eighty-Two
May 2002

On Monday morning, May 6th, Anissa reported to Juanita Dopton at the foreign language laboratory at Boston University, introducing herself with her new pseudonym, Ansasha Barnes. Juanita was the spitting image of her mother. She appeared to be in her early thirties, full-figured, with long brown hair pulled back into a ponytail. She wore a simple black dress with a string of pearls and diamond stud earrings that were about 2 karats. The black and white pumps finished off an elegant fashion statement.

"Good morning, Ansasha, nice to meet you," she said without a hint of a Spanish accent. "I've heard a lot about you from my mother. Come with me and let me show you around. Have you had a chance to see much of the city yet?"

"Just a little while I did some shopping," Anissa replied looking down at her new baby blue long sleeved silk blouse and navy skirt. "It's a nice city; I think I'm going to like it. I didn't see too many people of color until I got near the campus."

"I know the feeling. This city is divided into its little sects. I'll have to tell you about it. The Latinos live in one area, the Blacks in another, and the Italians in yet another. It's very interesting, but as long as you mind your own business, nobody bothers you. The kids here are great, I love working here."

"How long have you been here?"

"Three years. I came here with my husband. He's Dean of the Business School."

Anissa followed Juanita as she moved through the listening stations to a large booth to the left of the room. As they walked, Anissa noticed that the equipment was fairly new.

"So both of you work here. That's great. Do y'all have children?"

Juanita gestured with her hand to indicate that both spouses working at the same location was just so-so or as the French say, *comme çi comme ça*.

"It has its days. And yes we have two boys. Seven and eight years old. How about you?"

"No children," Anissa replied, feeling the ache of the child that could have been.

"You married?"

"I used to be."

They continued making small talk as Juanita showed her around. Anissa's duties would include retaining the headphones, having all assignments and lab manuals ready for each class, maintaining the schedule, and making sure that all students respected the lab rules. These rules of the laboratory were pretty straight forward: no student was to be admitted without a valid student ID badge; they were to occupy any vacant workstation that was assigned them; and any checked out materials were to be returned upon leaving the lab. The only variation in the procedure occurred during final exams. Her hours were from 9:00 a.m. until 5:00 p.m. It was a longer day than she was accustomed to, but she welcomed it. As long as she was busy, she didn't have time to think about Foley and where he might be.

"I'm fluent in French," Anissa added.

"That's good to know. You can help the French students. We are so happy to have you. Our last lab manager had an emergency and had to leave unexpectedly. We were about to panic when the call came about you. If I can help at any time, please don't hesitate to ask me. My office is right next door," Juanita said.

"I'm glad to be here." Anissa hugged Juanita. Soon the lab was filled with a Spanish class and the lab period officially began. Lunchtime arrived quickly.

A little café called Brenda's, a half block up and across the street, was by far the number one recommendation for lunch. Anissa had a turkey sandwich and chicken soup. On the way back she discovered Marsh Chapel, a small church on campus that housed the offices of the University Chaplain. She went in and sat on a pew and for the first time in years said a silent prayer of thanks and a plea that Foley would not find her. Going to the chapel at lunch became a ritual; praying made Anissa feel stronger.

Kathy cautioned her to be extremely careful. She was to become a woman of a few words.

"Limit your details. Details invite questions and you don't want to answer too many," Kathy advised.

"That's the truth. I think I'm going to become aloof and a loner."

Kathy laughed as they began the rehearsal of her new background story. This time she was from Seattle. She was divorced. Badly. Her ex had been horribly lazy, unable to keep a job. She'd been educated at the University of Washington where she'd earned a bachelor's degree in French.

Her new tactic was to be on the offensive, never waiting to be asked anything. Without hesitation, she was to ask "Where are you from?"

It was vital that she follow Foley's advice of never talking to strangers, because she never knew who might see her and connect the dots to Foley. It was a different life, but she was free for the time being.

She and Kathy talked every day. Kathy was planning to come and visit soon. She was still working on selling the house where Anissa had lived in Powder Springs. She'd had several interested parties, but so far no takers. She wanted Anissa to have the proceeds from the sale in cash, so that if she ever had to make a quick getaway she would be able to do so. Kathy could be depended upon, but she could not be in all places at all times.

"Foley will not stop looking for you, because you've embarrassed and shamed him. He can't tolerate that. In his mind, you should be grateful for all that he's done for you. Since you are not, he has to teach you a lesson. If he finds you, he will kill you. Don't ever doubt it!"

Every time they talked, Kathy re-emphasized this point. Her experience with battered women and their tendencies to return to the abuser stayed in the forefront of her thoughts at all times. As much as she laughed and joked, domestic abuse was a serious issue and a sore spot for Kathy—one that she was determined to address for the rest of her life.

Anissa settled into her new identity, spending her days at work, her nights at the apartment, and her weekends riding the 'T' all over the city. She started out on the green line, then changed to the red line, and then to the orange. She liked the red line best because it went to Harvard and MIT. She loved to browse their bookstores and to have coffee at Harvard Square because it was nice to be in the midst of so many young students. She'd recently posted a flier for French tutoring on the bulletin boards back at Boston U and Harvard. She hoped she'd get some takers because that would give her something to do in the evenings.

She'd also joined a gym. She felt like she needed to be strong if she ever had to face Foley again. Her plan was to spend thirty minutes doing strength training five days a week. Every morning she ran four miles before going in to work.

The looks from some of the guys at the gym were hard to miss, but she ignored them. Occasionally, she'd glance at herself in the mirrors and swell with pride at the sight of her toned figure. Especially her abs. It had been almost a year since she'd been hit in her stomach, and she thanked God every day that she had not suffered permanent damage.

"How are you today, Ansasha Barnes?" Anissa was so lost in thought that it took a few minutes for her to realize that someone was talking to her. She was Ansasha Barnes. She turned her head and looked into the face of Stan something or other, a personal trainer who'd explained to her how to use some of the equipment.

"I'm okay, Stan, how are you?"

"I'm so good that if I got any better I'd be scared. I see you smiling to yourself over there. You must have saved a lot of money with your auto insurance company."

Anissa couldn't help but laugh. Stan had a great sense of humor and he wasn't bad looking if you liked muscle.

"It's just good to be alive," Anissa answered walking away, but Stan had fallen into step with her.

"When are you going to let me take you out?" he asked.

"Never," she answered smiling at him.

"Ouch! That's cold. You know you just broke my heart, don't you?"

"You're a strong man, Stan, you'll get over it. Have a nice day." Anissa hurried through the door to the outside. She was not into looking for love. She was into staying alive.

Chapter Eighty-Three
May 2002

Merlot Candy had never been to Powder Springs, Georgia. Talk about a small town with nothing to do: this was it. But Merlot was not a snob, he was who he was and who he was could not be in Powder Springs after dark. The place where he liked to go first anytime he visited a city was where the brothers hang out. He wanted to see just how dangerous they were. He was dangerous and he knew it, but you could always run into somebody with something to prove. Better to meet them early.

It was amazing the information one could gather by simply starting a friendly conversation. But he didn't find any brothers. After cruising the main street, he drove to Valeria Middle School. When he pulled into the parking lot, there was a red SUV parked in the parking spot for employee of the month. It was not wise for a lone man to hang around a school for too long, but he decided that he would be safe for about five minutes. As it turned out that's all he needed.

A man came out of the building, and from his appearance, he had to be the custodian. He carried a ring of keys and was dressed in work khakis and a blue shirt. He was well into his fifties and appeared to be in good health. He had a bounce to his step. Merlot got out of the car just as the guy stepped down from the sidewalk and headed towards the SUV.

"Excuse me, sir?" Merlot called out.

The man stopped and turned toward him.

"How you doing, sir? My name is James Stockton," Merlot lied, extending his hand. The man had a strong grip and held on as he introduced himself.

"My name is Roger Wilson." He looked at Merlot expectantly.

"I live in Atlanta," Merlot continued. "I just heard from an aunt that my sister, whom I have not seen for three years, is working at a school around here somewhere. She's my half-sister, but blood is blood. Anyway, I wanted to surprise her, and I know that this is Saturday. I don't have any way of contacting her other than showing up and seeing her in person, but I just wanted to be certain that this is the right school. You may not even know her. It was just a long shot, but I thought I'd ask what with your being here and everything. Her name is Lynn Stockton."

Merlot noticed the slight change in the man's face. A telling change—Roger knew Lynn Stockton.

"Well, we got a lot of teachers working here. I can't be sure that I know who you're talking about. The best thing would be to come back here on Monday morning and talk to the principal," Roger said guardedly.

Merlot smiled, deciding not to push too hard.

"Thank you, sir. I didn't think you'd tell me, but I thought I'd ask anyway. I sure am looking forward to seeing her. I haven't seen her since our mother died." Merlot turned back toward his car.

"Did you say her name was Stockton?"

Merlot stopped and turned toward the man again.

"Yes, sir. Lynn Stockton, she's a French teacher."

The man spat on the ground and then put both hands in his pockets. He seemed nonchalant, but Merlot knew that the guy had sized him up and decided that he was harmless.

"Well, she did work here. They say she left a few days ago and nobody seems to know where she went. But like I said you can come back and talk to the principal. He knows more than I know."

Merlot knew that flattery was a good tool. He used it.

"In my day, sir, nobody knew more about my school than the custodian. Is that what you do here?"

Merlot did not miss the way the man suddenly straightened up and swelled his chest with a look of pride on his face

"Been with this system twenty-eight years. I was transferred here when this building opened. I live about five minutes from here and it's real convenient. I can get here quickly whenever an alarm goes off on the weekend." He puffed his chest out like a rooster.

"Twenty-eight years! Man, that's a long time! I guess they treat you good?"

"I can't complain. Listen, Miss Stockton lived off Macland Road in a new subdivision over there. I bet if you drive over through there and ask some of the neighbors, you might find out more than I can tell you. All I can say is that she was a real nice lady. All the kids seemed to like her. Sorry, I can't be of much help to you."

"Thank you, Mr. Wilson. That helps a lot. Maybe I'll see you Monday."

"I'll be here. Have a good day now and I hope you find out something."

Roger got into his vehicle and pulled out ahead of Merlot as he left the parking lot. He turned left. Merlot glanced quickly at his map and then turned right.

Forty-five minutes later he ended up on Ben Hur Drive where he learned from neighbors working in their yards that someone broke into Lynn Stockton's house the last time anyone saw her and killed her dog. Just cut his throat. There'd been a strange man sitting in his car, with a bandage on his face. The neighbor called the police, who had simply run him off. Merlot pondered the things he had heard and he thought about the scar on Foley's face and how much it looked like a dog bite.

Chapter Eighty-Four
May 2002

On Monday morning bright and early, Merlot arrived at Valeria Middle School. Parents were dropping off their kids and he could see school busses unloading in the distance. It appeared that the school was pretty balanced demographically. His research had shown that there were 30% Hispanic, 30% African American and 38% Caucasian students. The remaining 2% hailed from other parts of the world. He wore a navy suit and a Panama hat to match. He drove a different car, too. He hoped that the custodian was busy in another part of the school.

This time he pretended that he was looking for a school for his non-existent nephew. In the front office, he met the cute little brunette secretary, Esther who was anything but professional. She was dressed in a white low cut blouse that barely contained her boobs and a red tight skirt with black high heels. Obviously, she did not come to school to learn anything other than how she could get herself a boyfriend from the men who visited the school. She turned on her allure as Merlot cranked his charm up a notch. He had her eating out of the palm of his hands in less than five minutes. She told him all sorts of things that she wasn't supposed to. So, Merlot figured that the only fair thing to do was to ask her out.

The dinner date at Red Lobster proved to be very fruitful. He learned quite a bit about Lynn Stockton, most of it inconsequential, but a few things were helpful. She wrote a lot of administrative referrals and a lot of students were removed from her class and placed with other teachers, mostly African American kids. As a result, she earned a reputation for being prejudiced, or so the black kids said. Merlot had to ask the secretary twice if Miss Stockton was African-American, because it didn't make sense that she could be prejudiced to her black students if she was black as well.

"Miss Stockton was not afraid of the troublemakers or their parents. Most of the white teachers are. I think that's why they called her prejudiced."

"So she didn't really care what color a kid was if he was a trouble maker?"

"No, she didn't and I liked that about her," Esther smiled.

"Do you know where she's teaching now?" Merlot asked casually.

"No. We have a new principal and our German teacher, Ms. Schmidt, was transferred too. Really strange!" Esther was busy cracking into her crab legs.

"Did she have any friends who might know where she went?"

"She didn't have any close friends and she was not very friendly with the rest of the teachers. If you want to know anything about her, ask her kids. Why are you so interested in her anyway?" Esther asked with her dark brown eyebrows raised. She licked her lips with her tongue. Merlot didn't miss the gesture, he just wasn't interested.

"You know, I told you about my nephew? He heard that Miss Stockton was a fun French teacher from some of his friends who attend this school and I just wanted to know about her. My brother was thinking about buying a house in this area so that my nephew could come to your school and also go to that big high school," Merlot explained, keeping his eyes trained on hers.

"Well, Miss Stockton is gone. So let's talk about me. Aren't I interesting enough for you?" She winked at him. He decided to keep talking.

"Of course you are." Merlot gave her his most charming smile. He needed to keep her engaged. She was resonating compliance.

"I have a lot of free time, so I was just looking out for my nephew; you know you can't trust every teacher to really teach nowadays. I can't tell you how much I appreciate your helping me out like this." He was relieved that she'd finally questioned him. Her free fountain of information was beginning to make him seriously consider private school when and if he ever had children of his own.

Esther smiled at him. "She was a good teacher. But some parents complained and that got her in trouble with our former principal. He got transferred too. I've never seen them transfer so many people in a matter of days before," she dipped her crab in butter and put it into her mouth.

Merlot concentrated on his meal, giving her time to chew and swallow.

"I wonder if Miss Stockton went to another school in the county," Merlot asked as he put a shrimp in his mouth.

"No she didn't, because I would have processed her transfer papers. I have no idea where she's gone. The kids may know. Like I said, they can tell you about her."

"The kids? The kids would know about a teacher?"

"Honey, kids know everything except the things you want them to know. Most of the kids liked Miss Stockton. Even the ones she didn't teach. I'd overhear the troublemakers in here talking about how good she looked all the time. She was a snazzy dresser. She came dressed professionally every day. Not too many of them do, you know." She leaned in so that Merlot could get a good look at her breasts that were tugging at the fabric of her low cut dress. Who knew one could find a hot babe at school?

"Troublemakers liked her? That's funny." Merlot quipped, tearing his eyes away from her bosom.

"What's really funny is that most of them live in the same housing area. Over in the Forest. You can drive through there any time at night and find some of them out on the street. Gang activity. I had to drive a student home over there one night. I was nervous the whole time."

"The forest? Like Sherwood Forest?"

Esther laughed. "Its official name is Emerald Forest Place, it's a townhouse complex. The kids call it the Forest."

The rest of the evening was uneventful. Foley took her home and made the obligatory promise to call again. He had no intentions of following through.

Chapter Eighty-Five
May 2002

On Tuesday night Merlot cruised through Emerald Forest looking for troublemakers and lo and behold, he soon spotted a group of them. He rolled his black Escalade with the spinning rims that he reserved for his drives into the 'hood' right up to the curb next to them and got out.

He wore Sean Jean jeans, a black tailor made sports jacket, and a pink shirt.

"What up, guys?" he asked as he walked towards them.

"What you want, nigga?" one of the bigger boys asked. "And man take that pink shirt off, it's hurtin' my eyes." The other guys laughed. They all had their hands in their pockets, like that was supposed to incite fear.

Merlot laughed too. "I want to talk to you. And I like pink, it makes me feel like it's just me against the world," he added.

"I don't know you, man."

"That's right you don't know me. I might be a killer or I might want to buy some information," Merlot replied.

"Information? This ain't no Jeopardy game, man," a different boy spoke this time. They all laughed again.

Merlot smiled. "Do any of you guys attend Valeria Middle School?" he asked.

"You a cop?" The big one again.

"No," Merlot replied.

"I don't know shit!" The big boy spat.

"I can believe that," Merlot acknowledged. A 38 automatic was one of many guns that he owned. Remembering Esther's comment about gang activity, he'd come prepared for such a time as this. He reached behind him underneath his jacket where the gun nestled just inside his belt, removed it, and cocked it, putting a bullet in the chamber as the boys watched, then put the gun back where it was. "Let me rephrase," he said, eyeing the big guy who'd spoken. "Any you dudes go to the Middle School?"

"The fuck you wanna know for?" The big guy wouldn't quit.

Merlot took out a one hundred dollar bill from his pocket and fanned himself with it, still eye to eye with big boy, but watching the others carefully with his peripheral vision to make sure he had their attention.

"I know you guys get around and you see things that most folks don't know you see. I want to know about a teacher who used to teach at Valeria: Miss Stockton. She taught French. Every adult I talk to tells me that she didn't have any friends, but I know that ain't true. Do any of you guys know any of her friends?"

"Naw, man, we don't know nothing except we don't like that pink shirt. I like your whip though," this from another guy in the group.

"My car? Yeah it's nice. I like it too. If any of you want to make this bill, hit me up." Merlot pulled out one of his cards and placed it on the ground.

"Wheah you from nigga?" The same new guy was speaking, as he looked down at the card.

"I'm from the ATL," Merlot answered, directing his eyes toward the young man.

"Oh, so you bad then, huh? Big city nigga out heah slummin' wit us country boys." The big boy again, hands still inside his pocket.

"I can be pretty fucking scary if I have to be. Check ya'll later, homies." Merlot started back to his car.

"Hey, shawty, wait up," another young man called out, stepping away from the crowd. He walked up to Merlot.

"Miss Stockton had a white lady friend. The lady lives over on Bear Claw Trail. I was working on a project at one of my white friends' houses and we saw Miss Stockton go into the driveway next door to his house. The lady that lives there don't have no kids and she ain't no teacha, so Miss Stockton must be her friend."

"Where on Bear Claw Trail? What address?"

"I can show you. My mama don't care. She ain't nevah home, no way. Come on, man, ride me over there."

"Me too, man," the big boy chirped as he stepped out of the crowd.

Merlot turned to face the group. "I ain't crazy. I don't see any parents. Okay? So the answer to that is no, nobody is getting into my car but me." He made eye contact with each of them.

Then he looked at the young man standing in front of him. "I'll tell you what. You tell me how to get to where your white friend lives and describe the house that you saw Miss Stockton go into and if I like what I hear I'll pay you this one hundred dollar bill."

The boy's face lit up with anticipation.

"Start talking," Merlot commanded. "I'll give you the money if I believe what you say. And don't fuck with me. I know when somebody is lying to me and I don't like liars. Got me? Now what's up?"

"Yes, suh!" The boy started talking and Merlot listened, keeping one eye on the other boys who'd gone back to talking in their little group, except the big dude who kept his attention on Merlot. When the kid finished, Merlot gave him the hundred.

"Thanks, kid. Remember what I told you. I'll be back if what you told me doesn't check out. But I believe you. You look like a good kid to me. Now get off the street and go do some homework before these guys take your money. Where do you live?"

The boy pointed to the next building over and cast a glance back at the group.

"Go home. I'll watch you go."

Merlot stood there until he saw the boy go into the house. Then he got into his car and drove away. He'd done what he could. If the boy let the money get away from him that was his problem.

Chapter Eighty-Six
May 2002

Anissa had found it interesting to learn that Boston had been home to many Abolitionists during the antebellum era. This information, along with other historical facts, was posted along the very celebrated Freedom Trail, a tourist attraction for the city. Even in the 1960's, one Bostonian in an all-white elementary school in the South was the only teacher willing to teach a little black girl when the public schools were first integrated. She was the only black child in the whole school and the teacher had to teach her alone for over a year. Norman Rockwell's painting "The Problem We All Live With" memorializes the historical moment when four very tall U S Marshals accompanied her to school. Yes, this was Boston history too, but it seemed like the generations that followed made an unspoken decision to keep the races separate, or maybe the races decided to separate themselves.

Anissa finally met Lucille Doud, who made it clear that she had her problems with African-Americans. Anissa was coming in from work one evening, and, as usual, when she turned her key in the lock, Lucille's head appeared.

"Hi," Anissa turned suddenly, clearly catching the woman off guard. "I'm your new neighbor, Ansasha Barnes." Anissa crossed the hall and extended her hand to the woman as she reluctantly opened the door.

"Lucille Doud. You know, all the years that I've lived in this building, you are the first person of color to reside here," Lucille sputtered.

"Well, it's good to have some variety don't you think?" Anissa asked, smiling broadly at Lucille.

"I like things in their place. I don't know if you've noticed or not, but most of your kind live in Dorchester."

Anissa chose to ignore the part about 'her kind.' Lucille Doud was looking for a button to push and Anissa was not giving her one.

"Really? Well, I like it here don't you?" Anissa smiled again. She clearly enjoyed that she seemed to make Lucille uncomfortable. Every forward step that Anissa took, Lucille took one backward.

"That's not your apartment," Lucille said accusingly. "That place belongs to Kathy Stockton."

"Yes, I know. She's a *very* good friend of mine. I'm thinking about buying this place from her."

Lucille's face turned red as a beet.

"You might find that to be difficult. We residents make the decision as to who moves into our buildings." Lucille held her chin up with a smug look on her face.

"Well, it's good to meet a Bostonian, Lucille. Let's have dinner together sometime," Anissa offered.

"Harrumph!" Lucille grunted. "I'm from Texas," she added.

"Are you serious? I never would have guessed that you were from the South," Anissa smiled her sweetest smile.

"Well, I am," Lucille spat, closing her door soundlessly.

Anissa chuckled to herself. So that was Lucille Doud. A living, breathing, unabashed bigot. Waving her hands across her forehead, Anissa said aloud, "Erase, Erase." She literally wanted to forget having ever met that woman.

Anissa had cut her hair very short and dyed it jet black. She liked it. It gave her a more sophisticated look. It wasn't cut in any particular style, just low to her neck in the back and long enough for bangs in the front. She wore large sunglasses all the time, rain or shine. She'd purchased several large wide brim hats she could pull down over her face whenever she felt threatened. And she felt threatened whenever she saw a tall blond man from a distance.

Many times she spotted a man who resembled Foley. Her immediate response was to quicken her pace and get out of sight to assess the situation. She'd turn into the doorway of a book store, restaurant, library, clothing store, coffee shop, or whatever was close. Then she'd linger and watch the man from a distance until she was absolutely certain that it was not Dr. Foley Brogdon. Only then would she move on. She imagined seeing him at least once a week. Her heart would jump to her mouth, she'd shake for hours afterward, but she would not let her guard down.

Charles Street, a very pleasant and busy thoroughfare, was her favorite street in all of Boston. Antique stores, gift shops, boutiques, bakeries, fabric stores, arts and crafts shops, and even art galleries lined the street. She loved it. She'd start her walk early on a Saturday morning and spend hours going in and out of the little shops. She'd set a dollar amount, and promise herself that she'd buy one thing. She'd shop until she found something that fit her budget. She had picked up some really unique items that way.

In the past she'd always avoided crowds, but now she loved them—safety in numbers. The one thing Foley would not do was hit her in front of people. He never wanted anyone to know that he beat his wife. In fact, he never referred to it as beating. He called it discipline and training. He trained her to do what he wanted her to do and when she didn't do it, she had to be disciplined. "You're like a little child Niss; you can't seem to remember from one day to the next what I've told you to do or not to do. You have to learn, and discipline is the best way."

She shuddered. She didn't want to think about him. She shook her head—how she used to love that man! He just seemed so perfect. She could see him now with his running shorts on. His physique was slender, but he was muscular and his calves were so strong. He'd been a distance runner in college for two years before he gave it up competitively, but continued the training even after they were married. They had that in common—running.

Anissa and her friend Carlie had both been members of the track team in high school and were both great sprinters. Carlie ran the 2nd leg of their 4-by-100 relay team, while Anissa ran the anchor. They'd competed once against each other in the 100-meter dash in a county meet and Carlie had won, because Anissa had a false start. Considering herself the better athlete, Anissa practiced starting the race relentlessly until she was certain that she'd never lose a race again because of movement before the gun.

Their relay team won the state championship two years in a row, and Anissa still held the record for the 200-meter race at their high school. Her prowess earned her a scholarship to Tennessee State University to blaze the same track that

Wilma Rudolph had. Carlie wanted to attend TSU as well, but her father insisted that she apply to Johns Hopkins, and when the acceptance letter came, all thoughts of becoming a Tennessee Tiger Belle were driven from her mind; her father had worked too hard for her to give up an opportunity like that.

When Anissa and Foley were together she ran as often as she could, depending on her physical condition. When he beat her, she sometimes had difficulty walking afterward, and running would have been out of the question. He was up before dawn five mornings a week running. She wondered if he still did.

Chapter Eighty-Seven
May 2002

Foley walked through his gate and closed it. He bent forward and touched his toes. He then leaned backwards as far as he could, trying to stretch out his legs and his back. He looked very handsome in his jogging shorts and sleeveless Nike shirt. He started off with a nice trot. He waved at a few neighborly women who always seemed to be outside when he ran. He crossed over the street and picked up speed.

Running cleared his head. He had erased all evidence of Anissa's existence from his house. His next project was to have the wall that surrounded their property taken down. He no longer needed it. Nor did he need the house. His mother had made many not so subtle remarks about the residence.

"FJ, do you think you need this entire house? It's too big for one person," she'd said, implying that his wife would not return.

"I have no idea, mother. When Anissa comes back we'll decide together."

He'd left it at that. He didn't like talking back to his mother. He knew that she had a different sort of temperament. She could smolder for years and then explode. She'd done something to Foley's father to cause him to change. He had been a strong, virile man when Foley left to go to camp one summer. And then, he was in and out of the hospital with surgeries, and since then walked with a cane. He'd not been the same man, his hands and feet crippled with rheumatoid arthritis. He deferred to Lacy for every decision, and Foley could swear that his father had not laid hands on his mother for years.

Foley jogged in place at the corner as a car turned left across his path. He continued his run, thinking about his mother, and how she had become dangerous. But then, so had he. One reason he had no friends was because of his ruthlessness. A cool, calm veneer with pristine manners belied the malice brewing beneath the surface. He'd been planning the things that he'd do to Anissa whenever he found her. They would not be nice.

And as for Merlot Candy. If he was so doggone good at his job, why hadn't he found something yet? His father had spoken highly of him. In a weak moment Foley had felt helpless and begged his father to assist him, but too much time was passing. Anissa could be anywhere by now.

So he'd put out some feelers; gone underground and devised a plan of his own. This thing with Anissa had become like a game of chess, a game that Foley had mastered at an early age. The trick was to see your next three moves before you made your first.

Chapter Eighty-Eight
May 2002

When Kathy Stockton drove her Mercedes into her entry gate, she noticed a car that she had never seen before parked on the side of the road. That set off alarms in her head. Nothing like that ever happened on her dead end street. Each house sat on at least five acres of lawn, trees, or fenced in pasture for horses, and each house had a driveway long enough to accommodate a number of cars. There was no reason for a car to be parked like that in the middle of the day. Her own house was a long way from the road and almost hidden by a mixture of pine trees and large shrubs that flowered in the spring. She lived alone, so she had a gate to keep out uninvited guests. No one came to their street unless they were on a mission. So to see a car just sitting there was more than suspicious. It was a call to arms.

The first thing she did when she got inside was to call the police chief. She knew him personally. She'd made it her business to know as many people of authority as she could, because one could always use friends with power.

"George, this is Kathy Stockton. There's a car parked near my driveway and I don't like it. I want to know who it is. Can you get one of your guys to stop the car and go through the driver's license and registration routine? You know how we are about our privacy around here."

"No problem, Mrs. Stockton. I'll get someone right on it. Is the car there now?"

"I don't know. I just came in and it was there. It was a dark SUV. Maybe he's there or maybe he's gone, but he can only go left or right out of here and that's a long road to the next major intersection in either direction. If you hurry, your guys should be able to spot him easily."

"I'll get right on it and I'll call you back when I know something."

"Thanks, George, you're the best!"

Kathy hung up the phone and then made a routine check to make certain that all the doors and windows were locked.

She never went on the second floor unless she had guests. All of her living was done on the main level. She'd been knocked down those stairs so many times by her husband that she never wanted to remind herself by climbing them. After he died, she'd had a master bedroom built on the main floor. It was large and airy with lots of windows that let in the light. She'd spent too many days in bed in the dark with the curtains drawn when he was alive, trying to heal from his brutal beatings.

Living with that man and enduring all of his cruelty had taught her one thing: to never underestimate the resolve of a man. Foley Brogdon had money and influence. His pride was sorely hurt. His punching bag had escaped him and he would do anything to get her back. Since he had no idea where she was, he would no doubt hire help to find her. A good private investigator would do the trick. There were excellent men in that field, she knew that, and he would be willing to pay whatever they wanted to do the job. He wouldn't hire someone to kill her. He wanted to do that himself—of that she was certain. And there was no doubt in her mind that he would want her dead. There was just no other way to salvage his ego. He was a victim now. He had warned her that if she left him he would kill her. He'd told her that if he couldn't have her, no one else would. And as sure as the sun rises, he meant those words and he would carry out his threat.

She shook her head as she thought of the many battered women who'd shared with her that their husbands made the same threat—a threat that Kathy's own husband made. She believed that he would have killed her, and like nearly all abused women, she had been afraid to risk running. Now she knew that the key to running, to leaving an abusive man, was leaving after the first lick and never going back once you did. Leaving after the first violent act would catch most men off guard. They would not be prepared to carry out a threat, because they would not have been given time to make one. Unfortunately, most women in a persecutory situation convinced themselves that it would never happen again. But it always happens again. And again.

For the first time in her life, Kathy was involved in a real life game of cat and mouse with a woman who had actually taken that leap of faith into the unknown, risking everything to escape a life of being abused and demoralized. She was an outsider looking in at Anissa, the mouse and the big cat, Foley. True to the nature of the cat, once he had the mouse he would torture it for a while and then kill it. She would not let Anissa die. Foley could not catch her. Kathy believed in having a back-up plan, but now she needed a back-up to the back-up plan and then a sidebar to that.

She went to her room and pulled out her little black book. George would call her soon to let her know if he'd learned anything. In the meantime she had another call to make.

Chapter Eighty-Nine
May 2002

Merlot Candy sat in his car relishing his good fortune. He'd found the house that Lynn Stockton had supposedly visited and he now knew who lived there. The woman who resided in the home, Kathy Stockton, was loaded. She had old money, new money, and used money. If Anissa Brogdon, a.k.a. Lynn Stockton, got out of Georgia without a trace she had to have had money or a friend with money. This woman could be the missing link, and wasn't it a coincidence that her last name was Stockton too?

He needed to tie the two of them together. If Kathy had helped Anissa run, then chances were, they were in contact with each other. He would have to bug her phones, tail her, and get a look at her mail. For all of that he needed help. He never liked to be the face that people could remember later. He was too upstanding a citizen for that. He liked his work; he was good at it and he never hurt anyone unless they tried to hurt him first. He tried to stay on the right side of the law at all times. But he had a few acquaintances that would eradicate the law for the right number of dollars.

He was able to get a glimpse of the woman in the Mercedes when she turned into her driveway. She had red hair and was in no way a paleface. She had a nice tan even for this time of year. Her lips were red. She appeared to be late thirties or early forties. That's all he could tell. But she didn't see him. She never even glanced in his direction. He had counted on her being a woman like his mother, so confident in her little world that she was never aware that danger could be lurking in plain sight.

He started his car and pulled away. At the end of the street he stopped at the stop sign, looked both ways and then looked both ways again. He made a left turn and drove less than a mile when he noticed the blue light flashing behind him.

He pulled over and stopped. From his rear view mirror, he watched the officer get out of his car and walk toward him.

He stopped when he reached Merlot's window. Merlot hit the automatic button and lowered the window halfway.

"May I see your license and registration, sir?" the officer asked.

"What's the problem, officer? I wasn't speeding. I use cruise control for such a time as this."

"Just a routine check, sir. We've had an APB on a car fitting your description, so we're checking every one we see. Your license and registration please."

Merlot didn't like it, but he did as the policeman asked. The officer took the documents and walked back to his car to run the necessary inquiries. Merlot wondered what kind of APB he could have received. Was it the usual? All persons black? The police car had come out of nowhere. He didn't notice it when he pulled out. It didn't matter; he was an above-board citizen who had not broken any laws. It also occurred to him that Kathy Stockton might have seen him after all and had placed the call to the police. A woman with influence.

The police officer came back to the car about fifteen minutes later and returned his license and registration.

"I'm sorry to have interrupted your day, Mr. Candy. You enjoy the rest of your afternoon, and drive safely."

"And you do the same, Officer Tindy," Merlot said, wanting the cop to know that he knew his name. He had his badge number, too. "For future reference!" he said to himself as he drove away. He would do well not to underestimate the Stockton woman. If anything, she provided a challenge, and he loved a good challenge.

Chapter Ninety
May 2002

"Mrs. Stockton, this is George over at the police department. One of my deputies just stopped your man leaving a few minutes ago."

"That's good news, George. Who was he? Not an escaped criminal I hope."

George laughed. "No, ma'am. His name is Merlot Candy, spelled just like the wine and the chocolate. He lives in Atlanta, has no hits on his driving record, no record of any citations, accidents, nothing. My deputy said he was well dressed, well mannered, hadn't been drinking or nothing. He is a black boy, but he seemed to be a good one—an apparent upstanding citizen. Hope that helps you. If he was up to no good, he'll have better sense than to carry it out, because he now knows that we know who he is. If you see him around again, let us know and we'll get tough next time."

"Thanks again, George."

Kathy hung up and then immediately dialed a number.

"Speak," said the brusque voice on the other end.

"His name is Merlot Candy and he lives in Atlanta."

"I'll see what I can do."

Kathy hung up and sat for a few minutes staring at the phone. If it was as she had suspected, Merlot Candy was a private investigator hired by Foley Brogdon. If so, he had found her. But how? It really didn't matter how, what mattered was that he knew who she was. He could use her to get to Anissa, unless she was very careful. She had tried so hard to cover Anissa's tracks that she had never considered covering her own.

"This guy may be good, but so am I, and I've got friends who are better," she said aloud.

Now what? Now she had to be very careful. Now the most important thing was to make sure she didn't lead Foley and his investigator to Anissa. She'd have to change her plans to visit Boston for Anissa's birthday. Or maybe she wouldn't see her at all for a while. There was really no reason to do so. She considered Anissa a friend and friends liked seeing each other, but in a life- or-death situation such as this one you had to put sentimentality aside and use your head. And Kathy knew how to use hers.

She would have to tell Anissa that they should cool it for a while without alarming her. Maybe she'd tell Josefina instead. Anissa was human after all and could only take so much. There was no need to throw her into a panic; Kathy could do the worrying and the watching. She just needed to make certain that Foley never set foot in Boston while Anissa was there.

Chapter Ninety-One
June 2002

At 9:00 a.m. on Tuesday June 4th, Kathy was awakened by a buzz at the gate. She was expecting no one, so she was suspicious. She had kept her eyes peeled for an appearance by Merlot Candy, who, as she now knew, was a private dick, indeed, but so far he had not returned.

"Yes?" she spoke into the intercom.

"Telephone company, ma'am."

"Yes? May I help you?"

"I just wanted to let you know that we'll be working on the lines so you may get a little static, but we should finish up before noon."

"What's wrong?"

"Nothing, ma'am, just putting in new cable. We just like to let you know we're here."

"Thank you very much."

"No problem, ma'am."

Kathy lay thinking momentarily. That was odd. When was the last time the telephone company had been in their area? There was no new construction, no bad weather to down lines, so why were they here? And why did they announce themselves to the residents? That was a tad too much customer service. Was she getting too paranoid? No. Merlot Candy was a private investigator. But would he go so far as to bug her phones? She was not taking any chances. She smiled to herself, thinking that Merlot didn't know who he was dealing with. She got up and dressed to watch and wait. She spent a lot of time in the yard while they worked. As soon as they left the area she called a friend to request that some of his friends come and check the outside lines and sweep her house—the common vernacular for looking for bugged phones.

Chapter Ninety-Two
June 2002

Merlot was not your typical run-of-the-mill private investigator. He was shrewd and crafty—never taking anything at face value. Like most folk who are naturally suspicious, he knew that if a telephone company showed up at his door without his request, he would be on high alert, especially if he was involved in helping a woman who was presumed dead. He also knew that for Anissa to hide in plain sight, her friend Kathy would have to have connections. He was also pretty confident that she knew who he was based on that little trumped up traffic stop near her home and a tip from Glenn Baush that someone had recently run a thorough background check on him.

Any connected person worth his salt would advise a friend to have telephone lines checked after an unwarranted visit from the telephone company. So he sent some of his employees there in pretense of working on phone lines in order to place taps. He himself borrowed a florist truck from another business associate and drove down the street a few hours after his men had finished.

He grinned when he saw the cars parked near the road and a crew of men inspecting the telephone box and wires. They would find the taps and remove them. Kathy Stockton could go back to believing that she was safe. But then he'd place the next taps himself. If she knew Anissa Brogdon and if she was helping her, she was bound to speak to her sooner than later. All he had to do was wait; and borrow a lot of business trucks.

He had an associate who was very good at getting cell phone numbers, tapping cell phones, and using microphones to listen in on any conversation. Soon he would have an ear on Kathy Stockton.

Chapter Ninety-Three
June 2002

Kathy looked across the table at her best friend in the world, Geoffrey Winston. His blue eyes pierced hers. They were comfortably relaxed in the sitting area of her bedroom, languishing over cognac after a dinner of steak, salad, and green beans. Dessert had been apple pie with vanilla ice cream.

"Are you sure you want to keep this up Kathy? I'm worried about you," his voice showed his obvious concern.

"Of course I want to keep it up. I'm in it to win it. Anissa cannot go back to Foley. So we have to stay a few steps ahead of him at all times." Kathy sipped from her snifter.

"And if he ever does catch up to her, you could be in danger too. These men are quick to blame everyone except themselves. I don't want to see you get hurt. I won't allow you to place yourself in danger."

"I'm fine," Kathy replied as she lay back against the cushions of the yellow sofa. "Don't worry about me. I use you as a sounding board, not to get you emotionally involved in my problems. I can take care of myself." Kathy suddenly sat forward, placing her glass on the table. "Now listen, if this private investigator does find Anissa, I've got to have an exit plan for her."

"Exit plans are my strong suit," he smiled.

"She needs to be ready to leave town at the drop of a dime. I'm going to need new identification for her."

"As you wish. I'm one step ahead of you. We always used a system in the witness protection program that lets people use names that begin with the same letter as their real first and last names. That helps them to remember who they were. That's why I didn't like you calling her Lynn. But we're on track now. She's Ms. Ansasha Barnes in Boston. Going forward, if we need to, her initials will always be A.B. Okay?"

The fact that Geoffrey still had connections with the United States Marshal's office played heavily in Kathy's favor. It was no problem for him to ask for help with hiding someone who was in mortal danger, as long as they were not criminals. All he needed to do was make contact, and in twenty-four hours later he would hold in his hand pertinent documents to establish a new identity.

"I don't know what I'd do without you, Geoffrey." Kathy put her arms around his neck and snuggled in close.

'Unless you choose, you will not have to do without me, Kathy, I love you."

"Is it me you love or is it my money?" she teased. "Your money!"

They both laughed. He covered her mouth with his. She loved to kiss him and each time that he touched his tongue to hers, she resisted the strong urge to confess her love for him. Mutual love could mess things up. They were good together the way it was. No need to change things.

Kathy liked sex as much as he did. He pulled her sweater over her head and unsnapped her bra, freeing her breasts. He cupped both in his hands and began to knead her nipples as she moaned softly. He trailed kisses down her neck to her right breast. He circled the dark patch with his tongue and then sucked the nipple into his mouth. She moaned again. He lifted her skirt and when he inserted two of his fingers into her sex, she was ready for him. Later, in bed together, he showed her that it was not money he was after.

"I love you so much," he whispered.

"I know you do," Kathy sighed.

Minutes later he snored softly. Kathy slipped out of bed to phone Anissa.

"Hey, lady!" Kathy chirped into the phone.

"Hi, Kathy! How are you? Where have you been?" Anissa asked.

"You got my message from Josefina?"

"Yes, she told me that you wouldn't talk to me for a day or two. What's up? I've missed you!"

"Geoffrey wants to take me to Los Angeles for some one-on-one time. I've been sort of neglecting him lately. You don't mind do you? I need a little R & R. How are you doing? You still like your job?'

"I love it! I almost wish I'd graduated from Boston University. The faculty is great and the kids are really nice. I actually enjoy working in the language lab. I get a chance to talk to the students that want to be foreign language teachers. It's just great," Anissa gushed with excitement.

"I'm sorry about this. It just came up at the last minute. And I'd take you with me if I could, but I just don't think it would be a good idea." Kathy honestly felt sad that she wouldn't be there for Anissa's birthday. But it was safer if she stayed away for a while.

"Nor do I. You go ahead and get your freak on. Have fun and tell Geoffrey I said hello and thank him for me for the millionth time."

"I will. When I get back, I'm coming up and staying for two weeks; you'll get tired of me."

"Never, you're too good to me!"

"I do my best."

"And your best is good enough! Why this cloak and dagger routine with the phone call? I'm still safe aren't I? Josefina told me that you didn't want me to call you on my cell. Is something going on?" Anissa asked warily.

"Nothing. You know I always say that we can never be too careful. We'll talk when I get back. Love you, sweetie."

"I love you too, Kathy. Enjoy your trip. I'm sorry you're not coming up for my birthday; I planned to cook and everything. But oh well, I'll take the day off anyway, and do some more sightseeing."

"Good idea. Listen, I have to go, Geoffrey's here, but I'll talk to you soon. I'll phone you from Los Angeles, okay?"

"Okay, talk to you soon."

Chapter Ninety-Four
June 2002

Anissa held the phone in her hand for a long time. Something was wrong. Kathy had been evasive and something in her tone had been guarded. She'd tell her if Foley was on her tracks, wouldn't she? *Yes she would*, Anissa told herself firmly, trying to calm down. Perhaps something was going on with Kathy's personal life. After all, not everything in Kathy's life revolved around Anissa.

Anissa would have to find something else to do on her birthday. She'd planned to spend it with Kathy, the only confidant that she had. Except for Carlie. But their friendship seemed to have dissipated when Anissa got married. So many times Anissa had hoped that she would show up and realize that something was wrong. But Carlie had stayed away. She never called, wrote, or visited. Anissa had been thinking about her often since she'd heard her voice at Lenox Mall.

She couldn't blame Carlie for withdrawing. Anissa had not reached out to her either. Maybe Carlie felt that Anissa had withdrawn. Foley did not allow her to call or write or visit anyone. He kept her isolated from her former life, and made her live his. Maybe now would be a good time to find out if Carlie was still a friend.

Carlie Harper and her family had moved from New York City to Chester, South Carolina in September of their ninth grade year. Carlie's grandfather had owned seventy-five acres of farmland that her father, an only child, decided to sell. Carlie couldn't believe that she had to move to a dismal place like Chester. They'd met the first day of school and each was a breath of fresh air to the other. Carlie didn't talk like the rest of the kids and she didn't look like them. Not ladylike at all, she constantly said "I can't believe this shit!" referring to everything about Chester. She was a thinker. She never made a decision without thinking it through first, even down to parting her hair on the left or right or down the middle. Anissa liked that about her. She especially appreciated Carlie's brashness and her willingness to resort to fists if necessary.

Anissa had to smile when she thought about all this while using directory assistance to track down Carlie's father to get a phone number to reach her friend. She dialed it immediately, but hung up before the first ring. Should she call? What if Foley had arranged to have Carlie watched or her phones bugged? She couldn't put her friend's life in danger. She didn't really worry about Mr. Harper, because Carlie had always referred to him as a 'scary man.'

"We don't know what my father does for a living and my mother says don't ask. Just enjoy the good life," Carlie answered when Anissa asked about her father's employment.

"We think he's a spy, but that's hard to believe considering he's black and all. He'd have a hard time going under cover," Carlie laughed. But there was something very mysterious about Mr. Harper. He was gone a lot and when he was around he was very quiet. If anyone could be trusted with a secret, Mr. Harper was it. Deciding that she had nothing to lose, she dialed the number again.

"Hello," a male voice answered.

"Mr. Harper?"

"Yes."

"This is Anissa, Carlie's friend."

Silence on the end of the line became thick enough to cut. "Let me ask you something," he said. "What was the crazy response that you and Carlie had for anyone who pissed you off?"

Anissa paused.

"We said kiss our striped, rocking-chair behinds."

They'd really said 'asses' but Anissa did not feel comfortable using that language with an elder. She had not thought about that silliness for years. Carlie would tell people to kiss her black ass in a minute. But, according to her friend, Anissa could do no such thing.

"Your mother is black and your dad was white. That makes you a zebra. Technically you don't have a black ass. Yours is striped." The rocking chair part was added to make them laugh.

A long sigh on the other end. "This is a surprise, Anissa. I'd heard that you perished on 9/11."

For the next forty-five minutes Anissa told Mr. Harper everything. When she finished she was crying.

"I commend you for your decision. Now, if you want to see Carlie, we will have to be clandestine about it. I don't want either one of you hurt. I will send her an email. I will tell her that her striped, rocking chair friend has recovered and wants to talk. Then I'll buy two burner phones, overnight one to Carlie and one to you addressed to the maid who works for you, along with the phone number of Carlie's cell. When you get it, then, and only then, make contact. If Carlie comes to visit, tell her to take a wild goose chase. She knows what that means. She will take a route that only a bird could follow. And Anissa, be careful. Abusive men are dangerous. Now spell Josefina's name for me."

Anissa hung up, feeling cleansed and happy. Mr. Harper was indeed a scary man. He'd asked the most unusual questions to get the facts about Foley and his abuse. And then to use a code? And burner phones? Maybe he had been a spy. Or an undercover cop.

Two days later, after receiving the phone and thinking about it another day, Anissa dialed the number that Mr. Harper had enclosed with the phone.

"Hello?" Carlie gasped into the phone. She sounded like she'd been running.

"Carlie?" Anissa asked. The silence was loud on the other end of the phone.

"Carlie?" Anissa spoke again. "Carlie it's me. It's Nissa."

"With the striped rocking chair ass?" Carlie asked suspiciously.

"That's me, girl." Anissa couldn't help but laugh. It was so good to hear that brashness again.

"Anissa? You have got to be kidding me! Foley said that you died, but I knew that was your yellow ass I saw in Atlanta! I couldn't believe it when my dad emailed me the other day. What the hell is going on?"

Anissa took a deep breath and plunged ahead.

"He thought I died. I wanted him to think I was dead. Oh Carlie, you were so right about him. He was too good to be true. He's a monster, Carlie. He beat the daylights out of me all the time. On 9/11, when so many people were presumed dead, I saw a chance to escape from him and I took it. But I wanted to let you know that I'm okay. I heard you at the mall that day, but was too afraid to answer!"

"Girl ! I don't know what to say. First, I thought my dad had lost his mind, but he never gets anything confused. I didn't know anybody else with a striped ass so, it had to be you. I've been so nervous waiting for you to call. The last time I'd heard from you was this strange letter. Whenever I tried calling, I was told that you didn't want to talk to me. And then you're dead. I'm glad that you're okay and still alive and everything, but seriously why did you cut me off like that?"

Anissa was puzzled. What was Carlie talking about?

"What do you mean? What letter?" Anissa's hand began to tremble. She had not written a letter to Carlie.

"Right after your honeymoon you sent me a letter telling me you didn't want to have anything to do with anyone in your past. Sounded like you were suddenly too good for all of us. You freaking wished me a happy future! I tried to call you, but Foley always answered. At first, I didn't know what to make of it, but after calling several times and always getting the same answer, I let it go."

"I didn't write to you, Carlie. I wasn't allowed to reach out to anyone."

"Oh, come on, girl. The letter was all typed and everything, but that was your signature."

That's when Anissa remembered all those sheets of blank stationery with her signature—supposedly practicing for a signature stamp. Frustration, anger, and desperation caved in on her, and she couldn't help it, but she needed her friend.

"Just come see me, Carlie. I'll tell you all about it. I need to tell you everything."

"Anissa, I can't tell you how often I wanted to come to your home and ask you to tell me what was going on. It was as if you had disappeared from the face of the earth. I'm so glad to hear from you finally, girl!"

"Do you still have the letter?"

"Yes, why?"

"I'll explain later. Just bring it with you."

And then she took a leap of faith. “I’m in Boston. I’m living in a huge apartment all by myself and my birthday is coming up and I don’t want to be alone. Come help me celebrate!”

“When, honey? Just say the word.”

“Today! As soon as you can. We’ve got a lot to catch up on. Get a pencil and I’ll give you the address. Tell your boss it’s an emergency; of life and death, because it is. My life. Carlie, whatever you do, don’t tell anyone that you’ve spoken to me. Promise me.”

Anissa crossed her fingers even though she wasn’t the one doing the promising.

“And make everybody think I’m crazy? Don’t worry. Girl, I am a pediatrician with my own practice. I’m my own boss so I ain’t gotta lie to nobody!”

“And your dad? He must really be a spy. He said to tell you to go on a wild goose chase.”

“Girl, like I told you, we don’t talk about my father and what he does for a living. Hold on and let me get a pencil.”

Chapter Ninety-Five
June 2002

When Kathy Stockton ended her call, Merlot sat back in his pizza delivery car and smiled. He had Anissa Brogdon. She was in Boston. He didn't know exactly where she lived, but he knew where she worked. Boston University in the foreign language lab.

Bingo!

He should call Foley Brogdon and tell him, but something nagged at him, causing him to procrastinate. He had had this sensation in a few other cases in the past, and it had always been because he had missed something. What had he missed this time?

He had not yet followed up on the report he'd requested from Glenn. Glenn had dug up some sealed juvenile record which had yet to be unsealed.

Merlot trusted Glenn implicitly— he was sharp and he was methodical. He rarely missed anything and it was unusual for him to take this long to complete a report. It was time for Merlot to put some pressure on Glenn. He needed to know more about Foley, because he was sure that he was lying to him. So no, he would not call Dr. Brogdon just yet, not until he got Glenn's report. In the meantime, he'd continue the job on his own.

Merlot had learned that Anissa's house in Powder Springs had belonged to Kathy. Ergo, any place of residence owned, leased, or rented by Kathy Stockton in Boston or the surrounding area would be a very good place to start looking.

If Anissa used an alias in Powder Springs there was a good chance that she was using an alias in Boston. So he had two options for finding her: one, he could stake out the language lab at the University, or two, he could locate her place of residence. The latter would involve time, the former would not. He would start there.

Chapter Ninety-Six
June 2002

Juneteenth, a combination of the word June and nineteenth, is a holiday observed in the African American community to celebrate the emancipation of slaves in the state of Texas. The freshly penned Emancipation Proclamation signed by President Lincoln in 1862 had been ignored by Texas citizens. Therefore, federal troops led by union officer, General Gordon Granger, rode into Galveston to force the state to abide by the law. On June 19, 1865, General Granger read the proclamation to the public from a hotel balcony. The newly freed slaves began celebrating the holiday the following year.

Merlot Candy, a free man indeed, had thoroughly enjoyed his dinner at the Top of the Hub restaurant in the Prudential Tower on Boylston Street in the Back Bay neighborhood of Boston. The view was spectacular, so much so that he didn't mind dining alone. Boston was considered the unofficial capital of New England, and it was a great place to be.

He'd arrived early enough to do some shopping so he'd worn a new outfit for dinner. He was very pleased to have found a salmon pink shirt in one of the shops in the Prudential Center mall. He truly enjoyed a nice pink shirt. He knew that some men would find that disturbing, and others would understand, but he lived as he pleased.

The meal had been delicious. He started with soup and the arugula salad. He chose both because he had a very healthy appetite. The main course was a filet mignon with a loaded baked potato and asparagus on the side. For dessert, he had two servings of the chocolate tart. Afterward he went up to the skywalk observatory, to get a view of the city. Juneteenth was the coming Wednesday and he had no plans for the day. His purpose for being in the city was to find Anissa Brogdon.

He stood outside the foreign language building watching the students going in and out. It had been a long time since he'd been on the campus but he knew his way around. When he was at Harvard, he had dated several girls who attended

Boston University. With more than 30,000 students, it was one of the largest private universities in the United States, and with a faculty of approximately 4,000 members, it was the city's largest employer. Nobel laureate, Martin Luther King, Jr., Pulitzer Prize winner, Joseph Hallinan, and Guggenheim and Macarthur fellows like Romare Bearden and William Brumfield were among its faculty and alumni. And the basketball team played Division 1. Merlot had attended a lot of their games.

He waited until about 10:30 a.m. When he finally entered the Geddes foreign language lab, quite a few students were already hard at work. He stood just inside the door looking around when a soft voice behind him spoke.

"May I see your identification please?"

He turned to look directly into the brown eyes of Anissa Brogdon. He whistled softly inside himself. Her picture did her no justice. She was a living doll. The hair was different, short and black, but he was sure it was her.

"My identification?" was all that he could manage.

"Yes, your student identification."

"Oh! That. Well. I'm not a student. I'm actually looking for a job here."

"You've come to the wrong place. Job applications can be made on line or in person with Human Resources on the Charles River Campus or the Medical Campus."

"That's too bad, but the good thing is that I get to meet you, Miss…?"

"Ansasha Barnes, lab coordinator. And you are?"

"Marvin Bell. Nice to meet you. You like working here?"

"Yes, I do. And I want to keep my job, so I'm going to get to work and you're going to leave. Goodbye, Mr. Bell."

"Goodbye? I'm leaving?" Surely she wasn't dismissing him. Maybe he needed to pour on more of his allurement.

She laughed at his question, tilting her head to the left. He liked Anissa Brogdon. She had a nice laugh.

"You most certainly are. By the way I like that pink shirt!"

"Thank you." He smiled his most charming smile and moved in closer so that she could smell his cologne.

"Bye, Mr. Bell." Merlot's eyebrows went up a notch. Was this pretty lady ignoring his magnetism?

"Bye, Miss Barnes. It is Miss, not Mrs.?"

"That would be telling, Mr. Bell. Have a nice day!" She turned and walked down an aisle of listening stations, leaving him to watch the sway of her hips and to admire her form.

Try as he might, he could not imagine her having a drug problem. She didn't look the part. But what did he know? She'd smiled at him, they'd had a three second conversation, and now he knew her? No, he didn't. But then again, Foley Brogdon was a good-looking man with a lot of money. Why would a woman in her right mind leave that? He knew there was more to Foley than met the eye, and there was probably more to Anissa than met the eye, too. But his eye was a private eye and it was his job to see what others missed.

He had seen her. Now his next task was to follow her home. The feeling of triumph he usually felt at a time like this in a missing person's case eluded him. And he couldn't understand why. Nor could he understand the feeling of anticipation he felt at seeing her again. What he did know was that Glenn should have his report on Foley Brogdon on Merlot's desk by the time he returned to Atlanta. Merlot wanted to read it before giving away Anissa's whereabouts.

He waited at a coffee shop across the street for the lab to close. He wanted to follow Anissa when she left work. He wanted to get to know her routine. A good look around the campus made clear that exiting the front of the building on Commonwealth was the best way to get to the green line for the 'T' or a taxi. If she had a car he was out of luck today and would have to start over again tomorrow.

He sat at a small table near the window and sipped his coffee. He was lucky; at 5:17 p.m. she walked out. She was wearing a big brown floppy hat with a bright orange scarf around her neck. She was also wearing dark glasses, but he recognized the sway of her hips. He watched her as she walked towards the 'T' stop. With each step, his heartbeat quickened. He loved the way she moved. She knew how to use her hips for sure. He gulped the last of his coffee, walked out, and quickly crossed the street.

A crowd of people stood waiting, so he pulled up the collar of his jacket and blended in at the far end. There were at least fifty feet and about as many people between them. Anissa kept her head down, not looking at anyone in particular. The train arrived, and Merlot stepped on last. He grabbed onto the overhead rung near the operator, facing front. He would remain like so many travelers: inconspicuous.

At Park Street, where all lines merged, he hurried along to insure that he'd be on the same train as Anissa. Once again, she walked all the way down the track away from the crowd. Merlot hung back. When the doors opened he entered with the fray and had to stand again.

When the train stopped at Harvard Square, he was glad she was wearing that big hat; otherwise, he would have missed her. She got off with a large assembly of people and walked down the sidewalk. He had just enough time to get off before the doors closed. He crossed over to the opposite side of the street and kept his eyes on her. She slowed down to window shop. Suddenly he had an idea. He hurried ahead, and crossed over to her side of the street, and started walking back toward Anissa. His plan was to catch her eye and then begin their conversation where they'd left off.

It would not be a coincidence for him to run into her on the same day that they'd met, but he was confident that he could pull it off. She was still walking slowly, stopping to peer at the displays in the windows. Merlot was upon her.

"Hi! Miss Barnes, right? Boston foreign language lab? Remember me?"

Anissa turned to look at him, recognition showing on her face.

"Hi yourself? What are you doing here?"

"I'm heading to the bookstore. What are you doing here?"

"Minding my business. Enjoy your day, Mr. Bell." She continued down the sidewalk. He was impressed that she remembered his name.

"Wait a minute! Can we talk for a few minutes?"

"Why?"

"I don't know. Just to be friendly human beings?" This lady was a real escape artist.

“I’ve got things to do. I’m sure so do you,” she said not looking at him at all.

“I’m not in a hurry. Guess what? I think I may get a job at Boston U. Then we’ll be fellow employees, so we might as well get to know each other a little.” He smiled at her. Merlot was not conceited, nor was he a player. He knew he was handsome and he knew he possessed a considerable amount of charm. He had never had difficulty with the ladies. Nor had he ever had to push himself on a woman. Either she would give in or she’d at least smile and give him something to hope for.

“Good for you. Now don’t let me keep you any longer.” She smiled, waved her hand, and went into the store. Merlot looked inside and saw bars and bars of soap. It smelled so fresh and clean inside. He looked at the window and a saw that the store was called Lush. Part of him wanted to follow her and make a complete idiot of himself, yet the more rational part forced him to keep walking down the street. That was the first time he’d been given the brush off and he didn’t like it. Not one bit.

Chapter Ninety-Seven
June 2002

Anissa looked back as Marvin Bell walked away. He was a very attractive man, tall, and with a good sense of humor. Something about him carried a strong magnetic pull and it had taken all of her strength to walk away from him. Another time, another place. She picked up a bar of soap and sniffed it.

"May I help you?" asked the salesgirl.

"Please," Anissa responded, considering that she'd broken her rule of not talking to strangers.

Two days later, she was surprised as she passed Marvin jogging along the Charles River at 6:00 a.m.

"Hello again," he stopped, breathing hard. Anissa waved her hand and kept her pace. He turned and fell into step beside her.

"We've got to stop meeting like this," she said.

"I disagree. How are you?"

"I'm fine. If I didn't know any better, I'd think you were following me."

"Moi? Perish the thought. It's a public place, right? I've been running here every day since I moved here. I'm just early today. I usually run at 8."

"Well, I'm done by then. As a matter of fact I'm done now." She stopped, glancing at her watch as she jogged in place at a slower pace to cool down. "I usually get a cup of hot chocolate and the paper and walk back home. So I'll see you around." She walked away.

"May I join you?" Marvin called out behind her.

"Why?" She did not look back. She hated being rude, but she could not afford new friendships. She could not afford men.

"Why not? Look, I'm not a freak, I'm just lonely. Please let me buy you that cup of hot chocolate." He smiled at her as he caught up.

Every fiber in Anissa's being sounded an alarm. She knew that she should refuse, but he was just too darn good-looking, especially with that smile. A cup of hot chocolate couldn't hurt. She'd never tell him anything about her personal life. And maybe she could convince him that she was not to be pursued.

"Fifteen minutes and I have to get back, okay? I don't know how much conversation we can have in that length of time, but I'm game if you are." She decided then that her words would be short and curt.

Instead, they talked for almost two hours about nothing in particular and everything in general. Out of the blue, he'd asked about her plans for Juneteenth, and had appeared surprised that she knew about the holiday.

"What? I look ignorant to you?" she'd asked teasingly.

"No, it's just that a lot of . . . I mean," he'd stammered, clearly embarrassed. She knew what he meant. A lot of African-Americans were not aware of the holiday. She enjoyed watching him squirm, and everything else about him, too. She really liked Marvin Bell, and now more than ever she regretted that she was on the run.

Chapter Ninety-Eight
June 2002

Merlot knew that his job was to locate Anissa, find her roosting place, establish her patterns, and report to her husband. He had done all the research he needed to do and knew what he had been paid to find out, and yet he was not inclined to inform his client, Foley Brogdon. The longer he had talked to Anissa, the more he'd felt that there was pain in her life, yet not the kind of pain that comes with drugs or cheating. What he'd sensed from Anissa was deeper, darker, and laced with fear. She was terrified of something; Merlot had a sixth sense where fear was concerned.

The sight of a tall blond Caucasian male in the line ahead of them had made her hands shake. And a few minutes later, when another tall, blond Caucasian male had walked past the coffee shop right next to their table in the window, she had turned away her head as fast as possible, but not fast enough to hide the look of terror in her eyes. And then it hit him. Foley Brogdon was tall and blond and white. A woman running from her husband because she wants to live her life a different way does not jump out of her skin when she thinks she sees him. Instead, such a woman would brace herself for a confrontation, fueled by a power gained from living her own independent life. Anissa Brogdon behaved like someone who was running from danger. More and more it seemed that Foley Brogdon himself was that danger.

Merlot stayed until the end of the week and managed to 'run into' her one last time at the sandwich shop across from the university at lunch time.

"You again," she said with a smile when he discovered her in line.

"Me again. How are you?

"I'm fine," she answered turning her head toward the menu on the wall.

"*I'm* doing great! Thanks for asking."

Anissa laughed. He loved to hear her laugh. "That's good to know. Now excuse me, I'm trying to decide what I want for lunch," she said politely.

"I like their soup. Do you?" Merlot was fishing and he knew it. But he wasn't going to be put off that easily.

"No soup for me today."

"Do you mind if I join you for lunch?" She could say yes or no. Fine with him either way.

"Why, Mr. Bell? You and I are strangers and I'd like to keep it that way."

Okay so she tried to say yes. He just needed to help her out. "We're not strangers. We've had hot chocolate together, jogged a few feet together. People have moved in together knowing less about each other. We just don't know each other's taste in lunches well. But we can fix that."

"Listen, I usually eat in the lab. I order something to go and then back to campus I go."

This woman was a pro at playing hard to get. His pride was taking a beating, but no need to turn back now. He might as well lean into it.

"I really don't have a bacterial disease. I need to find the guy who started that rumor," he said lamely.

"You really do," she giggled.

"What do I have to do to persuade you to have lunch with me? Because I'll do anything."

"Anything?" she teased.

He looked into her eyes and felt his heart warming. "Anything," he responded.

"I guess if I'm that irresistible, I'll have to eat with you. But I pay for my own food."

Touchdown! She ordered a sandwich and coffee, and he took the chicken soup and a blueberry muffin with two cups of coffee—black.

"You know I don't think it's a coincidence that I keep running into you," Anissa said suddenly as they made themselves comfortable at a table for two in front of the window.

"I was supposed to have an interview this morning, but somebody else got the job. This looked like a nice place to grab something to eat and lick my wounds. I'll bet a lot of the people in here attend the university or work there. Is that a coincidence?"

Anissa openly breathed a sigh of relief. “Point taken. I’m a loner, Marvin Bell,” she said looking across the table into his eyes that held hers. “That’s how I like it and that’s how it’s going to remain. From this day forward, if you see me I’d appreciate it if you acted like you didn’t. ”

He looked at her and smiled. “Ansasha Barnes, I think you are a very nice lady and not bad to look at either. I promise you that after today you won’t see me again and I take no offense at your direct dismissal of me. Let’s finish our lunch,” he said earnestly.

They finished their meal with small talk about the weather, each concentrating on their food. Once outside she turned to say goodbye, but before she could get a word out, his mouth was on hers. At first softly, then with more pressure as he slipped his tongue inside her mouth and gently explored. She put her arms around his neck and kissed him back right there in front of God and everybody. For a few minutes there was nothing in the world but her mouth and his body close to hers. Then he abruptly pulled away. “Goodbye, Ansasha Barnes,” he said.

He turned and began to jog down the street.

Chapter Ninety-Nine
June 2002

Anissa was up early on Saturday morning. Carlie was due to arrive any minute. When the doorbell finally rang, she opened the door with such gusto that it rattled the doorstop. There stood Carlie, live and in color, with Louise Doud's head in the background, no doubt swimming with resentment at the sight of another of Anissa's kind in the building.

"Hey girl!" Anissa cried as she reached out to her friend with open arms.

"Hey girl!" Carlie responded. The two young women embraced and then stepped back and gave each other the once over. Anissa noticed that the door to Louise Doud's apartment closed.

"Girl, you look good! Death becomes you," Carlie exclaimed.

"Not as good as you. Come on in!" Anissa led the way inside and closed the door. "Look at you. Have you lost weight?" Carlie was beautiful. She was five nine, one hundred forty-five pounds, with a figure to die for. Her eyes were her most striking feature. Deep set with the most perfectly arched eyebrows and long silky eyelashes. Her pupils were light brown, but when she was emotional they turned very dark. Her skin color was dark chocolate.

"A few pounds. This staying up all hours of the night on call will do that for you. Girl, I'm tired, I want to sit down. Ooh, I like this place, whoever it belongs to!"

"My angel, Kathy Stockton. Let me show you how she rolls," Anissa took Carlie's bag, placed it on the floor, and took her by the hand to give her a tour of the apartment, coming to rest in the large family room with vaulted ceilings. The room was painted beige and in the center of the room sat a teal leather sofa. On the bar to the right, Josefina had prepared a bowl of salad and a tray of bruschetta with two place settings. Anissa poured two glasses of red wine.

"Let's eat, girl! I know those peanuts and biscotti on the plane did not do it for you."

"I'm not hungry, but I am thirsty" Carlie kicked off her shoes, carried the two glasses of wine to the sofa, and beckoned Anissa to follow.

"So tell me why you prefer death to life?" Carlie asked abruptly.

Anissa hesitated. She was stalling and she knew it. Telling Carlie about Foley was not going to be easy. How was she going to explain staying with him? Not being able to leave him?

Finally, Anissa took a deep breath. "Remember how you told me that you thought Foley was too good to be true?" she began. "And you said you wouldn't marry him?"

"Well, I didn't think he loved me, and that's important for the man I want to marry."

"Carlie, stop being silly! I need you to be serious."

"Okay. I remember. When someone appears to be perfect in every way, they usually aren't. Something about him struck me as dark. It was as if he had a curtain dropped on his real self and behind that curtain all sorts of things were going on and none of them good."

"You were right. And I should have listened to you," Anissa admitted as she carefully commenced the long horrible story of Foley's abuse. When she'd finally struggled through to September 11th she was crying. Carlie had sat still, listening intently the whole time.

"I'm so mad I could kill him," she said as she pulled Anissa toward her. They embraced for a long time. Finally, Carlie let go and offered to send Anissa to Africa.

"Girl, I got friends there! Their huts don't look as good as this place but I'll bet you won't catch Foley Brogdon tramping through the jungle looking for you! Somebody might shoot his ass with a poison arrow! And they got gangs over there that would put the Bloods and Crips to shame."

They both laughed.

"All kidding aside, Nissa, Africa is a great place to hide. Not necessarily to live, mind you, because you're accustomed to things like electricity and running water. Just say the word, I'll hook you up!"

"Maybe one day I will."

"Nissa, I don't mean to be hateful or rude, but I have to ask why you didn't act like Kunte Kinte and run? You're telling me all of these horrible things that he did to you and you just took it! I don't understand."

"It's hard to understand, Carlie. He loved me and made love to me so good that I was hooked from the very start. But when he went nuts on our honeymoon, all I could think about was getting away from him. And I did. I got away in the airport in Atlanta."

"What happened? Why did you go back?"

"He went to Chester to my mom's house. He said he'd hurt her if I didn't come back. So I did." Anissa began to cry. "He killed her anyway."

"What? Why didn't he go to jail?"

"Because he made it look like a heart attack. But I know better, because he told me how he did it. He gave her something that would make her heart stop and no one would be the wiser. He told me if I left him again, he would go after Nedra and her family next, and then you Carlie!"

"Me? I wish the motherfucker would come after me! I can kill in a lot of ways too. And one of them is with a gun. I don't know anybody that's bad enough that two taps center mass and one tap to the head won't kill."

"It's okay, Carlie. Kathy has friends and she has a plan. I'm safe for the time being and I'm sure he's too busy looking for me to think about you. But watch your back anyway," Anissa said reaching for Carlie's hands to calm her down.

"Let him step to me! He'll find out what abuse is. I am not scared of him. I got friends, too. And my dad has friends that nobody wants to meet. Anytime I ever had problems with anyone, I'd look around and they'd be gone. But like I said, we don't talk about my dad."

"I know it, Carlie," Anissa had not meant to upset her. She suddenly felt helpless.

"I've got to meet Kathy. I want to shake her hand," Carlie said, changing the subject as she went to the bar and poured a stiff shot of bourbon. "She sounds like a phenomenal woman."

"Indeed she is. And you will meet her one day." They finished another bottle of wine, cooked, watched movies, played scrabble, and drank some more. The tension between them melted away to make room for the closeness they had felt ever since they met as teenagers.

"Stay in touch, Anissa," Carlie said when they hugged each other at the airport.

"I will I promise. And you be careful not to mention my name to anyone," Anissa cautioned.

"You pray that I don't get the sudden urge to go and kill me a white boy in Tennessee."

"Don't you dare and stop thinking like that! You know you're not a killer."

"I might be. You don't know. Call me if you need me," Carlie waved and headed towards the Security check-in that had become so time consuming since 9/11.

She knew that she could trust Carlie. It had been risky to call her, but she was glad that she had. Carlie's 'wild goose chase' worked well. No one had followed her. She was certain of that.

Chapter One Hundred
June 21, 2002

When Merlot first started looking for Anissa Brogdon, he began by contacting people who were in the counterfeit document business. In order to disappear she'd need a new name, and in order to become a teacher or a language lab supervisor at Boston U she'd need valid identification, including a social security number and manipulated fingerprint records. Someone who was an expert had faked documents for her. Her original social security number had not been used since 9/11. How had she managed this? His background check of her acquaintances and lifestyle did not reveal any unsavory characters. No forgery entrepreneur he had talked to remembered doing anything for a woman with the last name Brogdon who fit Anissa's description.

He'd also talked to the longtime client who had referred him to the Brogdons. From him he learned that the elder Foley Brogdon had access to a lot of people that could help him accomplish anything, but there was no way that Brogdon senior would help his daughter-in-law deceive his only son. Kathy Stockton had the necessary money, but no obvious ties to criminal elements. So how was she doing it?

Something didn't add up.

The morning after he returned from Boston, Clint G.—a good friend of a friend, called him. Merlot had never known what the G stood for.

"Hey, you remember asking around about somebody named Brogdon a while back?' Clint G.'s voice boomed through Merlot's car phone.

"I sure do. But no worries, mate, I found who I was looking for," Merlot was done, but Clint kept talking.

"Yeah, I had no doubt; you're good at that. But that's not why I'm calling."

Foley glanced at his watch. Traffic was crawling on I-85. He'd have to call his secretary and let her know he was running late.

"Why are you calling, Clint? What's up?"

"Well, I was talking to an individual, who said he knew this old boy, a counterfeiter, who'd made a new driver's license and credit cards for a cat named Brogdon. Course, Mr. Brogdon, who paid for it all, don't know that they know his name, but he ain't supposed to. It's insurance for these counterfeiters, you know what I mean?" Clint laughed.

"No, I don't. But go on. Some guy made a bunch of phony IDs for a man whose last name is Brogdon. So what?"

"Good old Mr. Brogdon is a plastic surgeon from Brentwood, Tennessee, and happens to be the husband of the girl you're looking for. That's so what," Clint replied.

Merlot suddenly snapped to attention. Foley Brogdon? Why would he need phony papers? He claimed that he wanted to get back together with his wife. So why would a man with honorable intentions need fake credentials?

As soon as Merlot reached his desk, he spotted the report from Glenn. Ignoring the stack of phone messages, he quickly sat down and began reading. What he learned caused the hairs on his neck to almost walk down his back. Foley had been a very bad boy.

His sealed record revealed that on two separate occasions he had been accused of beating and raping girls in high school. One of the girl's parents died in a house fire that had first been suspected as arson, but then was ruled accidental, after all. Foley had been expelled from two schools for fighting. He'd also been a suspect in multiple breaking and entering incidents. When he was arrested for drug possession and carrying a concealed weapon, he ended up doing only a few hours of community service in the courthouse, courtesy of excellent lawyers bought by his father's money and influence.

But somehow it seemed that Foley grew into a responsible adult. Successful undergraduate and graduate studies, then an internship at a hospital, and finally, establishing his own practice in Nashville as a plastic surgeon to the country stars. All without incident. Then the wedding to Anissa. Soon after, a hospital report, claiming Anissa had sustained severe injuries from a fall down some stairs. The doctor registered his doubts, but Anissa refused to file charges. Glenn also talked to a doctor, who'd treated Anissa at home after an automobile accident.

There were no reports of domestic abuse to the police, and no one that Glenn talked to could say anything but good things about the Brogdons. If he was beating his wife, and Merlot was starting to believe along those lines, no one knew about it. Foley Brogdon fit the profile of the classic abuser. Behind that handsome face he was a vicious son of a bitch. What was he planning to do with the fake identification he'd obtained for himself?

Like all abusive men, he was angry that his punching bag had dared to get away. He would certainly hurt her, perhaps even kill her. That was why he needed a fake driver's license. He wanted to cover his tracks so no one would ever be able to prove that Foley Brogdon had been anywhere near Anissa, the wife he'd assumed to be dead since 9/11.

Merlot made up his mind. He'd tell Foley that none of his leads had panned out and that the trail had gone cold. He dialed the number.

"Dr. Brogdon's office," a female voice answered.

"May I speak with Dr. Brogdon, please," Merlot requested.

"I'm sorry, Dr. Brogdon is out of the office. May I take a message?"

Merlot's hand got sweaty. "Just for the day?"

"He is out of town on private matters."

"When will he return?" he asked.

"He didn't say when he'd return. Would you care to leave a message, sir?" she asked again impatiently.

"No thanks. I'll try another time." Foley was out of town, equipped with fake ID. It was time for Merlot to meet Kathy Stockton up close and personal. Someone needed to warn Anissa.

Chapter One Hundred and One
June 21, 2002

Kathy had prepared an egg-white omelet laced with spinach, mushrooms, onions, and red peppers. Cheddar cheese sprinkled on top added more color and flavor. Topped off with an English muffin and orange juice, her breakfast was fit for a queen. Glancing at the clock, she realized that she'd slept late, so technically she was having brunch.

Her palate screamed for strawberry jam, so she answered the call. She carried her plate to the table—making a second trip for the juice and jam. The kitchen in this house was her favorite of all the kitchens in all the houses she owned. It was completely white: cabinets, appliances, and even down to the white oak floor. The breakfast nook added the color. A white table surrounded by four white chairs with teal leather backs and seats anchored by silver nail heads sat in the center of a teal rug. Teal curtains hung neatly in the bay window.

The fresh cut flowers on the table added a sweet fragrance. She sat down, sliced the omelet with her fork, and lifted the fork to her mouth, anticipating its goodness. The buzzing at the entrance gate to her property stopped her momentarily. Seconds later she followed through with the fork to her mouth and savored the taste as she began to chew. The buzzer sounded again. She quickly took another bite, slightly miffed by the intrusion. Who could that be? The gardener had a code to the gate.

"Yes?" She answered the intercom.

"Mrs. Stockton, I'm Merlot Candy. I need to talk to you about Anissa Brogdon," a male voice replied. Kathy smiled. The fly had come to the spider. Well, he would not be welcomed into her parlor this morning.

"You must be mistaken. There's no one here by that name," Kathy replied truthfully.

"Please, Mrs. Stockton, we need to talk. Anissa's in trouble. I think Foley might know where she is. I think he might be in Boston."

Kathy's blood pressure went up a notch. Was this a trick? Her intuition told her that it was not. And if it was, she'd listen to him anyway.

"Come on in, Mr. Candy. I just opened the gate."

By the time he reached the door, Kathy had slipped a blue dress over her gown, ran a comb through her hair, and put on lipstick. As she headed for the door, she glanced longingly back toward the kitchen where her omelet was getting cold.

She was impressed by Merlot Candy. Not only was he tall, he was very handsome. He wore a dark green suit, a light green shirt and matching paisley tie.

"Hello, Mr. Candy. Kathy Stockton," Kathy extended her hand as she stood back from the door to allow him in.

"It's nice to meet you. I apologize for the intrusion but I know that you know how to contact Anissa."

"Mr. Candy, I must warn you that I don't play games very well, and I don't play fair. So if this is some kind of ruse..."

"I was hired by Foley Brogdon to find Anissa," Merlot interrupted. "I can't blame you for not trusting me, but I know that Anissa is in Boston. I met her. I talked to her. I even ate lunch with her. She works at the language lab at Boston U." Kathy, who was trying to keep an impassive face, stared at Merlot. He knew where Anissa was. She needed to hear more.

"You met her? How did you get her to eat with you? I know you didn't tell her who you are?" Kathy asked incredulously.

"Of course not. I introduced myself as Marvin Bell, looking for a job at the university."

"And she fell for that?"

"Come on, Kathy—may I call you Kathy?"

"Yes, Merlot," Kathy snapped. What had she told Anissa about talking to strangers?

"You have to admit I'm not easy to resist," he smiled. "Especially my natural charm. But seriously, I liked Anissa immediately, and I started to doubt the information that Foley had given me about her."

"But you told Foley where she is?"

"No, I didn't. I wanted to read my investigator's report first—I just got back into Atlanta last night. If we can sit down, I'll share what I found out this morning from that report.

"Forgive my manners, let's sit in the sunroom." Kathy led the way, wondering if she should hear him out or just call Anissa. No. What he had to say should not take long. There was no need to upset Anissa until she had facts.

"Would you like some coffee, or juice? I was having breakfast. I could whip you up an omelet," Kathy offered.

"No thank you. I don't think we have time for that. Foley has left Nashville for an out of town trip, carrying false identity," he stated abruptly.

Kathy listened while he continued to relate to her the things he'd learned this morning. He told her about Foley's sealed records, the very ones that Geoffrey had mentioned, giving her all the details. He told her about the phone call from a friend who was acquainted with a counterfeiter who'd made a phony driver's license for Foley. He shared that he'd learned about Foley's trip out of town from his receptionist. When he finished talking, Kathy knew that she needed to get Anissa out of Boston.

"If you don't mind telling me, I'd like to know how Anissa has been able to change her identities so smoothly," Merlot requested.

"Now that's a long story. Before we talk about that, I need to make a phone call. You sure you don't want something to drink?"

Kathy's brain was trying to figure out how Foley could know Anissa's whereabouts if Merlot didn't tell him. But before she could get to her cell phone she heard it ringing.

Chapter One Hundred and Two
June 21, 2002

Anissa was shopping on Newberry Street. She wore a grey pair of slacks, a navy blue long sleeved blouse, topped off with a bright orange scarf. Orange had always been her favorite color. She had not worn green since the day she left Foley in New York. She slipped her feet into a pair of grey flats. Everything she now owned was new, but some things were newer than others. Summer was coming and she needed lightweight clothes.

She looked at herself in the mirror. She looked good. A confident and strong black woman. She smiled sadly to herself as she thought about Marvin Bell. He'd been on her mind since last Thursday, but she had no room for distractions in her life. It was too dangerous.

At 10:00 a.m. she left the apartment. She had an uneasy feeling, but shrugged it off as guilt for being attracted to a man at a time like this. Every other person that she knew and talked to was someone that Kathy knew or a student— with the exception of Carlie. Well, the chaplain at the chapel, but she didn't believe that he or his cleaning staff had any ties to Foley. They worked too hard. And then there was Marvin Bell. Kathy didn't know about him yet, but maybe she'd tell her about him and have him checked out. If he was okay, maybe she'd accidently on purpose run into him. No man who knew Foley would dare to kiss her like he had. She took a deep breath of the brisk air and set out with a purposeful stride.

As usual, people were out in droves for the weekend. The 'T' was crowded so she had to stand. She really wished she had just walked, but as it was she would be walking a lot once she hit Newberry.

Arriving at the famed street, she spent the next hour window shopping. As she approached Burberry's she was overcome with nostalgia. Four Christmases ago, before she knew the monster within him, Foley had given her a beautiful Burberry purse. With her income now, she couldn't even afford a wallet from Burberry. She glanced in the window as she passed by.

A tall man stood at the register. At the split second that she spotted him, he turned his face to his right to speak to one of the salespeople. She saw a clear profile. The height was right, the aquiline nose was right, the long eyelashes were right, but the telltale feature was the mole on his cheek. His mother had one in the exact same spot. The hat was wrong, the mustache was wrong, but alarm signals were going off with everything else.

She quickly looked both ways and bounded across the street. Luckily there was just enough of a break in traffic to prevent her from being hit by a car. Once on the other side of the street, she entered a shop that offered a full view of the exit from Burberry's. She stood very still and trained her eyes on the doorway.

A few minutes later, the man emerged. He turned left. The sidewalk was crowded, and so he chose the outside edge near the traffic.

His elitist attitude made him avoid crowds whenever possible. In his mind, he didn't belong with the regular human throng; he stood out and had the capability to lead the masses. After all, he was Dr. Foley Brogdon, cosmetic surgeon to the country music world, pulling in a cool million every two months. As much as the attitude had bothered her when she was with him, now it allowed her to get a clear view of his gait and determine beyond a doubt that it was Foley. He walked with an uncharacteristic stoop, but it was him alright. Why was he walking like that? And why was he dressed in those baggy pants, a sweatshirt, and tennis shoes? Foley never went out in public unless he was dressed to the nines. There could be only one answer. He knew she was here and he didn't want her to see him coming. But why was he shopping? She shook her head to clear her thoughts. None of these things mattered.

Her heartbeat accelerated and her breath caught in her throat. She had to get as far away from him as she could. Every fiber in Anissa's body wanted to run, but she stayed and watched him until he was out of sight.

"May I help you, Miss?" asked a saleslady behind her.

"No thank you, I was just looking," Anissa answered over her shoulder as she walked out and turned to walk in the opposite direction. She walked quickly, careful to stay in the middle of the crowd. She had to get out of Dodge. She'd left all her emergency credit cards in a drawer back at the apartment. But she couldn't go back there. Foley had to know where she lived.

At the corner, she flagged a taxi. Safely inside she pulled out the special cell phone and dialed Kathy's number.

Chapter One Hundred and Three
June 21, 2002

Foley was one of the many people who would argue that the world's greatest chess player was Bobby Fischer, having learned the game himself when he was seventeen years old. Chess proved to be more than a game, it was a war between two minds, each trying to gain control over the other and capture the crown. Foley had learned how to positively channel his aggressive tendencies and to maintain control at all times by maneuvering the pieces on a chess board. Learning to master the different pieces also impressed upon him the need to take control over time, place, and people. Chess, a game of strategy, involved staying at least three moves ahead of your opponent at all times.

The day Foley met Merlot Candy, he knew immediately that the investigator did not like him. He'd turned him down at first and shown that he had absolutely no respect for Foley. He was obvious about it, especially when he'd asked whether or not he'd beaten Anissa. Hiring him had been Foley's first move, but he'd had his next three moves in sight already.

After a week with no word from Candy, Foley had made his next move. He'd hired another investigator, one who appreciated and treated Foley with respect, without asking snooping questions. His name was Robert Spick and he lived in Nashville. Foley told him the same sob story, but the questions Spick asked weren't the suspicious prying kind like Candy's.

Instead, Spick asked if Anissa had any childhood friends, and so Foley had mentioned Carlie Harper. Foley had no idea how to find Carlie, and didn't think Anissa would dare contact her, but Robert Spick did and he found her—and her father too. He was unable to put a tap on her father's phone, because he apparently had high tech equipment that detected the bugs immediately. Foley wasn't surprised. Anissa had said rumor had it that Carlie's father worked for the CIA. But Spick hacked into Carlie's computer and read her emails. She emailed back and forth with her father at least twice a week—the usual banal greetings, and sharing news.

He was beginning to lose hope that Anissa would ever contact her, when he saw a weird email from her father about a friend with a striped, rocking chair behind that wanted to see her. That seemed like code to Spick. He mentioned it to Foley, who at first thought it made no sense, until he remembered the story that Anissa had told him about the running joke between the two friends. Foley knew that the striped behind referred to Anissa. He ordered Spick to follow Carlie—not to let her out of his sight. She booked several flights to four major cities. Technologically savvy, Spick had to call on every skill he possessed to keep up with her, but he followed her right to Anissa's doorstep in Boston.

For the first time since he'd known her, Foley loved Carlie. She'd never know that she was responsible for her best friend's death. He almost wanted to call her and let her know when it was all over, but Carlie was foolhardy. Better for him to gloat secretly.

The first time he'd met her he thought she was a knockout, but she'd been a handful. She'd come to Nashville to visit Anissa before they were married. He'd picked her up from the airport, and he could feel her looking through him straight to his soul. To impress her he'd taken the two of them out to dinner at a posh restaurant called Scarlatta's. While they were having drinks and laughing, a strawberry blond woman walked by their table, gave them a disapproving look, then returned immediately to approach Carlie from behind as she sat facing Anissa and Foley.

"Excuse me, but you really need to rethink your laugh!" she spat at Carlie.

"Pardon me?" Carlie replied.

"You need to rethink that laugher. People can hear you all over the restaurant!"

Anissa's eyes grew large and she reached across to take her friend by the hand, but it soon became apparent that Carlie's temper was something to contend with and it wasn't pretty.

“Carlie, ignore her,” Anissa said quickly but she was too late. Carlie was on her feet. And Foley watched her and her temper live, in color, and in 3D.

“Who do you think you are? You have just talked too much to the wrong colored girl. I’m about to go straight ghetto on you!” Carlie stood with her hands on her hips. “Are you crazy? Are you such a miserable bitch that you have to get angry with me because I’m black and having fun? You don’t know me! You don’t know what I might do! You don’t bring your pale faced ass over here and say nothing to me about laughing. In fact, don’t say nothing at all. Do you understand me?” Carlie was in the woman’s face by this time and the blonde had turned scarlet. Foley finally stood and stepped between them.

“You need to walk away,” he said to strawberry head. “You are insulting my new friend. I don’t know you, but I promise I will tomorrow. Perhaps as early as brunch you will know that you made a big mistake tonight. I hope for your sake that you own your own business or that you are independently wealthy, because life is going to get extremely difficult for you. Every move you make from now on will be the wrong one, because you decided to open your mouth and let your racist mentality show. Now walk away.” His voice was calm and he had kept a pleasant look on his face with no hint of anger.

“Don’t you threaten me! I’m just shocked that you would allow this at your table,” she blustered.

Foley leaned in very close to her and said: “That wasn’t a threat, it was the truth.”

By this time, he had signaled the server who hurried to the table. Foley turned to him and explained the situation as the woman stalked off. Less than five minutes later, all three of them watched the woman and her companion being escorted from the restaurant. The manager and restaurant owner, Scarlatta, a buxom brunette with bright red lipstick and fingernails, came over to their table.

“I apologize for that, ladies and Dr. Foley,” she said looking directly at Carlie. “I want everyone who comes here to feel welcome and enjoy themselves. You order anything you want. It's on the house. And I'm sending over a bottle of my best wine."

"Thank you," Carlie said.

"Dr. Foley, it's always a pleasure to see you. I hope this distasteful incident does not ruin our relationship. Bon appetit!" Scarlatta continued, her eyes on Foley.

"I appreciate that, Scarlatta." When she walked away he turned to Carlie.

"I do apologize, Carlie. It was my choice to come here. I've never encountered anything like that as long as I've been a patron here, we can leave now if you want to," Foley said.

Carlie was still fuming, but managed a smile. "No, Foley, I'm fine, but I'd like a double shot of cognac please."

The evening continued uneventfully. The next day, as promised, Foley helped the racist blonde retire from her job, and made sure he mentioned it casually to Anissa, hoping that she would relay the information to Carlie. She did, resulting in the rude blonde unwittingly helping him to win approval from Anissa's best friend.

Chapter One Hundred and Four
June 21, 2002

Foley Brogdon emerged from the baggage claim area at Logan International Airport and hailed a taxi. He had several stops to make. The first would have to be for some quick shopping for his mother on Newberry Street.

It had been four years since he'd been to Boston. He loved this city, with all of the colleges, Boston Public Garden, and the park in the spring. He loved walking down Storrow Drive along the Charles River to Beacon Hill, named for the erstwhile location of a beacon at the highest point in the central Boston area, once located behind the Massachusetts State House. The north slope of the hill was once known as Black Beacon Hill and many famous black leaders such as Frederick Douglas and Harriet Tubman spoke at the African Meeting House on Joy Street. Beacon Hill was one of the most ardent centers for the anti-slavery movement during the Antebellum Era. His great aunt who lived on Beacon Street had shared all this history with him when he was a small boy. He and his father visited her at Christmas for several years. It had been his dream to one day own a home in this expensive and highly desirable neighborhood—maybe soon, now that his life was about to be in order again.

The city was beautiful, the weather nice. He asked the driver to let him out anywhere on Newberry. He wanted to walk a bit.

"I need to pick up a few gifts. I wonder if you would wait for me. I can pay you well for your time."

"My meter is running, sir," the driver replied.

"Will you keep it running for about thirty minutes, that's about how much time I'll need?" Foley asked politely.

"As long as you're paying, my time is yours."

"Here's a hundred dollars, get yourself a sandwich or some coffee and meet me back at this spot," Foley tossed the bill over the seat.

"Thank you, sir, my pleasure. Just take your time. I'll be back here in thirty minutes."

"I wouldn't advise you to pick up another fare; you may not have time to complete the trip in half an hour. And I like punctuality. I'm paying for all of your time until I get to where I'm going. Deal?"

"No problem, sir, see you soon."

Foley stepped out of the taxi and almost collided with a lovely African-America woman.

"Excuse me, I should watch where you're going," she said sarcastically, smiling with perfect teeth.

"Somebody should, I'm not doing such a good job," he'd winked at her with his most charming smile, his eyes starting at her feet and going all the way up her curves to rest on her clear brown eyes.

She winked. "You'd like it," she said, spreading her arms and tossing her hair over her shoulder as she kept walking. Foley smiled to himself. That was what he loved about African-American women—they sassed. Some other time Foley might have pursued the woman, asked her what she meant by her response. Get to know her, marry her, and then train her. But not today, today he had a more urgent matter to attend to.

He began to walk briskly down the sidewalk. His destination was to Burberry's. He wanted to buy his mother a new purse. She loved the Burberry styles and would be impressed with one from Boston. The purpose for his visit could wait just a little longer. He had the element of surprise on his side. He rubbed his hands together in anticipation of what was to come. He thought back to a phone conversation yesterday morning.

"Mr. Brogdon, Robert Spick."

"Good morning, Mr. Spick. Please tell me you have some good news."

"I do indeed, sir. After a veritable wild goose chase, I've located your wife. She's in Boston living in an apartment on Commonwealth. I have the address for you. I must tell you that you were absolutely correct about her appearance. She definitely does not look like herself. She's going by the name Ansasha Barnes now and she's wearing her hair short and dyed black."

"You say you have the address?" Foley asked.

"I certainly do. FYI, she runs every morning at 6 a.m., works at Boston U, and usually leaves for work around 8."

"Good job, Robert."

Foley's heartbeat quickened. She was in Boston, just two and an half hours away by air. He wrote down the address and made arrangements to transfer the money to Robert's account.

"I'll get back to you with details for another job when I get back from Boston. Thank you, Robert. Have a good day," he'd hung up with complete satisfaction.

He planned to fire Merlot Candy. He dialed the number and was told by his receptionist that Merlot was out of the office. Foley left a message, planning to call back later to inform him that he no longer needed his services. Robert Spick had proved that he was more than worth the amount of money he'd earned.

He'd decided to check into a hotel in Boston under an assumed name and then find the apartment building. He'd learned a little about the advantage of false identities when he'd found out Anissa had a new name. Some time ago, he had made contact with someone who was able to acquire a fake driver's license and credit cards for him.

He wore a hat and a fake mustache with a plain off the rack sweatshirt, a pair of baggy pants with a pair of Nikes. An outfit that he would ordinarily never be caught dead in publicly, but it served its purpose. He also managed to stoop his shoulders when he walked.

At Burberry's, he found just the right purse. He had enough cash to pay for his selection. He watched with amusement as the eyebrows of the salesclerk went up a notch when he pulled out his wad of cash. Usually, he didn't carry more than two hundred dollars in cash in his wallet. Today he had over five thousand, all in one hundred dollar bills.

He also had a ton of cash in his carry-on bag. That cabbie would have a stroke if he knew how much money he was riding around with in the trunk of that taxi. Money no longer meant anything to Foley. It was a tool to use to get things done. And he didn't know what he'd need to do in order to get to Anissa. He was ready to pay anybody any amount of money. He'd never been a boy scout, but he personified their motto of being prepared.

Chapter One Hundred and Five
June 21, 2002

Back in Powder Springs, Georgia, Kathy Stockton answered her cell phone.

"Hello?" she answered

"I have to get out of Boston right now. Foley's here. I just saw him on Newberry Street at the Burberry's. Shopping!" Anissa sounded hysterical. Kathy had expected to talk to her, but not like this.

"I knew he'd left Nashville, but wasn't sure he was coming to Boston. I wonder how he knew you were there," Kathy replied.

"How did you know he left Nashville?" She asked abruptly.

"I just had a very interesting conversation with his private investigator, Merlot Candy. He found you, you know. Only he told you his name was Marvin Bell," Kathy said.

Kathy heard Anissa gasp.

"He told Foley I was here?" Anissa asked incredulously.

"No, he did not. He came to see me. He wanted to warn you. He found out about Foley's past. It's pretty dark, sweetie. And he also learned that Foley is traveling, apparently with false documents," Kathy said, all the while wondering how Foley knew where Anissa was if Merlot had not told him. Had Anissa done something foolish after all the warnings she'd been given?

"You're right. He was wearing some sort of disguise when I saw him. What is he doing? Why didn't he come straight to my place? I wouldn't have been there but—wait! Do you think he knew I'd be shopping?" Anissa was panicked. Kathy could hear it in her voice.

"Anissa calm down and think. Somehow something has gone awry. Have you talked to anyone, or been any place that could get back to him?"

Anissa hesitated for a few minutes, breathing loudly. Then a sudden intake of air.

"Carlie," she whispered.

"Carlie? Your friend? The one from high school?" Kathy tried to control the tone and timber of her voice.

"Yes. I invited her here for my birthday. I didn't think she'd tell anyone."

Kathy was a firm believer that when a thing was done it was done. Carlie was the missing link. Somehow she'd done something to lead Foley to Boston. All the way to Anissa. There was no point in rehashing it.

"Where are you?" Kathy realized it was time to get down to business.

"In a taxi. To nowhere," Anissa replied. She was crying.

"Go to 195 Binney Street, Apartment 607. He'll buzz you in. Tell him your real name."

"Who?" Anissa asked.

"A friend of mine. His name is Major Tory. I've known him for years," Kathy reassured Anissa.

"Then what?" Anissa was going berserk.

"Listen to me and calm down. Someone will meet you with new identification and a bag with a new look inside. They'll drive you to the airport. You're taking a flight to New York LaGuardia where a car will meet you to bring you to my home. We're getting you out of the country this time. Where do you want to go?"

"Oh, Kathy, when is it ever going to be over?"

"Soon. Now do as I say and don't worry."

"Kathy you never cease to amaze me. How is it that you are ready for everything?"

"Because I plan, sweetie. You call me when you get to the airport." Kathy hung up.

Chapter One Hundred and Six
June 21, 2002

"195 Binney Street, and please hurry." The driver sped up and began turning corners like he was on rails, cutting in and out of traffic, running red lights, and honking his horn all the way.

When Major Tory opened his door, Anissa had the strong urge to run. He was tall and big, weighing at least three hundred pounds and standing at least six feet six inches.

"Come on in, young lady!" he boomed. His hair was salt and pepper and stood out all over his head. His eyes were clear blue and he had to be at least sixty years old.

"I'm … my name is …Kathy sent me here," Anissa stammered.

"Like I always say, what's in a name? You're her friend and that's all that matters to me. Have a seat and make yourself comfortable. You want a cup of tea? I was just about to make myself a cup when she called."

Anissa entered an old, well lit world. All of the furnishings were antique, and books were everywhere. There was no television, and every accent table, at least six of them, had a lamp. Two pedestal floor lamps and a large ceiling light completed the attempt to brighten the room. Anissa chose a large faded armchair.

"Yes, tea would be nice. Thank you so much, for everything. And call me Anissa," she said extending her hand.

"Good to meet you. Do you take cream and sugar?" He headed toward what Anissa guessed was the kitchen.

"No, just tea thank you."

Anissa took a deep breath. Foley was here, in Boston. He had found her again. Would it ever end? Would he chase her around the globe?

"Nothing like a good strong cup of tea to calm the nerves," Major Tory said as he carried in a silver teapot on a silver tray that also contained two steaming cups of tea, cream, and sugar. His huge hands offered Anissa a cup of the brew.

"Kathy has been a friend of mine for a long time. She's a smart girl and I trust her. I don't know your story and you don't have to tell me. I'm just here to keep you safe until you take the next step, which shouldn't be long," he said, taking a seat on the dusty looking sofa across from Anissa. He held his cup and saucer daintily in his hands. Minutes later the doorbell rang.

Two men entered, one of them carried a bag with everything necessary to change her appearance. When Anissa walked out with them, about an hour later, she was a pregnant platinum blonde wearing a big hat, sunglasses, and a light pink coat dress with the collar upturned to hide her face.

She arrived at LaGuardia airport in record time thanks to the pilot declaring that he was going to fly the plane like he stole something. She had a new name now but she decided to think of herself as Anissa from now on. She was glad that she would be leaving the United States soon. Maybe she would be out of reach on foreign soil. All she could think about on the flight was that she wanted to go to a country where she spoke the language. France would be nice.

When she reached the baggage claim area she saw the man holding the sign immediately, but it took a minute to register. Written in very rudimentary block letters was the name Angelina Beach, her new alias.

"I'm Angelina Beach," she announced.

"I'm your driver. Come with me please"

Soon she was settled in the back seat of a limousine speeding away from the airport. Ninety minutes later, she entered Kathy's home on the Upper East Side. It was just as she remembered it—warm and inviting and very comfortable. Kathy told her to choose any bedroom she wanted, so this time she decided to take the one that gave a view of Central Park. She went up and placed her carry-on bag on the bed. She stood there for a moment contemplating just how far she had come in the short nine months since September 11th. She had experienced life without the fear of being beaten and she knew now that she would rather die before going back to it.

The marriage to Foley Brogdon had been a false start, but that was in the past, nothing could change it. At this very moment, he was nowhere to be seen, and if all things went according to Kathy's plans, he would forever be a part of a past she longed to forget. It would not be easy to live in a foreign country, but it would be an adventure. She'd decided on Belgium. Her future held new experiences and she was young—she could handle it. She was already equipped to conquer one barrier: the language. She could speak French, a language she'd loved from the first words she heard spoken. For fear that Foley might look for her even abroad, and he'd likely start in France, she would not even plan to stay in one place too long. There were many francophone cities in the world other than Paris.

She came out of the guest room and headed upstairs to Kathy's office. She wanted to log on to the computer and check the weather in Belgium. She noticed that a light was on in Kathy's bedroom and went in to turn it off, admiring the furnishings and the rose colored bedding and draperies. As Anissa reached for the lamp switch, she noticed a photo of a smiling Kathy and a judge—standing in what must have been the judge's chambers. The judge was an attractive African American female staring out into the camera lens. Oddly, the woman looked familiar to her, but she shrugged it off. She'd never stood before a judge in her life.

Chapter One Hundred and Seven
June 21, 2002

Lacy Brogdon came into the house from shopping and noticed that her husband was not in his study. He was usually there for several hours in the afternoon reading his newspapers.

"Foley?' she called out.

"In here, Lacy." She followed the sound of his voice to his office. He sat at the desk, obviously distraught.

"What's wrong?"

"It's FJ. Seems he just left without saying a word. I've been calling him all morning and couldn't get any answers. I ended up calling his office and was told that he's out town. He wouldn't just do that. He's got to be chasing a lead to Anissa."

Lacy sat down in a chair and sighed. She was so tired of this business with her son and his formerly dead wife. He had not been the same since that tragedy in New York. Finding out Anissa was still alive was the straw that broke the camel's back. He'd lost his mind.

"Well, I hope for his sake that he finds some peace wherever he is."

"Lacy, you can hardly blame the boy. His wife is mighty ungrateful and inconsiderate to do a thing like this," he stared out of the window as he spoke.

Lacy was silent. No good could come from reminding her husband that their son was a wife beater just like his father. It had been a long time since she'd been the victim of a beating and she did not want to stir her husband up now. It was best to let him say whatever he wanted to say and to think whatever he wanted to think. FJ would be back with or without his wife and then he and his father could stop sitting around and feeling sorry for themselves. She got up, deciding to go in and help their maid put away the food. It had done her good to get out of the house and do the shopping—to mingle with other shoppers and exchange a few pleasantries.

"Where are you going?" Foley Sr. demanded.

"To put away groceries." Was there a note of dominance in his voice?

"We pay someone to do that. I need you to sit down and talk to me."

Lacy sat down again, not out of subservience, but amusement. She stole a glance at him. He was looking at her coldly.

They feared each other. Lacy had added poison to her husband's food several times after he'd attempted to strike her with his broken hands. He'd come up behind her once as she stood at the top of the stairs and almost managed to send her tumbling down.

"Why don't you hire a hit man, Foley? If you want me dead, pay somebody to kill me," she'd snapped at him. "Otherwise live and let live. God is in control in this house."

"I don't want you dead, Lacy. I want you crippled, like me," he'd growled. They'd made a silent pact that time. She'd placed her hand on the bible and swore to never harm him as long as he did the same. So far, they'd done well; he slept in his bedroom and she slept in hers.

"I haven't been able talk to anybody about this mess with Anissa. You just don't act at all like I think you ought to be acting about it. It makes me just want to throw up my hands and let everything go, this house, all your clothes, your car. You know what I mean?"

"Listen, darling, can I get you a cup of coffee or some tea? FJ's going to be alright. You said this private investigator was good. He'll find Anissa."

She went over and tried to put her arms around him. He winced in pain. His arthritis. His wonderful, incurable, make-believe arthritis. No longer was he able to inflict the pain with those fists that he used to dole out like candy. To help him save face she still tried to defer to his wishes whenever she felt like it. She did love him in an oddly twisted sort of way.

"Now look what you've done! You've caused my arthritis to flare up!" he whined accusingly.

Lacy looked at him with pity and shook her head.

"That's really too bad, dear. Now if you don't mind I'm going back to what I was doing."

She left him there. She wondered where FJ could be. If he'd found Anissa he'd never tell them. Lacy was positive that he intended to kill her.

Chapter One Hundred and Eight
June 22, 2002

Foley arrived at Anissa's apartment building on Commonwealth early Sunday morning in a rental car. He parked and sipped his coffee. After a while, he got out of the car and slowly walked by the building. He knew that Anissa would come out early and he wanted to be ready for her. Robert Spick said she ran every morning at 6 a.m. on the dot. He walked for several blocks, turned a corner and made his way back to the top end of Commonwealth. He looked at his watch, 5:59; she should be coming out soon. He quickened his pace because he wanted to be right behind her. By the time he reached her building it was 6:02 a.m., but no sign of Anissa. He slowed his pace and tried to alter his gait so that if she came out she would not recognize him by the way he walked. He crossed the street and turned to go back in the opposite direction when the door to the building opened. He looked hopefully, but realized that the person was not Anissa. He continued to walk slowly trying not to look conspicuous. Still no Anissa.

At 6:30 a.m., he decided to try something else. He walked to the door of the building just as he saw a man entering and went in right behind him.

"Good Morning," said the old fellow.

"Good Morning," Foley responded.

"Can I help you?"

"No, I'm visiting someone." Foley continued purposely to the elevator, cursing softly as the elderly man joined him.

"Who are you visiting?" the man asked.

"A friend."

"Who exactly?"

"I don't mean to be rude, but that is actually none of your business," Foley replied making full eye contact.

They didn't speak again, and the man got off on the second floor. Foley hoped he was senile and would not remember his face if someone ever questioned him.

Foley got off on the third floor, walked up to door 3127, and rang the doorbell. He waited. No answer. He rang again, lacing his fingers, and pivoting back and forth on his heels. No answer. He knocked harder, still nothing. He knocked again, even harder this time. No answer. The door to apartment 3126 across the hall opened. A woman of about fifty with tousled salt and peppered hair stuck her head out of the door.

"What's all of the fuss about?" she demanded.

"Well, if you must know I'm looking for Ansasha Baines." *Or was it Barnes?*

"If you mean that young woman that's been staying there she's gone. She must have left some time yesterday, because Josefina came out of there like a bat out of hell, and double locked the door. She only does that when she's going to be away for a while."

"Gone? She's gone?" Foley couldn't believe it. She couldn't be gone. How could she have known he was coming?

"Yes she is. So you can quit knocking and making enough noise to wake up the dead," the woman snapped, beginning to close her door.

"Wait," Foley demanded. "Do you have any idea where she went?"

"No, I do not. Why don't you ask the rich bitch?"

"What rich bitch?"

"The rich bitch from New York who owns the place. Kathy Stockton. Don't you know her?"

"Why, yes I believe I do," Foley lied. "Thank you so much for your help. I'll have to get up to Manhattan and see her soon. She does keep her home in Manhattan, doesn't she?"

"I don't know anything about what part of New York she's from although, I would imagine that it is Manhattan, because she thinks herself much too important to be from Brooklyn or Queens or the Bronx. Good day to you, sir." And with that she closed the door.

Kathy Stockton. Foley was sure that he'd finally found Anissa's guardian angel. And he realized that she probably knew he was here. He had no idea how, but that didn't matter. If he was right, she was probably busy getting Anissa to a different location.

When he got back to his room, Foley called Robert Spick. By mid-morning, he had the address of one Elton Woods in New York City. Elton, now deceased, had been married and fathered two children—a boy named Troy and a girl named Kathy. He surmised that the address was the family home and that Kathy probably used it when she was in the city. Robert had found out that Kathy was a widow. According to Spick, Kathy Stockton lived in Georgia, where Anissa had lived first, but Anissa would not go back there. New York was a short flight away with an international airport. Foley sat there thinking, realizing he had nothing to lose if he went to the Big Apple. He took a taxi to the airport and bought a one-way ticket to New York.

While he waited at the gate, he began to formulate a plan. He was still traveling under his alias, which was good because he would need to rent a car in Manhattan. He would need it to make a quick getaway once he found Anissa. He would go to Kathy's house and if Anissa was there—and he was certain that she was— he would force her to come with him. He was confident that he could coax her, if need be with a weapon. He smiled as he thought of the 38 in his suitcase, buried underneath all that cash. Anissa knew him well enough to recognize when he was displeased.

He was positive that he had taught her the importance of trying to please him when he was unhappy, and unhappy he most assuredly was. He knew just how to look at her and what to say to make her pay attention. His only concern was that she had been on her own too long and might think that she could resist him. That would not be wise. He didn't want to have to kill her immediately, but he would, in spite of the fact that he wanted her to suffer.

Once she was in the car, he planned to drug her and drive all the way back to Brentwood with her in the backseat. Once he got her inside his house, he could do with her as he wished.

But what if she wasn't alone in the house? Then what? He didn't want to hurt anyone else. He was her husband and he had a right to demand that she come home with him. He really didn't want to think about what could or couldn't happen. He would just take his chances.

Chapter One Hundred and Nine
June 23, 2002

Orella Bookings woke up with a headache. She groaned as her thoughts rushed back to Friday, arguably the worst day of her life. From the time she'd entered her chambers that morning there had been one problem after another. The most pressing issue had been a case involving a two- year-old girl who'd been molested by her foster father. Everything about the case was bad news.

Then she'd had to send her clerk home with a fever and couldn't get a decent sub. If that wasn't enough, the power cord for her computer had caught on fire and someone had ordered a Thai dish made with peanuts for lunch, which meant she'd had to eat crackers instead, because she was allergic to peanuts. And then, she'd ripped her robe. When it was 5:30 p.m., she couldn't get out of that building fast enough.

She was tired. She was a small town girl who had made it in the big city. It was true that if you could make it in New York you could make it anywhere. She was proof. The trouble was she was seriously considering trying her luck somewhere else.

She'd unlocked her SUV, and sat behind the steering wheel trying to put her will and her mind in the same place. She wanted a drink. What else was new? She always wanted a drink. And she usually kept some in her car. Her motto was 'have alcohol will travel.'

She had been able to handle it for a long time, but lately people were avoiding her. Her memory had become fuzzy, so there was no telling what she'd said or done to them. She even had one case where the people requested a different judge the moment she entered the courtroom. Sometimes, when she played back her recordings, she could hear the slur in her words. She had fallen several times and then had to cover it up with a lie about some type of medication. She was losing it.

When she made her first call to Alcoholics Anonymous, the person told her that she was likely experiencing blackouts. She begged to differ. A blackout meant unconsciousness. She had not been unconscious except when she passed out on the bed. She just couldn't remember. Everybody woke up with a hangover and couldn't remember, didn't they?

Attending that first AA meeting helped her realize that she had nothing in common with those people. They laughed and talked about their drinking experience like it was a joke. Orella had left that meeting feeling like it had been a complete waste of time. She'd gone to a bar right after that. But now she was seriously considering the possibility that she might have multiple personalities—those new clothes in her closet, waking up and not remembering going to bed, and having conversations with people who knew her, but she'd never met them.

She didn't start out drinking every day. First, it was mixed drinks, especially frozen fruity daiquiris, at parties in college. Once out of school and on her own, she'd experimented with all kinds of fruit and kept increasing the amount of rum, because after a while the drink would not be strong enough to work its magic. Then she'd tried leaving the hard stuff alone and only drank wine. Jesus drank wine, she rationalized, why else would he have turned water to wine? But it didn't get any better. It just kept getting worse and it scared her.

She'd finally had to change to vodka because she needed a drink in the morning to get her day started. She had a drink in the car when traffic was bad. She had a drink when she got to the courthouse to celebrate making it there in one piece. She had a drink just before she went into the courtroom, a watered down version during court, and then a drink when court recessed, a few drinks at lunch, and a drink after lunch. She had a drink on the way home, and by the time she reached home, she poured a stiff drink and the next thing she knew it was morning again.

She tried to think back to the last time she had a drink and really enjoyed it. It seemed like ages ago. Once she took that first drink she was on a roller coaster with endless rides. She could no more stop with a 'few' drinks than a cow could eat a few blades of grass.

The real fright was back in November, when the Police had knocked on her door to inquire about her red sports car.

All she could think was that they'd finally found her and she was going to spend the rest of her Thanksgivings in jail for vehicular homicide. After a few questions she'd realized that they were not looking for her; they wanted to know about the car, which she had to tell them she'd reported stolen.

She'd known that they'd checked her record and knew that she'd had a spotless career and was a highly esteemed family court judge. She'd played it cool, told her tale, and they'd believed her. They had not wanted to harass her.

She had been a wreck for days after that. She'd attended two more AA meetings, but it's a good thing she had alcohol to help her through it. The craving was so strong that she was almost blinded by it. All she could think about was going into a liquor store and picking up a bottle. She didn't want wine. She wanted something strong like whiskey, a big glass of liquor. They'd told her in the meetings to call her sponsor if she felt like drinking. She didn't have a sponsor.

After that horrendous day at work Friday, she'd cranked her car, driven to the liquor store, and bought herself a pint of the best cognac they had. She'd planned to have a drink before dinner and a drink afterwards and then pour the rest out.

But she'd ended up going back to the liquor store after the pint was gone and that was all she remembered. Until just now. She got out of bed and stumbled to the bathroom, thoughts still swirling through her head. And the guilt was back—that overwhelming guilt that came from being drunk and not remembering how she got to bed.

She flushed the toilet and walked back into her bedroom. There were no sheets on the bed and the house smelled of something burning. Alarmed, she made her way to the kitchen where she found a pan that had been charred and blackened. Something inside of it had burnt to charcoal. Who did this? She didn't cook anything yesterday. She opened the refrigerator to get some juice and was shocked to see that none was there. She distinctly remembered that she had a bottle of cranberry juice. She glanced at the trash can, and there was the empty juice bottle and an empty pint bottle of bourbon. Upon closer inspection, she found four empty pint bottles of bourbon. Where did they come from? There was not a soul to ask.

She looked at her watch and was filled with dread as she realized that the date was June 23rd. It was Sunday. What had happened to all day Saturday? She sank down into a chair and stared at her cabinets. She'd done it again. She'd had a blackout. And then she saw it—a gallon of wine on the kitchen counter. She had not noticed it earlier.

"I might as well have a drink to calm my nerves," she said aloud.

Chapter One Hundred and Ten
June 24, 2002

Foley stood on Fifth Avenue in front of Central Park staring at the house on 81st Street that belonged to the Woods family. He wasn't sure if Anissa was there. But he was going to watch the place for a while just to see. He was on his own now. Merlot was incommunicado. Plus he wanted to fire him anyway. Robert Spick had done all he could. It was time for Foley to take over. He was tired of playing this game of cat and mouse. He didn't dare break into the house. He couldn't walk up to the door and ring the bell. He knew that neither Anissa nor her friend would let him in. He was forced to skulk around like a common criminal.

It was early Monday morning, not even seven o'clock yet. He was uncomfortable standing still in the midst of pedestrians. He started walking so nobody would notice he was watching the house. As he walked, he kept his eyes on 81st for as long as he could.

When the house drifted out of sight he turned around, crossed the street and walked back toward it. He felt like a fool, but he could think of nothing else. He started kicking the sidewalk as he walked along, his anger beginning to rise. He just wanted to punch something! There were enough people that he could probably just elbow somebody and then apologize. He had to get rid of some of this frustration.

The last time he'd been in this city was the aftermath of September 11th. Total chaos. Hysterical people everywhere. Smoke, dust, and public servants blocking his progress. He looked around at his fellow sidewalk companions. They were all hurrying to get somewhere. And then he had an idea. An excellent idea. He just needed a few things first.

Chapter One Hundred and Eleven
June 24, 2002

Anissa woke with a start. It took her several minutes to realize where she was. She looked around at the unfamiliar room and its grandiose décor. The walls were a pale blue, adorned with large paintings of fields and flowers. The draperies were very white with ruffled tiered sheers. There was a very comfortable white brocade chaise where she'd discarded her clothing last night. She slept in a four poster Mediterranean style bed with mounds of navy and baby blue pillows and a very warm white down comforter. She rolled over to her side so that she faced the windows. She knew that behind those white draperies, a block away was the park.

She loved Central Park, a beautiful mecca, in the center of the city containing over seven hundred acres and receiving over twenty four million visitors every year. This fact alone made it the most visited urban park in the United States. It had been designated as a National Historic Landmark in 1963. Several artificial lakes and ponds that looked unbelievably natural, two ice skating rinks, the conservatory garden, the zoo, and an outdoor amphitheater all helped to create a wonderful place of repose in the middle of a buzzing metropolis.

Kathy would arrive in New York later today with a passport and new identity so that Anissa could get out of the country. She would fly to Brussels. Maybe after a month or two she would go to Switzerland and then to Africa to the Côte d'Ivoire, Sénégal, or Morocco. She giggled as she thought about her plans. How in the world was she going to afford travelling to all of those places? Maybe she could become a disciple of Kathy and share her mission to save abused women. There were wife beaters in foreign countries, too. She threw the covers off and stood.

At that moment, the doorbell rang. She dressed quickly and ran downstairs. She peeped through the curtains and saw a police officer and a fireman. *What in the world? Had something happened to Kathy?* She opened the door immediately and noticed that people were coming from their houses on both sides of the street, being escorted by authorities. The sidewalks had been cleared of pedestrians. Fire trucks and police cars lined the street on both sides. *What was the matter?*

"Good afternoon, ma'am," the fireman greeted her. "We've got a suspected gas leak and gasoline leaking in the street from an unknown source. We're going to have to ask you to evacuate. Is there anyone else here with you?" he asked

"No," Anissa said.

"Come with us, ma'am. We've got a safe place where you can wait," he gestured for Anissa to follow him. Anissa was scared. Obviously, she didn't want to perish in a gas explosion, but leaving her sanctuary was just as dangerous. Foley could be out there somewhere. But the policeman didn't leave her much of a choice. She fought down her fear and followed him. Surely there were enough police and people about that if she screamed, someone would come to her rescue.

Chapter One Hundred and Twelve
June 24, 2002

Foley was waiting for Anissa to come out. When he saw her, he imagined himself as the knight on a chess board. He was about to check the king, or queen in Anissa's case. He was almost giddy with anticipation. He felt like a time bomb. Tick. Tick. Tick. He'd had the gun on his side equipped with a silencer. Just in case he had to shoot her where she stood, because he didn't want to get caught and go to jail. His parents would be devastated; the family name would be ruined. No, he had to stay in control.

Foley walked at a deliberately brisk pace. He was in charge. She was just ahead of him, close enough for him to touch her. And this time she wasn't getting away.

He almost chuckled when he thought of how careful she was trying to be. Looking over her shoulder. Scanning every car she passed or that passed her on the street. Little did she know that danger was hiding in plain sight.

"Keep moving, everybody just keep moving, everything's going to be alright," Foley said to the crowd as he adjusted his cap.

He moved swiftly to where Anissa stood. She was looking down, but as he approached she looked up. He wished he had a camera to capture the look on her face. She was frozen. In shock. Time and space ceased to exist. The flight or fight response kicked in. She turned to run. But he was too quick for her. He caught her. But she jerked away so quickly it startled him. She started flailing her fists at him. She got in a few good shots. But he was able to subdue her. He pulled her toward him. He nudged the gun to her side.

"Hi, sweetheart, don't make me shoot you in front of all these people. I'm a police officer shooting a deranged woman in the line of duty," he whispered as people began to stare.

"I'm going to have to handcuff you now, bitch," he hissed. "You're under arrest," he said aloud as he spun her around and locked her wrists. "You have the right to remain silent…" he continued in character as he dragged her along to a police sedan. He slapped her head, lowering her into the backseat.

He walked around the car and quickly got into the driver's seat and drove away.

"Hello, Anissa, or should I say Lynn? Or Ansasha? That's some run you've had. It's over now." He glared at her through the rearview mirror. Once again he was aware of how good she looked. Angry, she locked eyes with him. The look was unmistakable. She wanted to harm him. Good. The feeling was mutual.

He drove for three blocks. Then pulled into a side alley. He got out and looked around. The alley was deserted. He opened the back door, grabbing her by the neck. He stood her on her feet and then punched her in the face. Twice. She was screaming at the top of her lungs. He'd expected her to do this. He put her in a chokehold and slapped duct tape across her mouth. That shut her up. He pulled a syringe out of his pocket and plunged it into her neck. The medicine would act quickly.

"We're leaving now. We're going home, baby. You're going to walk over to this car with me and you will not do anything to attract attention. If you do I will shoot you." He showed her the gun. "I may go to jail but you'll be dead. Do you understand me, Anissa?"

Her eyes were watery as she glared at him. Was that hatred in her eyes? He slapped her. He punched her in the stomach. He kicked her shin. All that just for looking at him like that. Now she had something to hate him for.

"I could kill you now you know. But I want us to go home. I want us to be together again. Don't you want that, too?" His mouth was so close to her ear. He pushed her forward, wrapping one arm around her waist. In the other he held the gun. He poked it into her side as hard as he could.

"Be nice, baby! I kid you not; these could be the last minutes of your life. Come on!"

Anissa did as he said. They stumbled over to the car. A green Toyota Camry.

"Your chariot awaits," Foley said through clenched teeth.

She was back to being the obedient little wife. Hoping against hope that if she would do everything just right he wouldn't get angry and hit her. Too late. He was already angry. He had already hit her. She had to know that there was nothing she could ever do right to stop the course that they were now on. He had won. He was in control. He shoved her into the back seat of the car. He locked the door just before he slammed it. She stared into the barrel of the gun pointed right at her face.

"Lie down!" he commanded.

She did.

Checkmate!

Chapter One Hundred and Thirteen
June 24, 2002

Anissa couldn't believe what had just happened. Disguised as a policeman, Foley had been able to abduct her in the presence of witnesses. And no one questioned his authority. Could she have done something different? No. He was the police. The Man. There had been no way to escape. He wore the uniform of those whose job it was to protect and serve. No matter what she could have said or done, nobody would have helped her.

Foley was rummaging on the floor in the front seat. She looked out through the rear window. She saw a woman crossing the alley farther down the street. Walking a dog. She looked at the car. Anissa tried to catch her attention by moving her head frantically. But the woman turned away quickly and continued down the street. Without another glance in their direction.

Anissa's mouth was bleeding. She could feel and taste the blood mixed with the rubbery taste of the tape. She felt herself becoming lightheaded.

She lay down on the back seat. Tears rolling down her cheeks. It was over. Foley was right. No one was coming to rescue her. Not Kathy. Not this time. Kathy would come home to an empty house and become frantic with worry. But she wouldn't come for her, because she'd never know what happened.

Maybe a neighbor might mention being evacuated. But that would never register. Who would suspect that Foley was responsible? Kathy would live out the rest of her life believing that Anissa had gone back to Foley voluntarily. Unable to live on the run any longer.

Back with him she was. For good this time. And she knew that she was going to die. A painful death. Foley would make sure of that. The sedative he had given her finally knocked her out.

Chapter One Hundred and Fourteen
June 24, 2002

Dr. Jennings Ford was late. He wanted to get to his grandson's basketball game. He'd missed the last three. This one was a tournament. He'd promised to be there. He'd taken this street thinking it was a short cut but it wasn't. He didn't know where he was. He had no business deviating from the usual route. He wasn't a native New Yorker. He got lost all the time, because, as his wife used to say his sense of orientation was virtually nonexistent. How long before he stopped getting lost? He swore silently as he checked his watch. Not knowing if he was ten or thirty minutes away. He wiped the perspiration from his brow. He tried to concentrate as he backed into an alley to turn around and head back in the opposite direction.

In his rear view mirror he saw the strangest thing. Down the alley, a policeman was struggling with a woman. He saw the officer slap the woman. Punch her in the abdomen! When he kicked her, Dr. Ford saw him pointing a gun at her. What the hell? That was police brutality! Here he was in one of the best neighborhoods in the city, and there was one of New York's finest beating a woman in broad daylight. Like a street punk. As he stared in the mirror, the cop pushed her into a Toyota Camry.

A Camry? Not a police car? Something was way off. Suddenly the woman turned her face in his direction as the cop slammed the door shut. He recognized that woman. The hair was different but he knew that face. It was Jessica Woods!

He'd never forget that face. He'd looked long and hard at her trying to figure out how someone so lovely could have ended up in a hospital bed suffering from such a cruel beating.

Just as a woman with a phone to her ear and a dog on a leash crossed the alley behind him, he shifted to drive and pulled out in front of a car. The driver laid on his horn. The doctor lifted his middle finger. He couldn't believe it! Once again he was faced with a mystery involving this woman. Why would a police officer take her out of a squad car and put her into another car?

He reversed the scene in his head. He flashed back to the back end of the car. Sometimes his memory was like taking a photo–his wife had always given him a hard time about it. In his mind's eye, he saw the license plate. And the number. Then the policeman's face! He had seen that face before, too. It was the man who'd knocked him down in front of the hospital and caused him back pain and huge chiropractor bills. He called himself a doctor. And today he was a cop. A liar is what he was. Dr. Ford hated liars. He hated men who mistreated women, too.

He reached for his car phone and dialed 911. That doctor/police officer was going to get some jail time today.

"9-1-1 emergency," answered a female voice.

"I'd like to report a cop beating a woman. He just threw her in the back seat of a green Toyota Camry," Dr. Ford declared.

He gave her a description of the man, the license plate number and the nearest major intersection. After he hung up he felt satisfied. He'd done what he could.

Chapter One Hundred and Fifteen
June 24, 2002

Foley drove very carefully. He did not want to attract attention. The last thing he needed was for someone to discover Anissa in the back seat passed out with blood all over her. When he stopped at a traffic light, he looked back at her. She looked disgusting. Her hair looked horrible. The clothes she wore looked horrible. And she'd dared to fight him. He had to hit her in the face. He didn't like to do that. He was angry with her. She provoked him. Made him lose control.

He was exhilarated, too. His idea had worked like a charm. It had cost him a bundle, but he'd had the cash for it. The most difficult part had been finding a costume store that had a police uniform. He'd purchased ten gallons of gasoline in containers around the city. He punctured holes in them and left them leaking onto the street from a parked rental car. Then he'd made a frantic anonymous call—yelling about a gas leak at one of the addresses near Kathy's house. Like clockwork the cops and the fire trucks showed up.

He'd watched them go from house to house to get people out of their houses. The smell of the gasoline was strong. The idiot cops never searched the cars on the street. They just went to work, evacuating residents. And then Anissa had appeared in the doorway. He'd just melted into the throng—looking like a cop on the job. It had been a long time coming, but it had come. She wouldn't be running anymore. Not after tonight.

He looked at his watch. He had a long drive ahead, but he would make it. If he had to stop overnight, so be it. A night in a motel room would be fun. Just like old times. He'd do anything and everything he wanted to her body. Give her the thrill of a lifetime one more time. He had enough medication to keep her out until they got back to Tennessee.

"I feel like celebrating!" he said aloud. He only drank on special occasions. If this was not a special occasion then what was? One glass of champagne! He'd buy a bottle. And some little plastic glasses. Anissa would toast with him. If not he could always pour it down her throat. And he was hungry. He'd get some chips too.

He spotted a liquor store and hesitated only for a moment. He jerked the steering wheel hard for a U-turn. He'd park on the opposite side of the street a little ways down. He had nothing to fear. Reason whispered that now was not the time to drink. What if the police stopped him? But he had stopped listening to reason a long time ago. He was rich, white, and willing to die. He was an American. He had his wife back. He could do anything he wanted to do. He made sure that the new blanket was over Anissa. Then he checked himself in the mirror. Looking good! He got out, locked the doors, confident that his wife would be there when he came back.

Chapter One Hundred and Sixteen
June 24, 2002

Kathy sat back into the soft leather seat of the limousine and kicked her shoes off. Her feet were killing her and she'd paid much too much for them to have to endure this kind of pain. Maybe it was because she ran in them. She'd had to race to get to her gate because she had been fortunate enough to get an early flight. She made a mental note that now was the time to buy a plane. Anissa was going to be so surprised. She was not expecting her for another four or five hours. It was good to be back in New York. Stopped at a red light, she passed the time looking at the people in the cars to her left. Where were they going? Were they happy? On her right was a black Mitsubishi SUV. Her eyes wandered to the driver. She suddenly gasped. She hit the buttons trying to roll down the window. The light changed before she could open the window. Orella pulled away much faster than the limo before Kathy could get her attention.

Orella Bookings! Kathy had not seen her for a while. The last time she'd been in New York was in September. With the World Trade Center attack, her brother's death, and Anissa, her mind had been elsewhere. She should have taken the time to call her friend though. She'd do it this time, once Anissa was in the air. Maybe they'd have lunch.

She'd met Orella years ago. They'd been at a frat party at NYU. Orella was at the bar when Kathy walked up and they'd started talking to each other. It turned out that Orella was a lot of fun, and she played tennis. They'd exchanged phone numbers and got together to play often. Those amateur matches led to a lasting friendship. When Kathy got married, they lost touch with each other. After Kathy's husband's death, she came back to the family home, and Orella was the first person she called.

Orella had invited her to lunch, requesting that they meet at the courthouse. Kathy thought it a strange place to meet, but went anyway. Upon arrival, she was met by a law clerk.

"Are you Mrs. Stockton?" the young woman asked.

"Yes, I am," Kathy answered hesitantly.

"I'm supposed to take you to Judge Bookings."

Judge Bookings? Kathy followed the woman down the hall and into a door. And who sat in chambers but Orella! They'd hugged and talked. Orella told her the story of how she'd become a judge. Kathy was so proud. She'd known that Orella's dream was to become a trial lawyer, but she was happy as could be about being seated on the bench. Over lunch Kathy had shared the story of her abuse and her desire to help other abused women.

"I see abused women at least twice a week in my courtroom!" Orella shared.

Kathy left a discreet card to be given to any woman who seemed to want to escape abuse. One woman, Ashley McHenry, had actually called Kathy recently and turned down assistance because her husband went to jail, but Kathy reminded her that he'd get out one day and when he did, he'd come looking for her. Ashley had promised to think about it.

Kathy was almost at her family home. Just a few more minutes and she'd be there with everything Anissa would need to leave the United States forever. And Foley Brogdon.

Chapter One Hundred and Seventeen
June 24, 2002

Orella, now on a brandy diet, had gone out earlier and got a bottle to help out with the housework. She'd cleaned house, she'd washed and folded clothes, and she'd danced to music until she'd run out of brandy again. She didn't believe in mixing liquors, and she was monitoring her drinking by not keeping a supply. Now she was on the street in an unfamiliar part of town. Looking for a liquor store. Whenever she bought liquor, she'd go to different parts of town. She didn't want to run into anyone that she knew. She had her music loud and she felt sexy. She didn't know that she was weaving from side to side in traffic. She heard the horns blowing, but ignored them.

She saw the red neon liquor sign ahead. She pushed down on the accelerator. Too late she realized that she'd passed the store. And no parking spaces in sight. She kept going. There had to be another one coming up soon. She turned up the volume.

"That's my song!" she said and began to sing along, scanning the storefronts for another liquor store. Suddenly she felt a thud.

"What the hell was that?"

She looked in the rear view mirror just as a city bus passed her and came to a screeching halt. She shrugged and looked at the road ahead of her. Not a single parking spot presented itself. Her only choice was to keep going. She'd find a side street where she could turn around and go back the way she'd come.

Chapter One Hundred and Eighteen
June 24, 2002

Foley walked along the street whistling. It was good to be alive. He had his wife back. Soon she would learn once and for all. She'd made a huge mistake by leaving him. He looked at his left hand. Bruising had already begun around the knuckles.

She'd lost her mind, fighting him in public. He shook his head to clear his thoughts. It was time to think of the future. He glanced back to make sure she wasn't getting out of the car.

Would he marry again? Probably. He liked being married. Having a woman at his beck and call. He thought about the pretty woman he'd bumped into in Boston. So many fish in the sea. He'd date for a while. Maybe settle down in two or three years. He'd decided that he didn't want children. Ever. He never wanted to look down the hallway or around a corner and see a child of his watching him as he punished their mother. The way he'd watched his own father.

As he neared the liquor store he saw a break in the traffic. He made a run for it. He was so wrapped up in his thoughts that he didn't see the car. Until it was too late. He saw the face of the woman driving the car. She was bobbing her head and singing for God's sake. She wasn't even looking where she was going. He raised his arm to make her stop. He was too late. Her car made impact with his body. He was flipped up. He fell down directly into the path of an oncoming city bus. His hips and legs burned with excruciating pain—but he was alive when he hit the pavement. For a split second he almost felt sorry for the pain he had inflicted on Anissa, instead he turned his head. And saw the front tire on the driver's side of the bus just inches from his face. That was the last thing he saw before he got the worst headache he'd ever had in his life. It was also the shortest. His world suddenly went black and silent—forever.

Chapter One Hundred and Nineteen
June 24, 2002

Once again, Felton Dade found himself stuck in traffic when a call came over the radio about an accident with a fatality. He was less than a block away. He parked his car and walked toward the scene, suddenly overcome by *déja-Vu*.

He'd stood with the boys last month a few blocks away attending a ceremony to end the eight month cleanup at the site of the World Trade Center. It had begun with an honor guard made up of fireman and policemen carrying a stretcher with an American flag that symbolized the many people who'd lost their lives that day. The stretcher was placed into an ambulance that was followed by a flatbed truck that carried the last 50 ton steel beam of the South tower covered with a black cloth while buglers played 'Taps.' It was sad, but it provided closure for Felton and the boys.

When he reached the site of the accident, what he saw sickened him. A fellow officer's head was under the front wheel of a city bus. But closer inspection revealed the uniform to be fake. The color was off and the badge was a toy.

Minutes later, emergency vehicles arrived and the body was extricated. The man's face had been crushed beyond recognition. Felton, being the first officer on the scene, had gone through the man's pockets and found his wallet. What he saw confused him at first. He stared at an Arizona driver's license, with the face of his nemesis, Foley Brogdon—older, but with the same sappy smile. Only the name didn't match the face—Bill Jones. Two credit cards with the same name were in slots with the license. In another section, however, behind several hundred dollar bills, he found another driver's license from Tennessee—Dr. Foley Brogdon.

You have got to be kidding me ! Felton thought.

"Well, guys, looks like Bill Jones a.k.a. Dr. Foley Brogdon just died in a very bad way," Felton said to the officers nearby. He fought back a smile.

They spent the next thirty minutes interviewing witnesses. A young boy said that the man had come from a green Toyota parked down the street. Felton looked in the direction the witness was pointing and saw two police officers helping a woman from the car.

"Just a minute, officers!" Felton yelled. He quickly ran down the street toward them. "Evening, guys. I'm Detective Dade. We just had a bad accident back there. A man was killed and we have a witness that says he came from this car."

Felton glanced at the woman who sported an upcoming black eye. He recognized her immediately. She didn't have the blond hair or the smile, but the eyes were the same. Sad eyes. This was Foley's wife, Anissa Brogdon.

"Well, we got a call from two witnesses about some cop beating a woman and driving off with her in this car," one of the officers said, pointing at the Camry.

"We spotted the car, got out, and found this lady drugged in the back seat," the second cop gave his version.

"Are you alright, ma'am?" Felton asked.

"I think so," Anissa replied. "What happened? Who called the police?" she asked.

Felton almost winced. She had taken a hard shot to the face and her hands on her abdomen suggested that she'd taken a blow there too. Foley had done this to her.

"Ma'am, can you tell us who hurt you?" he asked.

"I don't know. He drugged me and I went out. As you can see, I just woke up. I can't imagine where he could be. But I'm fine. If you don't need me I can get a taxi and get back home."

"You need medical attention, ma'am," Felton said quietly.

"No, I don't. I'm fine," she said with more conviction.

All three officers gave each other a look and shrugged their shoulders.

"There's been an accident up there and a man got killed. He carried two identities. One for Bill Jones, the other for Dr. Foley Brogdon. Do you know anyone by either of those names?" Felton asked Anissa.

She considered for a moment. "I used to know Foley Brogdon," she said simply.

"He's from Brentwood, Tennessee," she continued resolutely. "His father has the same name and lives about five miles from his son." She turned her attention towards one of the two officers. "I'd like that ride home now if you don't mind."

It didn't take a rocket scientist to figure out what was going on. This woman had been beaten severely. The man responsible was dead. Did she even need to identify him? No, let his parents do it. She'd given Dade enough information to have them tracked down. No need to put her through any more than she'd already suffered. And he definitely did not want to see or talk to Lacy Brogdon. Not ever. Although he almost wished he could see her face when she found out her darling bad boy son was gone. But he'd just hold the thought in his mind. The one good thing about the dead—with the exception of Jesus Christ—was that they usually stayed that way. Anissa's troubles were over.

The two officers tipped their hats at Felton, who nodded his approval. They put Foley's wife in the squad car and drove away. Felton took a deep breath. Justice at last for one female beating son of a bitch!

Chapter One Hundred and Twenty
June 24, 2002

Anissa sat in the back seat of the squad car, pondering the events of the last hour. She had believed she was on her way to certain death. A horrible death. Foley had drugged her and she'd passed out. Now he was dead.

The sound of tapping on the window had awakened her. She'd sat up to find two police officers, one on either side of the car, staring at her. The same two officers who now sat in the front seat of the police car that she was riding in. They'd identified themselves—Jeff Evers, young and handsome; and Phil Carr, middle-aged and tired.

"Ma'am, we're not going to be able to just let this go," Phil Carr stated gravely. He'd turned to look over the seat at her.

"Let what go?" Anissa asked.

"We can tell that you've been hurt. By a person or persons unknown," Carr replied. Anissa could tell that he was uncomfortable.

"Not unknown to me. I just want to go home," Anissa said.

"Look, ma'am," Jeff spoke this time, glancing at Anissa in the mirror, and then quickly back at the road. "We see this all the time. Domestic abuse, I mean. And we know that unless you do something, nothing is going to change."

"Believe me, officer, everything has changed. The man responsible for my injuries is dead. You just heard that from one of your own. I was abducted by him, beaten, and drugged. My life has been a nightmare since I met that man. But it's over. And I want to go home," Anissa said simply.

What more could she say? She had no intentions of going through a formal identification of Foley. Let the dead bury the dead.

"I'm sure you both know domestic abuse never gets better as long as the people involved stay together. Sometimes someone ends up dead," Anissa continued.

In the front seat, Carr looked over at Evers. They held eye contact. "What's your address, ma'am?" Evers asked.

Chapter One Hundred and Twenty-One
June 24, 2002

Orella was finally moving again. The police had diverted traffic around that big assed bus. Something had happened, she could tell, but she didn't know what. A quick glance in the mirror showed what looked like a body with the head caught underneath the front wheel of the bus.

All the commotion was in front of the liquor store so there was no way she was getting to that one today. She should have stayed on her side of town. She could have been back home by now, relaxing in her clean house with a drink.

"Oh hell," she said to herself as she saw four people standing in the street ahead of her. Two of them were police officers. She slowed down, lowered her music, and veered to give them room and show respect. She had after all been drinking all day. As she passed, she looked over again. Into the face of the woman who'd yelled at her to stop back on September 11th before she'd run over that woman. The hair was different, but the face was burned into Orella's mind. She never forgot a face if she was sober enough when she saw it.

"Dear God, don't let her tell, don't let her tell, if she doesn't tell I promise I'll never take another drink," Orella prayed as she gradually increased speed.

Should she run? Maybe the woman didn't see her. She checked her rear view. They hadn't hopped into their cars in hot pursuit yet. They weren't even looking in her direction.

She would go home. She would not stop at a liquor store. If they didn't come to get her she'd be the first person at the AA meeting tonight. She'd get a sponsor. She'd stop drinking. For good. She had to.

Epilogue

Kathy Stockton stood looking out over her vast lawn. It had been a wonderful idea to purchase this mansion in Florida. It was a beautiful piece of property that only improved with all of the modifications to the house. It had enough rooms for at least ten women with children to stay while they began to put their lives back together after breaking away from their abusive men.

She was finally realizing her dream. Anissa Brogdon had been her first success story. It was a shame that Foley had to die the way that he did. And poor Jessica Woods—she had died a senseless death. And yet good came from it. Anissa was alive and free.

No longer tied to the Brogdon name, she'd gone back to using her maiden name—Strickland. She was doing well, living in California, and teaching again. Merlot Candy had begged Kathy for her contact information, and Anissa had given her permission to give it to him. She wanted to thank him for not telling Foley where she was. They didn't fool Kathy one bit. There was more to it than a polite thank you.

Anissa was also keeping her eyes and ears open for any women who appeared to be victims of domestic abuse. She would direct them to her earthly savior: Kathy Stockton.

Kathy sighed. To think none of this would have been possible had she not finally gathered enough nerve to fight back. She'd met Paul, a chemist who was one of the first additions to her vast array of special friends, and he'd told her about a poison that could simulate a heart attack and could never be detected once absorbed in the blood stream. She had been ready that last night when her husband beat her and broke her nose. She'd managed to pull herself up and offer him his usual drink that she had laced with the poison. He gulped it down, and then tried to apologize to her. Not to worry.

"No apology needed, sweetheart," she'd said to him as he lay gasping on the floor. It was the last time he laid his hands on her or anyone else.

Ain't life grand? she asked herself as she turned away from the window and walked into Geoffrey's waiting arms.

They were a team. Like Batman and Robin, the Lone Ranger and Tonto, Sam and Dave. Someday she just might marry him.

ORDER FORM

Yes! Please send my copy of A False Start today!

Quantity	Item	Cost
_______	**A False Start** ($15.95 each)	$_________
	Shipping and Handling (Add $3.95 per book)	$__________
	Total	$___________

Name____

Address____

____

City__________________ State_________________________

Zip Code____________________

T.S.W. Wordsmith

3127 Gus Robinson Rd.
Powder Springs, GA 30127

(770)222-6482

tswwordsmith@gmail.com

COMING SOON

******* A New Novel by Kris Allis**

Read the first four chapters on the following pages:

Moving Screen

By

Kris Allis

Prologue

While most people in Atlanta, Georgia were struggling to get in those last few hours of sleep before daylight, Missy Kinner was struggling to stay awake. She almost fell asleep in a house that was obviously occupied by a woman; she could see perfume bottles on the dresser, and that frilly purple pillows had been on the bed. Of course they were on the floor now. She'd been too out of it to notice the frills and frou-frou when she came in, but now that one of her eyes was unglued and seeing straight, she could see everything. She saw the pantyhose hanging out of the dresser drawer; the photo of a couple on the nightstand, the bulging jewelry box on the chest of drawers bursting with gaudy necklaces and big gold bangles bursting forth, and the lavender-chamomile jar candles. The bag by the dresser from Victoria's Secret was another giveaway.

She stumbled to the bathroom, almost jumping out of her skin as she felt something crawling on her arms and then across her face. She felt blindly for the light switch. When the light came on she saw leggings of all shades hanging everywhere—she'd waded through them trying to turn on a light. "I've got to get the hell out of here!" she thought to herself as the light revealed more purple. Purple rugs, towels, flowers, candles—purple everywhere!

She hurried to finish quickly on the toilet. The last thing she needed was to have some uptight trick walk in on her and start a fight. She was not a fighter. The man she left in the bed must have been good, but not that good. Not worth a battle. No man was worth losing blood over, unless he was hung so big that he tore membranes and created vaginal bleeding. That kind of bloodshed she could use, she thought with a wry smile.

It was all a game with Missy. Getting high and getting laid. The object of the game was to see how much of any intoxicating substance she could handle in order to get to the point where she could achieve orgasm. With whom or with what did not matter. Only the orgasm. And after the orgasm there was only time to think about the next time. Release was her goal, because it stopped the flood of memories. It eased the pain and brought short, sweet moments of peace. It would definitely be short-lived peace if she didn't hurry and vacate the current premises. She knew it would be polite to wake the guy and thank him for a lovely evening, but she was not in a polite mood right now. She found most of her clothing on the floor, except for her panties. She tried feeling under the covers for them without any luck. She wasn't waking this dude. She slipped quietly out of the room, deciding to leave the panties as a souvenir. She giggled at the thought of the scene that would occur when the female occupant came home and found a pair of strange underwear in her bed. Oh well—YOLO, you only live once.

She glanced around the living room of the small apartment. It was pleasant looking, almost homey. A white sofa with what else? Purple pillows scattered everywhere. Two purple and white accent chairs sat across from the sofa with a big, mahogany coffee table in the center, and green plants here and there. And of course a television—nobody can live without TV. It wasn't like most of the low rent housing she'd been inside—usually bachelor pads, funky and morbidly depressing until a couple of thousand beers and then everything was peachy keen. She closed the door behind her and dropped her head to hide her face just in case the hussy was on her way home and turned the corner in the next five minutes. She finished dressing as she stumbled along, and decided that it was better to take the hill behind the building. It led up to Macadamia Street which was only three blocks away from her home where she lived with her aunt.

It was dark, and not a creature was stirring. She heard thunder in the distance and there was a slight breeze. She sensed rain was coming. Halfway up the hill, Missy leaned against a tree to get her bearings. Whatever she'd smoked and drank the night before still lingered and she hadn't spent much time in the gym in the last few years. She was having a hard time getting it together. She knew she hadn't put anything in her nose and she didn't believe in needles and what not to get a buzz. Smoking weed was enough trouble, what with having to hold the breath, and inhale—a nice bottle of vodka was the best thing for her. She ran her fingers through her thick hair, shaking it loose on her shoulders, and blinked several times. It was then she saw the weirdest thing—even in her state she could tell it was not good.

At the top of the ravine, about two hundred yards away, she saw a car pull up and a dark figure get out. In the early morning, the car and the person were almost silhouettes. The person opened the trunk, struggled to remove what appeared to be a rolled up rug, dropped it on the ground, and then bent over and rolled it towards the edge of the drop off. Missy saw a momentary flame, and watched as the rug was propelled over the edge and burst into flames. She watched as the blazing object rolled and tumbled down the hill. The person who'd sent the fire stood for a moment watching the glowing rug. The scene was macabre: a tall black outline with no face, long hair cascading from a cap, eerily frozen in time with a fiery entity as the focus of its concentration. Moments later the figure got into the car and drove away.

Missy stood perfectly still. *Did that person see me?* she asked herself as she slowly shook the cobwebs from her head again and continued to watch the blaze where it came to rest. Suddenly there was a crack of thunder and the heavens opened up. The rain came down so hard, that had the thing at the bottom of the ravine not been lit up, she would never have seen it. The flames fought with gusto against the rain, but began to wane, and soon became no more than a few sparks.

Missy's first instinct was to run, but she quelled her fear and began to climb—this was the only shortcut she knew. She was still half drunk, tired, and she wanted her bed. Her feet were beginning to slide, and the scattered undergrowth became a lifesaver, as she grabbed onto it to pull herself up. She was almost to the top of the hill now, and she glanced back at the place where the fire had been. She blinked, as a flash of lightning lit up the sky. The rain was pouring down her face, nearly blinding her. What she thought she saw couldn't be real, could it? It was an arm—from the elbow down and even in this light she could see the hand wore glow-in-the-dark purple nail polish. More purple! Could this be the woman that lived in the apartment she just left?

Naturally curious, she slid back down the slippery slope to get a better look—seeing up close was believing to Missy. The fire had mostly gone out. She found an iron pole, as the bottom of this ravine was obviously a dumping ground for people who didn't want to have a yard sale when they moved. She gingerly prodded the burned tarp-like fabric until she was able to see that there really was a person wrapped inside, clad in nothing but her birthday suit. As Missy leaned in closer, the acrid smell of burned flesh mixed with gasoline filled her nostrils. She gagged. She knelt down and felt the top of the woman's wrist for a pulse and got nothing. The woman was dead. Missy had seen dead bodies before, but never a naked freshly cooked one, and she didn't know much about taking a pulse, but she knew enough to know she was supposed to feel a heartbeat. As she stood up to move away she felt something get tangled in her feet and almost jumped out of her skin.

She thought girlfriend had come back to life and grabbed her feet. She collected her thoughts, then bent down closer to see that it was an old fashioned fanny pack—the kind that women used to wear when they didn't want to carry a purse. *The burnt chick would not need it any time soon,* thought Missy. And it felt like it had something in it. Maybe a wallet filled to the brim with money? Weirdness overcame Missy, she intentionally avoided looking at what was left of the woman's face, as she picked up the fanny pack and slung it over her shoulder. She shivered as she finally topped the ravine. It was still raining hard—she could barely see ahead of her. But she knew these streets. She turned toward home clutching her prize—without the slightest inkling that along with the prize, something wicked would be coming her way.

Chapter One

Winston Merlot Candy came to work Friday morning not expecting his life to take a turn down an untraveled path. His mother was a doctor of psychology and his father played professional basketball in Europe for a while. Both worked hard to make his childhood worry-free—even though divorced after five years. Like every kid whose parents break up, he felt responsible for it, especially since he was their only child, but despite the divorce he knew his mother and father were devoted to him. He soon learned that he had nothing to do with why they could not continue to live together. Interestingly enough, neither of his parents had remarried.

He was tall—6 feet four inches—fair skinned, curly brown hair, with a beautiful smile framed around perfect teeth. He had his mother's eyes, which changed colors from brown to almost green, and helped to make him one very handsome man. At age fifty without a single strand of grey hair he could have passed for late thirties on any given Sunday. He'd like to say that he didn't feel his age either, but that would have been stretching it a bit, for there were times when he got up too quickly and his knees would scream at him wanting to know just who he thought they were.

Merlot was one of those men who did everything well and with flair. He danced well, played golf well, could handle any pool shark, and had won his share of cash at the poker table. And he dressed to kill.

His grey suit jacket hung open, revealing a mint green shirt with a tie that was flecked with the same color green, and a little dash of pink on a grey background. His black leather shoes were shined, his nails manicured, his diamond pinky ring sparkled, and his cologne smelled exciting to him, no matter what others thought of it.

A day in the life of Merlot Candy meant looking for people who did not want to be found. He owned his own private investigating firm, of which he was the chief operating detective. Starting out in Boston working for a legal firm gave him the opportunity to cross paths with the district attorney of Fulton County, who'd been so impressed with Merlot that he'd offered him a job in Atlanta. That had been twenty years ago. Today he worked with one other person—Glenn Bausch.

He'd met Glenn at a basketball game at Boston University when they were both in college—Merlot at Harvard and Glenn at MIT. Merlot was at Boston U to scope out the competition; Glenn was at the game because he loved basketball. Merlot had seen him at home games in the stands. Most people referred to him as a weirdo, because his manner of dressing caused him to stand out. In a world of students dressed in jeans, tees, sweats, shorts, and sneakers—Glenn always wore neatly pressed brown slacks. He alternated between white dress shirts with ties or some shade of yellow polo, his feet perpetually clad in sensible brown leather shoes that Merlot felt were just plain unfortunate.

Glenn was smart. Merlot found out that his knowledge of basketball was extensive. With a dad who played professional basketball, and always had his basketball playing buddies around, the only son had no alternative—Merlot had to learn the game. He'd learned, but had not excelled. He knew he was not going to the NBA, but his skills allowed him to make the team in high school and at Harvard. As a forward on his team, Merlot often had to set screens. During every game he was called for moving screen violations at least three times. The coach would take him out of the game to ride the bench until fourth quarter. He missed a lot of action that way, until the night he sat next to Glenn, the weirdo, who'd explained the history of basketball screens and the techniques necessary to avoid getting called for a foul. This was something no coach had been able to do for Merlot.

"You must set yourself in the screen far enough away from the defender so that he can see you," Glenn had said calmly. He then proceeded to direct Merlot's attention to the players on the court, pointing out effective screens, and calling attention to the ineffective ones just before the ref blew the whistle. "If you are setting the screen it is the responsibility of the player receiving the screen to move—by faking or cutting. Not you. You don't move."

After that night Merlot could count the times on his fingers that he'd received a foul for illegal screens. He never forgot Glenn. And when he'd run into him at an alumni frat party, he'd offered him a job by making him an offer he couldn't refuse.

Glenn had graduated summa cum laude and was a whiz on the computer. Using the computer he could dig so deep into a life that the person had to backfill like a shovel to avoid him gaining ground. He was the best at what he did, and as a result, Merlot earned a reputation for being the best investigator in town. He and Glenn worked well together, they liked and respected each other and both were thorough to the extreme.

Merlot stood at the big window that faced out onto Peachtree Street, and looked toward Woodruff Park. Originally purchased as four acres by Robert W. Woodruff, the park was donated to the city of Atlanta in 1971 and since then had become one of the city's most decisive green spaces. An outdoor showplace, with lawn and plaza areas, a bandstand, and fountains, the park accommodated not only the lunch crowd, but special events as well. From where he stood, Merlot could see the curved fountain, located at the base of a wall with water flowing down like a waterfall. His thoughts were all over the place when the intercom on his desk buzzed.

"Mr. Candy?" his receptionist implored.

"Yes," Merlot responded.

"Louise Canola is here to see you. She says it's urgent."

Protocol called for an appointment. Rarely did Merlot see someone who walked in, unless it was a close friend or business associate. He directed Ivy, his receptionist, to always schedule an appointment and she knew that. Something must be different; otherwise she would not have interrupted him. Louise Canola. She was the young lady he'd met in

Centennial Park when he'd almost made a fool of himself because she looked like someone he used to know—and still loved. What could she possibly want with him? It had been months since they met. His curiosity got the best of him.

"Send her in," he said, not considering for a moment the significance of those three words. And as the door opened, it was not just to Louise Canola, but to a maelstrom that would change his life forever.

Chapter Two

It was still dark as Etta Wasp maneuvered her body so as to become more comfortable and to ease the aching "catch," as she called which seemed to plague the right side of her back. She'd heard tell of people with the same ailment, blaming it on hours in front of a computer in a non-ergonomic chair. She couldn't say the same. She rarely used a computer. It was good for searching out things—like where to order the best tulip bulbs in the fall, or the crocus in the spring—and catching up with the daily headlines if one had missed the news three times in one day.

Weighing in at 274 pounds, she was finding it more and more difficult to get out of bed. In her youth, her small frame carried a scant 107 pounds, and she stood only 5 feet 4 inches. Etta had been a pretty girl. Her hair in those days had been brunette—her eyelashes thick and her brows were naturally arched. But nowadays every hair on her body was grey.

When the doctor informed her that she had type 2 diabetes she'd immediately gone into the state of denial. During her time in that state she gained 100 pounds, and by the time she came up for air the disease had become full-blown, and despite the scriptures about healing and the stripes of Jesus, she'd had to take medication.

Her diet had not improved much, although she tried to stick to vegetables and lean meats. She had not slept much this last night. It had to be because of the green bean casserole that Pearl, her sister, had made for dinner. It had too many onions in it. How many times did she have to tell that woman that she couldn't eat onions?

She was now positioned just right in the chair, pain-free, and she slowly turned toward the bay window. She was very fortunate to have chosen the room with windows facing the street as the master bedroom. She thoroughly enjoyed watching the world go by. Even in the wee hours of the morning, like now, with the thunder and the downpour of rain, she could catch a glimpse of something or someone. Once quite active, with gardening—flowers not vegetables—travelling a bit, going to movies, and attending the occasional social function, she now gained satisfaction from the lives of those around her. She still attended church every Sunday and bible study on Wednesdays, and whenever there was something going on in the neighborhood. She got out for a walk at least twice a week to keep her legs limbered up for getting down on a cushion to plant a geranium or a pansy. Etta loved her flower beds.

At age sixty-five, she had come to accept that death was inevitable—really accept it. Every day that she lived was something to be grateful for. Her late husband, who'd died ten years ago, had done everything in his power to keep her smiling because she truly believed that he was aware of how much he annoyed her. She missed him, but not his silly questions. A good conversationalist he was not, having read somewhere that the best way to strike up one was to ask questions. He didn't read far enough into the article to find out that the questions were never to be rhetorical. God rest his soul. Sometimes a memory of a long afternoon with his questions would still aggravate her.

Folks always said she had the prettiest smile. She was grateful that she still had her teeth. It just would not have been good for her vanity to lose all her teeth so that she had to both wear dentures and take medicine for diabetes. She chuckled to herself. Her sister Pearl kept her teeth in a little container by the bed at night.

Etta looked appraisingly at the peach ruffled curtains that adorned the huge window. The white shears were so light and delicate that she could see clearly through them, and for the most part could not be seen from the outside. She kept the lights off at night and during the day she sat back from the window. She never wanted to be accused of snooping. The original house plans had not called for a bay window. It had been added later. Two white wing-backed chairs flanked the window, leaving just enough space for her to place an oversized ottoman to put her feet on and be comfortable as she sipped a good cup of chamomile tea while reading a good book or looking out of the window to watch as the world passed by.

The street was quiet except for the rain. It was coming down hard—too hard for any living soul to be out. She glanced at the clock on the table in the center of the window. It was 5:30 a.m. Soon things would start stirring—folks would be leaving for work, the newspaper would be delivered, the dogs would start barking, and the five children next door would begin running and screaming. There was nothing to see, really. Not tonight. Etta was just about to get up to start breakfast when she saw a figure weaving down the street. She pulled her binoculars from the back of her chair where they hung perpetually just in case she needed to see something up close. She peered out through the rain.

"Missy Kinner!" she exclaimed, shaking her head. "That little slut's been out all night again!"

Missy staggered down the street. No coat, no hat. Etta thought it was a miracle she had on shoes. She would be soaking wet. Imagine coming home at this time of morning, drunk as a skunk in all probability, or high as a kite as Missy liked to say. That girl made the news ever since she moved in with her aunt, Connie Henderson, three houses down on the left. Etta and Connie had been friends for years, being the oldest homeowners on Hydrangea Court in Inman Park, the first planned suburb of Atlanta. They'd been neighbors for over thirty years now.

Connie was a hardworking Christian woman who'd taken in her niece—her only living relative—when the child fell into hard times, having promised her only sister, Missy's mother, that she'd always look out for the child. Missy had moved in with a lot of baggage—and not the kind by Samsonite. She'd had problems with her marriage. Her husband left her and was awarded custody of the couple's only child, a little girl. Connie never talked about what happened, but Etta didn't know many men that could live with a drunken wife. Missy was a grown woman and she ought to do better. Etta was just itching to get close enough to her to slap some sense into her. The way she was living her life she was never going to see her child again.

She watched as Missy stumbled past. She was usually good for a show, because she knew of Etta's habit of sitting in the window.

"Hey old woman! Whatcha looking at?" she'd yell at Etta whenever she caught a glimpse of her.

Etta never answered her. It just wasn't the Christian thing to do. Missy's sins were going to catch up with her soon enough. Sometimes Missy didn't make it to the door. From time to time Etta would see her lying out in the yard all night. Etta could see Connie's yard from the window. Now she watched her stumble up the steps and linger on the porch for a few minutes before finally entering the house.

Etta glanced at the clock again. She pushed herself up from the chair. It was time to get to the stove and start the water boiling for their daily oatmeal. The only variety and spice of life for the gruel came with the cinnamon and the fruit of the day. Today would be blueberries. And a dash of agave nectar—she had to have some sweetness. As she rubbed her back, Etta wondered what in the world Missy was carrying. It looked like a little purse, but everybody knew that Missy didn't believe in purses—she couldn't keep up with them. Neither Etta or Missy, as drunk and careless as she was on this rainy morning knew that Missy had just stumbled off the path of an unfit mother onto the long and winding path of redemption.

Chapter Three

Louise Canola had started the morning off in traffic, and as the rain beat down on her windshield, she had pulled off the road, feeling no need to try to proceed any further. Driving was impossible without a field of vision. That was one of the reasons that she didn't like rain. Actually, the only time she enjoyed the rain was in the summer when she had nothing to do except what she wanted to. And the operative word was "want."

"I want to go home, wake up again, and everything will be alright," she said aloud to the raindrops pounding on the roof of the car.

But she wasn't going anywhere. Not anytime soon. I-75 was a parking lot. "Traffic!" She thought. "The scourge of humanity." Louise looked at her watch. It was nearly 7:00 a.m. The first bell for homeroom rang at 7:15 and she wasn't going to be there. Late again! "If anything can go wrong it will go wrong." Those words floated through her head. "Who said that?" she asked herself. Was it Occam's razor? Or the Pythagorean Theorem? For the life of her she could not remember. And that bothered her. Things like that always bothered her when she couldn't remember who said what. Statements blurted out to her with authority and assurance, things that she read, things that she saw on the news, stuff she'd heard professors rant about—all of that stuff was in her head and most of the time she could think for a few seconds and retrieve it. When most students took the words of so-called expert teachers as if from the Bible, Louise never did. She needed proof. Substantial proof. She spent many extra hours on homework trying to prove or disprove something she'd heard a teacher say. Even in college. If she found any discrepancies she couldn't wait until the next class to let the teacher know.

She never wanted to be that teacher. She checked and double-checked before she said anything. She didn't want a student coming to her to correct something that she'd said. It wasn't hard to do in a Spanish class because most of the students didn't know anything. But occasionally she'd get a child that had lived in a Spanish speaking country for a while. So she stayed on her toes. But the answer to who said things can go wrong escaped her this morning.

Slender, dark hair with piercing blue eyes, Louise was striking. Pretty in a different sense—as in a combination of everything about her working all together at the same time— but she'd come to think of herself as just alright. Her figure was not flawless, but good nonetheless. And she got double takes often enough so she knew she looked okay to the opposite sex. Not that she was interested. She'd been in love once and that was enough.

Her one vice was clothes. She loved pretty clothes. And shoes. She looked down at her blue pumps. She'd found them on a clearance rack at Saks Fifth Avenue. They were a fine pair of leather footwear. Prada. They went well with the black dress and the red and white scarf with one wide stripe of blue that matched the shoes perfectly. She pulled down the visor and scrutinized her make-up. She'd done well again. Not too much eye shadow, a hint of blush, and a nice red lipstick. She commanded her Bluetooth to call the school. She might as well let them know that she was going to be late. They had to understand. It was raining cats and dogs and everyone in Atlanta knew how bad the traffic could get on a sunny day.

"Southwest Allegheny High School," the secretary answered.

"Murphy's Law!" Louise blurted into the phone. "Oh excuse me, Mrs. Clay," she said, catching herself. "I had something else on my mind. This is Louise Canola. I'm stuck in traffic on I-75. Someone will have to take my homeroom." Louise smiled proudly. If anything can go wrong was Murphy's Law.

Mrs. Clay cordially accepted Louise's call and promised to get the information to one of the administrators. Louise disconnected the call and sat back against the smooth tan leather upholstery and closed her eyes. She was going to wait out this mini-hurricane if it took hours.

"Whatsoever things are pure, whatsoever things are lovely and of a good report, think on these things." Where had she heard that? The Bible of course. Philippians. Her mother had read that to her whenever Louise felt down about something. New York. Home. She'd think about New York as the rain beat on the roof.

She should never have left New York. It was home. Despite the crowds, the crime, the slums, the high cost of living, 9/11—it was her home. Broadway. Atlanta had the fabulous Fox Theater, but it could not compare with Broadway, where one could choose from plays the way people in Atlanta chose which movie to see. She sighed as she remembered what a tough decision it was to make the move to a strange city alone. It was what she needed at the time—to get away from everything familiar and start again.

But life has a way of catching up with you. It came up on Louise and threatened to send her travelling when her sister, Chanel showed up. Chanel was trouble. She didn't mean to be, it was like the stars had aligned and dusted her with trouble attractors. She'd left home five days ago and not returned. It was not unusual for her to stay out all night—the unusual thing was the fact that she'd not called. She and Louise had a long conversation. That was one of the conditions by which she could continue to share her home with Chanel. She had to keep Louise updated because Louise was done worrying. Life was too short.

But she was in stop-and-go traffic, worried about her sister. She'd gone to the police station and filed a missing report three days ago, but nothing had happened. She'd made up her mind to try one more thing during her planning period today.

She shook off the thoughts of the morning as she now waited in the office on Peachtree Street. She looked at the business card in her hand as she sat back in a comfortable yellow leather chair. *Winston Merlot Candy, specializing in lost and found*.

"Ms. Canola? Mr. Candy will see you now. Follow me please," the very capable receptionist announced.

Louise got up and followed, rehearsing what she'd say when she saw him again. She wasn't being foolish, and she wasn't jumping the gun. Something had to be done. This was not like Chanel at all. Granted she was a wild child, but she respected Louise's rules—more than that she looked up to her, and deep down, they loved each other. Something was wrong. Something was terribly, terribly wrong. She had no clue that 'old man trouble' was headed towards her like a freight train.

Chapter Four

Merlot felt his heartbeat quicken at the sight of Louise Canola. Café au lait skin color, flawless figure, and athletic legs almost made her a double for Anissa Brogdon—the woman he loved unashamedly. The major difference was the eye color—Anissa's brown eyes that seemed to draw you in like a warm cup of hot chocolate on a frosty day were in contrast to Louise's icy blue irises. The mystique disappeared the minute Louise spoke.

"Hello again, Mr. Candy," she said in her husky voice, completely shattering the spell.

"Hello. Have a seat and tell me to what I owe this pleasure," Merlot replied, indicating one of the two red brocade arm chairs in front of his desk, as he sat in his leather executive chair that was upholstered in the same shade of red.

Louise took a deep breath. "My sister is missing," she blurted, suddenly losing control as tears ran down her face.

Taking a few tissues and handing them over to her, Merlot became concerned. He sat back again in anticipation. He always waited for his clients to speak first while surreptitiously watching their body language and their eyes. Eyes always told the story. Louise's eyes were filled with tears that served as a shield for the pain she was feeling. He could tell it was real pain. She was not being a drama queen.

"When was the last time you saw her?" he asked quietly.

"Five days ago. I was leaving for work, she told me she'd be out late. That was Friday."

"What do you think has happened to her?"

"I think something bad has happened. She never does this. I mean she has all-nighters, but she always calls to let me know that she's okay and to give me some sort of idea when she'll return. I've not heard a thing from her. And I've got this feeling. She and I were close—closer when we were younger. I would get this weird feeling and each time it happened, Chanel had either broken her arm, fallen out of a tree and knocked herself out, or drove her car into an embankment." Louise blew her nose and looked into Merlot's eyes.

"Chanel. Nice name. Sounds like she's a bit accident prone. Have you checked the hospitals?" he asked.

"Yes. And I've filed a missing person's report with the police. I've come to you because I'm desperate and you claim to specialize in finding the lost," she said, wringing the tissue.

As was his custom, Merlot continued to watch Louise—wanting to see how well she fared under his intense scrutiny. She held his gaze as long as he held hers. Without looking away he asked the pivotal question.

"Is there any reason that she would not come home and consequently feel justified in not telling you anything?"

Louise finally broke eye contact as she focused on the big windows that had recently been the object of Merlot's attention. From her vantage point, the top floors of the various hotels and office buildings were in clear view. After a few seconds in thought she redirected her gaze to Merlot.

"If you mean a man—if you're saying she ran away with a man to …I don't know…start a new life, if she somehow fell in love and lost her mind—the answer is no. On the other hand if you mean she was abducted and developed Stockholm Syndrome for her abductor—the answer is no. The answer to your question, no matter how you mean it, is no, no, NO!" Her voice increased in tempo with each no, so that the last one was quite loud, expressing her anger, frustration, and agitation.

"Okay. That's settled. So the next thing is my fee," Merlot stated. He didn't want her emotions to continue to escalate.

"That's a good segue. How much is your fee, Mr. Candy?"

"Please don't be formal. You and I met in a park and you turned me down for a date, so I'd say we're on a first name basis. People say this all the time in sales pitches, but I mean it," he said with a warm smile. "For you my fee is first a $5,000 retainer and then I bill an hourly rate of $300. If I need outside help the fees go up, but I start out on my own and I've been quite successful in the past."

"Don't do me any favors. I teach and I know how everybody thinks we don't make much money, which is true—though some of us have other resources, and I happen to have a trust fund, so charge me like everybody else. I don't want to have to owe you when this is all over." She winked conspiratorially at him, with the smile he remembered from the first time they met.

“Thank you for that info. If I have to hire outside help you will pay like everybody else. And all you’ll ever owe me is the bottom line on your invoice. I don’t go out like that—getting dates through my business. Do I look like I need to bargain for a date?” He stood, held his arms wide, and pivoted left to right. One of the things that Merlot knew without a doubt was that he was definitely boy candy. He was hot. He was fine. He usually kept that little tidbit to himself and let nature take its course.

Louise laughed out loud as she opened her purse and pulled out a checkbook. She quickly wrote out a check and handed it to Merlot.

“Thank you, Louise. And now I want you to sit down with my assistant and answer her questions thoroughly. Don’t hold back anything. The least little thing could provide a big clue.” He paused for a second. “Do you have a picture of Chanel? Is her last name Canola as well?”

“Yes, I do, and no, her last name is Compton,” Louise said as she began to flip through her Iphone. She produced five images of a smiling, very pretty, Chanel—a confident face without a hint of disorientation. “What rabbit hole have you gone into?” Merlot asked himself as he scrolled through the photos, studying her face.